Chain of Death
and
Death's Premium

TWO CLASSIC ADVENTURES OF

by Walter B. Gibson
writing as Maxwell Grant

Foreword by
Richard Wormser

with a new historical essay
by **Will Murray**

SANCTUM BOOKS

International Standard Book Number:
978-1-60877-033-5

First printing: September 2010

Series editor/publisher: Anthony Tollin
sanctumotr@earthlink.net

Consulting editor: Will Murray

Copy editor: Joseph Wrzos

Cover and photo restoration: Michael Piper

The editors gratefully appreciate the contributions of J. Randolph Cox and Robert, Lindsay and Ira Frederick Skutch in the preparation of this volume.

Published by Sanctum Books
P.O. Box 761474, San Antonio, TX 78245-1474

Visit The Shadow at www.shadowsanctum.com.

Volume 41

CONTENTS

Two Complete Novels From The Shadow's Private Annals As told to Maxwell Grant

Thrilling Tales and Features

**Cover painting by George Rozen
Back cover art by George Rozen and Graves Gladney
Interior illustrations by Tom Lovell and Edd Cartier**

THE SHADOW REMEMBERED

by Richard Wormser

While it seems impossible any literate person is not familiar with *The Shadow*, that austere—yet genial—publication, a few facts might be recorded for history.

The original business of Street & Smith had been the publication of a so-called story paper, *The New York Weekly*, which printed a third of a novel at a time; sometimes installments of two or three stories in each issue. The price of an issue was three or four cents, later rising to a nickel.

Then, Francis Smith tried reprinting a novel in full, while selling it for a dime. By 1880 or thereabouts, these "dime novels" had driven their parent weeklies out of business.

In turn, the dime novel spawned its own competition, the pulp paper magazine. Each of these weeklies, semi-monthlies or monthlies had a brightly colored cover and contained serial installments, short stories and novelettes.

Under such editors as Bob Davis of Munsey, Frank Blackwell of Street & Smith, the much younger Jack Byrne of Fiction House and others, the pulps produced and trained—I would estimate—two thirds of the successful American writers of my generation and the one before it.

A few years before I got to Street & Smith, the pulps had put the last of the dime novels off the newsstands. I think the last one to go was *Nick Carter....*

The Shadow was really retrogression, a return to the past on the part of the sentimental Smiths.

Sometime in late 1930, Street & Smith had tried radio advertising to promote their magazines. Some ingenious advertising man had thought up an announcer who, in eerie tones, called himself The Shadow. Laughing nastily, he would introduce a story from *Detective Story Weekly*, or—I think, although I never heard the program—*Love Story*, the biggest sellers on the S. & S. list.

People started asking for *The Shadow Magazine*, so to protect their title, the Smiths told Lon Murray to get out a *Shadow* pulp. They told him to mark it as a quarterly, though one publication would secure the title.

There was only a small amount of money allotted for the editorial contents of this one-shot. Lon, a brilliant, if erratic, editor, gave the assignment to a man who'd never written a word of fiction in his life.

He was Walt Gibson, Walter B. Gibson, a professional magician and advance man for other magicians.

Walt had a few eccentricities. For one, he never blinked; you could talk to him for hours, and his eyelids never closed. For another he was addicted to wearing several layers of clothing, in or out of the house, the upper portions of which he didn't care to button. Thus he'd reveal successive strata of overcoat, suitcoat, raglan sweater, vest and shirt. The last was buttoned, except sometimes at the collar.

Also, he didn't have too much faith in his new career as a novelist, and wanted to keep in shape in case he had to go back to the vaudeville stage. So, as he chatted, various things appeared and disappeared in his hands: rubber balls, knives, forks, playing cards, red roses, glasses of water colored to look like wine. He never deigned to look at these props; he just stared at you, unblinking.

Once, after *The Shadow* was a success, he came into the office with a helpful suggestion. He had worked out some suction cups for his feet and hands; if Lon would give him the money to buy an outfit like The Shadow's—big black hat, black cape swirling to his ankles—he would, when he came to confer at Street & Smith, enter by the outside wall, human fly style, instead of coming by the elevator. It would be a good publicity stunt, Walt felt.

Lon was not up to approaching Mr. Verne Smith or Mr. George Smith about this, and he felt it was too important a matter to take up with the vice-president, Bill Ralston, so the idea died. It wasn't needed, anyway, for *The Shadow* was an immediate success. The first issue was snatched off the stands within a day or so; Lon got orders to go monthly, and then, almost at once, twice a month.

In format the magazine was a compromise between a regular pulp like *Detective Story*, and the old dime novels. Each issue contained a full, book-length (60,000-word) novel about The Shadow, and was then filled out with four short stories. The Shadow was a vague, eleemosynary character who went around righting wrongs, frustrating criminals, cleaning up cities, rescuing the innocent and punishing the guilty, all without fee. What his real identity was is still not known; for a long time it seemed as though he was, when at rest, a wealthy man named Lamont Cranston, who seemed to have nothing to do but take his ease at the Cobalt Club.

Then, when the readers were sure of this, Walt had Lamont Cranston and The Shadow appear together.

I'd sure like to know who The Shadow really was.

Walt Gibson brought to the job a couple of talents that have seldom been rivaled. For one thing, he could write a full-length novel in four days—not once—several writers have done this—but every four days if called on.

For another, he was endlessly ingenious in devising gimmicks, or get-aways, or escapes. He could get The Shadow into any kind of a trap, writing steadily, never blinking, and then, without faltering at the keyboard, get him out again.

He typed those things, clean copy. In a pinch, you could—if you were a senior editor—hand his pages to the printers without reading them, confident that there wouldn't be a typo in all the two hundred pages.

Walt wrote two of those novels a month from early 1932 until the middle of the Second World War, when the paper shortage caught up with Street & Smith. On the side, for a hobby, he wrote, edited and published a professional monthly on magic. He was always after the editors to let him do the short stories, too, but he

had no facility for turning around in short spaces.

An hour before closing time on a Friday, we were told that *Headlines* magazine was suspended. So was *Sports Story*, so was *College Story*, so was every other magazine Lon Murray put out except *The Shadow.*

Lon was fired; his chief assistant Mike Tilden was fired; Rosie Ginter was fired. That left only two of us in the department: John Nanovic, a reader who had no part of *Headlines*, and myself. Since we both got thirty dollars a week, it was a tossup which of us would be kept; but he'd been there longer, and was told he was now editor of *The Shadow*—full editor....

Lon and Rosie and Mike and I had a few drinks at the Clam House on Fourteenth Street—a speakeasy—and separated for a bleak weekend.

But after the bleak weekend, I rallied. Monday morning, I recalled that in my part-time capacity as

It was a strange patient the hospital ambulance was carrying—a case that had been picked up along the railroad tracks at night.

MURDER ON DEATH AVENUE

By Richard Wormser

Richard Wormser wrote numerous short stories for the back pages of *The Shadow Magazine* but only two appeared under his own byline, including this one published in the same issue as *Chain of Death*.

reader of short stories for *The Shadow*, I had had no luck in finding stories under two thousand words in length that were passable for publication.

A pulp was a very rigid thing. Each ten-cent issue was 128 pages, one third of a pound of paper, no more, no less. Advertising, contracted for months ahead of time, occupied four or six pages; Walt's novel, eighty-eight to ninety.

In what was left went four short stories. Those were orders from the Smiths. If the editor found two good six-thousand-word stories, he had to piece out with two shorter ones. If he found two six-thousanders and a four-thousander, the last story had to be short to the point of editorial desperation.

I happened to know that two issues of *The Shadow*

were held up, one for lack of a twelve-hundred-word story, one for need of a masterpiece of eighteen hundred words.

At nine-thirty, I was back in the old paper warehouse. The new editor bought his first story from me; I sold my first piece of fiction to him by ten o'clock. Twelve hundred words at a penny apiece: twelve bucks.

That afternoon I was back; I knocked off eighteen dollars this time.

In one day I had made as much money as I would have in a week if I hadn't been fired.

The benevolent fates had given the English language a new fiction writer.

The English-speaking world, the United States,

Walter Gibson pounded out two Shadow novels each month during the 1930s and early 1940s.

New York, in fact, my immediate acquaintances and relatives were remarkably indifferent. I am sure that when the first few ashes fell on Pompeii, the busy inhabitants brushed them off their shoulders and went on selling oil and wine to each other.

On one of my mad gallops that day, between Street & Smith and my typewriter on 44th Street, I ran into Frank and Marian in Grand Central Station.

"Hey," Frank said, "Marian sold a story to *College Humor.*"

I didn't mention my twelve-dollar triumph.

The boy who had taken over the job as editor of *The Shadow* later became, I understand, a very good editor; I've met writers who said he was a help and a guide to them in their formative years.

But when I met him, he was probably a little surprised by his sudden promotion. As junior reader in the department, he'd been a tiny step above the office boy we didn't have; and now there was no one over him but Mr. Ralston, who was too busy to help him much. The editor's incompetence was probably a break for me, at first. I don't think he would have taken half as many stories from me if he'd known better.

On the other hand, he set up some difficulties; for one thing, I soon learned that he had put an arbitrary limit on my earnings. Sixty bucks a week was tops, and no more.

One week—this was a couple of months later, when I felt confident enough to try to sell on merit, instead of on straight convenience of length—I sold him a six-thousand-word story on Monday. Wednesday I brought in two more, one thirty-five hundred, one twenty-five hundred. He needed those, read them at once, accepted them—and then handed me back my six-thousand-worder.

I submitted it again in a couple of weeks, and he took it.

Of course, I was seldom published under my own name. Some issues had all four short stories by me—under four names. I had thirteen different names that I used regularly.

Many Street & Smith writers used pen names for another reason. Walt Gibson, for instance, signed The Shadow novels as "Maxwell Grant," no relation to the famous Maxwell Land Grant of New Mexico.

This was a name owned by Street & Smith, who took no chances on one of their writers getting famous and getting away from them. They had made two of their writers use the name "Maxwell Grant" before they assigned it to Walt; in that way he had no legal rights to it.

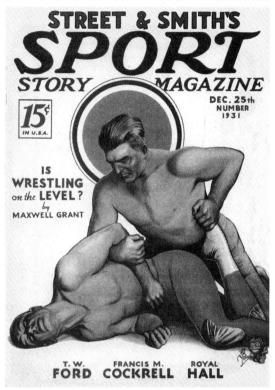

The "Maxwell Grant" byline was briefly used by non-Shadow writers.

I ground out stories for *The Shadow* all that summer. I was still doing some trade paper correspondence, but not much; business papers suffered more and more as the Depression deepened. Pulps, on the other hand, prospered; for a dime a family could get several evenings' entertainment. This was cheap, in a time when radio was not the storytelling medium it later became and when movies cost thirty-five and forty cents a person.

The editor let me know, not too subtly, that he would consider it disloyal of me to try to sell to anyone but him. I really didn't care; sixty dollars a week was charming money in 1932.

The Shadow prospered. Walt wanted them to let him write a novel a week, but Mr. Ralston said the Smiths didn't think he could do it without sacrificing quality.

I think they were wrong. I think if Walt had learned how to dictate, or if the electric typewriter had been invented then, he could have done a novel a day.

Of course, he'd have had to take a Sunday off once a month to get out his magic magazine. •

Richard Wormser's remembrance of The Shadow Magazine *first appeared in his posthumously published memoir,* How to Become a Complete Nonentity; *edited by Ira Skutch and published in 2006 by iUniverse (ISBN 0-595-38467-6), available from Amazon.com. Reprinted by permission of Robert, Lindsay and Ira Frederick Skutch.*

Like the multiple-headed Hydra of ancient times, so works this new, modern organization of crime, a

CHAIN OF DEATH

A book-length novel taken from the private annals of The Shadow

As told to

Maxwell Grant

CHAPTER I
PLANTED DEATH

MISTY night had settled on Manhattan. A chilly drizzle was creeping in from the bay. The bright lights of Times Square blinked and blazed in defiance of the gathering fog. This district maintained its brilliance despite the elements.

A young man, pushing his way through Broadway throngs, turned suddenly as he neared a subway entrance at the corner of Forty-second Street. He stopped to purchase an evening newspaper. His face showed keenly in the light. It was a well-featured countenance, with thick, dark eyebrows and a black, pointed mustache as its most conspicuous features.

Though his face was a trifle haggard, as though from overwork, the young man showed no signs of weariness in his action. As he stepped away from the newsstand, he headed briskly for the subway entrance and hurriedly disappeared down the steps.

A dozen minutes later, the same young man reappeared from a subway exit in a different section of Manhattan. He had reached the Wall Street area. His footsteps again were hasty as they carried him through a man-made canyon between two towering buildings.

Blanketing fog had created a strange effect in the lower district of Manhattan. The chilling drizzle had come in more heavily from the Battery. It was accompanied by low-hanging clouds that swirled in mistlike fashion about the upper stories of closely packed skyscrapers.

Towering office buildings rose out of sight. Like mountains of stone, they thrust their shafts into the enshrouding fog. Passers in the street were few. The chasms between the massive monoliths were silent and almost deserted. The business day ended, this district seemed a city of the dead.

Straight ahead, at a corner of the narrow street, was a tall white building that appeared magnified by the fog. Light glimmered from its open doorway. Above, at scattered intervals, were the lights of offices, which marked the presence of businessmen who had remained to work late.

Still higher, from spots where the building itself was invisible in the fog, shimmers of faint light marked other offices that were occupied. This was not unusual. The huge Zenith Building, which the young man now approached, was one of the best-tenanted of skyscrapers. Every night found some late-stayers in the thousand-odd offices that were located within its eight-hundred-foot walls.

THE young man entered the lobby of the Zenith Building. The place was scantily lighted. On the left was a desk, where a watchman remained on duty. On the right, beyond, was a row of elevator shafts.

One elevator door was open. It was toward this objective that the young man turned his steps. He was nearly at his goal when the stentorian voice of the watchman stopped him. Turning, with a slight grin, the young man came back to the desk on the left.

"Forgot all about it, George," he remarked, as he picked up a pencil and began to sign the register book. "I was in a hurry. I come in and out so much during the day that I never think to register at night."

"That's all right," growled the watchman. "I'm here to tell people when they forget."

He watched the young man sign his name as Howard Norwyn; after that, the number of the office to which he was going—3318. Then Norwyn marked the time of entry as 9:15, taking it from a clock above the registration desk.

"Your boss went upstairs fifteen minutes ago," remarked the watchman. "Guess that's why you're in a hurry, eh?"

Norwyn nodded. He had read the name of his employer, George Hobston, on the register. He had also noted the time of Hobston's arrival as nine o'clock.

Howard Norwyn hurried to the elevator. The sleepy operator had no challenge. The man was standing slouched in the corner of the car; he took it for granted that anyone who entered had registered. The checking of names was the watchman's job, not his.

The elevator reached the thirty-third floor. Its lone passenger alighted. Howard Norwyn paced along the gloomy marble corridor as the elevator doors clanged behind him. He reached the door of 3318. It was the entrance to a suite. On the glass panel appeared the legend:

HOBSTON & COMPANY
INVESTMENT ADVISORS
GEORGE HOBSTON
PRESIDENT

Norwyn found the door unlocked. He opened it and entered a darkened outer office. He seemed a trifle puzzled. Ordinarily, George Hobston would have kept this room illuminated. It was light from an inner room that allayed Norwyn's worries. He strode in that direction.

The inner office was Hobston's own.

Norwyn had an appointment with his employer, so he naturally supposed that Hobston was awaiting his arrival. But as he reached the door, Norwyn paused upon the threshold. He stared straight across the dimly lighted inner office.

OPPOSITE was the entrance to a strong vault room where George Hobston kept all money and securities. The vault room had a massive door of metal grillwork; beyond it, the vault itself was set in the wall. This arrangement made it possible for Hobston to guard himself while opening the vault, through the simple expedient of closing the grilled door behind him. Yet at the same time, air was obtainable through the open metal work.

The grilled door was always kept closed. Tonight, it was wide open. A light was burning in the small vault room. Its rays showed the vault, also opened wide, with papers scattered everywhere. The vault room, however, was empty!

Howard Norwyn stood petrified. Robbery was evident; still, there was no sign of the thief. In wild alarm, Norwyn thought of his employer. Where was George Hobston? Spontaneously, Norwyn looked about the gloomy office. His eyes fell on a figure that was slouched in a desk chair.

HOWARD NORWYN, innocent employee of George Hobston, who is framed in the murder of his chief.

It was George Hobston. The president of the investment company was dead. His body was crumpled forward, almost as if someone had placed it there. One motionless hand lay beside a telephone on the desk. As Howard Norwyn's bulging eyes stared back and forth, they saw that George Hobston's back was on a straight line with the open door of the vault room.

Mechanically, Howard Norwyn stepped forward. As he did, he sensed a sound from in back of him. He wheeled toward the door to the darkened outer office. A man came springing from the gloom. As Norwyn's hands came upward, husky fists caught his throat and sent him backward to the floor. A short quick pounding motion banged Norwyn's head upon the thick carpet. Groggy, the young man sprawled helpless, with arms outstretched.

Norwyn's attacker, a thickset, leering rogue, arose to survey his work. A pleased grin showed on puffy lips. The man had evidently accomplished what he sought. He had stunned Norwyn but had not seriously injured him. Within a few minutes, the young man would come back to his senses.

Hoisting Norwyn's body, the thickset man carried his burden into the vault room. There he propped Norwyn against the wall. He applied a handkerchief to the young man's throat, to remove the grime of fingerprints. From his pocket, he drew a revolver. He wiped it with the handkerchief and placed it in Norwyn's right hand. Using the cloth as a covering

for Norwyn's fist, the man squeezed Norwyn's hand tightly about the weapon.

Stepping back, the evil-faced man delivered another leer. Howard Norwyn was moving weakly. His eyes had not yet opened; but it would be minutes only before he regained full consciousness. With handkerchief on hand, Norwyn's attacker clanged the metal door shut. Through the grill, he could still see Norwyn moving feebly.

FOR a moment, the man became cautious. He had given Norwyn a loaded weapon; a sudden recovery would enable the victim to fire from the vault room. Norwyn's attacker drew a revolver of his own. He raised the weapon; then lowered it as he observed Norwyn slouch back into a stupor.

The villain's work was done. In the dull gleam of the office, which was lighted only by a corner lamp, the thickset man's pockets showed heavy bulges that represented stolen money and securities. The man approached the dead body of George Hobston; he frisked the pockets in a manner which showed that he had already gone through them, but was merely making sure that his search had been complete.

Placing his handkerchief upon the left hand of the dead man, the ruffian clamped the lifeless fingers to the telephone receiver. He used Hobston's hand to knock it from the hook.

With the revolver pointed to the open window of the office, the murderer stood in readiness for clicks through the receiver. His vile face showed its vicious grin. Evil had gained a triumph.

Murder had been this villain's first crime. Then had come robbery. The third step in the sequence was under way. This man who had slain George Hobston; this crook who had rifled the investment dealer's safe, was ready to complete his evening's work.

Simply, but with craft, he was planting his crimes upon Howard Norwyn, the young man who was lying helpless behind the locked bars of the vault room!

CHAPTER II
FROM THE NIGHT

WHILE grim events were taking place on the thirty-third floor, the lobby of the Zenith Building still maintained its hollow quiet. Two men came walking in from the outer door; simultaneously, the clang of metal announced that the elevator had reached the ground floor.

Two passengers alighted. Like the two men who had entered, they went to the registration desk to sign. The watchman was busy, checking the names of two persons who had entered and watching the departers tabulate the time that they were leaving.

Other eyes observed the cluster at the table.

These were the eyes of a watcher at the outer door. Standing against the wall, in from the sidewalk, was a tall figure that was remarkably inconspicuous.

Dressed in dark suit, this spying visitor might well have materialized from the blackened fog. He formed a shape that was almost spectral. Brief minutes had passed since his arrival here; he seemed to be awaiting an opportunity that had come.

The watchman's back was toward the lobby. The tall figure moved inward through the door. It became the form of a man whose close-fitting suit was glistening with moisture from the drizzle. In his right hand, this arrival carried a black briefcase.

There was something amazing in the stride of this tall personage. Where other footsteps had clicked upon the marble flooring of the lobby, his paces were swift and noiseless. Swinging to the right side of the lobby, where the window of a darkened shop showed black, the intruder was almost invisible as he headed for the elevator.

The watchman turned to see the two men who had registered go toward the elevator. Swinging about, he observed the other two men making their departure. He missed a glimpse of the extra arrival who stood a dozen paces from the elevators.

It was when the watchman turned toward the outer door that the tall intruder came suddenly to life. His quick, noiseless steps brought him to the elevator; he moved into the car just as the operator was about to close the doors.

The two men who had registered were engaged in conversation. The operator was sleepy and had no interest in his passengers. No question was put to the carrier of the briefcase. The operator closed the doors. The elevator was ready for its upward trip.

It was at that moment that the watchman found another duty. A buzzer had been sounding beside the registration table. It indicated a call from an office. The watchman picked up a telephone and growled into a mouthpiece.

"Hello... Hello..."

The watchman received no reply. Instead, he heard a sound that startled him. Over the wire came the report of a revolver. Then a gasp, a gargling, incoherent groan. A voice tried to mouth words. It failed. The thump of a falling receiver was the final token.

"Hello... Hello..."

The watchman looked at the board. He saw the number of the office from which the call had come: 3318. He hung up the receiver and wheeled toward the elevators. The lone night car had started upward. Its dial showed that it had stopped at the eighth floor.

The watchman hung up the receiver. He waited for breathless seconds. Then he raised the receiver with shaking hand and put in a call to the police. He

knew that crime had struck within the Zenith Building. He was sounding the alarm.

THE elevator was leaving the eighth floor. Two passengers had left it—they were the men who had registered—and only one remained. The operator looked toward the tall personage who held the briefcase.

"Thirty-five," announced the passenger.

The operator nodded. The car sped upward. It reached the thirty-fifth floor. The passenger alighted. The doors closed and the elevator began its downward trip.

A soft laugh came from the lips of the visitor who stood in the corridor of the thirty-fifth floor. Long, white hands opened the briefcase. From it, they drew the folds of black cloth.

This became a cloak which slipped over shoulders. A slouch hat settled on the visitor's head. Black gloves were drawn over white hands. A brace of automatics came from the briefcase and disappeared beneath the folds of the cloak.

Then the case itself was rolled into small compass. It went out of sight beneath the cloak as the tall visitant moved in the direction of a stairway. This being who had passed the watchman was indeed a creature of the night.

It was The Shadow who was descending from the thirty-fifth floor of the Zenith Building.

Crime had already struck in the Zenith Building. No word of its completion could have reached The Shadow. Yet he was here, in the building where one man lay murdered and another was held a prisoner, to have crime planted upon him. George Hobston's suite of offices was on the thirty-third floor. The Shadow had alighted at the thirty-fifth. His course had become a descent. He reached the thirty-third floor and there he stopped.

The corridor was silent. A full four minutes had elapsed since the watchman in the lobby had received the telephone call from 3318. The Shadow had been in the elevator when the watchman had gained word.

An automatic bristled in The Shadow's fist as the black-garbed visitant stopped before the door of 3318. The free hand turned the knob. The Shadow entered the suite. A tiny flashlight appeared in his left hand. It sent a shining disk of light about the outer office.

The room was empty. Striding to the inner office, The Shadow saw that this dimly lighted room contained but a single occupant. That lone man was dead. The body of George Hobston lay sprawled where the murderer had left it.

THE SHADOW saw the telephone upon the desk. The receiver, lying beside the instrument itself, was proof of what had happened. The Shadow knew that a call had been made below. That call, moreover, had been given during the last four minutes.

Approaching the body, The Shadow detected something else. It was the trace of revolver smoke; a faint odor of burned powder that was most noticeable close to the desk. The Shadow's eyes saw the swirling of heavy fog from the opened window. The Shadow knew the answer.

A shot had been fired close by this desk. Yet, as The Shadow viewed Hobston's body, he could tell that the man had been killed from a greater range. A soft laugh came from The Shadow's hidden lips. It sounded weirdly through this room of death.

Subtle in his conclusions, The Shadow could see factors that others would not note. Hobston's dead left hand was clamped to the fallen receiver. His right hand, however, was loose as it stretched toward the telephone.

An inconsistency that others might pass; yet to The Shadow, it was evidence of what had actually occurred. Beginning with the scent of powder—an odor that would soon be disseminated throughout the room—The Shadow had gained a starting point.

A murderer, he knew, had deliberately given an alarm. Why? The answer must be here. Already, The Shadow was looking toward the spot where it could be found—the grilled door to the lighted vault room.

The Shadow had observed that entrance before he had viewed Hobston's body. All the while, he had been sending keen glances toward the metal door. Howard Norwyn, slumped behind the grillwork, was motionless. The Shadow had glimpsed the outline of his body; but had left the inspection of the vault room until later.

A sound came upward from the street. It was the whine of a siren. A police car was arriving through the fog. Again, The Shadow laughed. Like a living phantom, he strode to the grillwork and worked upon the automatic lock.

His keen eyes flashed as they surveyed the form within. Lack of motion by Howard Norwyn had indicated that the young man might be dead. But as The Shadow worked, Norwyn moved. He blinked. He stared at the grillwork; he could see the motion of blackness beyond it.

Then Norwyn realized that he held a revolver. The fact impressed itself as he was rising. Thinking that an enemy stood without, the young man emitted a hoarse cry, just as the door swung open in The Shadow's grasp.

Norwyn raised his gun too late. Like a living avalanche, The Shadow came sweeping in upon him. A blackened fist clipped Norwyn's chin. The young man slumped to the floor. The revolver clattered from his hand.

The Shadow gained the weapon. He opened the chamber and spied one empty cartridge. A soft laugh came from his lips as he pocketed the weapon. Standing above Norwyn's slumped form, The Shadow gazed at Hobston's body.

THE situation was plain. Someone had murdered George Hobston. The killer had thrust Howard Norwyn into the vault room, planting the gun upon him. The grillwork offered numerous loopholes. It would have been easy for a man to have killed Hobston from this room.

The false evidence looked plain. Apparently Hobston and Norwyn had quarreled. Hobston had managed to lock Norwyn in the vault room. Then Hobston had put in his call; Norwyn, coming back to his senses, had shot his employer in the back.

The openings in the grill were too small to push a revolver through. Hence Norwyn could not have gotten rid of the gun until released. Had the police arrived before The Shadow, they would surely have arrested Howard Norwyn as the murderer of George Hobston.

The police! Again, a siren's whine came cutting up through the foggy night. The Shadow's laugh was grim. The Shadow could see the truth of what had happened here. He knew that Howard Norwyn must have been overcome by some swift-acting foe.

The real murderer was gone. To leave the wrong man here for the police to quiz would be in keeping with the murderer's desire. Too late to apprehend the killer himself, The Shadow, at least, could balk the criminal's schemes.

The Shadow had a double opportunity. First, to release Howard Norwyn from his dilemma; second, to leave the police looking for the murderer. The man who killed George Hobston could not have gone far. Doubtless, he was still in the building; secure in the thought that murder would be blamed upon Howard Norwyn. The Shadow saw a way to save an innocent man from trouble; also to force the police to the search, which the murderer thought would be delayed.

Turning toward the vault, The Shadow stooped and raised Norwyn's body over his shoulder. Carrying the unconscious young man as a trifling burden, The Shadow strode toward the outer office.

In his possession, the black-clad investigator was carrying the revolver which contained the empty cartridge. The Shadow reached the corridor. It was as silent as before; yet The Shadow knew that any minute would bring men of the law into this hallway.

Swiftly, The Shadow gained the stairway. Still carrying his burden, he turned upward. As he did, a shuddering laugh of triumph came from his lips. Echoes died along the hall. The Shadow was gone;

Howard Norwyn with him. Silence reigned for the space of seven seconds.

Then came the clang of the opening elevator doors. Three men leaped into the corridor. Detectives had arrived from headquarters. They were here to view the scene of crime. They did not know that a visitor from the night had arrived before them.

For The Shadow, swift and decisive, had left no trace of his mysterious presence. Yet he had carried away the man on whom crime had been planted; and with him, the weapon that the murderer had used to deliver death.

CHAPTER III
THE DEPARTURE

THE detectives had left the door of the elevator open. The operator, no longer languorous, was lingering in the corridor until their return. He did not have long to wait. Two detectives came on the run from 3318.

"A guy's been murdered," one of them informed. "You're going to take me down to the lobby, so I can bring up the rest of the squad. Say— we'll have to start a search of this whole blamed building."

"You're right," returned the other dick. "Have 'em keep a close watch in the lobby all the while. There's no way for the murderer to get out of this building except by the elevators. That's a cinch."

"This is the only car that's running," remarked the operator. "The others are all down in the basement."

"Good," commented the detective.

While this conversation was under way, The Shadow had reached the floor above. At a spot directly over the heads of the detectives and the operator, he had laid Howard Norwyn on the floor. Strong hands were at work on the closed doors of the elevator shaft. With an instrument of steel, pried between the sliding metal barriers, The Shadow released the catch.

The doors opened; peering downward, The Shadow saw the top of the elevator a few feet below. He could hear no sound of talk; for the elevator was a solid car that completely filled its portion of the shaft.

Easing downward, The Shadow gained a footing on the top of the elevator. His strong arms stretched forward and drew Howard Norwyn into the shaft. The Shadow rested the young man on the car; his gloved hand eased the doors shut.

In the midst of solid blackness, The Shadow crouched to the top of the elevator and gripped Howard Norwyn in a firm grasp. The space was ample; so long as The Shadow held Norwyn on his precarious perch, no harm could befall the man who had been rescued.

Yet The Shadow was not a second too soon. Hardly had he completed his preparation before the muffled clang of the doors sounded from the thirty-third floor. The elevator began a record drop on its way to the ground floor.

The Shadow clutched Howard Norwyn tightly during the three-hundred-foot descent. His grip was firm as the car came to a stop at the lobby. Doors clanged again. Footsteps shuffled from the elevator; but voices could not be heard in the lobby.

THE SHADOW was counting, however, upon another interval. Sliding over the side of the car, he slipped downward until his feet rested upon the top of an elevator that was on the basement level. From this adjoining shaft, The Shadow could just reach Norwyn's feet. He drew the young man toward him as Norwyn's body came limply from above. The Shadow caught it and rested the stupefied man upon the lower elevator.

Seconds passed; then doors clanged. A whirr of air as the first elevator sped upward. Its shaft was clear. The Shadow edged over the side of the basement elevator and worked upon the lower doors. They came open. The Shadow dropped to his objective.

Getting Norwyn through was a more difficult task. The Shadow was standing at the edge of the shaft which contained the one operating elevator. Below was a pit of considerable depth. The Shadow was equal to the job. He brought Norwyn's light form over the edge of the elevator, caught the slumping body and swung it to safety. In the basement, The Shadow closed the doors to the shaft.

During the day, the basement of the Zenith Building served as a concourse to the subway. At night, however, heavy doors were closed at the top of the stairs to the lobby. Hence the basement was deserted; not only that, the police who had arrived in the building had not started a search in this direction.

Howard Norwyn was coming to his senses. The whizzing trip down through the elevator shaft had produced a reviving effect. But The Shadow gathered him as before and carried him along the deserted concourse.

A turn in the wall brought The Shadow to a heavy barrier. A pair of metal doors, dimly discernible outside the range of the basement lights, were closed and locked. These, during the day, stayed open against the walls. At night, they were shut. A huge bar, dropped from one door into a catch on the other, added strength to the lock.

The Shadow again rested Howard Norwyn on the floor. By this time, the young man was almost entirely conscious. He was rubbing his chin ruefully, trying to take in his surroundings. He stared toward

The Shadow, who was by the doors, but he could barely discern the black-clad shape.

The Shadow was picking the lock. Clicks responded to his efforts. He forced the big bar upward and poised it carefully as he opened the door on the right. Turning, The Shadow gazed toward Howard Norwyn. His gleaming eyes saw that the young man was recovered, but still dizzy. The Shadow stepped beyond the door.

There he dropped coat, hat and gloves. The black garments went into the unfolded briefcase. Depositing the bag, The Shadow stepped back through the door and approached Howard Norwyn.

"Come." The Shadow's voice was a quiet, commanding tone, different from his sinister whisper. "We must leave. Do not delay."

Howard Norwyn nodded. He sensed that this was a friend. The Shadow aided him to rise. Norwyn passed through the open door. The Shadow drew the barrier slowly shut; then gave it a quick jerk that caused a slight clang. From inside came the answer; the poised bar dropped from the jolt and clattered into position. The doors were barred on the inside as before!

THE SHADOW and Howard Norwyn were in a gloomy underground passage, where the only light came from a hundred feet ahead. The Shadow paused to work upon the lock that he had opened. With the aid of a special key, he again locked the door. Picking up his briefcase, he gripped Howard Norwyn by the arm. Together, they made their way along the underground passage.

Norwyn blinked as he came into the light. For the first time, he realized where he was. They were entering the subway station, one block from the Zenith Building. The Shadow had opened the way between the skyscraper and the station.

Howard Norwyn followed his rescuer through the turnstile. A train was coming into the station; The Shadow urged Norwyn aboard. As they stood on the platform of the car, Norwyn studied this stranger who had brought him here.

He did not recognize The Shadow as the one who had encountered him at the door of the vault room. Nor did Norwyn recall the strange journey through the elevator shaft. He remembered, dimly, that he had found George Hobston dead. He could recollect an enemy striking him down; then this friend who had brought him to the subway.

The face that Norwyn viewed was a singular one. It was a countenance that might have been chiseled from stone. Thin lips, inflexible features; these formed the masklike face. Most noticeable, however, were the eyes that burned from the sides of a hawklike nose.

Those steady optics held Howard Norwyn with their gaze. Dizzy as he clutched the inner door of the speeding subway car, Norwyn lost all sense of other things about him. The roar of the train precluded speech. The dominating eyes commanded trust and obedience.

The express came to a stop. A sliding door moved open; The Shadow's hand caught Norwyn's arm. Nodding, the young man followed his commander to the platform. The Shadow headed for an obscure flight of steps. He and Norwyn reached the street.

They were at Fourteenth Street. Half a block from the station, Norwyn's rescuer stopped beside a limousine. A chauffeur bounded to the street. He opened the door. Norwyn felt a steady hand thrust him into the car. Then his companion joined him.

"New Jersey, Stanley," spoke a quiet voice through the speaking tube.

THE car rolled away. Howard Norwyn settled back in the cushions. He began to feel a sinking sensation. The back of his head was aching as a reminder of the pounding that it had received from the antagonist in Hobston's office.

"Where—where are we going?" questioned Norwyn, faintly.

"You will learn later," came the quiet reply.

"But—but what has happened to Mr. Hobston?" protested the young man. "Who—who killed him?"

"That we shall discover."

"But I—I should be back there. I—I must explain to the police. If they—if they—"

"If they find you, they will hold you for murder."

Howard Norwyn clutched at the strap which hung beside the window of the limousine. He tried to bring himself up from the cushions to stare at the quiet speaker. All he could see was the outline of the other rider.

The words still rang in Norwyn's ears. Sickened, the young man dropped back. He realized the truth of those steady words. He understood what the murderer had intended. Much had been stolen from Hobston's vault. Enough, however, remained to incriminate whomever the police might have found in the vault room.

"The revolver!" gasped Norwyn, suddenly. "I—I had it in my hand. Was it—was it—"

"It was the gun that killed George Hobston. It was in your possession. I have brought it with us."

A sigh of relief came from Howard Norwyn. It was followed by a groan as the young man realized that a predicament still existed. Norwyn's aching head rolled back against the top of the seat. Dazedly, his mind was yielding to drumming thoughts of new danger.

A hand stretched forward. It held a small vial. As Norwyn grasped the little bottle, he heard the command from beside him:

"Drink."

Norwyn pressed the bottle to his lips. He swallowed its contents. His head became light. The vial slipped from his hands. Swimming thoughts faded; under the influence of the opiate, Howard Norwyn slumped against the cushions and became quiet.

His worries were ended for the night. On the morrow, The Shadow would hear his story. The limousine had passed through the Holland Tunnel. It was heading into New Jersey, carrying its pair of passengers from Manhattan.

Howard Norwyn was traveling from the scene of crime. His course would not be traced. The Shadow had brought him from the spot where he had been left to bear the brunt of crime. Yet The Shadow knew that Norwyn's safety could be no more than temporary until the real murderer should be uncovered.

A soft laugh came from the darkness of the limousine. The whispered mirth of The Shadow faded. The rescue of Howard Norwyn had been effected. Work of more importance lay ahead.

That laugh presaged determination. It was The Shadow's challenge to hidden plotters who had gained their aim of crime. Against them, The Shadow had scored one point: the rescue of the man on whom they had sought to shoulder murder.

There was other work to be accomplished. The murderer of George Hobston must be discovered; with him all who had concerned themselves with that crime. The Shadow could foresee a mighty task.

Perhaps it was the subtlety of the murder itself; perhaps it was quickness with which the actual murderer had made his getaway—either of these points might have impressed The Shadow. Whichever the case, there was something strangely grim about The Shadow's laugh.

The master of darkness recognized that he was dealing with unusual crime. He could see that this episode might be but one in a sequence of malignant events. The Shadow knew the need for counterstrokes against a hidden menace.

Well did The Shadow divine hidden facts! Tonight, he had encountered a phase of crime that was merely the surface indication of what lay beneath. The Shadow had but reached the threshold beyond which he was to find insidious evil.

For in his rescue of Howard Norwyn, The Shadow had gained only a first and minor thrust against the most amazing organization of crime workers that he had ever encountered!

CHAPTER IV
THE POLICE SEARCH

ONE hour had passed since The Shadow had carried Howard Norwyn from the Zenith Building. In that space of time, much had taken place within the walls of the towering skyscraper. Office 3318 had become the headquarters of a massed investigation.

Three men were standing by the desk where George Hobston's body lay. One, a grizzled veteran of the police force, was Inspector Timothy Klein. The second was a police surgeon. The third was a stocky, swarthy man, whose keen dark eyes were watching the other two as they spoke. This was Detective Joe Cardona, ace sleuth of the New York force.

Though Klein was technically in charge, Cardona was the man upon whom the investigation hinged. As a hound upon the trail of crime, Cardona was conceded to be the best in Manhattan. He was listening to the surgeon's report: the statement that death had been caused by a bullet wound; that the shot had probably been fired from a dozen feet away.

When Klein turned to Cardona, he found the detective ready with theories. Joe stepped toward the door to the outer office. He pointed toward Hobston's body.

"A shot would have got him from here," volunteered the detective. "Suppose Hobston came in and sat at his desk. A fellow sneaking in from outside could have picked him off before he had a chance."

"That looks likely," agreed Klein. "But what about—"

"The vault," interposed Joe. "That's right. I'm coming to it. Suppose Hobston had opened the vault. He might have gone back to his desk. The theory still stands."

"Why would he have left the vault open?"

"Only because he suspected no danger. Because he knew that the only visitor would be a man whom he could trust. Like this fellow."

Cardona produced the registration book. It had been brought up from the lobby. He pointed to the name of Howard Norwyn.

Klein nodded. "I think you've got it, Joe," he declared. "Norwyn must have come in; seeing the vault open, he took a shot at Hobston. He started to rifle the vault; then got scared and made a getaway."

THERE was commendation in the inspector's tone. The detective, however, made no response. Cardona was studying his own theory, putting it to a stronger test. At last he came to a point that puzzled him.

"The phone call," he declared. "I can't figure it."

"Why not?"

"Picture it this way." Cardona strode toward the open door of the vault room. "Hobston opens the gate. He goes to his desk"—Cardona paused while he approached the body in the chair—"and while he's there, Norwyn enters. He sees two things that interest him."

Cardona paused emphatically and backed toward the door to the outer office, to indicate that he was playing the part of Norwyn from this point on.

"He sees the open gate over there," resumed Cardona, with a gesture, "and he sees Hobston sitting by the desk. He's got a chance to grab what's in the vault. All right, Inspector. What does he do?"

"He takes a shot at Hobston," answered Klein. "Puts a bullet in his back, as you suggested before."

"Yeah?" questioned Cardona, wisely. "And after Hobston is shot, he picks up the phone and calls downstairs, where the watchman hears the shot all over again?"

"I see your point, Joe," nodded Klein. "Norwyn must have covered Hobston from where you're standing. He threatened him. Hobston picked up the telephone to call the watchman. Norwyn fired."

"Wrong again." Cardona shook his head. "Norwyn wouldn't have given him a chance to do all that. I'll tell you where Norwyn found Hobston, Inspector. He trapped him at the door of the vault room."

Keeping the role of Norwyn, Cardona crept toward the open vault room. He suddenly made a leap, as for an imaginary antagonist. He stopped short and faced Klein.

"That's what happened," announced the detective. "Norwyn didn't pull a gun. He tried to knock out Hobston; but his boss must have handed him a haymaker instead. Then Hobston shoved Norwyn in the vault room and went over to make the phone call."

Klein was nodding unconsciously as he listened to Cardona's deduction. The police surgeon was standing attentive. He, too, seemed deeply interested.

"Norwyn woke up," resumed Cardona. "He was here, in the vault room. He heard Hobston trying to make the call. He pulled his gun—Hobston probably didn't know he had one—and either shoved the door open or shot through a hole in the grillwork. Come over here; take a look at the body from this angle."

The police surgeon accompanied the inspector to the door of the vault room. Klein was the first to nod as he studied the angle. He looked toward the police surgeon; the physician added his nod.

"I've got a hunch," decided Cardona, "that Norwyn was behind the door. Maybe Hobston jammed it, but didn't get it locked. The point is that Norwyn was in too much of a hurry to get away. He didn't have time to grab up the swag he wanted."

"He only had a few minutes," agreed Klein. "Our men got here mighty quick after the watchman reported the shot. It's a sure bet, Joe, that Norwyn is still here in the building."

"Right," declared Cardona. "That's why there's no use going into more detail on this reconstruction. Our job is to find Norwyn. Suppose we go down to the lobby and find out how the search is coming."

THE three men left the office. A uniformed policeman was standing in the corridor. Klein ordered him to take charge of the body. The inspector led the way to the elevators and rang the bell. The car arrived and the trio descended.

They were met in the lobby by Detective Sergeant Markham. Klein's inquiry regarding the search received a negative response.

"They're reporting in from every floor," declared Markham, as he went to answer a buzz at the telephone. "Not a ripple. Here's another report." He picked up the receiver and uttered a few short sentences; then hung up and turned to Klein. "That was Grady from the twenty-fourth. Nothing doing on that floor."

"What about the elevators?" demanded Cardona.

"Only one operating," spoke the watchman, from beside the registration desk. "You know, when I heard that shot and reported it, I watched the elevator dials like a hawk. Not a move from any of them—except the car that was in use."

"None of these fellows is Norwyn," stated Markham, pointing toward the end of the lobby.

Cardona turned to see a group of a dozen men under guard of two policemen. The watchman approached the detective in pleading fashion.

"You took the book upstairs, sir," he reminded. "It has the names of all these gentlemen in it. They were in their offices when the police entered."

"Here's the book," declared Cardona. "We can check on these men right now. Sorry to trouble you, gentlemen, but there's been a murder in this building. There's one man we want to get. His name is Howard Norwyn."

One by one, Cardona quizzed the men. He made each sign his name; then compared the signature with the one that the man had written in the book. He also checked each name with the watchman.

By the time this procedure was finished, five more men had come down under police guard. Cardona went through the same formality with them.

"Look at this, inspector!" Cardona's exclamation was a triumphant one. "We've checked on every name except one. That's Howard Norwyn."

"But he's the one you need," said Klein, glumly.

"Sure," resumed Cardona, "but if we get anybody now, we'll have a suspect. By rights—according to this register book—there should only be one man left in the whole Zenith Building. That's Howard Norwyn."

"I get it," nodded Klein. "There might be somebody else here; somebody that sneaked in."

"Yes." Cardona turned suddenly as the elevator door clanged open and men appeared. A disappointed frown showed on the detective's face. The final squad of searchers had arrived, without another man with them.

Reports were checked. The lobby teemed with foiled searchers. The manhunt had started promptly after the police had discovered George Hobston's body. Outfitted with pass keys, detectives and officers had gone through the skyscraper from top to bottom.

Even the basement was to be searched, according to Klein's new decision. The watchman was positive that Norwyn could not have gone there, but the

**The manhunt had started promptly after the police had discovered
George Hobston's body.**

inspector was determined to make this last effort to trace the one man who had registered and who had not reappeared.

CONFERRING with Cardona, Klein decided not to hold the other occupants of the building. None of them had been found in the vicinity of the thirty-third floor. All had legitimate business that had brought them to the building. Cardona quizzed each man closely and checked with the officers who had taken them into custody. That formality ended, the lobby cleared. Inspector Klein and Joe Cardona waited for the small squad of searchers to return from the basement.

While the detective was making another check-up with the watchman, a policeman entered and advanced to Joe Cardona. This officer was one of two who had been stationed outside the building.

"Some newshounds out there," began the blue-coat. "I told 'em they couldn't come in. Said you'd see them later—"

"That's right," growled Cardona. "Let them wait. The weather's good for them."

"But there's one guy that raised a squawk. Says you'll want to see him. His name's Burke—he works for the *Classic*."

"Burke, eh?" Cardona laughed. "Tell him to come in. I'll talk to him."

The officer left. Cardona swung to Klein and spoke a few words of explanation.

"You know Burke," said Joe. "He's all right. We've got to let the newspapers have this story. If Burke acts as spokesman, he'll give them the right slant. He'll hand us the credit that's our due. None of this stuff about a futile search by the police."

As Cardona finished speaking, a young man appeared from the outer door. He grinned as he removed his felt hat and splashed water from the brim. Clyde Burke was a typical newspaperman. His manner was keen; his expression genial. He was wiry but not husky. His eyes began a prompt survey of the lobby.

"Hello, Joe" was his greeting. "Say, have a heart, won't you? Let the boys in out of the rain. They're sticking around to get the story and they're pretty sore because their police cards won't get them through."

"I'll let them in pretty soon," returned Cardona. "They'll cool off when they get the story. But I want to talk to you first, Burke.

"Get this straight. In less than ten minutes after the watchman here heard a shot over the telephone, there were three detectives in room 3318, where the shooting took place. There were five men more down here in the lobby.

"The murderer had no chance to get out. So far as we know, he's still in the building. We're completing the search. We haven't found him; but it's not because of any slip-up on our part."

"What about those men who filed out of here?" questioned Clyde. "Some of the boys were going to duck along after them. I held the fellows, though, by promising to get them in to see you."

"Those men," explained Cardona, "were business-men who were in their offices. We checked them on the register and released them. We have accounted for everyone except the one man we want.

"You give that to the other newspapermen. See that they get off to the right start on the story. Then bring them in and I'll answer questions."

"Leave it to me, Joe."

CLYDE BURKE hurried back to the door. Joe Cardona smiled as he turned to Timothy Klein. The searchers were returning with the news that the basement was unoccupied except for the employees in the engine room. Cardona had expected that report. His elation was due to the way in which he had handled Clyde Burke.

"A real fellow, that reporter," declared Joe. "I'm glad he got this assignment. More brains than any other newshound I ever met. Why he sticks to the *Classic* job is more than I can figure."

There was logic in Joe Cardona's statement. There was also an answer to his speculation regarding Clyde Burke. It came half an hour later, after the reporters had entered, gained the details of the murder and search, and left for their respective offices.

Clyde Burke, nearing the *Classic* building, stepped into a cigar store and entered a telephone booth. He called a number and heard a quiet voice respond:

"Burbank speaking."

For the next few minutes Clyde Burke delivered terse details of the police findings at the Zenith Building. These facts were not for the New York *Classic*.

Clyde Burke was an agent of The Shadow. Through Burbank, The Shadow's contact man, he was reporting all that he had learned. His statements would be forwarded as soon as his call was finished.

Thus The Shadow, who had played so important a part after the murder of George Hobston, was to learn the vital news that no killer had been found in the Zenith Building.

The fact that Howard Norwyn was suspected and missing was one that The Shadow expected to hear. But The Shadow was to learn another fact that he would find important: namely, that no unregistered prowler had been found at large.

That fact was to play a part in The Shadow's coming plans. It was to give him the inkling that the murder of George Hobston had been well planned beforehand. It was to place The Shadow face to face with the truth; that craft had been used in murder.

The planting of crime on Howard Norwyn had been the first evidence of cunning preparation. The disappearance of the actual murderer was even more remarkable. Already, word was on the way that would make The Shadow prepare for new and unseen crime!

CHAPTER V
MURDERERS TALK

IT was nine o'clock the next morning. The Zenith Building's business day had begun. The massive skyscraper, glistening like a marble pinnacle in the sun, was thronged with hordes of workers.

Morning newspapers had blared the story of George Hobston's murder. To the workers in the Zenith Building, the killing in 3318 was a subject of intense discussion. Few of them had ever heard of George Hobston. The dead man's name was but one of hundreds on the big boards in the lobby. Yet the fact that he had been murdered in the Zenith Building was real news to the working inhabitants of that particular skyscraper.

A portly, gray-haired gentleman heard the talk of Hobston's death as he rode up to the thirtieth floor. Alighting from the elevator, this man approached an office that bore the name:

CULBERT JOQUILL
ATTORNEY AT LAW

Entering, he nodded pleasantly to the office force, which consisted of two stenographers and a young man who looked like a recent graduate of law school. He continued through a door marked "Private."

This man was Culbert Joquill. He was in his own office. Massive bookcases lined the walls; from floor to ceiling they were filled with buckram-bound volumes that pertained to the law. Joquill seated himself behind a mahogany desk and stared in beaming fashion from the window.

A stenographer entered with the mail. Joquill opened letters, read them, and dictated replies in the stentorian tone that he might have saved for addressing a jury. This finished, he arose and walked to the door as the stenographer went back into the larger office.

"I do not care to be disturbed for the next half hour," he announced. "If any clients call, tell them that they must wait. I am preparing an important brief. I shall notify you when I have finished."

To emphasize his statement, Culbert Joquill closed the door of his inner office and turned the key. Walking back toward the window, he stopped at a bookcase and removed two volumes from a lower shelf. Pressing his fingers into a crevice, he clicked a hidden catch. Stepping back, he drew a section of the bookcase outward on a hinge. The action revealed a small room, no more than six feet square.

A man was seated on a rumpled couch. He arose with a grin as the bookcase opened. He stepped into Joquill's private office. The light from the window showed the evil leer upon his lips. It marked his face as that of the man who had murdered George Hobston and thrust Howard Norwyn into the vault room of 3318.

CULBERT JOQUILL closed the bookcase. He waved the ugly-faced man to a chair; then took his own position behind the desk. He smiled placidly as the man from the little room put an eager, whispered question:

"Did you read the newspapers?"

Culbert Joquill nodded.

"Did they get him?" the man questioned. "Did they get Norwyn? What did he have to say?"

"They did not get him," responded Joquill, in a quiet tone. "However, it does not matter. His name is given in the newspapers; he is suspected as the murderer of George Hobston. What is more important—to myself as well as to you—is the name they did not mention. The newspapers say nothing regarding Garry Hewes."

The ugly-lipped man grinned. This statement referred to him. He could see a pleased look on Joquill's face. He settled back into the chair.

"Substantially," declared the lawyer, in a soft tone, "the story is this. George Hobston entered his office at nine o'clock. At nine fifteen, Howard Norwyn arrived. Apparently, Norwyn must have threatened Hobston, who overpowered him, placed him in the vault room and called the watchman.

"Norwyn, however, had a gun. He managed to shoot Hobston. Then—probably due to Hobston's neglect in locking the grilled door—Norwyn escaped. The building was searched. No trace was found of him."

"The police found the gun?"

"No."

"You just mentioned that they said he had one."

"I was stating the theory as advanced by the police. The evidence against Howard Norwyn is purely circumstantial. Read the newspapers after you leave here. Form your own conclusions."

Garry Hewes was staring from the window. His face was speculative. Culbert Joquill seemed to be awaiting his henchman's reply. Garry spoke in a puzzled tone.

"Here's what happened, Joquill," he stated. "I stayed here after five o'clock yesterday afternoon. I kept in the hideout behind the bookcase. I heard the scrub women come in and go out. I waited until half past eight.

"Then I went up to Hobston's office. I found a good place to hide in his outer office. I intended to threaten him; to make him open the vault before Norwyn arrived. That was where I got a break. Hobston opened the vault himself. I didn't lose any time. I piled in from the outside office and plugged him in the back.

"With Hobston dead, the game was to plant it on Norwyn. So I lugged Hobston to the desk and fixed him so his back was toward the vault room. I turned out the light in the big office. I waited there until Norwyn arrived.

"He saw the open vault room. He saw Hobston's body. Then I whacked him. Shoved him in the vault room and put the death gun in his mitt. I figured he'd come to inside of five minutes. So I made a phony call to the watchman in the lobby. I fired a shot out through the window; made a couple of gargles; then beat it.

"I left Norwyn to be the goat. I never thought he'd manage to get out. That lock on the vault-room door must have jammed. Norwyn had sense enough to beat it when he came to his senses.

"Anyway, I came back here. I laid in the hide-out; I heard searchers coming through this office. I figured that Norwyn must have been found; that he said the real murderer was somewhere in the building. I thought they were making a search to find out if he was right. Now you tell me that it was Norwyn they were hunting for."

"Precisely," nodded Culbert Joquill. "Joe Cardona, the smart detective, fell for your idea. He decided that Hobston overpowered Norwyn and shoved him in the vault room. Hence, as I remarked before, Norwyn's successful flight has made him a marked man. No one will believe his story when he is captured. He is definitely a fugitive."

"Good," said Garry, with a grin. He nudged his thumb toward the bookcase. "The swag is back there—all those securities and the cash that Hobston owned for himself. I left the other stuff—the stocks and bonds marked with the names of clients—in the vault room to make it look bad for Norwyn."

"Did you get Hobston's private book?"

"I did. Here it is." Garry produced a leather-bound pocket memorandum. "It tallies exactly with the swag. More than half a million total."

CULBERT JOQUILL took the little book and smiled as he thumbed the pages. Finished with his brief inspection, the gray-haired lawyer chuckled.

"This office is very similar to Hobston's," he remarked. "Like his suite, this one has its strong-room." He pointed toward the bookcase. "However, I found it most suitable to close off my little alcove.

"Lucky, isn't it, that the police never suspected a space behind that bookcase? They took it for granted that this was just an ordinary law office. Those books, with the thin woodwork behind them, form a better barrier than the grilled door to Hobston's vault room."

"I found that out last night," returned Garry.

"This office," remarked Joquill, as an added thought, "differs in one respect from Hobston's. It has a door of its own leading to the hall. That is essential in a lawyer's office. It is always poor policy to usher clients out through the anteroom.

"So you, Garry, can leave by my private exit." The attorney pointed to a door at the far end of the room. "You were here yesterday before the watchman went on duty; you are leaving during business hours today. Communicate with me later—about the end of the week."

Garry Hewes arose. He turned toward the exit. He took a few paces; then turned and came back to the desk. He stood there with a quizzical expression on his face.

"Listen, Joquill," he stated. "You and I are in the same boat. You ordered Hobston's death and I went through with it. That was the best arrangement, because you and I are different.

"You're a big-timer. I'm nothing but an ordinary gorilla that you imported from the Middle West. I've got sense enough to stay away from gangsters here in New York because you've paid me good money to play I was respectable.

"You're smart, Joquill. You moved in here a month ago; you fixed this hideout in simple fashion. But you didn't pick the Zenith Building just for fun. You took it because you were gunning for George Hobston. Am I right?"

"Certainly," smiled Joquill.

"Well," resumed Garry, with an uneasy shift, "that's what bothers me. The hideout worked; the job's gone through; but there's a couple of points that don't look so good.

"How did you find out that Hobston was hoarding his securities—that he had a lot of real dough stored in his vault with no record except the little book in his pocket?

"How did you arrange it for Hobston to come to his office last night; and how did you fix it so that Norwyn would be there for my frame-up?"

Garry Hewes paused. Culbert Joquill frowned. His tone was cold as he replied to his henchman's questions.

"Those matters," asserted the old lawyer, "do not concern you, Garry. Forget them."

"I can't forget them," pleaded Garry. "They do concern me. I figure you must have known Hobston personally. What's more, you must have pulled some gag to get him and Norwyn into the office last night. Suppose the police get working right.

Suppose this smart dick, Cardona, finds the trail to you. What then?"

A broad smile appeared on Culbert Joquill's crafty lips. The lawyer's frown was gone. Joquill had taken Garry's questions as an unwarranted attempt to pry into affairs which did not concern him; but the henchman's explanation of his qualms were justification.

"Do not worry," purred Joquill, in a confidential tone. "You have admitted that I am smart. Take my word for it that the police will never trace me. I knew that George Hobston had that secret wealth in his vault. I knew that he and Howard Norwyn would be at the office last night.

"Yet I made no effort to trace those facts. To me, George Hobston and Howard Norwyn were nothing more than names. Let us regard the whole matter as one of coincidence. Better, let us state that I acted upon sudden inspiration; that the possibilities of crime came to me as in a dream.

"I am serious, Garry." Joquill set his fist upon the desk. "Between those facts and myself is a breach that can never be leaped. No one will ever know how I came to enter into this successful episode of crime. You think of me as a crafty schemer, do you not? Let me tell you more: I have a certain possession—we might say talisman—that makes my position invulnerable.

"I did not need you for a henchman. I chose you simply because I knew your past; because I was positive that you were a strong-armed worker upon whom I could rely. I do not care to play an active part in crime. I have taken you as an instrument with which to work.

"I am the brain, so far as you are concerned. You know that I planned Hobston's death some weeks ago. It occurred on perfect schedule. Do you think that my plans came to an abrupt ending with last night?"

Rising, Culbert Joquill approached his henchman. He clapped his hand upon Garry's shoulder; then drew the ugly-faced killer toward the door to the hall.

"Forget your worries," suggested Joquill. "You are safe because my position is secure. My part in this entire episode has been one of complete concealment. I am a recognized attorney; the fact that I have an office in the Zenith Building means nothing.

"I am but one of hundreds of other tenants. So far as Hobston's death is concerned, I am but a chance reader of the newspaper accounts. You understand?"

Garry Hewes nodded. His qualms were allayed. Turning, this tool who had performed murder stalked, unseen, from Culbert Joquill's private exit.

THE old lawyer chuckled as he returned to his desk. Taking pen and sheet of paper, he inscribed a series of odd-shaped circles. They apparently formed a code.

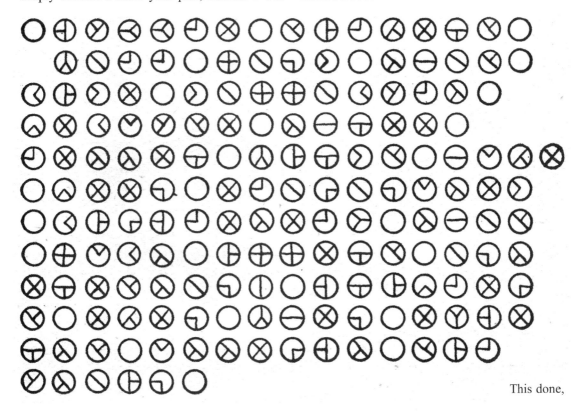

This done,

Joquill began another peculiar inscription, formed with a succession of blocklike characters in several lines.

[coded symbol inscription — four lines of blocklike cipher characters]

Joquill placed the sheets together; he folded them and put them in an envelope. From memory, he made duplicates of each sheet, folded these pairs together and put them into a second envelope.

The lawyer addressed the envelopes and placed stamps upon them. Rising, he strolled to the door of the outer office, unlocked it and walked from his own room. He nodded to two clients who were seated on a bench and remarked that he would soon be back to interview them.

Stepping into the corridor, Joquill continued toward the elevators. There, he posted his letters in the mail chute. Wearing the ghost of a smile, the gray-haired attorney came back through the outer office and continued into his private room. He pressed a buzzer. A stenographer appeared to find him behind the desk.

"I am ready to see the gentlemen who are waiting," declared Joquill, quietly. "You may usher them in here."

With hands folded upon the desk, Culbert Joquill looked the part of a conservative English barrister. His task of crime had been completed; the mailing of those coded notes had been the aftermath of his talk with Garry Hewes.

The hideout closed; its occupant gone; the spoils of George Hobston's vault stowed safely from view, Culbert Joquill had no worry. He was resuming the role which he could play so well because it was his actual capacity: that of a consulting attorney.

Murder remained unavenged; and Culbert Joquill was confident that no investigator in all New York could possibly trace crime to him.

CHAPTER VI
THE SHADOW WAITS

WHILE Culbert Joquill and Garry Hewes were discussing their successful crime, the murder of George Hobston was receiving close attention elsewhere. A tall, calm-faced personage was seated in a bizarre room, reading the complete accounts in the morning newspapers.

He was the same hawk-faced stranger who had rescued Howard Norwyn on the previous night. His chiseled countenance was steady, even when relaxed. His eyes seemed burning as they scanned the headlines.

The room in which this personage dwelt at present was remarkable to the extreme. Its walls were furnished with a remarkable assortment of curios.

Tapestries, adorned with golden dragons; a huge Malay kris suspended from the ceiling like the sword of Damocles; a portion of an Alaskan totem pole; a mummy case standing in a corner—these were but a few of the articles that made the place look like a museum.

The hawkish face turned toward the door as a knock sounded. Thin lips gave the order to enter. A servant appeared and bowed from the doorway.

"What is it, Richards?" questioned the occupant of the curio room.

"Your guest is awake, sir," replied the menial. "I have served his breakfast. He is finished."

"And now he wishes to speak with me."

"Yes, sir."

"Usher him to this room."

Richards departed. He returned a few minutes later with Howard Norwyn. The young man was attired in a dressing gown that Richards had evidently provided. Norwyn blinked at sight of the odd curio room. He stared toward the seated figure; in response to a gesture from his host, he entered and seated himself on a cushioned taboret. Richards departed.

HOWARD NORWYN recognized his host as the person who had conducted him to the subway. Yet the young man seemed bewildered. He had slept steadily and had not awakened until late in the morning. The effect of The Shadow's opiate had caused prolonged slumber.

"I presume," came the tones of a quiet voice, "that you are somewhat befuddled regarding your surroundings. Perhaps you are a bit uncertain as to the circumstances which resulted in your arrival here."

"I am," admitted Norwyn. "It seems as though I have had a nightmare; yet events were too realistic to have been false. I know that my employer—George Hobston—was murdered. I realize that I was in a predicament from which you rescued me. But—but—"

"But you do not know where you are." Thin lips formed a slight smile. "Nor do you know who I am."

Howard Norwyn nodded.

"I shall explain," resumed the tall personage. "My name is Lamont Cranston. Perhaps you have heard it."

"Lamont Cranston!" exclaimed Norwyn. "The famous globetrotter?"

"Yes. This is the curio room of my New Jersey home."

"I begin to understand," declared Norwyn. "You purchased stock from Mr. Hobston some months ago. I remember him mentioning you as a customer."

The thin lips still retained their smile. There was a reason for the expression. The face which Howard Norwyn viewed was the countenance of Lamont Cranston; but its wearer was not he.

The real Lamont Cranston—a singular individual who traveled as fancy suited him—was at present in Afghanistan. He would not be back in America for six months to come. When he made his long excursions, Cranston never announced his destination. His friends as well as his servants had no idea when he might return.

There was one, however, who kept a close check on Lamont Cranston's journeys. That one was The Shadow. When The Shadow knew that Cranston was far away, he frequently found it useful to take advantage of the millionaire's eccentricities.

Cranston always kept his establishment in operation. He never talked with his servants regarding his travels. They were trained to expect him home at any hour, on any day; and they were used to his strange departures. Hence The Shadow, during Cranston's absence, often assumed the character of the globe-trotting millionaire. The secluded New Jersey mansion served him well as a headquarters.

"I was one of Hobston's clients," stated The Shadow, in the quiet tones that characterized Lamont Cranston. "I called his club last night and learned that he had gone to his office. So I went there, myself, to call on him."

"You registered in the lobby?"

"No. I happened to pass the man who was on duty. It was not until the elevator was going up that I realized that I had neglected to sign. There was no use in my returning to the ground floor. As matters developed, it was fortunate that I did not register."

Norwyn stared as the speaker paused reminiscently. He saw significance in the quiet smile.

"When I reached Hobston's office," resumed The Shadow, "I found his body. George Hobston had been murdered. There was a light in the vault room. I opened the door—"

"But it was locked!"

"Not quite." Again the smile. "It was jammed and it caused me a bit of trouble. You were in the vault room, coming to your senses as I worked with the door. When it swung open, you apparently took me for an enemy."

"I remember. I had a gun—"

"Which I took from you. There was no time for palaver. I was forced to overpower you and carry you away, for your own good. I feared that the police might find you."

"And blame me for the murder?"

"Yes. As they have already done."

WITH these words, The Shadow passed a newspaper to Howard Norwyn. The young man paled as he saw his name in the headlines. The newspaper trembled in his hands. Then came the reassuring voice of Lamont Cranston.

"By good fortune," remarked The Shadow, "I brought you to the basement; thence to the subway. My chauffeur was waiting with the limousine on Fourteenth Street. He drove us here. No one knows where you are—no one, except myself."

"But—but I must surrender to the police!" blurted Norwyn. "I—I must tell them my story."

"And thereby play into the murderer's hands. That is not the proper course. No, my friend. I have decided that you shall remain here as my guest."

"Until when?"

"Until this case has cleared."

Howard Norwyn uttered a sigh of relief. He remembered the confidence that he had gained from this stranger last night. He was beginning to feel more at ease. He realized that Lamont Cranston was a friend upon whom he could rely.

"Make yourself quite at home," declared The Shadow, in an easy tone. "Free yourself from all qualms. No one will ever guess where you are staying. Richards, my valet, will see that you are provided with whatever you may need."

With this reassurance, The Shadow became silent. Howard Norwyn realized that it was his turn to speak. The steady eyes were inquiring; they wanted his story.

"I didn't expect what happened last night," asserted Norwyn. "It all began around half past eight, when I received a telephone call from a customer named Seth Deswig. It was Deswig's secretary who called. He insisted that he must have some stocks that belonged to him—shares of Middlebury Preferred—and I knew that Mr. Hobston had them in the vault.

"So I called Mr. Hobston at his club. He said he would go to the office and open the vault. I was to join him there. When I arrived, I—I found him dead."

"And the vault?"

"Was open. Envelopes and folders were scattered on the floor. Before I could investigate, someone landed on me. When I woke up, I was in the vault room. You were opening the door. I had a revolver."

"The gun that was used to kill Hobston."

"So I realize. It—it must have been planted on me."

"Exactly. With you were envelopes containing listed securities that belonged to Hobston's customers. It looked as though you had been trapped, while committing robbery."

"I understand that. But what I can't guess is why the murderer didn't take those securities that he must have come to get—"

Norwyn paused abruptly. He saw a new smile forming on Lamont Cranston's lips. He waited, expecting an explanatory statement. It came, as a question.

"Did Hobston," questioned The Shadow, "ever show you an itemized statement of the securities in his vault?"

"No," admitted Norwyn.

"Did he ever mention," resumed The Shadow, "that he had invested a considerable amount of money in securities of his own choice?"

"He said that he never missed opportunities when they came his way."

"You have given the answer. You were not the only person to whom Hobston made that statement. Let us suppose that Hobston had purchased—privately, of course—securities worth about half a million dollars. Where would he have kept them, assuming that he might wish to sell at the most opportune time?"

"In the vault."

"Under whose name?"

"His own."

Silence.

THE truth dawned on Howard Norwyn. He realized that wealth had been taken from that vault. The murderer had rifled the strongbox of Hobston's own possessions—of wealth known to the dead investment man alone—of securities that would not be listed in the office records.

The burglar had deliberately passed up the stocks and bonds that Hobston held in other names. Many of these might have been poor investments; others might have proven non-negotiable. The unlisted wealth had been taken; the rest had been left to add proof to the frame-up against Howard Norwyn.

"That is why," declared The Shadow, "your story must remain untold. There is much to learn; until we have the murderer's trail, you shall remain here."

The tall speaker arose. He opened the door of the curio room and summoned Richards. He told the servant to see to his guest's comfort. With that final order, he departed.

Howard Norwyn, returning to the room which had been assigned him, heard the purr of a motor. Looking through the window, he saw the limousine rolling from the driveway of the broad-lawned estate.

TWO hours later, a light clicked in a darkened room. Bluish rays shone upon a polished table. White hands—one wearing a gleaming gem that sparkled in the glare—appeared upon the woodwork.

The Shadow had reached Manhattan. He was in his sanctum, a strange abode known only to himself. Clippings appeared upon the table; with them, reports in ink, inscribed in code.

Writing faded as The Shadow finished reading these reports. Such was the way with messages that The Shadow gained from his agents. Passing to the clippings, The Shadow studied them with care.

These newspaper reports were of various dates. They told of unsolved crimes in different cities. To them, The Shadow added items that pertained to the death of George Hobston. The hands rested upon the table.

George Hobston's murder was the latest of several crimes that seemed disconnected except for one vital point. All had remained unsolved. Was that coincidence, or did it mean an actual connection? This was the answer that The Shadow sought.

Reports from agents told of possible crimes that might be committed. When The Shadow was temporarily balked in the face of crime, he looked for opportunities that might attract crooks.

This was how he had learned of George Hobston. On a sheet of paper, The Shadow was writing the name of Rutledge Mann. A secret agent of The Shadow, Mann conducted business as an investment broker. He had informed The Shadow that George Hobston had made large purchases of stock that might logically be kept in the vault at the Zenith Building.

The Shadow had not mentioned Mann's name to Howard Norwyn. But he had already sent word to Mann to perform another duty on this case. A light was gleaming on the wall beyond The Shadow's table. The white hands removed earphones from the wall. The Shadow spoke in a whisper. A quiet voice responded:

"Burbank speaking."

"Report," ordered The Shadow.

"Report from Mann," declared Burbank. "He called Seth Deswig. The man is in Florida."

"Deswig's secretary?"

"Deswig has no secretary."

"Report received."

The earphones clattered to the wall. A creeping laugh sounded within the enshrouding walls of the sanctum. From Rutledge Mann, the message relayed through Burbank, The Shadow had learned that Howard Norwyn had been hoaxed.

Had Norwyn stated to the police that he had received a call from Seth Deswig, the checkup would have proven another mark against Norwyn. Had the young man added that it was Deswig's secretary who had called, his statement would have sounded like an excuse.

Norwyn knew Deswig as one of Hobston's customers. Had Norwyn, as the police supposed, gone to murder and rob George Hobston, only to be trapped, his natural action would be to give some reason for summoning Hobston to the office.

To lay the call on Deswig's non-existent secretary would have proven disastrous. Here was another point that showed how well-planned the frame-up had been. The Shadow knew that he had work ahead. Cunning men of crime had played a crafty game.

Men of crime. The Shadow's laugh indicated that the master sleuth knew the game involved more than a single individual. His hand was making notations, that came as written thoughts, disappearing after the ink dried.

SOMEONE had learned that George Hobston had great wealth in his vault. That might have been any one of many who knew Hobston. Someone else had learned that Seth Deswig, one of Hobston's customers, had left Middlebury Preferred in Hobston's keeping. Someone else had arranged the murder and the robbery. Crime had been planted on Howard Norwyn through multiple scheming.

Again the earphones clicked. In response to Burbank's voice, The Shadow gave an order.

"Instructions to Vincent" was his whispered command. "Cold-canvass the Zenith Building. Look for suspicious tenants. Check on those who have recently taken offices."

"Instructions received," came Burbank's reply.

The earphones clattered. A *click* sounded as the bluish light went out. A grim laugh sounded in the blackened sanctum. It awoke shuddering echoes that died in hollow emptiness.

The Shadow had departed. As yet, he could rely only upon a long shot—an investigation of persons in the Zenith Building, through the aid of Harry Vincent, a capable agent. The Shadow knew that he was on the right trail; but it was one that would take time and might prove hopeless.

Coming crime. The Shadow scented it. For the present, he had shredded clues that might lead in different directions. All of them, The Shadow knew, would end abruptly. Criminals of a strange sort had cooperated in clever crime.

The dying laugh had been foreboding. Mirthless in its sound, it had told The Shadow's thoughts. At times, this master investigator found himself confronted by problems that could not be solved before crime struck again.

New robbery—perhaps with murder as its accompaniment—this was the token of the future. Though The Shadow might not gain the opportunity to prevent it, another episode of evil might bring him close enough to strike.

The Shadow knew that he was facing super-crime. He expected to encounter methods that he had never met before. In that assumption, The Shadow was correct.

CHAPTER VII
CRIME INCORPORATED

Two days had passed since the murder of George Hobston. New news occupied the front pages of the New York journals. The police were still looking for Howard Norwyn. This fact was proclaimed in short columns on inside pages of the newspapers.

The Shadow, too, had gained no progress. He had learned that Seth Deswig was coming home from Florida; Harry Vincent, canvassing offices in the Zenith Building, had discovered nothing. Slender clues were bringing no immediate results.

Somewhere in Manhattan—not in one place, but in several—The Shadow might have found the answer to perplexing problems. He knew that men of crime could be forced to speak, if discovered; but he had not gained the opportunity to learn their identities.

The police search for Howard Norwyn had passed from public interest. Yet there were people who still gave it their concern. On this new evening, when the night was as misty as the time of Hobston's death, a querulous old man was thumbing through the final edition of a newspaper, looking for new reports on the futile manhunt.

The old man was a wizened creature. He was lying propped upon the pillows of an old-fashioned bed. Beside him, on the table, were numerous bottles of medicine. His breathing came in wheezy gasps, with intermittent cackles of senile joy. From the mist beyond the half-opened window, the occasional *flap-flap* of tires on asphalt indicated that he was in the second story of an old house on a secluded street. The glare that hung within the swirling fog told that the house was within twenty blocks of Times Square.

The old man had found the evening item that pertained to the police search. His eyes blinked as he read the new report of failure. His lips spread in a smile of sordid delight. Again the cackle; then a coughing spell that racked the old man breathless. As the wizened face sank back into the pillows, the door opened.

The man who entered was a dry-faced individual whose countenance was solemn and gloomy. He was evidently an attendant who had the old man in his care. He approached the bed and stood in readiness while the convulsion ceased.

"You are prompt, Garwald," cackled the old man, when he had regained his breath. "Well, you need not worry. Your duties will soon be ended. When this finishes me"—the old man coughed as he clutched his thin throat—"you can find more suitable employment. After all, you are a secretary, not a trained nurse."

"I am in your employ, Mr. Talbor," returned the solemn man, quietly. "I take what comes."

TALBOR shot a look at Garwald. A knowing smile appeared upon the old man's lips. The secretary noted the expression, but made no comment. He stood silent as Talbor chuckled with wild glee.

"You take what comes! Ha—ha—ha—" The old man trailed a laugh. "You always take what comes. You're right, Garwald. Quite right. You take what comes."

Unsmiling, Garwald shook his head. His action indicated that he could not understand his employer's mirth. Still cackling, Talbor gripped the newspaper and thrust it into Garwald's hands. He pointed, with scrawny finger, to the news account that concerned the search for Howard Norwyn.

"Read that, Garwald," he ordered. "Read it. Tell me what you think of it."

"Very well, sir."

Garwald read the item in solemn fashion. When he had finished, he looked toward Talbor for an explanation. The old man was sitting up in bed. His paroxysm ended, he was studying his secretary, smiling as he did so.

"What do you make of it, Garwald?" questioned Talbor.

"Make of it?"

"Yes. Do you think that Howard Norwyn murdered George Hobston?"

"Most certainly. The evidence is apparent."

"Ah!" The old man's eyes gleamed. "You have been reading previous accounts, eh, Garwald?"

"Yes," confessed the secretary, "I must admit that I have."

"Good." Talbor settled back into the pillows.

"Very good. I am glad to learn it. Now, let us see. I am Barton Talbor—an old man—dying. You are my secretary, Fullis Garwald, nursing me in my last illness.

"In your spare time, you read news concerning crime. You read about a murder. Good. Why do you read about murders, Garwald?"

Fullis Garwald made no reply. He stared at Barton Talbor and blinked in owlish fashion. The old man chuckled.

"I'll tell you why," asserted Talbor. "You read about murders because they interest you. The reason murder interests you is because you have considered murder yourself!"

Garwald nearly forgot himself. He stepped toward the bed, his fists clenching. A look of sudden fury came upon his face and faded. Talbor chortled.

"You would like to kill me," laughed the old man. "You would kill me, if you thought that the blame could be shifted to someone else. But you have decided to let me die; and you hope that you will be alone here when I pass to another world."

Garwald made no response to the impeachment. He betrayed no new sign of nervousness. He waited quietly to hear what else Talbor might say.

"You think, Garwald," declared the old man, "that I have wealth hidden in this room. You would like to find it; to rob my heirs of their due. I can't blame you, Garwald. My relatives are a shoddy lot; but they will get my money just the same. It is stowed in safe deposit vaults. My lawyer has the keys, along with my will.

"I'm sorry for you, Garwald. I've seen you eyeing this room, looking for some hiding place. So I'm going to help you out. Go, there, to the mantel. Press it, as I tell you."

FULLIS GARWALD

FULLIS GARWALD hesitated. A frown showed upon his solemn face. Hesitation ended, he turned and followed the old man's bidding. He reached the mantelpiece that projected above the old fireplace.

"Press inward," ordered Barton Talbor, with eyes half closed. "Then to the left. Inward again. To the right. Draw outward—"

Garwald was following the instructions. As a climax to the old man's final statement, a sharp click sounded from the fireplace. Garwald stooped to see that the rear of the fireplace had dropped. Something white showed in the cavity beyond.

"Bring out the envelope," came Talbor's order. "Then close the fireplace. It will lock automatically. Carry the envelope here."

Garwald obeyed. He appeared at the bedside, holding the large envelope that he had found behind the fireplace. Talbor gripped it with his scrawny hands and opened it with ripping fingers. From the inside, he drew two objects. One was a smaller envelope; the other, a folded paper. He retained the envelope and passed the paper to Garwald.

"Open it," ordered Talbor.

Garwald did so. To his surprise, the sheet of paper resembled a stock certificate. He started to read its wording; he arrived no further than the title.

There, in large printing, he observed the statement:

CRIME INCORPORATED

A chuckle came from Barton Talbor. The old man's eyes had opened. His hands were holding the envelope; they gestured toward a chair beside the bed. Fullis Garwald sat down. He listened while the old man spoke.

"Garwald," declared Talbor, in a solemn tone, "I have left my heirs half a million dollars. I am giving you a legacy worth twice that amount. The certificate that you now hold will mean your fortune.

"Crime Incorporated. A wonderful name, eh, Garwald? A wonderful organization, also. One that you can appreciate. Particularly when you learn its history from the founder—namely, myself— Barton Talbor."

Garwald had folded the document. He was staring intently at his aged employer. Keen enthusiasm was showing on his usually solemn countenance.

"I have made my fortune," stated Barton Talbor. "I gained my wealth through crime. Not ordinary crime; but craft. Subtle methods were my forte when I was younger.

"I learned that there were others, as crooked as myself. Also, like myself, they kept their methods covered. It occurred to me that men of our ilk should be banded into a cooperative organization. That, Garwald, was the beginning of Crime Incorporated.

"I was the founder; but all are equal. I chose two men; I knew that both were crooked. I told them

each my scheme. I gained their cooperation. These two men do not know each other. I am the only link between them.

"I issued myself this share of stock in Crime Incorporated. To each of them, I gave similar certificates. I supplied them with codes for correspondence. Thus we formed a chain of three, with myself as the connection.

"Each of them, in turn, solicited another member. Those new members gained one man apiece. That plan has continued, until Crime Incorporated now numbers more than twenty chosen persons, each a crafty master of crime, in his own right."

THE old man paused to rest upon the pillows. He cackled reminiscently. With eyes shut, he continued:

"I saw at once that stock bearing the name Crime Incorporated would be a dangerous possession. So I changed the name on the other certificates. I am the only man who owns a share of the original stock. The others bear the title Aztec Mines, a name which struck my fancy. But every holder of such stock knows its true meaning. Aztec Mines is simply a synonym for Crime Incorporated.

"This envelope contains the names of my two original associates. With it are details—bylaws and procedures—all in special code. Every member of Crime Incorporated holds a share labeled Aztec Mines; also the names of the two men whom he knows; and a coded table of instructions."

Talbor paused wearily. The explanation had tired him. Garwald, observing the opportunity, interposed a question.

"What is the purpose of Crime Incorporated?" he asked. "How does the organization operate?"

"We further subtle crime," explained Talbor, slowly. "One member sees opportunity for great gain. He sends coded messages to his two contacts. They copy the note and send it along. A statement of planned crime goes through the entire chain.

"Then come the replies. Each member adds his own suggestion. If cooperation is required, volunteers make known their readiness. We call ourselves by numbers—not by names."

"And of all the twenty," questioned Garwald, "you know only two?"

"Yes. Each man knows but two. Those at the end of the chain know only one, until they gain new members. Sometimes, a message goes along the line, suggesting names of members to be solicited. But they must be followed up by those at the ends of the chain."

Again, Barton Talbor paused. Fullis Garwald unfolded the certificate of holding in Crime Incorporated. He was beginning to understand the value of this sheet of paper.

"Each share is transferable," remarked Talbor,

opening his eyes. "That certificate, Garwald, is my legacy to you. In this envelope, you will find the names of the two men whom I know. We shall send them messages tonight, informing them that Fullis Garwald has replaced Barton Talbor as holder of certificate number one."

GARWALD opened the envelope as Talbor thrust it in his hands. He found a sheet of paper, with a peculiar code of oddly blocked letters. He also found two smaller envelopes. He was about to open one when Talbor stopped him with the clutch of a scrawny hand.

Garwood stooped to see that the rear of the fireplace had dropped. Something white showed in the cavity beyond.

"No, no!" exclaimed the old man. "Those are for emergency only!"

"How so?" asked the secretary.

"They are from the two men whom I know," explained Talbor. "Each contains the name of the man next beyond in the chain. Thus I know two men; I also have the names of two others. You will notice that the envelopes are coded, to tell from whom they came.

"Suppose that one of my friends should die suddenly. Suppose that he should have no opportunity to do what I am doing now—make a transfer of his certificate. What would happen?"

"The chain would be broken."

"Precisely. But by opening the proper envelope, it would be possible for the man next in line to learn the name beyond the broken link. The breach would close automatically. Crime Incorporated would continue without interruption!"

There was triumph in the old man's cackle. The secretary nodded his understanding. He realized the cleverness of his employer's organization.

"We are sworn," declared Barton Talbor, "not to open those envelopes except when actual emergency compels. My oath, Garwald, is transferred to you."

"I understand."

The old man shifted in his bed. From a table, he plucked a letter which had come in the afternoon mail. He drew out two sheets of paper. One contained letters in the block code; the other a succession of quaint circles.

"This came today," declared Talbor. "It tells that crime has been successful. Can you guess to what crime it refers?"

"The murder of George Hobston?"

"Yes. That deed has been planted on Howard Norwyn. One member of our chain planned it. Others aided in its completion. All along the line, we have been waiting for that crime to be finished. Someone else now has the chance to suggest a masterstroke. This time"—Talbor chortled huskily—"it will be my turn. No"—his tone saddened—"not mine. Yours, Garwald, as my successor."

"You have a crime already planned?"

"Yes. One that can be accomplished only with the aid of Crime Incorporated. I shall reveal it to you, Garwald, and you can send your word along the chain. But first—most important—is the code. That depends upon a key, here"—Talbor tapped his forehead—"and if you bring paper and pencil, I shall reveal it to you."

"There are two codes from this letter," reminded Garwald, as he produced a notebook and a pencil. "One consists of circles; the other of blocks, like those which were with the certificate."

"You must learn both," stated Talbor. "The circled code is a blind. It is simple to decipher. So we use it for trivial, useless messages. The block code is the one of consequence. It will never be deciphered. It is too subtle. It will baffle the greatest of cryptogram experts; for it depends upon a special principle."

"Why the useless code?"

"To mislead any who might find a message. Any experimenter would shift to the circles as the easy one to solve. Finding a useless message, he would think these codes to be a puzzler's game. Finding the block code too difficult for ordinary solution, he would regard it as something of no importance.

We are crafty, Garwald, we who form Crime Incorporated!"

Propping himself upon the pillows, the old man took the pencil in his scrawny right hand. Letter by letter, he formed the alphabetical arrangement of the codes: first the circles, then the blocks.

GARWALD stared as Talbor dealt with the second code. He realized at once that the old man had spoken true when he had stated that it would baffle experts. Simple though it was, the block code adhered to a principle that Garwald had never suspected.

Minutes passed. Old Talbor's hand was slowing. It completed the final task. With a gasp, the old man settled backward. Garwald caught pencil and pad as they dropped from his loosened hands.

Barton Talbor's breath was coming in long, choking wheezes. His feeble fingers were pressing at his throat. Staring at his stricken employer, watching the pallid face with its bluish, closed eyelids, Fullis Garwald realized that death was soon to come.

Standing with the certificate of Crime Incorporated in his hand, holding the coded names and bylaws, clutching the translated formula that the old man had inscribed in the notebook, Fullis Garwald smiled.

No longer did he seek to hide his evil nature. His curling lips were proof of Barton Talbor's assumption. The servant, like the master, was a man of crime. Barton Talbor had passed his greatest legacy to an heir as evil as himself.

Soon, Fullis Garwald knew, Barton Talbor would recover strength. Then the old man would reveal his scheme for crime. After that, word would go forth along the chain of members who formed Crime Incorporated.

Days would pass before the new scheme would be perpetrated. Before that time arrived, Barton Talbor would he dead. In his place, the new Number One of Crime Incorporated, Fullis Garwald would reap the profits of Barton Talbor's scheme.

Swirling mist crept into the gloomy room where plans were to precede death. The same chain that had worked toward the murder of George Hobston would soon work again. Unbroken, the links of Crime Incorporated would deal in profitable murder.

CHAPTER VIII
ONE WEEK LATER

IT was late afternoon. A chubby-faced man was seated at a flat-topped desk, staring meditatively through an office window. Beyond was the skyline of Manhattan. Towering buildings, shadowy shapes in the dusk, showed glimmering twinkles from their lighted windows.

The chubby man clicked a desk lamp. He set to work sorting a stack of clippings. He made a reference to penciled notations and began to inscribe a message that consisted of coded words in bluish ink.

This individual was Rutledge Mann. A contact agent of The Shadow, Mann was compiling data for his master. During the day, he had received reports from such workers as Harry Vincent and Clyde Burke. These were ready to be forwarded to The Shadow.

Rutledge Mann was gloomy. He knew that progress had been lacking. Harry Vincent's travels through the Zenith Building had brought no results. Clyde Burke had learned nothing new at detective headquarters.

Clippings, gleaned from recent newspapers, showed that the search for Howard Norwyn still continued. Mann did not know that The Shadow had provided refuge for the missing man. Mann knew only that until some new phase of investigation developed regarding the Hobston murder, The Shadow would not be satisfied.

Mann referred to a penciled notation that marked a telephone number. Nodding to himself, he picked up the telephone and put in a call. A voice answered.

"Hello..." Mann's tone was pleasant. "Is this Mr. Seth Deswig?... Good. My name is Rutledge Mann... Yes, I called before. I understood that you would arrive home this afternoon.

"Yes, I am an investment broker... Let me explain my business. It regards a client of mine... His name is Lamont Cranston... Yes, the millionaire. He is interested in the purchase of a certain stock... Middlebury Preferred... Yes, I was informed that you might have some shares of it.

"I see... You do not care to sell?... That is too bad. Mr. Cranston will be disappointed... Perhaps he may wish to see you in person. Would it be convenient?... Good. Tonight, then... At your apartment... Yes, I shall inform Mr. Cranston..."

Rutledge Mann inked another brief message. He tucked it in a large envelope along with other sheets and clippings. He scanned the newspapers for a final checkup. He found no news item that he thought worthy of clipping.

IN one journal, Mann noted a brief item that referred to the estate of an old recluse named Barton Talbor. This man had died a few days ago. Mann thought nothing of this short account. To him, Barton Talbor was a person of no consequence, even though the old man had left large sums to some dozen-odd relatives.

Rutledge Mann never realized that he was passing up a clue of vital consequence. Had some hunch caused him to take interest in the affairs of Barton Talbor, Mann would have accomplished much for The Shadow's cause. As it was, the investment broker merely tossed the newspaper in the wastebasket.

Sealing his large envelope, Mann pocketed it and left his office. He appeared upon Broadway a few minutes later, hailed a taxi and rode to Twenty-third Street. There he sauntered to a dilapidated office building that stood as a relic of a forgotten business period.

Entering this edifice of the past century, Mann ascended a flight of warped stairs. He reached a blackened door; its dingy glass panel was scarcely discernible. Painted letters displayed the name:

B. JONAS

Mann dropped the envelope in a door slit beneath the glass panel. He went back to the stairs

and left the building. All remained gloomy behind the frosted pane that bore the name "B. Jonas." Yet Rutledge Mann's visit had been no blind errand.

He had dropped the envelope in The Shadow's letter box. Communications deposited through that obscure door invariably reached the personage for whom they were intended. Though no one ever observed a person leaving or entering that deserted office, The Shadow had some mode of getting within.

THE proof of this occurred an hour later. A light clicked in The Shadow's sanctum. White hands appeared, holding the envelope that Mann had dispatched to The Shadow. Fingers tore the wrapper. Keen eyes studied clippings and reports. A soft laugh sounded from the gloom beyond the range of focused light.

A click. The bluish rays were extinguished. Again, the laugh shuddered weirdly through The Shadow's sanctum. Then came silence amid the Stygian walls. The master who inhabited this strange abode had sallied forth on new business.

ONE hour later, a visitor was announced at the apartment of Seth Deswig. The arrival was Lamont Cranston. Seth Deswig, a thin-faced, middle-aged gentleman, told his servant to usher in the visitor. A few minutes later, Cranston and Deswig were shaking hands in the living room.

"I am pleased to meet you, Mr. Cranston," declared Deswig in a thin-pitched voice. "I am afraid, however, that your visit will be to no avail. Your broker—Mr. Mann—called me in regard to a stock which I own. Middlebury Preferred."

"Yes," returned Cranston, quietly. "The stock is not on the market; and I am trying to obtain some shares."

"I choose to hold mine. I was fortunate in purchasing Middlebury Preferred. I am doubly fortunate in that I still own my shares."

"How so?"

"The stock was in the hands of my broker, George Hobston. It was in his vault."

"You mean the man in the Zenith Building? The one who was murdered in his office?"

"The same. I left my stock with him a long while before I went to Florida. Fortunately, nothing was stolen from Hobston's vault. The police turned the stock over to me, after they learned that I was the rightful owner."

"You are really fortunate," observed Cranston, in a thoughtful tone. Then, with a change of expression, he added: "Mr. Mann has informed me that you do not care to sell. I thought, however, that you might know of other persons who held this stock. Perhaps you could name someone from whom I might buy."

"I know of no one," returned Deswig, with a shake of his head. "I purchased the stock a year ago."

"Did Hobston hold it all that time?" questioned Cranston, in a casual tone.

"No," responded Deswig. "I left it with one of his assistants—young Howard Norwyn—along with other securities, about three months ago."

"I see. I presume you purchased the stock through Hobston, originally."

"Yes. I did."

"Too bad that Hobston is dead," mused Cranston. "He would have been the proper man for me to see regarding a purchase of Middlebury Preferred."

"No; you could not have done so." Deswig was positive on this point. "You see, I wanted to buy more of the stock through Hobston. He was unable to acquire any of it. Hobston was in the market for all that he could get.

"I mentioned the matter to various friends. I told them that I had bought Middlebury Preferred from Hobston; that if they knew of anyone who held such stock, to give their names either to myself or Hobston."

"I understand," nodded Cranston. "You tried quite frequently to locate holders of Middlebury Preferred?"

"I did. In fact, I discussed the stock with people up until the time I left for Florida. I mentioned it several times to friends at the Merrimac Club."

"And told them to see Hobston if they learned that more stock could be obtained?"

"To see either George Hobston or Howard Norwyn. I stated that I had turned over my present shares to Norwyn, who had deposited them in Hobston's vault for safekeeping. You see, I intended to go away—"

"Do you believe," came Cranston's casual question, "that any of those club members might have uncovered some Middlebury Preferred during your absence? I suppose that you remember the names of the men to whom you spoke?"

"Unfortunately," declared Deswig, seriously, "I never mentioned the matter to any particular individual. Investments become a group discussion at the Merrimac Club. I remember only that I spoke of Middlebury Preferred in a general way—to whomever happened to be on hand when the talk turned to securities."

"Well, Mr. Deswig"—Cranston's tone signified readiness for departure—"it appears that we are both in the market for Middlebury Preferred. Should you learn of any shares that you do not intend to purchase, I would deem it a favor, should you communicate with Mr. Rutledge Mann."

Five minutes later, The Shadow was leaving the

apartment house where Seth Deswig lived. The visit had proven one point: namely, that Deswig's name had been used by the unknown person who had called Howard Norwyn, prior to the murder of George Hobston.

UNFORTUNATELY, Deswig had been unable to name definite persons to whom he had mentioned that his shares of Middlebury Preferred had been placed in Hobston's vault through Howard Norwyn. Again, The Shadow was balked in his tracing of a clue.

The odds pointed heavily to some member of the Merrimac Club as the one who had duped Norwyn. But there were as many members in the Merrimac Club as there were offices in the Zenith Building.

Sifting, alone, could find the culprit. It would be a process that might require many weeks. All that The Shadow had gained was a negative opportunity. Should he find a suspect who belonged to the Merrimac Club; should he find one who had offices in the Zenith Building, he would know that he had men of crime before him. But to reverse the process was a prolonged task!

Coming crime! Again The Shadow scented it. But when and where was it to strike? Who would be the men responsible for it? While the police still followed their hopeless hunt for Howard Norwyn, The Shadow was far in advance. Yet the master sleuth, like those of lesser skill, had encountered an impasse.

Coming crime! While The Shadow considered its potentialities, the beginnings of such evil had been planted. On this very night, cunning crooks were to spring their next attack.

IN the room where Barton Talbor had died, Fullis Garwald was standing alone. The former secretary of the dead plotter was smiling as he tore two sheets of paper and applied a match to them.

Garwald was living in Talbor's home. It was his headquarters for the present; this house would be his abode until he chose to move. The sheets that he had torn were coded messages. They were the final replies to communications which Garwald, at Talbor's instruction, had sent along the chain of Crime Incorporated.

Evil which Barton Talbor had plotted was to find its completion tonight. Aided by other members of the strange criminal group, Fullis Garwald was ready to fare forth. His smile was one of recollection, coupled with confidence of the outcome.

For Barton Talbor had schemed well. Crime Incorporated had promised its full aid. Before this night was ended, the law would find itself confronted by a mystery fully as perplexing as the murder of George Hobston!

Fullis Garwald dropped the burning papers in an ash receiver. With a chuckle that was reminiscent of his dead employer, the solemn-faced man walked from the room. He descended to the street and stepped out into the night.

Two blocks from his starting point, Garwald hailed a taxicab. He gave the driver an address on Seventh Avenue. As the taxi swung into the broad thoroughfare, Garwald, looking far ahead, saw a distant sign that blazed this name:

HOTEL SALAMANCA

Again Fullis Garwald chuckled. The address that he had given the taxi driver was in the block this side of the glittering sign. Fullis Garwald's actual destination was the building that carried the flashing letters.

Bound on crime, Garwald intended to alight and complete his journey on foot. The Hotel Salamanca was his goal. Arrived there, he would be ready to complete the scheme of evil that Barton Talbor had designed.

CHAPTER IX
THE CHAIN PREPARES

WHILE Fullis Garwald's taxi was swinging north on Seventh Avenue, a man was entering the Hotel Salamanca. Stoop-shouldered, faltering of gait, with a mass of white hair bulging from beneath his oddly shaped hat, this individual appeared to be a mild-mannered man of learning.

Arriving in the lobby, the man's face showed like parchment in the light. His bowed figure hobbled forward; a heavy cane enabled him to proceed at a fair pace. In his left hand, the elderly man was carrying a bag. A bellhop sprang forward to take the burden; the old fellow waved him away and continued his faltering stride to the desk.

"Any word for me?" he inquired, in a pleasant voice: "Any messages for Professor Devine? Professor Langwood Devine?"

"No, sir," replied the clerk with a smile. "No mail this afternoon."

The old professor turned and hobbled from the desk. He entered an elevator and nodded to the operator as he ordered the man to take him to the twenty-fourth floor.

Like the clerk, the operator smiled. Professor Langwood Devine was a new and eccentric guest at the Hotel Salamanca. He had come here only a few days before; he had a penchant for carrying his own luggage and he seemed to relish walking sticks. The cane that he carried tonight was different from the last that the operator had seen. Heavy, with a rounded silver knob, it formed an interesting curio.

The professor nearly tripped as he stepped from

the elevator. The operator caught his arm and kept him from falling. The old man's hat dropped off, revealing the full mass of his bushy white hair. The operator handed him the headpiece; Professor Devine bowed in thanks. Wheezing from the sudden jolt, he hobbled toward his suite, which was on the south side of the twenty-fourth floor.

The professor entered a room marked 2410. He passed through a little entrance and hobbled into a living room. Here books lay piled in disarray. Opened bags showed masses of manuscripts. Three canes—all different in appearance—were stacked together in a corner. The professor placed his bag upon a chair. He laid the cane beside it. He hobbled to the bedroom that adjoined and turned on a light. Hobbling back toward the entry, he turned out the living room light.

Semidarkness was the result. The only shaft of illumination came from the door of the bedroom. The old professor moved back toward the chair where he had placed bag and cane.

HE still hobbled, but not so noticeably as before. Though actually advanced in years, his strength was by no means gone. Professor Devine seemed somewhat younger and more virile now that his actions could not be observed.

By the chair, he picked up his walking stick. He twisted the silver knob; then pulled it. The cane lengthened in telescopic fashion to twice its original length. The old man unscrewed the knob. A spool of fish line came in view. The old man rolled the spool along the floor; then hobbled after it and completed the unrolling. Methodically, he found the free end of the fish line and tied it to the handle of his bag.

Carrying the lengthened cane to the window, the professor removed its tip. A sharp spike showed in the end of the double-sized walking stick. The professor set the cane against the radiator and opened the window.

This suite fronted on a side street. Across the thoroughfare was an old building—a decadent apartment house some twenty stories high. The flat roof showed its dull surface behind a parapet. Off from Times Square came the glow of brilliant lights; but the indirect illumination revealed nothing upon the silent roof.

Placing fingers to his lips, Professor Devine gave a low, peculiar whistle. He waited. A reply—similar to his signal—came from behind the parapet, forty feet away and thirty feet below. The professor picked up the cane. From it ran the long fish line that terminated at the bag handle. Making sure that the cord was free, the old man gripped the six-foot cane as one would grasp a harpoon.

He used his left hand to steady his shaky legs.

Leaning against the radiator, Professor Devine drew back his right arm. That limb had lost no precision. With a forward swing, the professor sent the harpoon whizzing through the air. The fish line whined as it followed. The weighted shaft cleared the opposite parapet by fifteen feet and struck point downward in the surface of the roof.

Quivering back and forth, a white line in the darkness, the transformed cane remained at an upright angle. The entire roof had been the professor's target. The old man had not missed.

Hobbling back to the bag, the professor opened it and produced a coil of light cable. Meanwhile, the remainder of the fish line was paying out. Someone on the opposite roof had picked up the harpoon. The line became taut; the cord had been gathered in from the other end. The professor chuckled as he attached the thin cable to the end of the fish line. This was a simple procedure; a loop in the end of the cable made it possible.

The professor tugged the line that he had released from the handle of the bag. One signal was sufficient. The fish line moved toward the window; the cable followed it. The professor watched until the cable was nearly paid out. He grasped the loose end and carried it to the radiator. Here he slipped the end loop over a knob that projected from a heavy pipe. He gave a tug. The man at the other end pulled the cable taut.

Back again to the bag; this time, Professor Devine produced a small bar attached to a pair of tiny wheels. He carried this to the window and clamped it on the cable, so that the wheels ran free. The bar formed a little car which a man could grip and hold in safety.

Peering from the window, the professor saw the line of his cable. It ran above the parapet of the building opposite. It was attached, apparently, to the iron pillar that supported a water tank on the roof. The cable showed as a dull silver line from this height. Yet anyone looking upward from the street below would never have detected its presence.

Hobbling from the window, the professor picked up the silver knob and the silver tip of his harpoon cane. He carried these to the corner and attached them to a plain walking stick. Chuckling to himself, the old man picked up the bag and took it into the bedroom.

FIVE minutes passed. When Professor Langwood Devine again entered the living room, he was clad in pajamas. He was holding an opened book in his left hand. He hobbled to the outer door and turned the knob. He pulled the door a half inch inward. Though it apparently remained closed, the automatic latch was loose so that anyone could open the door at will.

Returning to the bedroom, the professor turned out the light. A few seconds later, he pulled on a lamp above his bed. Seating himself beneath the covers, the old man leaned his head against a propped up pillow. He reached to a table beside him, picked up a pair of spectacles and began to read.

Professor Langwood Devine made the perfect picture of an elderly savant, engaging in comfortable study. His peering eyes were intent upon the pages before him. He seemed unperturbed by the outside world.

Yet in the space of the few previous minutes, Professor Devine had marked himself as other than a scholar. His unique method of communication to the roof of the opposite building; his act of stretching a cable and providing a car—both proved that he had prepared for some event to come.

Professor Langwood Devine was a member of the insidious chain that constituted Crime Incorporated. The worker on the opposite roof was another factor in that evil group. Between them, they had prepared for coming crime. They were the aides who had sent back their suggestions to Fullis Garwald.

Crime was due to strike tonight, here in the Hotel Salamanca. Fullis Garwald was coming alone, to begin the evil work. The way was paved for his escape. Suite 2410 would be his goal after his accomplishment of crime.

Aided by the brains of men whom he had never met; taking up bold efforts that dead Barton Talbor could not have accomplished, Fullis Garwald was already assured of success.

CHAPTER X
A MURDERER STRIKES

PROFESSOR LANGWOOD DEVINE had retired, content that his aerial cable could not be seen from the street below. The professor's assumption was well formed. Already, peering eyes were gazing upward, trying to spy the slender line of steel from the chasm of the thoroughfare.

Fullis Garwald had arrived at the corner on which the Hotel Salamanca was located. A pleased leer appeared upon his lips as he stared toward the dull glow of the sky. Garwald could not see the cable. That was why he smiled.

The arriving man's eyes turned as they looked upward. On the top floor of the hotel—one story above the twenty-fourth—a tiny sparkle showed at a window. The twenty-fifth floor was a penthouse; and someone was at home.

Entering the lobby of the Hotel Salamanca, Garwald strolled to a corner where the house phones were located. He called the penthouse and spoke in a voice that was gruffer than his usual

tone. He asked for Mr. Gaston Ferrar. A short pause; then Ferrar himself was on the wire.

"Good evening," declared Garwald, in a gruff tone. "I have come to see you about the green."

"Ah! My friend!" A suave voice came across the wire. "You have decided upon the matter? I thought perhaps that I would not hear from you. Come up, at once."

Garwald smiled as he hung up the receiver. He entered an elevator where several people were already standing. He waited as the car stopped at various floors. When the twentieth was reached, Garwald was the only remaining passenger.

"Penthouse," he stated, in a gruff tone.

The elevator man turned as the door clanged. He did not see Garwald's face. The passenger was studying a dinner menu posted at the back of the car. The operator hesitated.

"Who are you going to see?" he questioned.

"Gaston Ferrar," answered Garwald, without turning. "He is expecting me."

The operator started the car upward. He stopped at the twenty-fifth. Garwald stepped forward while the doors were opening. His head was faced slightly toward the side. Again, the operator failed to note his features.

The car remained stationary with the operator watching while Garwald rang a bell at the opposite side of a little anteroom. Garwald's back was toward the car. When a servant opened the door, the visitor stepped through. The operator closed the door and descended.

"You wish to see Mr. Ferrar?"

The servant was questioning Fullis Garwald. The solemn-faced man made no effort to hide his features. He looked the servant squarely in the eye.

"Yes," he said testily. "I came to see Mr. Ferrar. Tell him that I am here."

"Your name?"

"Tell him I am the friend who called from downstairs."

The servant went into an inner room. He returned and motioned Garwald to the door. As the visitor entered, the servant closed the barrier from the outside. He was evidently following instructions which he had just received from his master.

FULLIS GARWALD was standing in a small, but magnificent room. Every item of furniture—from heavy chairs to massive table—was an antique of value. Garwald's eyes went toward the corner, where a languorous man was seated at a bulky writing desk. Brown eyes stared from a pale, pinched countenance as Gaston Ferrar looked toward his visitor.

"Who are you?" questioned Ferrar, in surprise. "I do not know you. I expected to see—"

He paused, apparently loath to utter the name. Fullis Garwald supplied it, smiling as he did so.

"Barton Talbor," he declared. "He was the man whom you expected."

"He could not come?"

"No."

"Why? Is he ill?"

"He is dead."

A troubled look appeared upon Gaston Ferrar's face. Fullis Garwald did not display concern. He calmly seated himself in a chair opposite the writing desk.

"My name," he stated, "is Fullis Garwald. I was secretary to Barton Talbor. Before he died, he told me of his acquaintanceship with you, Mr. Ferrar. Perhaps if I give the details of his statements, you will know that my claim is genuine."

"Proceed," suggested Ferrar, sinking back in his chair.

"Barton Talbor," declared Garwald, "once possessed some rare gems. He sold them—all except a certain emerald, of Siamese origin, which he kept. You, as a collector of such gems, came to Talbor privately and offered to buy the stone. You had learned that it was in Talbor's possession."

"That is true."

"You said that if Talbor chose to sell, you would buy. You also stated that if he wished to take other jewels in its stead, you would let him choose from your collection, up to a value greater than that of the emerald."

"Correct."

"Barton Talbor told you to visit him again. When you came, he said that he would never part with the emerald unless circumstances should force him to do so. He added that if such circumstances arose—such as poverty or financial failure—he would never want it to be known that he had been forced to sell."

"That is right. Go on."

"So Talbor—who was quite eccentric in his ways—said that should he come to you, he would mention neither his name nor the emerald. He declared that he would announce himself by simply stating that he had come to see you about the green."

"Those were his exact statements."

Fullis Garwald settled back easily in his chair. From his pocket, he produced a small jewel case. He placed it on the desk as he leaned forward. He sprang the cover. A sparkling emerald glistened in the light. Gaston Ferrar crouched forward, his pale face keen with eagerness.

"The Siamese emerald!" he cried. "How did you gain it?"

"As a reward for faithful service," stated Garwald, in a solemn, convincing tone. "Barton Talbor died wealthy. He divided his existing estate among his heirs. He gave me the emerald before he died."

"Poor Talbor." Ferrar shook his head. "I can see him plainly—a weary man—as he was when last I visited him. He loved that emerald; and would not part with it, much though I coveted the stone."

"My own circumstances," said Garwald, "are very moderate. I value the emerald because of its actual value. Talbor told me that if I came here in his stead, I could dispose of it to you."

"Certainly," assured Ferrar. "I am still anxious to purchase it. Of course"—he paused doubtfully—"I should first make sure regarding your statements. I have only your word as proof that Barton Talbor is dead. I seldom read the daily newspapers. Under what circumstances did Barton Talbor die?"

GARWALD produced a clipping from his pocket. It was Barton Talbor's obituary notice. He passed the item to Ferrar. The pale-faced collector nodded. The clipping convinced him.

"How much money are you asking?" he inquired.

"I do not want money," replied Garwald, with a touch of shrewdness in his voice. "I would prefer gems from your collection—on the same terms that you promised Barton Talbor."

"But your circumstances are moderate."

"Frankly, they are. I am simply following advice that Barton Talbor gave me. He said that all collectors have gems that mean but little to them. He added that collectors frequently purchase more than their means allow.

"It follows that a collector, like yourself, would give greater value in jewels than in cash, when purchasing a rare item. I can readily dispose of gems. So I would prefer to exchange, rather than to sell."

Gaston Ferrar frowned momentarily; then he leaned back and laughed. Garwald's calm frankness amused him. It did more; it gained his full confidence. He picked up the jewel case, removed the mounted emerald and smiled as he saw the beauty of the gem. Replacing the case upon the desk, he arose and went to a safe located in the wall.

"You shall have your terms," he laughed, as he turned the combination. "I shall abide by my offer to Barton Talbor. I shall show you my entire collection; then I shall pick out gems from which you can choose. You are right; I can spare gems more than money. I promise you that I shall give you value beyond that of the emerald."

Ferrar produced a long, flat jewel box. He turned to face Garwald. His lips trembled; his arms began to shake. Fullis Garwald had risen. In his right hand he was holding a revolver.

"What—what—"

Ferrar's exclamation came in a gasp. It brought a command from Garwald. In response to the crook's order, Ferrar staggered to his chair and dropped the jewel box upon the desk.

"You fool!" spat Garwald. "You have fallen for the game. Not my game, mind you, but Talbor's. This is what he intended to do. He baited you with that emerald, so that he could capture your entire collection.

"Why do you think he wanted his name kept quiet? Why do you think he insisted that he would speak of the 'green'—not of the 'emerald'? Simply to make his path an easy one. That is all."

Ferrar sat stupefied. Garwald's face showed its evil leer. Suddenly, the collector broke forth with a challenge.

"You cannot escape from here!" he exclaimed. "If you take the jewels, you will be traced. You must have been Talbor's secretary. The law will find you."

"Not through your testimony," scoffed Garwald. "You will never speak, Ferrar. I am here to murder you—in that very chair where you now sit."

THE fiendish words had the very effect that Garwald wanted. With death facing him, Ferrar took recourse to desperation. He howled for his servant.

"Larmond!" he cried. "Help me! It's murder—murder—"

Garwald stood rigid. He had purposely refrained from firing. A shot might have sent the servant scurrying for help. A cry, however, was bringing him on the run. Footsteps sounded outside the closed door as Ferrar began to rise. Garwald swung a quick glance. He saw the door knob turning. Swinging his eyes toward Ferrar, he fired point blank.

Ferrar collapsed in his chair. The bullet had been aimed straight for his heart. Garwald did not wait to witness the result. Turning, he covered the servant, who was caught flat-footed in the doorway. With a hideous laugh, Garwald pressed finger to revolver trigger.

Larmond made a frantic dive for cover, just as the revolver spurted. Garwald saw the servant stagger. He heard his body clatter in the hall. Pocketing his revolver, the murderer leaped to the safe. Jewel boxes came forth in his eager hands. Garwald packed them in his pockets. He added the box that was on the table; for the finish, he seized the little case that held the Siamese emerald. He started for the door of the room.

A look of startled surprise appeared upon Garwald's morbid face as the killer reached the outer room. Larmond, the servant, was not in sight.

Leaping to the door of another room, Garwald saw the man slumped at a table, telephone and receiver in his hands.

Too late, Garwald realized that his shot had merely crippled Larmond. The wounded man had managed to reach the telephone. He had given the alarm. Fiercely, Garwald raised his revolver. Larmond, seeing him, tried to move from the table. He sprawled upon the floor. Garwald furiously fired two bullets into his helpless body.

Positive that his shots had not been heard outside the penthouse, Garwald had lingered in Ferrar's room. Larmond's call for help had changed the situation. Even while Garwald was backing from the spot where the servant's body lay, the door of the anteroom opened. Swinging, Garwald saw a man who was evidently the house detective; beyond the fellow, the open door of the elevator with the operator standing at the control.

Garwald whirled to fire. The house dick, not expecting the sudden attack, made a plunge back toward the elevator. Two bullets whistled from Garwald's gun as the detective made the car. The third shot flattened itself against a closing door of the elevator.

Reaching the anteroom on the run, Garwald observed a bolted door at the right. He yanked back the bolt; opened the door and sprang down a stairway. With long leaps, he gained the hall below. He was on the twenty-fourth floor. Straight ahead was the path to the elevators.

Garwald fired as a man poked his head around the corner. This time a shot responded. The house dick had alighted at the floor below. He was exchanging bullets with the killer. One of Garwald's shots nicked the detective's arm. As the man staggered out of sight, Garwald sprang forward.

THE dick was diving for the stairway that led to the floors below. Garwald aimed toward him; he stopped as an elevator door clanged open and a uniformed policeman came into view. Garwald backed toward the hall, firing as he retreated. The second operator—like the one who had brought the house dick—slammed the door as a protection against the fire.

Garwald was in the corridor. He was trapped. A policeman from the elevator; the house dick on the stairs; both could hold him until reinforcements came. Garwald, however, made no new attack. Panting as he ducked back into the corridor, he reached the door of 2410.

A quick glance told him that he was momentarily free from observation. He pressed the door; it opened inward. Garwald was in Professor Devine's entry. Breathless, he closed the door behind him. Pocketing his revolver, he scurried for the window.

Turning, he covered the servant, who was caught flat-footed in the doorway.

Whistles were sounding from Seventh Avenue. Whines of police sirens answered the shrill blasts. The alarm had been sounded. Fullis Garwald had no time to lose. He had come here for a purpose. He saw the trolley-bar resting on the radiator. He gripped it with one hand as he clambered to the sill.

Blackness ruled below. The side street was an asphalt ribbon at the bottom of a gaping chasm. Garwald hesitated; for the first time he seemed to sense the sounds from the avenue. Gripping the bar with both hands, he swung his body from the window.

Wheels clicked as the weight of Garwald's body

sent the carlike bar whizzing down the cable line. Gathering momentum, Fullis Garwald became a rocketing form that sped swaying toward the roof of the old building opposite. The trip was a matter of brief seconds. Garwald's flight carried him above the parapet; it ended as he released himself upon the solid roof.

Swiftly though Fullis Garwald had acted, there was another who moved as rapidly. Professor Langwood Devine, coming from his bedroom, hobbled with remarkable speed to the window. He saw Garwald's figure tumbling upon the opposite roof. The old man chuckled.

In his hand, Professor Devine was holding another object that he brought from his bag. It was a cardboard mailing tube, a coil of fish line wrapped about it. The professor thrust this cylinder beneath the radiator. He gripped the cable that was around the radiator pipe, wrenched it free, and attached the end of the fish line. He slapped the end of the cable as a signal.

Someone was pounding at the door of the suite. Unperturbed, the professor watched the cable start outward from the window. Chuckling in satisfaction, he turned and hobbled to answer the door.

Crime had been completed. Fullis Garwald had escaped. The last evidence was making its automatic departure. Professor Langwood Devine, member of Crime Incorporated, had no qualms to annoy him.

CHAPTER XI
THE SHADOW'S FINDING

As Professor Devine neared the outer door, he clicked on the light switch. He fumbled with the door knob; then turned it. Standing with book in one hand, he stood gaping in bewildered fashion as the door swung inward. He was face to face with a swarthy, stocky-built man.

"What—what's the trouble?" stammered the professor. "Has—has any trouble happened?"

"Yes." The reply came in a growl. "There's been a murder in this hotel. Did anyone come through here?"

"I—I don't think so," protested the professor. "I was dozing over my book, there in the bedroom. I am sure that this door was locked."

"I'm Detective Cardona from headquarters," informed the stocky man. "I just arrived here. I'm in charge. We're searching this entire floor. Come on, men.

Professor Devine hobbled toward his bedroom. Cardona was forced to smile at the bewilderment of the bushy-haired old man. Two policemen followed the ace detective to search the suite.

While Cardona was staring about him, he failed

to see a motion beneath the radiator. There, the mailing tube was completing its final revolution. Across the sill of the opened window, a streak of green fish line was marking its final course. Cardona missed that sight also. When the detective strode in the direction of the window, the cord was gone.

Leaning from the window, the sleuth flicked the rays of a flashlight along a narrow cornice. Satisfied that no one could be clinging to the wall, he turned and entered the professor's bedroom. The old man was pulling on trousers and coat.

"You'd better put on slippers, too," urged Cardona. "We're sending everyone down a floor, while we complete this search. We're up against a murderer. It's not safe here."

The professor nodded. He donned his slippers and hobbled into the living room. Cardona ordered a bluecoat to accompany him. Reaching the hall, the professor joined a group of other guests who had been aroused on the twenty-fourth floor.

FIFTEEN minutes later, Joe Cardona was standing glumly in the corridor, when an elevator door clanged open and a wiry young man stepped from the car. The arrival grinned as Cardona stared in his direction. The newcomer was Clyde Burke.

"Say!" Cardona's tone was indignant. "How did you pull in here? I told them downstairs that reporters weren't to get by until I gave the word."

Burke drew back his coat. On his vest was a glittering detective badge. The reporter grinned as he watched Cardona's expression.

"I picked it up in a hock shop, Joe," laughed Clyde. "It fooled those dumb clucks downstairs. I told them I was coming up here to join you."

"You've got plenty of nerve," growled Cardona. "You'd better stow that medal, before I put some bracelets on you. If you like tinware, I'll let you have it."

"Forget the handcuffs, Joe," suggested Clyde, plucking the phony badge from his vest. "You've got plenty to do without pinching me for impersonating an officer. I'm in—that's all I wanted—and I won't make any trouble."

"All right," decided Cardona.

Clyde Burke proceeded to make himself inconspicuous while Cardona gave new orders to a squad of detectives who were still engaged in concentrated search of the twenty-fourth floor. When the ace turned to go up the stairs to the penthouse, he motioned Clyde to follow.

At the top of the stairs, they found Inspector Timothy Klein. The red-faced official was talking with the house dick, whose grazed arm was bandaged. Two elevator operators and a policeman were also in evidence. Clyde Burke recognized that the four must have played some part in the murderous affray. He listened while Klein spoke with Cardona.

"I've been checking on these statements, Joe," announced the inspector. "The house detective says that the murderer was a gloomy faced fellow."

"Looked like an undertaker" informed the house dick.

"I seen him," added one of the operators. "He was a solemn looking bloke, if you ask me."

"They are positive," resumed Klein, "that he could not have gone below the twenty-fourth floor. The house detective covered the stairway. The officer was in the elevator. The killer must be somewhere hereabout."

"But where?" demanded Joe. "I've got men on the roof—others in here—still more on the twenty-fourth. I've even had a report from the street, to make sure the guy didn't jump to his death."

"How about the guests on the twenty-fourth?"

"They're down on the twenty-third floor, under guard. The manager is there to identify them."

"We'll go down there," asserted Klein, "as soon as I post men to stay on watch."

CLYDE BURKE was a member of the group that descended to the twenty-third floor. In a spacious suite, he saw the guests who had been driven from their rooms. There were not more than half a dozen. The hotel manager was with them. He arose protestingly as Klein and Cardona entered.

"Gentlemen," he announced to the officials, "I can vouch for every one of these guests. It is preposterous to suppose that any could be the culprit for whom you are searching."

Cardona nodded as he eyed the group. Most of the guests were half clad. They had been aroused by the excitement. None of them answered the descriptions given by those who had seen Garwald.

The ace, however, insisted upon the formality of an identification. He questioned the two operators and the house detective, as well as the policeman. All four were positive that none of these guests could have been the fully clad murderer who had loosed shots during his mad flight.

The test was convincing. Cardona, himself, saw that these people must be innocent. Of all the half dozen, Professor Langwood Devine impressed him as being the one who was least suspicious. The hobbling old man, with his bushy white hair, could not possibly have been the active murderer in the penthouse. The other guests seemed nearly as innocuous as Devine.

"Here's what I suggest, Inspector," decided Cardona. "No elevators are running to the twenty-fourth floor. The stairway is blocked. Let these people go to other rooms, below. In the morning, we can have their belongings brought down to them. In the meantime, we'll make another search. We'll go through every spot on the two floors above; and we'll do it so clean that even a rat won't escape us."

The inspector nodded his agreement. Cardona strolled from the room with Clyde Burke in his wake. Growling, the detective swung and faced the reporter.

"Listen, you with the tin medal," asserted the sleuth, "I'll give you the details of this case. Then you can beat it and write your story. You're out so far as this search is concerned."

"But suppose you find the guy—"

"You'll hear about it."

"How soon?"

"Call me on the telephone. Give your name; ask to be connected with the penthouse. But don't bother me more than once an hour. Is that understood? All right; get out your pencil and copy paper and take down the details."

Fifteen minutes later, Clyde Burke appeared upon the street outside of the Hotel Salamanca. He strolled to a store a block away. He put in a telephone call to Burbank. Methodically, Clyde gave all the details of the double murder in the Salamanca penthouse.

In addition, he listed the names of the guests who had been cleared and dismissed. He added the numbers of their rooms. That finished, Clyde Burke left the phone booth and headed for the *Classic* office.

ONE hour elapsed. The search was still continuing in the Hotel Salamanca. Cardona had begun with the twenty-fourth floor. He had then headed up to the penthouse, leaving two detectives to patrol the twenty-fourth floor. Not a possible hiding place had been missed.

A third detective was standing by the elevators. He was within earshot of his companions. His duty was to watch the stairway. He was following the same procedure that had made it possible for Clyde Burke to come upstairs as a false detective: in brief, he was watching to see that no one left the twenty-fourth floor, not to look for any arrival.

Hence his eyes were not toward the stairway. They were turned toward the corridors where the patrolling detectives were in charge. These men were pacing back and forth; occasionally one strolled up to the penthouse to report to Joe Cardona.

The stairway that led below was black. From its solid darkness came a strange, moving patch that extended along the floor. It became the silhouette of a hawklike profile. It rested almost at the feet of the detective who was standing by the elevators.

The patch moved inward. It was followed by a form. The sinister figure of The Shadow came in sight. Noiselessly, the tall being approached until he reached a corner of the wall beyond the elevators. The single detective was standing near the corridor. The Shadow was less than three feet from him.

Silently, The Shadow waited. The detective, wearied of what seemed a useless vigil, drew a cigarette from his pocket. He followed with a match. He turned as he applied the flame to the cigarette.

Strolling from the entrance to the corridor, he approached the elevator. The flicker of the match showed his face to The Shadow. The sleuth, however, busied with his light, did not observe that tall black shape in passing.

The Shadow swung noiselessly from his hiding place. He swept toward the corridor. The doors of rooms were opened. A patrolling detective was moving in the opposite direction. Before the man had reached his turning point, The Shadow had glided into one of the empty rooms.

There The Shadow waited until the man had passed in the opposite direction. Again, the black-garbed phantom moved into the corridor—across—then through another open door: the one marked 2410.

Safe in Professor Devine's suite, The Shadow began an intermittent investigation. He timed his actions to the passing of the detective. Whenever the man's footsteps approached, The Shadow slid to cover; at other times, he continued his examination.

THE SHADOW had chosen this suite with a purpose. The Hotel Salamanca, though tall, was a narrow building. It fronted for half a block on Seventh Avenue. Its north side was high above an empty lot that awaited new construction. Its western exposure was a solid wall. Its south side, however, loomed above the dark cross street. There were but four rooms on this side street. Two were in an unoccupied suite; the others belonged to Professor Devine.

The Shadow had picked 2410 before examining the empty suite. His keen eyes, peering about the professor's living room, told him that there could be no one hiding here. But they saw items of interest which Cardona had not noticed.

Beneath the radiator beside the opened window, The Shadow spied a cylindrical object. Swiftly, he crossed and picked up the mailing tube. He carried it to the bedroom. He opened the capped end. The tube was made of more than cardboard. It had weight, due to a hollow metal cylinder within. A faint, whispered laugh came from The Shadow's hidden lips.

Peering from the bedroom, The Shadow noticed three canes in the corner. He glided forward, touched each in turn; then moved back to the bed-

room with the cane that the professor had furnished with tip and knob.

Removing the silver ornamentations, The Shadow examined the cane. He saw that it was a plain one; that no scoring had been provided for cap and ferrule. The Shadow replaced the cap and the tip. He waited until the patrolling detective had passed the door of 2410; then he went into the living room and put the cane in the corner; the mailing tube beneath the radiator.

Returning to the bedroom, The Shadow observed the professor's empty bag. He noted the bed lamp, which was still lighted. Again, The Shadow moved into the living room. He paused beside the open window. He noted scratches upon the sill; stooping, he saw where paint had been rubbed from the iron pipe of the radiator.

This time The Shadow was forced to move swiftly before the detective again passed the door of 2410. Gaining the bedroom, the black-cloaked investigator waited calmly while long minutes passed. At last came the sound of voices. Men had arrived from the penthouse. Joe Cardona was talking in the corridor, near the open door of 2410.

"Somebody's gone looney," the ace detective was announcing. "We've gone through this whole place clean. There's no sign of the guy we want. He must have made some sort of getaway down those stairs.

"I figure he passed the house detective. At any rate, he's not on this floor; he's not in the penthouse; he isn't on the roof. I even sent two men up into the water tank.

"The hunt is off. I'm leaving two of you men up in the penthouse; but that's all. So far as this floor is concerned, there's no use watching it."

Tramping footsteps were followed by the clangor of the elevator doors. Then came silence. The Shadow was alone on the twenty-fourth floor. Gliding out into the living room of the suite, he turned off the main light; then moved to the open window.

THE roof of the opposite apartment house lay dull beneath the city's glow. The Shadow's gaze looked toward the parapet; then beyond it, to the upright of the water tower on the deserted roof.

As clearly as if it still stretched above the chasm of the street, The Shadow could visualize the cable line that had been provided for Fullis Garwald's escape. The mailing tube was evidence of the final fish line. Knob and ferrule, attached to the wrong cane, were proof of another shaft—the one which had been used like a harpoon. The empty bag told of the cable itself.

The Shadow had found the answer to the killer's escape. He had not learned the identity of the murderer who had made a getaway with Gaston

Ferrar's highly valuable collection of gems; but he had settled upon one person who had been accessory to the crime.

With Clyde Burke's detailed description of the crime; with the reporter's added comments upon the guests who had removed from the twenty-fourth floor, The Shadow had picked one member of the crime chain. Though he had not yet learned of Crime Incorporated, the master sleuth had made his start toward the unknown goal which he had determined to reach.

The Shadow had gained the identity of one man through whom others might be forestalled before new evil struck. By working backward as well as forward, he had opportunity to solve baffling cases of the past while he worked to prevent crime of the future.

Through one man, whom he would trail with unrelenting skill, The Shadow could find the facts that he needed. A sibilant laugh came from The Shadow's unseen lips. Whispered mirth floated above the stilled canyon that lay between the high-walled buildings.

The laugh of The Shadow was eerie as it faded. Lingering echoes sighed from the night air. Echoes like laughter boded ill for Professor Langwood Devine!

CHAPTER XII
THE CREEPING SHADOW

"HERE'S your mail, Professor."

"Ah, yes. Place it here on the desk, Rupert."

Professor Langwood Devine leaned back in his chair as a hunch-shouldered serving man put three envelopes on the desk by the window.

"Your appointment, sir," reminded Rupert.

"That's right." Devine nodded. "I had almost forgotten it. How soon is Detective Cardona due to arrive, Rupert?"

"In fifteen minutes, sir."

The old professor leaned forward. He rested his elbow on the desk and placed his chin in his withered hand. He stared toward his servant; Rupert waited.

"Matters were bad, three nights ago," observed Devine. "They were most annoying to me, Rupert, particularly because I had given you the evening off. Murder is very trying to one's nerves, Rupert, when it occurs at close range."

"So I can imagine, sir."

"Think of it, Rupert!" Devine paused to picture the events of which he was speaking. "While I was seated in bed, placidly studying theorems in Calloway's admirable volume on non-Euclidian geometry, there was a frightful tumult at the door of my suite."

"The police, sir?"

"Yes. In fact, the very detective who is coming here tonight. He was searching for a murderer."

"They have not found the man yet, sir."

"So I have noticed by the newspapers. Well, Rupert, it was a most horrible experience. I was forced to leave my suite on the twenty-fourth floor. I am thankful that I did not have to return there."

"This new suite is a better one, sir."

"Yes." Professor Devine nodded in studied agreement. "You are right, Rupert. This is a superior suite; better than my old quarters. Of course, it is only on the eighteenth floor; but with this northern exposure"—he waved his hand toward the window, where the glittering lamps of Central Park showed as tiny sparkles in the distance—"I command an excellent view. Furthermore, this suite is more spacious than the one which I formerly occupied."

"Yes, sir."

"And the furnishings are more luxurious. I must commend the management, Rupert. They made up for my troublesome experience by offering me a selection of any quarters that I might choose."

The old professor turned about in his chair. He gazed with approval as he surveyed the living room. There were three doors in view. One led to a spacious anteroom; the second to the professor's bedroom; the third, located almost at the professor's shoulder, opened into an extra bedroom which was unoccupied.

The furniture was of more expensive design than that of the suite on the twenty-fourth floor. Moreover, the living room had the appearance of a large study, for each doorway was curtained with thick draperies of dark green velvet.

"Within a few days, Rupert," remarked Professor Devine, in a pleased tone, "I shall have you move into this unoccupied bedroom. Previously, you have had your quarters elsewhere. In the future—since no extra expense is involved—you may as well live here."

"Thank you, Professor," returned the servant. "I can arrange to move at the end of the present week."

THE professor stooped forward and reached for his mail. That was a sign that he was through with Rupert. The serving man went out into the anteroom.

As soon as Rupert had passed the curtains, Professor Devine glanced shrewdly upward. Satisfied that Rupert was in the anteroom, the old man selected an envelope that bore no return address. He opened it.

Two folded sheets of paper slid upon the desk. The professor spread them. Each bore a cryptic code; but the two sheets differed in appearance. One was marked with circled characters, which read:

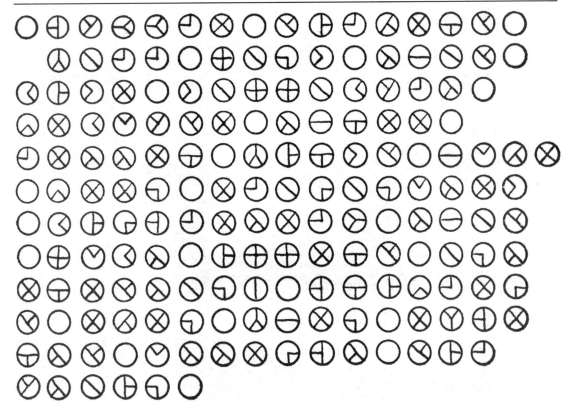

Professor Devine placed this sheet aside. Carefully, he began to study the second, which he obviously regarded as of more importance. It contained a succession of blocks, which bore the message.

Drawing forth two sheets of paper, the old professor picked up a quill pen and began to copy the codes. He worked rapidly; his own inscriptions, while accurate, differed from the originals as one person's handwriting might vary from another's.

The work required only a few minutes. Professor Devine covered the original sheets with a large book. He folded his copies, placed them in an envelope and addressed the wrapper in cramped style.

As the professor was completing his action, the curtains behind him moved. There was no sound to their motion; they parted almost as though governed by some mechanical force. Burning eyes appeared between the hangings. Along the floor, a strange patch of blackness crept forward, forming a hawklike silhouette.

"Rupert!"

As Professor Devine uttered the crisp call, the creeping shadow paused. The prompt appearance of the servant brought about an instant withdrawal of the blackness on the floor. The curtains wavered by the anteroom; as Rupert stepped into view, those behind the professor closed.

"Mail this letter," ordered Devine. "At once, Rupert. Then return."

As he passed the envelope to Rupert, the professor held it so the address was turned downward. Eyes that were peering through the tiniest slit of the closed curtains could not observe the writing. The Shadow, hidden in the unoccupied room, was balked in his attempt to learn where the letter was going.

Rupert departed. Professor Devine referred to the coded sheets upon the desk, he chuckled. He picked up a newspaper that lay beside him. He turned the pages until he came to the announcements of steamship sailings.

THE SHADOW'S eyes were at the curtain. The drapery had spread. Again, the sinister patch of blackness was creeping forward. The Shadow could not see the codes; the professor's newspaper obscured them. But the master sleuth's keen optics spotted the name upon which Devine's bony forefinger stopped as it ran through the list of ocean liners. The name of the boat which the professor marked was the Steamship *Mauritius*.

Devine dropped the newspaper. He reached for the codes. The phantom stretch of blackness was almost to the desk. Then came footsteps. Rupert was returning. The professor slipped the codes beneath the book. The Shadow's form faded behind the curtains.

"I mailed your letter, sir," announced Rupert, from the door of the anteroom. "There will be a mail collection within five minutes."

"Excellent," responded the professor.

"The telephone was buzzing when I returned, sir," added Rupert. "It was Detective Cardona. He is in the lobby, sir. I told him I would notify him as soon as you would be ready to receive him."

"Very good, Rupert. I am pleased that Detective Cardona is prompt. Do you know, Rupert"—the professor paused in meditative fashion—"I have been quite worried ever since Gaston Ferrar was murdered. I told Detective Cardona of my qualms, for he seemed to be a capable chap in his own profession.

"I have valuables here in this suite. They are considerable enough to attract a robber. So I decided to post Detective Cardona regarding them. I felt that I should seek his advice as to the protection of my possessions. That is why he is coming here tonight."

"A very good idea, sir."

"I want him to see you, Rupert," spoke Devine. "I would like his opinion concerning your potential ability as my sole attendant. I shall tell him that I intend to have you reside in the extra bedroom.

"Of course, if Detective Cardona decides that I need more protection, your situation will not be jeopardized. I shall simply employ another man to serve with you."

"I understand, sir."

"Call the lobby, Rupert. Then go directly to the elevators, to meet Detective Cardona when he reaches this floor."

Rupert turned and walked toward the anteroom. Hardly had the servant passed the curtains before Professor Devine lifted the book and seized the coded papers. He was about to tear them, when he desisted. Knowing that he had a few minutes ahead, the professor leaned back in his chair to chuckle over the messages.

IT was then that the curtains behind Devine moved with greater swiftness. As they spread, a tall form moved slowly forward. Before it, a patch of blackness crept with steady swiftness. The silhouette reached the table; it seemed to spring upward. The creeping shade covered Professor Devine's white hair. It cast an umbra upon the papers which the old man held.

The Shadow was seeking a long glimpse of the coded messages. His new opportunity ended as suddenly as it had arrived. There was a reason for the professor's conclusion of his reading—a reason which The Shadow could not observe, for he was in back of the old man.

Devine's sharp eyes happened to note the top of one sheet. There, upon the whitened paper, he saw the edge of the creeping profile. Staring warily beyond the coded sheet, the old man observed the remainder of the silhouette.

Whatever his emotions might have been, the crafty professor did not betray them. He pressed the coded sheets together. He folded them in a casual manner, as though they were of little consequence. He laid them on the desk and arose, apparently preparing to leave for the anteroom.

The creeping silhouette glided backward. Blackness faded from the floor. Professor Devine began his hobble from the desk; as an afterthought, he stepped back and leaned heavily upon the woodwork as he opened a desk drawer.

The old man's hand was momentarily out of sight. As it withdrew from the drawer, his body covered it. Again, the professor shifted away from the desk; then, with a quick wheeling motion, he turned squarely toward the curtains that covered the entrance to the unoccupied room.

A flash from Devine's hand. Metal sparkled in the light; a bony finger made a snapping motion. The professor had clutched a revolver from the desk drawer. Spurting flame came belching from the mouth of the .32 as the crafty crook loosed his sudden fire.

The professor had recognized the token of The Shadow. He had prepared his answer to that unseen presence. Decisive in his action, he had loosed a murderous bullet straight for the spot where the eyes of The Shadow had peered between the velvet curtains!

CHAPTER XIII
DEATH STRIKES

PROFESSOR LANGWOOD DEVINE had aimed for blackness. Yet he had not aimed blindly. Craftily, he had gauged The Shadow's spying action. He had fired to kill—straight for the exact spot where The Shadow had been hidden.

One bullet—two—deadly missives sped from the old villain's revolver. These were but the outset of the volley. Without pause, Professor Devine swung his weapon downward. His action showed his super cunning.

Swift though he had moved, Devine knew that The Shadow might have acted with the same prompt rapidity. No living being could have sprung away before the firing of the shots; but a dropping form, falling with simultaneous speed, might have escaped the deadly aim.

It was this instantaneous thought that prompted Devine's downward move. The .32 described a falling arc; a bony finger was ready to loose the entire volley of the gun. With amazing precision, Devine had chosen the exact spot where a huddled or crouched body might be situated.

The proof of the insidious professor's exactitude came from the curtain itself. Like an answer to the white-haired villain's thought came a roar accompanied by a tongue of spurting fire. The doorway echoed with the thunder of The Shadow's automatic.

Devine's finger faltered. His hand loosed. The

.32 dropped from his clutch. Gasping, the old man floundered to the floor. The slug from a .45 had ruined the chances of the .32. Devine's one mistake had been to The Shadow's gain.

The being behind the curtain had dropped with Devine's first aim. As the professor's hand had swung downward, The Shadow's fist had been acting in return. Devine had gained the first shots; but they had gone above The Shadow's head. The villain's second guess had been too late.

The curtains parted. From between them came a shape that seemed to rise like an avenging specter. The Shadow, pressed to a duel of death, had struck. Langwood Devine, abettor of crime, potential murderer, lay upon the floor before the cloaked master, coughing his last breaths.

UPON the desk lay the folded papers, the clues to Devine's part in crime. The Shadow, towering weirdly in the light, from the desk, was turning to reach for them when an unexpected interruption came from the outer door.

Rupert had left the door of the suite open. At the elevators, the servant had heard the sound of gunfire. He had dashed back to the professor's room.

His startled eyes saw Devine's dying body on the floor; above it, the form of an eerie intruder.

Devine's crimes had been concealed from his servant. To Rupert, the presence of The Shadow was proof of the fears that the professor had advanced tonight. This was the enemy whom Rupert's master had dreaded!

Frantically, Rupert shouted for help as he flung himself across the room, straight for the black-garbed form. Turning from the desk, The Shadow swept to meet the plunging servant. With Rupert, The Shadow had no quarrel. Yet in this moment of emergency, he could not stop.

Servant and Shadow met. Black arms caught Rupert's springing form. Twisting in The Shadow's clutch, Rupert went rolling sidewise across the room. His spreading arms encountered the wall. The Shadow, turning, was in the center of the room.

Gamely, Rupert staggered to his feet. Fiercely, he came up beside the desk where Devine's body lay. His eyes glimpsed the revolver close to the fallen form. Rupert seized the weapon.

The servant's action was folly. The Shadow could have dropped him with a single shot. By such procedure, The Shadow could have gained the folded ciphers, which Rupert was unwittingly guarding. To The Shadow, however, Rupert's blind loyalty to an unworthy master was but proof of the servant's character.

The Shadow whirled toward the door to the anteroom. His action was an acknowledgement of Rupert's bravery. Langwood Devine was dead. The codes were safe from destruction. Much though The Shadow had wanted them, he was ready to entrust them to the future.

As Rupert turned to fire at the being in black, The Shadow was sweeping through the curtains to the anteroom. Rupert was frantic as he employed wild aim. His hasty bullets zipped wide of their mark. The Shadow was gone.

A shout came from the hall. It was Joe Cardona, coming on the run. The Shadow stopped abruptly; his tall form faded behind the opened door as the detective came dashing into the anteroom, revolver in hand.

Springing through to Devine's living room, Cardona came face to face with Rupert, standing above the dead professor's corpse. The tension ended, Rupert gasped vague words. Cardona, thinking that Devine's assailant had taken to the room behind the desk, hurried in that direction.

SWIFTLY, The Shadow came from behind the door. He turned toward the corridor. As he did, a form came plunging directly through the doorway. It was the house detective, who had come up on the elevator with Joe Cardona.

The Shadow's form dropped. Before the house dick realized what had happened, he was hoisted upward by two arms that gripped his waist with the power of steel rods. The Shadow sent the man rolling across the anteroom. When the bewildered house detective came to his knees, his assailant had vanished.

The door of the elevator was open. The operator was peering, wild-eyed, down the corridor. The Shadow, profiting by Clyde Burke's description of the scene at Ferrar's murder, fired a warning shot. As the automatic echoed, the operator dropped from sight and clanged the doors.

The Shadow gained the stairway, a soft laugh rippling from his hidden lips. His form vanished in the darkness. The echoes seemed to continue as the weird intruder continued his downward course.

The elevator that had brought Joe Cardona and the house detective was moving downward to give the alarm in the lobby. The operator had hesitated behind his metal doors, wondering if he should wait until the detective returned. That was a point that served The Shadow.

A second elevator was coming down from the twenty-fourth floor. Its operator knew nothing of the excitement on the eighteenth. Seeing a stop signal for the sixteenth story, he halted his car and opened the doors.

A tall passenger entered. The operator noted a keen, hawklike visage. He glimpsed a briefcase that the entrant was carrying. In methodical fashion, the elevator man closed the doors. He let the car descend. There were no more stop signals. The car reached the lobby ahead of the one that was bringing the alarm.

Calmly, the passenger with the briefcase strolled out through the lobby. He reached the sidewalk just as the other elevator came to the bottom of the shaft. The alarm had arrived; it was too late to trap the being who had caused it. The tall personage who had left the Hotel Salamanca was The Shadow.

CHAOS had come again to the Hotel Salamanca. In the furor which followed the operator's report, one man alone maintained a steady composure. That was Detective Joe Cardona. Although faced with what appeared to be a third murder mystery, the ace sleuth was calm.

He had summoned police. He had reported to headquarters. He had gained incoherent statements from both Rupert and the house detective. But amid it all, Cardona had seized upon a potential clue. He had found the folded papers upon Langwood Devine's desk.

Joe Cardona was an unusual detective. He had a keen ability for gaining hunches; a remarkable aptitude for silence when it was needed. Instinctively, Joe had decided that those coded messages might hold the key to the death of Professor Langwood Devine.

Murder at the Hotel Salamanca! The alarm had gone rapidly. Tonight, reporters were on the job almost as quickly as Inspector Klein and the police surgeon. Through their early arrival, the news seekers managed to reach the eighteenth floor before they could be stopped.

The spokesman of the journalistic throng was Clyde Burke. To this reporter, Joe Cardona gave terse statements regarding the death of Langwood Devine. But the ace sleuth said nothing of the discovery that he regarded as the keynote to the case: those coded sheets that he had plucked from the dead professor's desk.

WHILE Cardona was still at the Hotel Salamanca, a bluish light was burning in a secret room. The white hands of The Shadow were taking earphones from the wall, where a tiny bulb was glowing to signify Burbank's call.

The Shadow's weird voice called for the report. Across the wire came the details that Clyde Burke had gained from Joe Cardona. There was no mention whatever of discovered codes. The earphones clattered back into their place.

Out went the bluish light. A sardonic laugh quivered through the sanctum. Ghoulish echoes came from blackened walls. The Shadow's mirth was strident.

For tonight, The Shadow had gained much despite the unexpected events which had obstructed his path.

He had learned that Langwood Devine was but one member in a group of criminals. He had seen the dead villain forward word along the chain.

The Shadow knew that the key to hidden crime lay in those coded sheets that Devine had failed to destroy. Moreover, The Shadow knew that the all-important papers had fallen into good hands.

Joe Cardona held the coded messages. They would be safe—more than that, their existence would be unknown—while they remained in Cardona's hands. The Shadow knew who held the cryptic papers. With that knowledge, he could find a way to learn their exact contents.

The fading tones of The Shadow's laugh were again foreboding. Previously, that mirthful cry had presaged trouble for Professor Langwood Devine. On this occasion, it foreboded ill for Crime Incorporated!

CHAPTER XIV
THE CHAIN CLOSES

AT nine o'clock the next morning, Culbert Joquill entered his office in the Zenith Building. There was a serious expression upon the dignified lawyer's face. Joquill's greeting to the office staff was no more than a curt nod.

Reaching the inner office, Joquill seated himself behind the desk. He drew a folded newspaper from his overcoat pocket. With forehead furrowed, the attorney began to read a news account that he had studied while riding hither in the subway.

The headlines told of death at the Hotel Salamanca. Professor Langwood Devine, a scholarly old recluse, had been slain by an unknown assailant. Details were complete. The newspapers mentioned that the fray had commenced while Professor Devine was alone in his suite. His servant, Rupert, had returned from posting a letter to see the professor alive for the last time.

Still frowning, Joquill tossed the newspaper aside. His eyes looked toward the tray upon his desk. There, projecting from the morning's mail, was an envelope which caught the lawyer's attention. Joquill seized the missive. He ripped it open.

Out came two folded sheets. One carried the circled code; the other, the series of blocklike characters. These were the copies that Professor Devine had made.

No wonder Culbert Joquill had been alarmed by the reports of Devine's death. The professor and the lawyer were connecting links in the chain of Crime Incorporated!

Joquill settled in his chair. He pondered. A smile showed on his benign features. The lawyer was considering the circumstances of Devine's death as revealed by this forwarded copy of the word which Devine had received.

CULBERT JOQUILL

Some member of Crime Incorporated had started a request along the line. Last night, Devine had received his notes. He had copied them and forwarded the request to Joquill. That work had been accomplished before Devine had faced the danger which had brought his death.

Culbert Joquill was positive that Langwood Devine must have destroyed the coded message that he had received. That step, normally, should have preceded the forwarding of copies. The newspapers contained no mention of any papers found at Devine's.

Joquill chuckled. The chances seemed certain that Devine had destroyed his messages. What if he had not? It made no difference. Joquill had confidence in the code itself; he was positive, also, that Devine must have kept some excellent hiding place for his documents that pertained to Crime Incorporated.

Knowing Devine, Joquill recalled that the old professor had a special lodging somewhere in the city—a place where he seldom went—and the chances were that his stock certificate and coded bylaws were concealed there.

The fact that Devine's letter had come through the mail was all that Joquill needed to feel absolutely secure. Freed from sense of menace, the lawyer became methodical. Taking pen and paper, he copied the coded messages that he had received. His own writing showed a difference from Devine's.

WHILE his copies were drying, Joquill picked up Devine's notes and tore them to shreds. He raised the window and let tiny fragments of paper flutter out into the breeze. Intermittently, like flurries of confetti, the bits of Devine's notes were scattered beyond recall.

Returning to his desk, Joquill picked up his own copies; he sealed them in an envelope. He wrote an address, sealed the letter and strolled from his office. He posted his letter in the mail chute by the elevators; then returned to his private office.

Culbert Joquill had sent the request along the chain. The promptitude with which he had copied Devine's notes and mailed them proved that he could see no way in aiding coming crime. In fact, the satisfied smile that showed on the lawyer's lips indicated that he felt he had done his share.

The theft of George Hobston's private wealth had been a big job. Culbert Joquill was holding vast spoils for later division among the members of Crime Incorporated. He regarded himself, for the present, as no more than a connecting link.

Yet Joquill had another duty. An emergency had arisen. Professor Langwood Devine was dead—

killed under circumstances that had obviously rendered it impossible for the old professor to transfer his franchise in Crime Incorporated. There would be no substitute to take the dead man's place. A link was broken in the chain.

Culbert Joquill went to the door of his private office and softly turned the key. Crossing the room, he opened the hinged bookcase. He stepped into the secret room. There he faced the solid back of the bookcase. He pressed a panel. It moved upward, revealing a narrow space between two vertical surfaces.

From this cache, Culbert Joquill removed an envelope. From the container, he produced two smaller envelopes. He chose one that he knew had come from Langwood Devine. He replaced the other, closed the trick panel, and moved from the secret room, shutting the bookcase from his office.

At his desk, Joquill ripped open the sealed envelope. He found a piece of paper that bore a coded name. Joquill chuckled. This was the name of Professor Devine's other friend. In all probability, that man was at present opening an envelope of his own, to learn the name of Culbert Joquill.

THE lawyer inscribed a note in the circled code. His rapid writing showed that this was merely a formality; that the succession of circles was merely a blind.

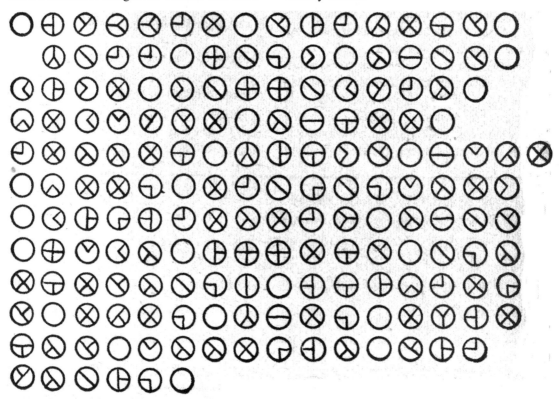

Then he followed with a second message, which he prepared slowly, pausing to choose his statements.

This was in the blocked code. Finished with his hieroglyphics, Joquill pondered over the message. It read:

Smiling, the lawyer folded both sheets and placed them in a plain envelope. Methodically, he tore up the little slip of paper that revealed the name of Professor Devine's other connection. He tossed the bits from the window. Then, from memory, he addressed the envelope:

Chalmers Blythe,
Merrimac Club,
New York City.

Carrying the letter, Joquill used his private exit to reach the hall. He returned a few minutes later, without the envelope. He unlocked the door to the outer office, seated himself behind the desk and picked up the morning newspaper.

Casually, the attorney turned to the page that listed steamship sailings. He chuckled as he found the name of the Steamship *Mauritius*. The liner was not scheduled to sail for one full week.

Someone knew that crime could be launched upon that ship. The plotter of evil had stated his case to his fellow members in Crime Incorporated. Word had come to Chalmers Blythe; from him to Langwood Devine; then to Culbert Joquill; and the lawyer had sent it further on.

Replies would be immediate. From somewhere in the chain of crime, a crook equipped to do the task requested would pledge his cooperation in the stroke that was required. Members of Crime Incorporated would act in teamwork aboard the Steamship *Mauritius*.

The plotter had probably sent requests in two directions. Perhaps cooperative aid would come from someone beyond Joquill; possibly it would come from the opposite end of the chain. In either event, the waiting plotter would be assured of aid before the *Mauritius* sailed from New York.

Culbert Joquill chuckled. He had done his part. Not only had he forwarded the request; he was ready to send along the reply when it arrived. But he would send no message to Professor Langwood Devine. The dead man had been eliminated from the band of supercrooks. The new recipient of Joquill's messages would be a man named Chalmers Blythe.

Already, Joquill had phrased a coded note to Blythe. He would probably receive a similar epistle from Blythe himself. Unknown to each other in the past, Joquill and Blythe were now joined as friends. They had bridged the gap left vacant by the death of Professor Langwood Devine.

The Shadow had been forced to slay Devine. That, in a sense, had been a victory for The Shadow. But it had again brought him to the end of a blind trail. The Shadow had simply broken one link in the chain of Crime Incorporated.

The break had been joined. Devine, dead, was a discarded unit. Culbert Joquill and Chalmers Blythe were unencumbered. Crime Incorporated could proceed with its heinous plans, its evil members hidden as effectively as before!

CHAPTER XV
CARDONA MEETS A VISITOR

"I AM going out this evening, Norwyn. Perhaps we can play our chess match after my return."

Howard Norwyn nodded as he looked up from the chessboard. Before him, he saw the tall form of his congenial host, Lamont Cranston. Dinner ended at the New Jersey mansion, Norwyn had retired to the smoking room while Cranston made a telephone call. They had planned a chess match during dinner; now it would have to be deferred.

"You are going into the city?" questioned Norwyn.

"Yes," came Cranston's quiet reply.

Norwyn seemed pleased. Though his host was a leisurely, noncommittal sort of personage, the young fugitive sensed that Cranston's frequent visits to New York were in his behalf. Norwyn's worries had quelled considerably during his extended stay at Cranston's.

"The limousine is waiting, sir."

Richards made the announcement from the hallway. With a friendly nod to Norwyn, Cranston turned and left the smoking room. A minute later, the limousine purred away from the drive, with Stanley at the wheel.

IT was nearly an hour later when a light clicked in The Shadow's sanctum. White hands toyed with clippings. They reached for earphones. A voice came over the wire:

"Burbank speaking."

"Report," whispered The Shadow.

"Report from Burke," informed Burbank. "He has left headquarters. Cardona is still there, working on the Devine case."

"Any mention of the codes?"

"None."

"Report received. Burke off duty."

"Instructions received."

Earphones clattered. Again, the hands were at the clippings. A soft laugh sounded in the gloom beside the focused light. Among the news items was one that had been mentioned in a previous report. It was a planted story in the New York *Classic,* put there by Clyde Burke through The Shadow's bidding. It announced that Mynheer Hansel Vaart, prominent economist from the Netherlands, was due to arrive in New York.

Burke's story—of half a column length—consisted of a reputed interview with the Dutchman. The article was conspicuous enough to attract the attention of the average newspaper reader.

The Shadow's light went out. A soft laugh sounded in the gloom. The sanctum was empty. But The Shadow had not left the neighborhood of his abode. Another light clicked in a second room. Its burning glare was reflected by the polished surface of a mirror.

Away from the light, motion was in progress. At last, a shape moved forward, close to the polished looking glass. The blackness of The Shadow's cloak came into view. The sable garment was drooping from the shoulders that wore it.

The slouch hat was gone. A face was revealed in the light. It was not the masklike countenance of Lamont Cranston. It was another visage that The Shadow, master of disguise, had chosen to don as one would put on a new garment.

The face that showed in the reflected light was a puffy, robust one. Above it was the edge of a close-fitting wig that was topped by thin hair of iron gray. White hands, moving upward, smoothed the line where the wig began. Deft fingers, pressing against cheeks and lips, were molding the countenance as one might work with clay.

Bushy eyebrows came into place. They fitted perfectly above the keen eyes. They matched the color of the hair. The work of disguise continued; it ended when a soft laugh came from large-formed lips. The Shadow's task had resulted in the perfect formation of a countenance that presented a virile man of nearly sixty years.

Out went the light. The folds of The Shadow's cloak were drawn upward. Then came silence. Masked by his chosen disguise, ready to put aside his cloak and hat, The Shadow was departing upon a definite errand.

DETECTIVE JOE CARDONA was seated at his desk in headquarters when a fellow sleuth entered and passed a card to the star detective. Joe studied the Old English lettering. It bore this legend:

Mynheer Hansel Vaart
Amsterdam

"Hm-m," mused Cardona. "Say—this must be the Dutchman that I read about in the *Classic.* Coming in from Holland on his way to a big convention in Chicago. What does he want?"

"He wants to see you. He won't say why."

"Show him in here."

The detective left. He returned with a tall, stoop-shouldered man who was attired in a heavy overcoat, with large fur collar.

Cardona found himself staring at a remarkably distinguished countenance. Hansel Vaart seemed keen-eyed; his robust cheeks marked him as a man in fine health. His dignity and friendliness combined to create confidence.

"What can I do for you, sir?" questioned Cardona, in a polite tone. "I hope that you have encountered no trouble since your arrival in New York?"

"Trouble for me? Ah, no." The visitor's voice

seemed saddened. "That trouble hass happened, yess, to someone who iss a friend off mine. While I wass yet upon the steamboat, coming to New York. It wass three nights ago."

"You mean something happened on the boat? What ship?"

"The boat, no. It wass here, in New York. *Mein freund*, Herr Professor Devine. He iss dead. It iss too bad, yess."

"Ah!" Cardona was interested. "You knew Professor Devine?"

"Yess." The visitor nodded. "He hass written to me sometimes; but not for a long time since. I wass to see him when I haff come to New York. But he iss dead."

"Devine had very few friends," stated Cardona. "He lived at one hotel, then another, finally at the Salamanca, where he was killed. Did you ever write to him?"

"Not for a long time since."

"Where was he living then?"

"At a hotel. It wass called the Darien."

"That must have been before he hired Rupert," mused Cardona. "His servant said nothing about the Hotel Darien. Tell me, Doctor, can you give me any clue regarding Professor Devine?"

"Doctor, no." The visitor chuckled. "I am joost Mynheer Vaart. That iss all. But it wass to ask you about something that I haff come here. Haff you found the Herr professor's goads?"

"His goads?" Cardona seemed puzzled.

"Yess," nodded the visitor. "The goads. The writing which iss in what you call the cipher."

"You mean codes!" exclaimed Cardona, his face lighting with elation.

"Yess," replied Mynheer Vaart.

"Like this?" questioned Cardona, forming circles with a pencil. "Or like this?" He made rough blocks. "Are those the codes you mean?"

"*Nein.*" Vaart's head was emphatic, in its negative shake. "Like this."

He took the pencil and made a succession of crisscross lines. It was Cardona, this time, who shook his head.

"None like that," said the detective, in a decisive tone. "But perhaps you can tell me the purpose of these codes that Devine used."

"It wass to him a hobby," asserted the visitor, solemnly. "When he would write to friends, he wass accustomed to use such ways. It wass not because the writing should not be read by other people. It wass because he wass fond of those goads. With me, he sent them first to make me be confused I think. But each time that he haff made the goad different, I haff guessed it, word by word and haff sent him back the answer."

"How long do you expect to be in town?" questioned Cardona, suddenly, as he rose to his feet.

"I must go by a train at midnight," insisted the visitor. "It iss to Chicago that I must go from here."

The detective glanced at his watch. He nodded; then spoke tensely to the placid Dutchman.

"We found two coded messages at Devine's," confided Cardona. "I turned them over to a cryptogram expert, Doctor Lucas Mather.

"Doctor Mather had no trouble with one code— the message with the circles. But the other has stumped him. The circle message was not important. It appears to be exactly what you have described— a game that someone sent to Devine.

"But those blocks are puzzlers. We need all the advice we can get on them. If you have had experience with codes written by Devine, perhaps you are the very person whose aid we need.

"Suppose I take you out to Long Island. We'll see Doctor Mather and talk with him. We'll give you a look at the codes. It's only nine o'clock. I'll guarantee to have you back in town in time to catch the midnight limited."

FIVE minutes later, Detective Joe Cardona and his companion were riding eastward in a speedy automobile. They were bound for the home of Doctor Lucas Mather, the cryptogram expert who resided on Long Island.

Joe Cardona was elated. The ace detective had accepted Mynheer Hansel Vaart at face value. Through the possible aid of this friendly visitor from Amsterdam, Cardona hoped that he might gain a clue to the identity of the person who had slain Professor Langwood Devine.

Joe Cardona was looking for a murderous crook. Not for one instant had he suspected that such a brand belonged to the dead professor. Hence Cardona's actual purpose summed to this: he was hunting the slayer of Devine.

Cardona would have been amazed had he known that beside him in the speeding car was the very person who had killed Langwood Devine, in self-defense. Mynheer Hansel Vaart appeared too genuine—particularly because a newspaper report had preceded his coming to New York—to be regarded as an impostor.

Such a revelation would have astounded Cardona; the real identity of Mynheer Hansel Vaart would have left the detective bewildered. For Joe Cardona, totally oblivious to the truth, was taking a most remarkable visitor to view the codes at Mather's home.

The star detective was riding side by side with a supersleuth whose skill made Cardona's ability at crime detection seem like a puny power. Without the semblance of a hunch that might have given him a lead, Joe Cardona was falling for the game of a mastermind.

Cardona had good reason to suppose that the taking of this visitor to Doctor Lucas Mather might bring great results in the solution of a baffling crime. But Joe Cardona had no inkling of that actual reason which was so important.

The ace sleuth was taking a tremendous step toward the ending of insidious crime, despite the fact that he was acting blindly. He was about to lay the all-important evidence before the one master sleuth who could use it best.

Joe Cardona was taking The Shadow to visit Doctor Lucas Mather!

CHAPTER XVI
A QUESTION OF CODES

"THE solving of this circled code was child's play. The man who wrote the message sought to make the message difficult. Instead, he opened it to simple attack."

Doctor Lucas Mather made this statement as he faced Detective Joe Cardona and Mynheer Hansel Vaart. Mather, seated behind a table in a room which served him as a study, was pointing to the first of the two papers that Cardona had brought from Professor Langwood Devine's.

Adjusting a pair of large spectacles, Mather peered toward the paper. A smile appeared upon his thin, pale lips. The cryptographer laughed scoffingly as he ran his fingers along the inscription:

"Let me explain my simple process of solution," suggested Mather, in a methodical tone. "I noticed, first of all, that the message forms solid lines of characters. That would mean a jumble of words, unless a special character were utilized to indicate a space.

"Counting the various characters," proceeded Doctor Mather, "I found that two symbols each appeared with more frequency than the others. Each of those particular symbols appeared exactly twenty-six times. Here are the characters in question.

"The most rudimentary fact regarding statements in the English language," resumed Mather, "is that concerning the letter E. It will appear more often than any other letter of the alphabet, provided that no effort is made to reduce it by tricky wording.

"Hence, in my basic study of this message, I had two characters—the crossed circle and the plain circle—either of which might stand for the letter E. I began a prompt comparison of those two characters; and I made an immediate discovery.

"The crossed circle could easily stand for E. The blank circle was doubtful. You will note that the message begins with a blank circle and ends with one. That was one oddity. The second peculiarity was the intervals existing between blank circles. The third was the fact that no two blank circles appear together.

"Assuming that the blank circle was either E or

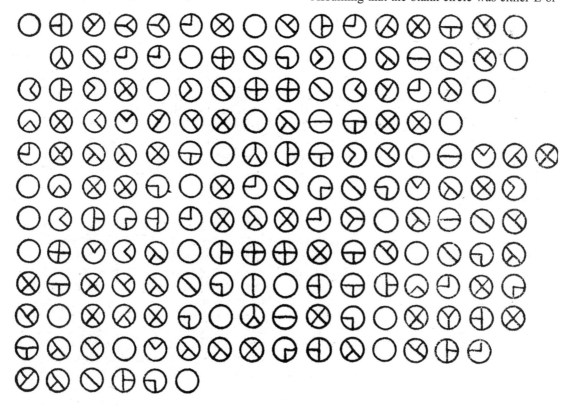

some other frequent letter such as 0, or T, the intervals and lack of doubles stood against it. So I went back to my original theory, namely, that some character stood for a space between the words. The character could not be the crossed circle; for it twice appears as a double. It must be the blank circle. So I eliminated all the blank circles and made this revised message."

The cryptographer produced a sheet of paper which bore the following code:

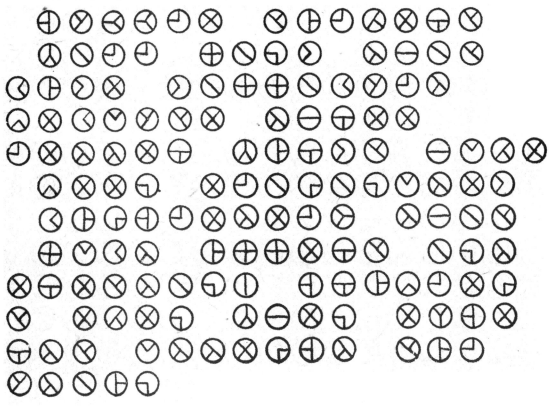

"Beginning again," explained Mather, "I used the crossed circle as the letter E. I was immediately impressed by the ninth word in the message. It consists of five letters, ending in a double E.

"Referring to my dictionary of word endings"—the speaker paused to tap a book that lay on the table—"I found very few words of five letters that end with a double E. One such word stood out from all the rest. It was the word 'three'; so I used it for the ninth word of the message, thus."

The bespectacled man wrote on a blank paper.

"The fifth word of the message is identical with the sixteenth. Both are words of four letters, beginning with TH. My choice was 'this' or 'that'; of the two, I took 'this' because the words did not end in the character that I had established as T.

"The procedure gave me two new letters: I and S. Studying the tenth word of the message, I saw that I had five of its six characters. It ended in E, T, T, E, R. That meant that the first symbol was probably B or

L. It eventually proved to be L. I shall tell you why.

"In the meantime, I had noticed the third word. Its second letter was I; it ended with a double character that was the same as the first symbol of the tenth word. So I chose double L, as double B would not have followed the letter I. The tenth word proved to be 'letter'; the third word 'will.'

"I supplied T wherever it belonged. I used the letter S, thus gaining plurals. With B, I, R and H at my disposal, I made speedy progress. The deciphered message needed only a few fills. The twenty-second word—four letters—spelled W, H, E; so I finished it with N. The last word of the message, with five letters gained, obviously spelled 'solution'."

THE cryptographer was working with his pencil as he gave his illustration. He was copying characters upon blank paper at a rate that made Joe Cardona stare in wonder.

"All checked," concluded Mather, "with the exception of a few isolated letters that I reasoned out with ease. For example, the first letter of the message. I read it as P, U, then two unknown characters, both alike, and finally L, E.

"What was the double letter indicated by those central characters? The answer was simple. Inserting double Z, I gained the word 'puzzle'. I might have used double D"—Mather smiled wanly—"but dealing with a puzzle and not with a puddle, I chose Z.

"Here, gentlemen, is the deciphered message. It is merely a cryptogram, I take it, that some friend sent to Professor Devine to see if he could solve it."

Mather printed letters upon a plain piece of paper. He handed the sheet to Detective Joe Cardona, who nodded and placed it in the hands of Mynheer Hansel Vaart.

The message read:

> PUZZLE SOLVERS WILL FIND THIS CODE DIFFICULT BECAUSE THREE LETTER WORDS HAVE BEEN ELIMINATED COMPLETELY THIS FACT OFFERS INTERESTING PROBLEMS EVEN WHEN EXPERTS ATTEMPT SOLUTION

"And here," added Doctor Mather, drawing a paper from the desk drawer, "is the code itself, arranged in alphabetical order. You will note that I have merely guessed at characters which could be used for the letters J, K and Q; for those do not appear in the message."

you got from Professor Devine?" questioned the detective. "Did yours follow the same line?"

"Yess." The reply came methodically. "But some were more hard to read. Yess, much more hard. This one, it seems easy. So our friend, the good Doctor Mather, hass said."

"Easy to you, maybe," responded Cardona, "but it looks tougher than a dozen crossword puzzles to me."

"Mynheer Vaart," asserted Mather, "agrees that this code is rudimentary. But I am positive that he will find the other message to be a complete riddle. I have been unable to make any headway with it."

So saying, the cryptographer produced the second message. He passed it to the visitor. Keen eyes sparkled from beneath the false eyebrows as The Shadow studied the blocked code. Lingering minutes passed while Cardona and Mather watched him. Then The Shadow spoke, in the thick voice of Mynheer Vaart.

"It iss indeed a different thing," he announced. "Never haff I seen one goad that iss like this one. Nothing, never hass Professor Devine sent me like this."

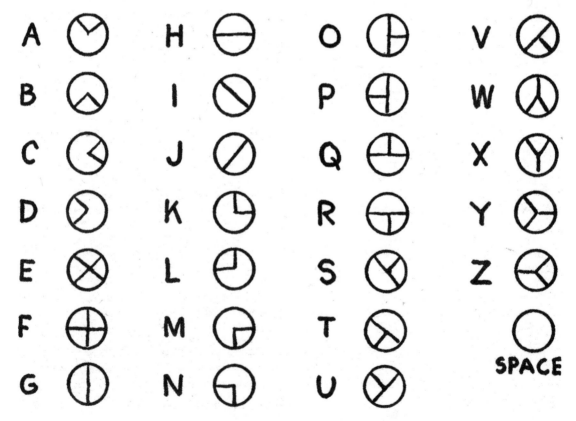

The cryptogram expert looked upward through his rimmed spectacles. He saw the nodding head of Hansel Vaart.

"Is that the way you figured out the messages

"Prevailing characters lead one nowhere," observed Mather. "I have tried every form of cryptogram solution, but to no avail. I have resorted to foreign languages. I have considered the use of extra symbols for certain letters; such as two—or perhaps three—different characters to represent the letter E. Yet I have been balked incessantly."

"But if it iss like this one," suggested The Shadow, in his disguised tone, as he pointed to the solved code of circles, "why should it be that you haff tried so long? Perhaps it iss another message off no important meaning."

"That's what we don't know," interposed Cardona. "Maybe the easy code was a blind to make this one look like it meant nothing."

"Perhaps," came the tones of Mynheer Vaart, "it iss a hoax that someone hass played upon mein poor dead friend. He wass very good at these goads, wass Professor Devine. Maybe this wass made to giff him trouble. Maybe these blocks and so forth wass intended to mean nothing."

"Say!" exclaimed Cardona. "That's an idea! You mean a jumble of crazy-looking figures that never were coded at all?"

"Yess."

"That is possible," agreed Doctor Mather. "Nevertheless, I shall still persist in my efforts to solve this intriguing cipher. If it is actually a coded message, I believe that it must be of importance."

Joe Cardona, studying the two persons before him, felt renewed reliance in the keenness of Mynheer Hansel Vaart. The Hollander was studying the blocked message with a gaze of concentrated interest. Cardona gained a sudden inspiration.

"Doctor Mather has photostatic copies of this message," remarked the detective. "Perhaps you would like to take one with you, Mynheer Vaart. I know that I can rely upon you to keep it out of sight; if you have a chance to work on it while you are in Chicago, you might strike the key."

"Ah, yess," came the reply, with a nod. "If I could haff one copy of this goaded message, I might haff time to solf it, yess. Off course, since it iss not solfed by Doctor Mather, it may be that it cannot be solfed by me."

"I don't know about that," returned Mather, dryly. "Freak codes like this one are very, very tricky. Perhaps, through over-concentration, I may have passed by a simple key to the solution. Here is a copy, Mynheer Vaart. I shall be pleased to have your cooperation in this difficult task."

IT was eleven o'clock when Mynheer Hansel Vaart shook hands with Detective Joe Cardona at the entrance to the Grand Central Station. The Hollander waddled into the huge terminal. Joe Cardona returned to headquarters. Shortly after midnight, he decided to leave for the night.

Smiling to himself, Joe pictured Mynheer Hansel Vaart aboard the midnight limited, pondering over the cryptic message which Doctor Lucas Mather had given him. Joe felt sure that the methodical Dutchman would work steadily upon the absorbing problem.

Cardona would have been surprised had he known where the copy of the message lay at present. It was not in the possession of Mynheer Hansel Vaart aboard the midnight limited, for no such passenger had boarded the Chicago-bound train.

The copied message was tucked safely in the pocket of a tuxedo jacket worn by a personage who looked amazingly like Lamont Cranston, the globe-trotting millionaire. The message was resting for the present; for its holder was engaged in playing chess with Howard Norwyn, fugitive from justice, in the smoking room of a New Jersey mansion.

The Shadow had played a clever part. He had gained the message which Professor Langwood Devine had received before his death. The Shadow knew that there would be time to work upon its solution.

That task would begin upon the morrow. In the meantime, returned to his guise of Lamont Cranston, the master sleuth was concerned with his game of chess. His gambits and his checks were too much for Howard Norwyn's defense. The blacks—moved by the long fingers of The Shadow—were picking off the whites that Norwyn handled.

There was something prophetic about this friendly match. Pawns and rooks were The Shadow's quarry tonight. Beginning with the morrow, he would plan moves to capture living men. Like pieces on a chessboard, the members of Crime Incorporated awaited the entry of The Shadow into their game.

CHAPTER XVII
THE SHADOW SOLVES

A LIGHT was burning in The Shadow's sanctum. Those bluish rays had been glaring steadily for a space of many hours. Hands, unwearied despite their constant task, were inscribing characters upon a sheet of paper.

The Shadow, like Doctor Lucas Mather, had struck a Tartar in the block-formed message. He knew, through experience, why the cryptogram expert had been willing to admit that the strange symbols might be meaningless.

The Shadow, himself, might have accepted that very conclusion had he not been present in Devine's room when the old professor had received the message. To Devine, this page had been quite readable.

The Shadow was sure that the solution of the code depended upon some simple key. Yet the vital point was absent.

The pencil poised above the scrawled sheet. Keen eyes focused themselves beyond, to the center of the table, where the photostatic message lay blue-tinged beneath the light. The Shadow's hand reverted to the simple circled code which Doctor Mather had so easily deciphered. The pencil, moved by steady fingers, inscribed a blank circle.

Spaces! This blocked message, like the circled one, was solid. There must be some allowance for space between the words. That might prove the one

The Shadow was sure that the solution of the code depended upon some simple key.

point of similarity between the easy code and this difficult one.

The Shadow had looked for characters that might mean spaces. He had found none; but he was thinking of spaces in a different light. Why characters for spaces when spaces already existed? If certain spaces in this coded message could be designated as blanks, they would serve their natural use.

With his thought, The Shadow began to study the message between the symbols, instead of viewing the actual characters themselves. He was looking for some little touch that would point to separations. He was comparing each character with the one that followed it. Suddenly, he struck the point he wanted.

Wherever a character showed a projecting line at the bottom, on the right, the one that followed it showed a projecting tab to the left. These coincidences occurred at intervals through the message, in a manner that could well signify spaces.

It was from this clue that The Shadow commenced a reasoning process that brought him to an amazing deduction. One point gained, he forged ahead until he discovered the weak spot in the code—a detail which the writer had never realized as an existing weakness.

The Shadow had begun by studying what he believed was a sample word. It read as follows, in the code:

At the left was a symbol with a lower tab to the left. At the right was a symbol with a lower tab to the right. There were seven characters in all. Did the lower tabs, alone, represent space indications, thus leaving a word of seven letters; or did the end

characters depend entirely upon their tabs, thus being total blanks with five letters between?

The Shadow sought the answer in the code itself. He found a combination that intrigued him. It read as follows:

Each of these four characters, according to The Shadow's belief, had a space indication. Therefore the entire symbols could not be spaces. Two spacers might come together; one at the end of a word; the next at the beginning of a word; but not four.

Therefore, The Shadow reasoned, each symbol must be a letter. The tabs alone were the pointers to spaces. In brief, the two central characters were the letters of a two-letter word.

It was then that The Shadow's hand poised above the paper. A full minute passed. From hidden lips came a soft, whispered laugh of understanding. The Shadow had struck upon a factor that another might have overlooked.

SUPPOSING that the two central symbols constituted the letters of a two-letter word, each with a space-pointing tab, what would the writer have done had he chosen to inscribe a word of only one letter? Where could it have gone? Only in one spot—between those central characters.

That, however, would force the existing characters into being nothing more than ordinary spaces—something which The Shadow had already reasoned they could not be. The Shadow's eyes burned toward the blank spot between the tantalizing symbols. The laugh that followed was the final answer.

The space itself bore the message! Such was The Shadow's verdict. Letters depended upon the relationship of one character to the next. These block—like figures were doubled symbols.

The Shadow's eyes gazed steadily upon the coded photostat while his hand inscribed the first four characters as they actually appeared.

Then The Shadow rewrote those same symbols in a new formation; he spread them apart to make their meaning plain.

The first character—a lone half at the left—was merely a blank indication. The second and third were each halves of the original blocks that had stood at one and two. They represented a letter.

The same with the next pair of symbols; and the next; until the isolated half character that stood alone, its bottom tab pointing to the right. It was a spacer.

The Shadow had discovered a three-letter word. He did not pause with it for the present. His keen, deductive brain was working upon a clue which he had gained at Professor Langwood Devine's—the name in the sailing list which The Shadow had so readily observed.

Running through the code with great rapidity, The Shadow found the symbols that he wanted. He did this, by looking for two words, each with nine letters that were side by side. He inscribed one above the other:

That done, The Shadow broke the symbols in his own fashion. He wrote them in revised form; in the spaces between each proper pair, he wrote the letters that he knew they must represent. His finished task appeared.

The game was won! The letter S, appearing twice in the upper word coincided with the final symbol of the lower S. The letter I in 'Steamship' was properly duplicated in 'Mauritius'. T and U proved themselves to be the correct letters. The letter A was right.

With this start on the alphabet, The Shadow had passed the final obstacle. His hands, moving with amazing swiftness, seized a fresh sheet of paper; the pencil inscribed the photostatic message in broken form.

WHEN he had completed this, The Shadow was prompt in his deciphering of the message. On a new piece of paper, his hand wrote out the final solution:

THE REPRESENTATIVE OF A BRITISH SYNDICATE IS RETURNING TO LONDON ON THE STEAMSHIP MAURITIUS WITH RARE PAINTINGS VALUED AT ONE MILLION DOLLARS I AM GOING BACK TO EUROPE BY THE SAME SHIP THE MAN WE SEEK WILL HAVE THE PAINTINGS IN HIS CABIN UNGUARDED INFORM ME HOW TO PASS HIS NAME TO THOSE WHO WILL BE READY

The Shadow laughed. He could see the workings of a hidden chain. This message had been sent to Professor Langwood Devine, who in turn had sent it along to some one else. The request must have reached some person who could aid. A reply would therefore have come back along the line.

Yet no coded letters had been delivered to Professor Devine's empty box at the Hotel Salamanca. The Shadow, in two nights that had followed his visit to Joe Cardona, had made cleverly faked long distance calls from Chicago, pretending to be Mynheer Hansel Vaart. Cardona, assured of the Hollander's sincere interest in solving the troublesome code, would certainly have mentioned it if new messages had been gained.

The Shadow realized that the chain of crimeworkers had closed. The gap made by Devine's death had been bridged. The Shadow also saw that crooks would not be intimidated because of Devine's elimination. The message had gone through. Cardona had suppressed the news regarding his finding of the codes.

Some hidden crook had make a fatal mistake by referring to himself as "I" in the message that he had forwarded through the band. That was not all. He had left a clue to his identity in this genuine message.

I am going back to Europe—

That signified that the crook had come from Europe. He had not come from England; for he referred to a potential victim who was returning to that land. The Shadow divined that the author of the plot to steal the valued paintings must be a foreigner; while the man whom he intended to point out would be an Englishman.

The Shadow's hand began a methodical inscription. It was tabulating the alphabet. Letters J, Q, X and Z were missing in the translated message; noting a formula, The Shadow promptly supplied the first three and added a possible Z; finally, the symbol that signified a space.

⌐A⌐	⌐F⌐	⌐K⌐	⌐P⌐	⌐U⌐	
⌐B⌐	⌐G⌐	⌐L⌐	⌐Q⌐	⌐V⌐	⌐Z⌐
⌐C⌐	⌐H⌐	⌐M⌐	⌐R⌐	⌐W⌐	⌐ ⌐
⌐D⌐	⌐I⌐	⌐N⌐	⌐S⌐	⌐X⌐	SPACE
⌐E⌐	⌐J⌐	⌐O⌐	⌐T⌐	⌐Y⌐	

A weird laugh broke through the sanctum as the bluish light went out. Paper rustled in the darkness. Strident echoes shivered back their response to The Shadow's burst of mirthful triumph.

The Shadow's task was ended. He had gained the cipher that he needed. He had solved one of the most unique methods of cryptic writing that had ever been devised.

Spaces, not the solid symbols between them, had told the final story. Through long hours of ceaseless activity, The Shadow had discovered the secret method of writing originally devised by Barton Talbor—the system which the crafty old crook believed to be invulnerable.

Stillness reigned in The Shadow's sanctum. Hollow, soundless blackness announced the departure of the master who inhabited this strange abode. The Shadow had departed to deal with crime. With him, ready for future use, he was carrying the deciphered code of Crime Incorporated!

Dusk lay over Manhattan, as a gliding figure of blackness moved westward along a narrow street. Evening was approaching, bringing a night that was to prove eventful. For at ten o'clock this evening, the Steamship *Mauritius* was scheduled to sail from its North River pier.

Criminals—potential murderers—would be aboard that liner. Their sole purpose would be to rob and kill a helpless victim. But crooks, alone, would not be on the scene.

The Shadow, master of vengeance would be aboard the Steamship *Mauritius*, ready to thwart the evil scheme of which he, too, had learned!

CHAPTER XVIII
OUTSIDE THE HARBOR

IT was nearing midnight. The Steamship *Mauritius* had passed the lower harbor, outward bound. The liner was ploughing at a slow but steady pace as it pushed through the calm sea near the seven-mile limit.

The *Mauritius* was an antiquated tub that had led the ways back in the late nineties. A fine ship in its day, the old boat had stood the test of time. Renovated and equipped with new motors, it still plied between New York and Liverpool.

Most of the passengers were men. The total list was less than two hundred. The low rates offered on this slow liner were attractive to persons who valued money more than time. The *Mauritius* was a one-class ship; the logical meeting place for its male passengers was the smoking salon.

A young man was seated in this remodeled section of the ship. He was one of a few dozen who had chosen not to remain on deck. As he read a book, this clean-cut chap occasionally surveyed the occupants of the salon, by directing well-gauged glances over the top of his book.

This passenger was Harry Vincent. An agent of The Shadow, Harry Vincent had received new instructions through Rutledge Mann. These had included ticket and stateroom reservation on the *Mauritius*.

Harry knew that The Shadow was also aboard. His chief was engaged in an important search. It was Harry's task to aid. Here, in the smoking room, the agent had opportunity for observing various passengers.

Mann had come to the boat to see Harry off. He had passed the agent an envelope which Mann had received at his club, shortly before sailing time. This had given Harry new information. He was to watch all foreigners other than Englishmen.

This was not a difficult task. Harry had already noted that the majority of the passengers in the smoking salon were either English or American. He saw two men whom he took for Swedes or Norwegians; he observed another who might be a Frenchman.

The latter had caught Harry's final attention. The man was puffing at a cigarette; it was the third that he had lighted in ten minutes. He had paid one visit to the bar; at present, he was seated at a card table in the corner, playing solitaire.

AS Harry continued his intermittent vigil, he saw the Frenchman pack the cards in their case. Thrusting the case into a space between the table and the wall of the salon, the man walked over and introduced himself to three Americans who were looking for a fourth player in a game of bridge.

Harry heard the man introduce himself as Raoul Darchonne. The Americans clapped him on the back and congratulated him upon his remarkable moniker. They called him "*Monsieur*" and the Frenchman smiled beneath his pointed mustache. Harry observed at once that the man spoke perfect English and understood the American conception of a joke.

The bridge game began. Harry watched it occasionally, but he also kept looking toward the door of the smoking salon. He saw an American enter. The man was a heavy, bluff-faced fellow who had the build of a football coach. This man looked about the salon in a casual way. He finally strolled over to the table where the Frenchman had been playing solitaire.

There, he picked up the pack that he found between table and wall. He deliberately opened the case and started to deal cards one by one. A dozen cards fell face up, in rotation; with a shrug of his shoulders, the big fellow gathered up the pack, replaced it in its case and tossed the whole on the table. He arose and strolled from the smoking salon.

Harry Vincent pondered. He had been instructed to watch for contact between strangers, particularly any such action that seemed unusual. To Harry, the episode of the card case appeared more important than the Frenchman's act of joining the bridge game.

The card players had finished a hand. One of the Americans was calling for drinks. No steward was close by; the American arose and waved the others along with him to the bar. Raoul Darchonne followed.

This was Harry's opportunity. Dropping his book, The Shadow's agent arose and moved toward the table where the card case lay in view. He picked up the desired object; then turned and went out on the deck.

Reaching a companionway, Harry descended. He arrived at his own stateroom. He entered, drew a fountain pen from his pocket and inscribed a brief note that he put in an envelope. He left this with the card case on the writing table. When Harry left the stateroom to go up to the smoking cabin, he did not lock the door.

This would be a signal to The Shadow. That door, unlocked, was the word that Harry had left a message. This was in accordance with the final instructions that Harry had received from Mann.

FIVE scant minutes passed after Harry had left his cabin. A figure appeared in the passage. It was The Shadow, garbed as an ordinary passenger. The Shadow opened the door and entered Harry's room.

A single light was burning on the table where the card case lay. The Shadow seemed a vague shape as he approached. His white hands showed beneath the light; the gem on his left third finger gleamed with sparkling flashes.

The Shadow opened Harry's note. He read a terse, coded message that explained what had happened in the smoking salon. The writing faded; The Shadow let the blank paper slide into a wastebasket. His fingers opened the card case.

Harry had described the exact actions of the heavy-built American. The Shadow knew that the cards had been gathered as they had been dealt, one by one. The Shadow let the pasteboards fall faces up upon the table.

Ten of diamonds; five of spades; six of hearts; queen of clubs; five of clubs; queen of diamonds—

The Shadow stopped, holding the next card face up. It was a black card; the duplicate of one that he

MYNHEER HANSEL VAART, code expert and friend of one of the principals in the story, whose help is obtained in solving cypher messages.

had already dealt. In his hand, The Shadow was clutching a second five of spades!

The thrumming pound of the liner's engines was the dull sound that formed an interlude while The Shadow's hands remained motionless. Then came a soft, whispered laugh as The Shadow dropped the duplicate card upon the table.

While his left hand held the pack, The Shadow's right produced a pen and wrote on paper with a bluish ink. The Shadow had discerned the reason for this extra card in the pack.

One agent of crime had arranged to pass word to the other. That message could be but one thing— the name of the man aboard this ship whose cabin held its million dollars worth of paintings.

Each suit in the pack of cards consisted of thirteen values. Inasmuch as there were twenty-six letters in the alphabet, it was plain to The Shadow that one color—say blacks—would give letters from A to M inclusive; while the other color would tell letters from N to Z.

Taking the blacks as the first thirteen, the reds as the last, The Shadow transcribed the letters as he read them. Ten of diamonds, W; five of spades, E; six of hearts, S; queen of clubs, L; five of clubs, E; queen of diamonds, Y.

The cards spelled the name Wesley. The duplicate five of spades was an E, starting the second name. The Shadow continued the deal; after the five of clubs came the queen of spades, the jack of spades, the nine of clubs, the ace of hearts.

The last name was Elkin. The Shadow knew the identity of the man whose life was at stake. Skulking crooks were laying low; The Shadow had not encountered them in his extended journey through the ship. They would soon be on the move; for they knew their quarry. The Frenchman, Raoul Darchonne, was the man who had sent the message along the chain. The husky American was another man of crime; the one who had agreed to follow Darchonne's tip.

The Shadow moved from the stateroom. He ascended a flight of deserted stairs and stopped outside the closed window of the purser's office. The passenger list had been posted. The Shadow saw it behind a glass frame. He spied the name of Wesley Elkin. The stateroom number was 128.

The Shadow descended the steps and arrived at Harry's cabin. From beneath a berth, he drew out a flat black bag. He opened it; the folds of the black cloak came into view. Then the slouch hat; donning the garments, The Shadow plucked a brace of automatics from the bag.

UP in the smoking salon, Harry Vincent had picked up his book. He read the volume a while; then laid it down and strolled toward the deck.

Raoul Darchonne followed him with a steady gaze. The Frenchman had suddenly lost interest in the game of bridge.

Prepared to establish an alibi, while others did their work, this crook had found a task for himself. Coming back from the bar, he had noted the absence of the card case. He had seen Harry Vincent return to the chair where the book was lying.

Harry Vincent was on his way to his cabin, to find if his message had been delivered. Raoul Darchonne, excusing himself from the game, arose and started on Harry's trail. A conflict between them was impending.

For The Shadow, at that moment, was gliding from the door of Harry's stateroom. Armed for combat, the black-garbed master was starting toward the spot where danger lurked. His goal lay on the opposite side of the ship.

Aft—the walls of the engine room, one deck below on the starboard side of the liner—such was the location of stateroom 128. Past the stairway, then to a bulkhead beyond; there The Shadow would reach the companion way that led to the lower deck.

Like a living phantom, The Shadow reached the bulkhead. He stopped as he neared a darkened spot. Enshrouded in gloom, The Shadow turned to peer back along the path that he had followed.

A figure appeared beyond the stairway. It was Harry Vincent, returning to his cabin. The Shadow watched, guided by some keen intuition. A crouching man came into view, following Harry Vincent's path.

One glimpse of the sallow, mustached face told The Shadow that this must be the Frenchman whom Harry had named as Raoul Darchonne. The crafty crook was on the trail of The Shadow's agent.

A shape emerged from the blackness by the bulkhead. Though time pressed, though crime was in the making, The Shadow was returning toward Harry's stateroom. The life of his agent was at stake. The menace of Raoul Darchonne must be eliminated before The Shadow could proceed to stateroom 128.

CHAPTER XIX
SHOTS ON BOARD

GRIM complications were combining aboard the Steamship *Mauritius*. While the broad-beamed liner was pounding steadily seaward, passengers aboard it were setting the stage for startling events.

The Shadow, planning a lone battle against crime, had gauged the situation. He knew that Wesley Elkin, traveling as an ordinary passenger on this slow ship, was probably secure in the belief that no one suspected the value of the secret cargo in his stateroom.

During his tour of inspection through many passages, accomplished prior to Harry Vincent's discovery of Raoul Darchonne, The Shadow had noted various persons and their actions. Among those whom he observed leaving staterooms was the man who occupied 128.

The way was clear for crime; and The Shadow knew that it would be carried through by stealth. A search of Elkin's stateroom; the removal of the valuable paintings—these deeds would require time. Such action might already be under way; yet a delay in arrival would not defeat The Shadow's cause. There was time to take care of the predicament which Harry Vincent faced.

PROOF of The Shadow's accurate calculation lay in stateroom 128. The door of that cabin was ajar. Within the lighted room, three men were at work. Elkin's cabin was a spacious one. It contained three wardrobe trunks. These had been opened by the trio. Upon the floor lay long metal tubes, each the container of a valuable portrait.

From behind the drawers of the wardrobe trunks, the riflers had brought framed canvases. The trunk had been specially prepared to hold the paintings. The spoils of crime—nine framed paintings and a dozen more in tubes—were being gathered for removal.

At the door, keeping the barrier almost closed, stood the husky American whom Harry Vincent had seen in the smoking salon. He was the leader of the trio. His hard eyes watched the workers. Then came a change upon his countenance. He raised a warning hand and hissed an order.

The riflers moved to the wall of the stateroom. Carefully, their leader peered through the crack of the door; then closed the barrier. He looked about and saw that his men had ducked from sight. He stepped forward and crouched beyond the central wardrobe trunk.

He was just in time. The door of stateroom 128 was opening. A moment later, a heavy, bluff-faced Englishman stepped into the room. Consternation showed upon his middle-aged visage. Wesley Elkin had returned unexpectedly to his stateroom, to find the door unlocked. Entering, he stood in amazement as he saw the wide open trunks and his treasures, stacked upon the floor.

Elkin backed toward the door. His thought was to sound an alarm. He did not gain the opportunity. A man's head and shoulders bobbed above the central trunk. A harsh voice commanded Elkin to halt. A revolver glistened in the hand that showed atop the trunk.

"Close the door," ordered the leader of the crooks.

Mechanically, Elkin obeyed. Unarmed, relying solely upon the belief that no one knew of his art treasures, Elkin was helpless. He faced the muzzle of the revolver.

"Don't make any trouble," growled the chief crook. "It will be too bad for you if you do."

"Who—who are you?" stammered Elkin.

"Let me introduce myself," scoffed the man with the gun, as he stepped from behind the trunk. "They call me Richard Glade. That is the name which I employ when I resort to crime. These gentlemen"—he waved his free hand toward the side of the cabin—"are my gang."

Glade's two cronies stepped into view. Each man held a revolver. Glade pocketed his own weapon while his minions covered Elkin.

"Passengers aboard the *Mauritius*," scoffed Glade, again indicating his men. "All except myself. I merely came aboard to superintend their work. Our purpose, as you see, is to remove the paintings that you are taking to England.

"Your plan was rather clever, Elkin. Traveling as the obscure representative of a large British syndicate, you thought it best to bring back these art treasures in a very inconspicuous fashion. Your plan, however, has failed. You cannot save your valuables; but you still have the opportunity to keep your life. I advise you to do nothing foolish."

Glade motioned the Englishman toward the inner end of the stateroom. Weakly, Elkin backed against a porthole and stood with arms upraised. Glade spoke to his men.

"You keep him covered, Hank," ordered the crook. "Come on, Terry, we'll move the swag. The boys are waiting."

Opening the door of the stateroom, Glade gave a low hiss. Two men appeared promptly from a passage just beyond the stateroom. It was an opening that led directly to the lower deck—the most deserted spot aboard the ship.

AT the same time, a door opened in a stateroom across the passage. Another pair of huskies stepped into view. As Glade and Terry bundled up a load of paintings and left the doorway marked 128, a second pair of men came in to gain a similar burden.

Glade and Terry reached the deck. Four boxlike trunks were set there, forming a huge cube. These burdens had been brought from cabins. Loaded on as ordinary luggage, emptied of their original contents, the four containers made a massive block.

While Glade and his companions were loading their stolen goods into one of the trunks, the next pair of men arrived with their burden. Glade yanked open the tight-fitting front of a second trunk, to admit the next supply of paintings. He then turned to a small box that lay on the deck. He uncoiled a length of wire, one end of which was fastened to the little box. He fixed the free end to the handle of a trunk.

Within his stateroom, Wesley Elkin was standing backed against the port hole. Hands still upward, the Englishman was watching the third pair of crooks as they gathered up the final spoils. Hank still held his quarry helpless. Elkin could not move while the revolver muzzle covered him. Yet a look of determination was creeping over the Englishman's face.

SIMILARLY, in a cabin one deck above, a man was standing covered by a gun. Harry Vincent, trapped in his stateroom, was staring into a shining barrel held by Raoul Darchonne. Harry had left the door of his stateroom unlocked. The Frenchman had stealthily followed his into the cabin.

In a low, snarling voice, Darchonne was baiting the man whom he had surprised. Darchonne was demanding information. He wanted to know what Harry Vincent had learned regarding crime aboard ship.

Tensely, Harry was facing his captor. Harry knew that Darchonne would not risk a shot while plans were still in the making, unless Harry, himself, committed the folly of an attack.

Silent, The Shadow's agent refused to reply to Darchonne's questions. Staring straight toward the snarling Frenchman, Harry maintained an expressionless gaze as he saw the door of the stateroom opening.

The Shadow!

Harry knew that his chief had returned. Darchonne's form obscured the center of the door. The only manifestations of The Shadow's arrival were the motion of the door and the blackness that seemed to creep forward as the barrier closed.

"Come on!" Darchonne's tone showed suppressed fury. "Speak! I'll give you five seconds longer!"

Darchonne was half crouched. His left fist was clenched in front of him. His right held the gun close to his body. A mass of shrouding blackness loomed behind the Frenchman. Burning eyes showed above Darchonne's head. Then, like living tentacles of darkness, a pair of arms came winging in from either side. A grip, as firm as it was swift, caught Darchonne's form and pinioned the Frenchman's arms.

The Shadow had stooped speedily. His obscured form shot backward with a powerful snap. To Harry's staring eyes, Darchonne's body seemed to act of its own accord. The Frenchman's feet shot upward. His body flew to a horizontal position in midair. Then, as The Shadow released a downward swing, Darchonne came smashing flat upon the floor.

The Frenchman lay stunned before Harry's eyes.

His arms spread. His revolver went bounding sidewise across the floor. Looking up to the spot where Darchonne had stood, Harry saw the swishing folds of The Shadow's cloak, as its wearer whirled toward the stateroom door. A whispered laugh was The Shadow's token. It came as the master fighter opened the door. Then Harry's rescuer reached the passage. The door closed, leaving Harry safe and Raoul Darchonne helpless.

MEANWHILE, the last pair of burden carriers had left stateroom 128. Facing Hank, Wesley Elkin stood with twitching hands. The Englishman was desperate. He was barely managing to restrain himself, despite the threat of the looming revolver.

The door opened. It was Richard Glade. The chief crook did not enter. He gave a hiss toward Hank; the minion shot a glance toward the door. He nodded as he heard Glade's whisper. The door closed. Hank approached closer to Wesley Elkin.

The Englishman sensed the verdict. Though he had not heard Glade's whisper, he had caught the involuntary gesture of a downward pointed thumb. Glade had ordered Hank to hold his prisoner a few minutes longer—then to kill.

Hank was but a few feet away; Elkin knew why. When ready for the shot, the rogue would jam the gun forward, to muffle the shot against his victim's body. Elkin shifted as though his arms were weary; then, with a sudden spring, he launched himself upon his captor.

The act caught Hank off guard. With a sweeping clutch, Elkin caught the fellow's wrist. As he grappled with his captor, Elkin twisted. The revolver clattered to the floor. Hank, writhing in pain, wrenched himself free. Then, as Elkin pounced upon him, Hank met the attack with powerful force, he flung Elkin toward a wardrobe trunk.

The Englishman slipped. His head struck the edge of the trunk. His slumping body yielded. Wesley Elkin rolled unconscious to the floor. Luck had come to Hank. The villain pounced to the floor and grabbed his gun.

Elkin had received a heavy blow. The man was out; it was plain that he would not recover consciousness for some time to come. Holding his revolver, Hank grinned as he leaned toward the slumped form and shoved the gun muzzle directly above Elkin's heart. His finger was on the trigger, it was a sound from the door that prevented Hank from firing the fatal shot.

Thinking that Richard Glade had returned, Hank turned. The door was open. There, framed in the gloom of the corridor was a black-cloaked figure. Hank, a product of New York's gangland, recognized the awe-inspiring shape.

"The Shadow!"

Hank gasped the name as he swung in desperation. He aimed his revolver squarely toward the door. Before Hank could press the trigger of the gun, a burst of flame came from an automatic wielded by a black-gloved fist. Hank sprawled upon the stateroom floor.

OUT on deck, Richard Glade heard the report. An oath came from the chief crook's lips as he stepped back from the trunk in which he had stowed the final paintings. Glade turned to two of his men.

"Back in there!" he snarled. "See what that boob Hank has done! I told him to hold that shot!"

Two ruffians dashed into the ship. They reached the end of the passage outside of 128. The Shadow, just within the stateroom door, heard their footsteps. With a backward swing, the black-garbed warrior swerved into the passage.

Glade's henchmen were holding drawn guns. They stopped short as they saw the blackened shape which confronted them. The burning eyes of The Shadow were orbs of fearful vengeance. As one man scrambled wildly back toward the opening to the dock, his companion fired at The Shadow.

The man's shot, delivered from a rising gun, was wild. The rogue never gained a chance to deliver a second bullet. The Shadow's response halted the ruffian's rising aim. Tongued flame came from a mighty automatic.

The crook crumpled. The second of Glade's henchmen had failed. His body, like Hank's, lay motionless upon the floor. The Shadow was moving swiftly forward, past the man whom he had downed.

For The Shadow knew the route that crooks had taken. He had seen the chaos in Elkin's rifled cabin. He knew that the paintings had been carried from 128. His opportunity still existed.

Alone, The Shadow was after desperate men. Warned by the crook who had fled back to the deck, they would be prepared for battle. A chilling laugh came echoing from The Shadow's lips. One against five, The Shadow was ready for the fray!

CHAPTER XX
SPOILS OF BATTLE

THE SHADOW'S first shot had alarmed Richard Glade, the white-shirted leader of a mobster crew. The Shadow's second burst, coupled with the report from the revolver of his victim, had roused the ship.

Echoing through the long passage, the shots had carried with surprising loudness. Above the throbbing of the liner's pounding engines came shouts raised by those who had heard the gunfire.

Harry Vincent was listening at the door of his stateroom. In his right hand, Harry was holding Raoul Darchonne's gun. The Frenchman still lay senseless on the floor. As he harkened, Harry could hear the aftermath of The Shadow's first skirmish. Scurrying footsteps sounded past the stairway.

Another man was listening to the noises that came through the stateroom door. Raoul Darchonne, suddenly reviving, had risen to hands and knees. Blinking, the Frenchman saw Harry Vincent staring out into the passage.

With surprising recovery, Darchonne arose and crept forward. Then, with a sudden leap, he precipitated himself toward the man at the door. Harry Vincent swung just in time to meet him. Turning at the sound of Darchonne's approach, The Shadow's agent met the Frenchman just within the door.

Before Harry had a chance to fire, Darchonne delivered a clip to his chin. Harry staggered across the stateroom. He caught himself against the writing table. Darchonne's intended knockout had failed. The Frenchman, however, had gained a break. Before Harry could cover him with the revolver, Darchonne yanked open the door and reached the passage.

As Darchonne rounded the corner to the stairs, he ran squarely into a steward who had come from above. The man was holding a revolver. Darchonne pounced forward and swung a heavy fist. The steward crumpled. Darchonne seized the gun that fell from his hand.

Continuing onward, the Frenchman sped toward the companion way that would take him to 128. Knowing that his part in crime had been discovered, Darchonne sought to join the other rogues aboard the steamship.

Meanwhile, events were happening below. Glade and his men had gained their warning from the crook who had fled to the deck. Glade had ordered two of his men to guard the side passage. With Terry and another, the chief crook was hoisting the four-blocked trunks to the rail.

Shouts continued. People aboard had not located the source of the trouble; yet Glade knew that time was short. Bracing the trunks against a post that extended above the rail, Glade snarled an order to his men.

"Get him!" Glade's words were ferocious. "There's four of you! Get him! It's your only out!"

The crooks understood. The ship was in a furor. They were in for desperate trouble, even without The Shadow. His presence made their plight hopeless. As Glade poised the large, but light trunks, the two men who stood beside him leaped to join the pair at the passage.

THE SHADOW had been waiting. He had known that an attack must come. He was in the passage by Elkin's stateroom. Already, he could hear shouts at the further turn. He had deliberately waited, in order to bait Glade's men to an attack. He could linger no longer.

Brandishing an automatic in each hand, The Shadow sprang to the passage that led on deck. He arrived there, just as the first pair of crooks were lunging inward. Flashing revolvers were in readiness. Fingers were pressing triggers.

It was a matter of split seconds. These minions of crime were prepared for The Shadow's thrust; the master fighter, in turn, was ready for them. Thin-gloved forefingers were on the triggers of the automatics.

Three shots crashed within the little passage. Two came from The Shadow's guns. The third, an instant later, was from a crook's revolver. The second of Glade's henchmen never fired.

Fired at five-foot range, The Shadow's bullets had found their mark. Crouching as he loosed the bullets, The Shadow had burnt a leaden slug into each lunging form before him.

One crook had fired also, almost at the moment when he staggered. His bullet, sped toward a dropping shape, whistled through the upturned collar of The Shadow's cloak, barely singeing the hidden face within.

The Shadow's form came up as gunmen's bodies slumped. A terrifying laugh burst from The Shadow's lips. Springing forward, this fierce fighter was on his way to deal with men outside. At the door to the deck, The Shadow encountered the second pair of henchmen.

One automatic jammed against a gangster's jaw. The second gun came clashing down upon the other fellow's wrist. As the first mobster sprawled, The Shadow seized the second to drag him back into the passage. This man was Terry.

There was strategy in The Shadow's odd attack. He did not know the numbers of his foemen. Disposing of one, he had grabbed the other's body as a shield. The move was wise.

Standing against the braced trunks, Richard Glade was holding a revolver. He was ready to down The Shadow if his minions failed. While The Shadow grappled with Terry, Glade could find no mark at which to aim.

All that Glade could see was a lunging form—Terry's—as it swayed like a dummy figure in The Shadow's clutch. Then, from beneath Terry's arm, came the flame of an automatic. The shot was loosed toward Glade; only a slump of Terry's body spoiled its direction. The Shadow's bullet clipped a corner of a trunk beside Glade's ear.

Wild shouts from within the ship. Glade hesitated no longer. Turning, the chief crook lunged upward against the trunks. The blocked boxes toppled outward into the ocean. Gripping the pillar, Glade launched himself forward into the water below.

His leap was just in time. The Shadow had hurled Terry helpless across the deck. With one fierce spring, he too reached the rail. He turned as he gripped the pillar. His black form, outlined against clouded moonlight, formed a spectral target for a man who was leaping out from the passage.

IT was Raoul Darchonne. Wielding the steward's revolver, the Frenchman aimed for the figure that he saw upon the rail. As Darchonne fired, an answering blast came from the blackened shape. It was the final shot from The Shadow's left hand automatic.

Then came the amazing climax. As Darchonne clumped heavily to the deck, a venomous groan came from his lips. His eyes, bulging downward, did not see what happened to The Shadow, although his ears heard a strange, outlandish sound.

With Darchonne's shot, The Shadow's figure hovered outward. As though timed to the slight swell of the sea below, the black-garbed figure lost its hold upon the post beside the rail. Outward, in a weird, spreading dive, The Shadow curved head foremost into the deep.

A trailing laugh, fading like a weird reminder of his prowess, was the sound that marked The Shadow's departure overboard. The throb of the ship, the shouts of arriving men—these drowned any sound of the splash that must have followed.

With dying eyes, Raoul Darchonne looked upward. Flat upon the deck, the insidious Frenchman glimpsed the post where The Shadow had been. He recalled the black-garbed shape at which he had fired. He remembered that it had loomed, tall and bulky, upon the rail. That shape was gone.

Men were raising Darchonne's body. Their excited voices were loud upon the deck. But Raoul Darchonne did not hear them. The triumphant grin that had formed upon his evil lips was an expression fixed by death.

Raoul Darchonne had died without a murmur. His passing thought had been a flash of evil victory; the realization that he had gained a chance to deliver death to the enemy whose bullet had spelled curtains for himself.

Passengers and members of the crew had arrived upon the deck. Terry and his gangster pal were overpowered before they could put up a groggy fight. Darchonne's body was carried into the ship, along with those of the two gangsters in the passage.

A cry marked the discovery of chaos in 128. Hank's body was found dead upon the floor.

Wesley Elkin, still unconscious from the gash aside his head, was carried to the ship's hospital.

THE *Mauritius* was plodding onward at a twelve knot speed through the easy, rising swell. Certain of the passengers managed to remain upon the deck where strife had been rampant. Among them was Harry Vincent. The Shadow's agent wore a face that was glum and solemn.

There had been no cry of man overboard. Yet Richard Glade—whom Harry knew only as the leader of the crooks—was missing. Moreover— and this was the factor that left Harry morose— there was no sign of The Shadow.

People had arrived from all directions, less than a half minute after the final shots. Harry had been among the first. He was sure that he, at least, would have spied The Shadow.

Harry felt helpless aboard this moving boat. He could not order the stopping of the ship. That might prove the worst step possible, for it would connect Harry—agent of The Shadow—with the ended battle. Harry could only hope that The Shadow was still on board. Yet Harry was gripped by a terrible belief that The Shadow had gone over the vessel's side.

Moving toward the rail, Harry noted scarred marks along the top. The same indications showed upon the post. These were the marks made by the blocked trunks that Richard Glade had followed overboard.

Higher, Harry found another mark that made his face turn grim. It was the long nick of a bullet that had skimmed the edge of the supporting post. Instinctively, Harry knew that The Shadow had been the target for that shot.

Sadly, The Shadow's agent went inboard. He appeared later, upon a high rear deck. Looking backward, Harry viewed the swelling ocean, streaked with shadowy blackness from the clouds that dimmed the struggling moon.

No speck was visible upon the surface. The ship had traveled several miles since the conflict had ended on the lower deck. Again, Harry sought surcease of melancholy in the hope that The Shadow had miraculously gained some hidden spot within the boat.

FAR back on the horizon which Harry Vincent had viewed, a cubical float was bobbing in the easy swell. Glade's four trunks, watertight with their precious spoils inside, were no longer within sight of the *Mauritius*.

Clinging to one side of his well-formed buoy, Glade was drawing up the little box that bobbed at the end of the connecting wire. The moonlight showed a pleased grin on the crook's dripping face.

Peering outward from a rising swell, Glade could no longer see the distant lights of the Steamship *Mauritius*.

The man's gaze turned first to one side, then to the other, timed by the periods when the floating trunks were raised by the sea's motion. Off to the right, almost parallel with his position, he spied the object of his search. It was the low, flat hulk of a moving boat.

Glade wrenched at the covers of the little box. The watertight lid came off; the box rested on top of the trunks. Glade drew forth a tapered object. A click sounded from his hand. With the hiss of a Roman candle, a flare splashed a deluge of crimson flame from the crook's hand.

Almost immediately, sparkles glimmered from the moving boat. The beam of a searchlight came now, across the water. As the buoy neared the high point of another swell, Glade set off a second flare. This time, the searchlight's rays picked up the floating trunks.

Lights formed a moving circle on the water as the purr of a motor sounded across the space between the boat and Glade's improvised buoy. The eye of the searchlight wavered, but again picked its mark. Glade was on the near side of the trunks, waving one arm as a signal.

The boat slowed as it came alongside the trunks. It was a trim motor launch; lights aboard showed three men leaning over the side. A line splashed in the water. Glade seized it; willing arms drew the boxes to the side of the thirty-five-foot craft.

Glade grabbed the side. He was hoisted aboard. Two men caught the ropes that bound the trunks. The burden came up easily until it was halfway out of the water; then the men levered it on the motorboat's side. Glade and the other man joined it. With a yank, they tumbled the resisting burden down into the cockpit.

"Head for port," puffed Glade. "There's no more to do—"

A sudden sound froze the words on the crook's lips. A weird echo had broken at the side of the boat; from the very spot where the trunks had stopped on their way aboard. Glade leaped up as the sound broke into the tones of a chilling laugh.

Revealed by the glimmering lights aboard the launch was a looming figure in black, poised upon the side. Like a spirit of vengeance from the deep, The Shadow had come to settle scores with Richard Glade!

CHAPTER XXI
THE SUMMONS

TO the three men who manned the boat that had rescued Richard Glade, the appearance of The

Shadow was unexplainable. To Glade, himself, the answer to the riddle came with drumming realism.

Glade knew that this amazing enemy must have followed him overboard; that The Shadow had easily spied the bobbing trunks and had clung to the side of the buoy opposite Glade himself.

Glade had been on the near side of the trunks when the searchlight had played upon them. When the trunks were hauled aboard the launch, The Shadow had dived under them. The resistance of the trunks, when they balanced on the side of the boat, had been due, in part, to The Shadow's added weight.

Glade had no weapons. He had dropped his revolver when he had plunged from the *Mauritius*. He did not realize that The Shadow, too, was weaponless. Plunging to safety when Raoul Darchonne's shot nicked the pillar beside him, The Shadow had let his automatics go.

His weird, vengeful laugh, delivered toward Glade and the crew of the launch, was an act of important purpose. Glade's three companions were rooted as they viewed this brine-dripped shape half crouched upon the side. Against the dullish sky, The Shadow's cloaked shape seemed bulky and formidable as it rose upward with long, spreading arms.

One man acted. That was exactly what The Shadow wanted. Hand to pocket, the startled member of the crew began to yank a gun. The deed marked him as The Shadow's first antagonist. The black form plunged forward into the cockpit, landing squarely upon the hapless victim.

As the fellow dropped, another man fumbled for a gun while the third dived into a low cabin at the front of the cockpit. The Shadow, swinging up from his first victim, delivered a sweeping blow that sent the second man sprawling against the side. A gun clattered from the fellow's hand. It landed at the feet of Richard Glade.

Desperately, the crook pounced to clutch the weapon. He would never have reached it had it not been for the unexpected intervention of the third member of the crew. As The Shadow swung toward Glade, the man who had dived for safety came lurching from the cabin, swinging the huge crank handle of the motor.

BEFORE The Shadow could stay the stroke, the husky man brought the metal bar forward with a mighty swing. It passed beneath The Shadow's rising arm. With a crackling thud of rib-breaking force, the handle smashed against The Shadow's side and sent his tall form sprawling toward the stern.

Glade had gained the gun. He fired late at the falling form in black. Once—twice—his hand paused for a certain aim as The Shadow's body slumped in the rear of the cockpit! As Glade's gloating lips oathed their triumph, as his finger rested on the trigger of his gun, The Shadow's hand swung upward.

A twist of the wrist; the glitter of the revolver which The Shadow still clutched safely—these came almost simultaneously with a rapid shot. Aiming fast while Glade steadied, the black-garbed fighter beat the snarling crook to the all-important shot.

Glade never pressed a trigger again. His form crumpled. The revolver left his hand. He had thought The Shadow incapable of meeting his attack. Yet The Shadow, despite the terrific impact of the flying crank handle, had delivered the needed stroke.

Two men were lying half-unconscious in the cockpit. The third, the big fellow with the crank handle, was staring into the muzzle of The Shadow's revolver. Before him lay the huddled form of Richard Glade. The crook had received The Shadow's bullet through the heart.

The Shadow arose. His triumphant laugh broke weirdly above the swell. The man who had struck him down stood helpless before the pointed gun, wondering how any living being could have withstood that mighty blow.

"Start the motor."

The hissed command came from The Shadow's lips. Backing from the tall, bulky warrior in black, the man inserted the crank handle and obeyed The Shadow's order. Stooped above the motor, he did not see The Shadow's next maneuver.

Spreading his dripping cloak, The Shadow released straps that hung across his shoulders. The reason for his bulkiness was explained as a thick, sturdy life belt plopped down in the cockpit.

The Shadow had anticipated a trip overboard. He had girdled himself with the belt when he had donned his black attire in Harry Vincent's stateroom. The Shadow had not needed the lifebelt in the water, for his silent swim to the floating trunks had been a short one; but it had served him in good stead later on.

Those thick, pleated sections of compact cork had been as effective as armor against the hard swing of the crank handle. The blow had sent The Shadow sprawling. It had not crippled him.

The man at the motor had given up all thought of resistance. He had drawn the crank handle from its shaft. Submissively, he tossed his erstwhile weapon back into the cabin. The Shadow, looming high in the rear of the cockpit, was at the tiller.

The other men were coming to their senses. Like their fellow, they decided to offer no attack. The Shadow's right hand kept the revolver in readiness. His hissed tones warned them to stay where they were.

THE SHADOW had guessed the mettle of these men. They were not gangsters; they were of less dangerous ilk. The launch was an ex-rumrunner; its crew, furtive men who had eked out a living by meeting ships outside the twelve-mile limit, to bring contraband cargo ashore.

Richard Glade had evidently hired them to trail the slow-moving Steamship *Mauritius* as soon as it had left the harbor. They had been paid their price. They did not even know the contents of the trunks that Glade had brought aboard. They were counting, perhaps, upon a further payment when they landed. That was all.

Cowed by their fear of the strange being who had followed Glade aboard, the three men awaited further orders as The Shadow turned the boat toward the Long Island shore. They did not know their destination; they could see, however, that the new pilot was steering for some defined objective.

From each rising swell, The Shadow was guiding by a distant headland that showed black beneath the moonlight. The launch, well-motored, purred rhythmically onward. It neared the shore.

A hissed order. One of the men slowed the motor. The Shadow piloted the launch between two points of land. The lights were out by his order; the moon provided sufficient illumination for The Shadow to watch his prisoners and to guide the craft as well.

The launch had entered a small cove. The motor was stopped at The Shadow's bidding. The boat grounded on a level, sandy beach. It swung sidewise, due to a final twist of the tiller. Three men arose as The Shadow hissed an order. They pitched the trunks over the side with the willingness of seamen ridding themselves of a Jonah.

"A flashlight," hissed The Shadow.

One man produced the required object. He gingerly extended it toward the being at the tiller. The Shadow clicked the switch. He blinked a signal beam toward the shore. Thudding footsteps sounded on the sand.

Two men arrived. They were Clyde Burke and Cliff Marsland, agents of The Shadow, who had been stationed here through final instructions from Burbank. They hauled the trunks ashore. At sight of two new enemies beneath the moonlight, the crew of the launch remained motionless, even though The Shadow no longer held his gun.

The Shadow was leaning over the dead form of Richard Glade. He was drawing water-soaked papers from the crook's pockets. He found a wallet among these effects. The rays of the flashlight were focused steadily upon Glade's dead face.

A soft laugh rippled from The Shadow's lips as keen eyes took in every feature of the dead man's countenance. The members of the crew shuddered at the sound. The Shadow picked up the gun that lay beneath Glade's body. Leaving the crew

weaponless, he stepped forward; three men shuffled aside as he advanced.

The Shadow reached the cabin. He stepped upon its roof. With a single leap, he gained the shore, where Clyde and Cliff were standing by the lashed trunks. The men on the boat, realizing that they were free, hurriedly started the motor. The former rum runner chugged in reverse. Its occupants were wild in their effort to get away from that spectral shape which stood upon the shore.

Cliff and Clyde nodded as they heard The Shadow's whispered command. They unlashed the trunks while The Shadow's figure faded in the darkness. When the agent brought the first trunk toward a spot where each had left a car, they heard one motor leaving. The Shadow had taken a coupé brought by Cliff. He had left Clyde's sedan.

The trunks were too large for the sedan. The Shadow's agents opened them and removed the contents. They loaded the car and consigned the trunks to the bushes. Clyde took the wheel and headed in the direction which The Shadow had taken toward Manhattan.

Two hours later, a spectral figure entered an apartment in the nineties. The Shadow had arrived at the residence of Richard Glade. He had learned the address from the dead crook's papers. Methodically, the investigator began a search of the place.

An electric heater, designed in imitation of a coal-grate, was standing in a fire place. Its upper section was filled with chunks of darkened glass that looked like lumps of coal. With a soft laugh, The Shadow stooped and tipped the heater forward. The false coal came clattering to the hearth.

Lying on the wire screen above the unused heater was a large envelope. The Shadow ripped it open. He found a stock certificate labeled Aztec Mines. He found a document inscribed in the blocked code which he had deciphered. He found two smaller envelopes which he opened.

The Shadow's laugh reechoed softly through the room. At intervals, the reverberation was repeated, while The Shadow studied the coded bylaws that he had uncovered. At last, the hands of The Shadow appeared, ungloved, beneath a desk lamp in the corner of the room.

In Glade's documents, The Shadow had learned the names of the dead crook's contacts. He had also discovered the names of two men beyond, through the inner envelopes with their coded messages. He had also discovered points of interest regarding the working of the chain to which Glade had belonged.

The Shadow inscribed a message in the blocked code. He added another—a trivial cryptogram with the circled code—to serve as the blind that went with all messages sent through the chain. He folded these sheets and inserted them in a plain envelope that he found in a desk drawer.

The Shadow duplicated the messages and sealed them in a second envelope. He addressed each letter separately. Gathering envelopes along with documents, he pressed out the light.

Faint light of dawn showed through the window when The Shadow raised the shade. The tinged rays revealed a vague form of black, making its departure. The laugh of The Shadow whispered its forbidding chill.

The Shadow's mirth was again an omen. It was inspired by the letters which this master sleuth had prepared. Those coded messages were to carry news along the chain of evil workers.

There was good cause for The Shadow's laugh. The master fighter had profited through the death of Richard Glade. With craft and with certainty, The Shadow had issued a summons that Crime Incorporated would obey!

CHAPTER XXII
THE DIVIDEND

EIGHT days had passed. Another night had come to Manhattan. The lobby of the Hotel Grammont was ablaze with light. This hostelry, for years a central spot near Broadway, never failed to attract throngs of evening visitors.

A stocky man approached the manager's office. He flashed a badge that gave him admittance. It was Detective Joe Cardona. The star sleuth entered to find two men awaiting him. One was the manager; the other a hotel detective.

Introductions completed, Cardona stated his business. He spoke in a manner that was gruff, but speculative. Joe had come here on a doubtful errand. He did not want it to appear that he might be the victim of a hoax.

"You know what tip-offs are," explained the ace. "We get them right along and chances are they're phony. Just the same, if they sound like something might be doing, we play along to make sure.

"Well, I got a tip-off to-night. I was told to be in the lobby of this hotel at nine o'clock. What's more, I was told to have a squad follow me. That's a big order—when it comes without anything else—but there's a reason why I took it up."

Joe paused for emphasis. He saw doubtful looks upon the faces of the men before him; and he delivered the statement which he had planned for them.

"It was on your account that I came here," resumed the ace. "The Grammont's a big hotel, with lots of people going in and out. Sometimes a tip-off means that one smart crook is trying to get even with another.

"If there's one chance in a thousand that gun business might start in this crowded lobby, it's worthwhile to be ready for it. That's why I'm staying—and there's six plainclothesmen coming in before nine o'clock."

The manager nodded in agreement. He saw the wisdom of protection. Cardona arose and sauntered to the lobby; the house detective followed. The time was five minutes of nine.

Joe Cardona had not stated the real reason for his prompt following of the tip-off. The ace held the hunch that business was due tonight. The call that informed Cardona of potential trouble in the Grammont lobby had come to headquarters. Over the telephone, a weird, whispered voice had delivered its instructions in a creepy monotone.

Cardona had heard that sinister voice before. He believed that he knew the identity of the caller—that was, so far as the actual identity of the personage could be traced. Joe Cardona had recognized the whisper of The Shadow.

GIRDING the Grammont lobby was a glittering balcony. Twenty private meeting rooms opened from that mezzanine. On this evening—as on nearly every other—more than half of the chambers were occupied.

In the Gold Room, where curtains of dull orange hung in clustered draperies and walls were ornamented with gilded frescoes, a group of men were gathered about a massive table. Furniture, like decorations, glistened in golden hue. The color seemed appropriate, considering the affluence of the men assembled.

All looked prosperous. There were eighteen present; seven to a side and two at each end of the long table. According to the statement which appeared on the day-board in the lobby, this was a meeting of the Aztec Mines owners. Perhaps that was why the management had designated the Gold Room for the meeting.

Aztec Mines seemed to indicate gold; and wealth was the subject of this meeting. But none of the eighteen had come to discuss treasure wrested from the earth. They were here to speak of profits gained through murderous endeavor. These were the members of Crime Incorporated.

The meeting had been set for eight forty-five. No one had been late. A man with a solemn countenance had risen at one end of the table. It was Fullis Garwald, self-appointed chairman of the meeting.

"According to the bylaws of the Aztec Mine Organization," began Garwald, in a dry tone, "the holder of certificate number one is to preside at any meeting of this group. I am the owner of that certificate. I shall produce it in due time.

"We have come here to declare a dividend. No

time was scheduled for this meeting. Our bylaws state that it could be demanded by a member who could present sufficient reason for its calling. Such reason has been given. I turn the floor over to the man who gave the word. Let him state his identity."

A figure arose at the far end of the table. It was that of a tall individual whose bluff-faced countenance was hardened in a fixed expression. Staring steadily toward Fullis Garwald, this member announced himself:

"I am stockholder number six."

"Your name?" questioned Garwald.

"Richard Glade."

"Identifying members?"

Two men stood up as Garwald looked about the group. Their nods were all that the chairman *pro tem* required. They were the contacts of Richard Glade.

"Proceed," ordered Garwald.

"In my message," came the harsh voice, "I stated that danger threatened our organization. I added that the menace could be avoided by a prompt declaration of a dividend. I gave my reason: the fact that one member of our group had been slain. One, to my knowledge. Possibly more.

"My request for the appointed meeting brought back messages. We know from them that two of our chain have died. The consensus of opinion proved the value of my request.

"I call for a statement of dividends."

"Is it agreed?" questioned Garwald, as the speaker sat down.

"Agreed," came the reply, in unison.

GARWALD drew a folded paper from his pocket. It was his certificate: the only one that bore the title "Crime Incorporated." It passed around the table. Members nodded as they viewed it. This certificate proved Garwald's title. It bore authentic transfer from Barton Talbor.

"My contribution," declared Garwald, dryly, as he regained the certificate and laid it on the table before him, "has not yet been converted into cash. It consists of rare gems now in my possession. I estimate their value as approximately a quarter million."

Other members took their turn, to declare their contributions to the dividend fund of Crime Incorporated. Some were holding cash in large amounts. Others had appropriated trust funds. Culbert Joquill, introducing himself, announced that he had converted securities that were worth a hundred thousand dollars; and that he still held others worth three times that amount.

The statement of Richard Glade brought a buzz. Paintings worth nearly a million were stacked in an apartment, awaiting disposal through profitable channels. There were members of Crime Incorporated who could do their part in fencing art treasures.

More reports came through. Confident in their security, these rogues made little effort to veil their crimes. Everyone had his share. Chalmers Blythe, who had pointed the way to crime for Culbert Joquill, had gained a full million on his own, aided in half a dozen crimes by members of Crime Incorporated.

One member did not report. Professor Langwood Devine was missing. But the crafty savant had provided for his wealth in case of death. He had informed one of his contacts, regarding the location of a cache where he had stowed the products of his evil genius. Devine's loot was estimated at nearly half a million in cash and rare items cherished by collectors.

"Through a committee headed by myself," announced Fullis Garwald, "our assets will be liquidated. Each stockholder will be apportioned his proper share. Some have gained more than others; all have produced, however, through the full cooperation of our organization. Therefore, we shall share alike. Are there any remarks before adjournment?"

All eyes turned to the opposite end of the table. The member who had announced himself as Richard Glade had risen. Steady words came from his lips. His face showed masklike in the gold-reflected light.

"I spoke of a menace" was his stern pronouncement. "I shall name it. Crime Incorporated has finished its career. The menace that you face will bring destruction. I am the menace!"

WEIRD hush fell upon the room. The glittering walls, the silent draperies seemed to hold the final words. Gilded surroundings were a mockery. Strange fear crept over the seventeen who listened.

Then came the burst of a fierce, fear-provoking laugh. The rending cry was from the false lips of Richard Glade. It belied the identity of the face that startled men were facing. It was the taunting challenge of The Shadow!

With his cry of mirth, The Shadow whirled toward the draperies at the end of the room. His long hands, coming into view, were whisking automatics from deep pockets. Muzzles pointed toward the massive table as wild-eyed men leaped to their feet.

Desperate villains, some of the members of Crime Incorporated had wisely armed themselves before coming to their meeting. Revolvers flashed in answer to The Shadow's challenge. The roar of automatics preceded the revolver fire.

Aiming at rising arms, The Shadow loosed crippling shots. Hot bullets sped toward backing foemen. His outlandish laugh ringing in new mockery, The Shadow whirled as scattered shots were fired in his direction. Through the curtains at the end of the room, he found a hidden opening. The clash of a sliding door marked his departure.

Frenzied crooks were balked. They feared to follow. The Shadow had closed a barrier behind him. The shots had given the alarm. Three members of the group were clutching wounded arms; three others were slumped upon the floor.

Escape! That was their only hope. With one accord, half a dozen of the beaten crooks sprang toward the door to the mezzanine, brandishing revolvers as they took to flight.

Shots greeted them from the balcony. Cardona and his squad had heard the firing. Reinforced by house detectives, they had come up from the lobby. They fired at the armed men whom they saw coming from the Gold Room.

Wild crooks fired in return. That was proof of enmity. Police revolvers sent tuxedoed rats rolling on the carpeted mezzanine. Trapped, the members of Crime Incorporated sprang back into the Gold Room. One man—Culbert Joquill—tried to close the heavy door to form a barricade.

A SHOT staggered the crooked lawyer. It came from the curtains at the end of the room. Fullis Garwald was the first to turn in that direction. He was the first to see the menace that had returned.

The Shadow was standing by the opened doorway. No longer did he display the guise of dead Richard Glade. He was garbed in cloak and hat of black. His blazing eyes, keen above leveled automatics, spelled doom to Crime Incorporated.

Garwald aimed, hoping to clear the way for escape through the end door. An automatic answered. The crooked successor of Barton Talbor fell coughing to the floor. The others preferred to meet the law. Head on, the surging members of the crime chain leaped for Joe Cardona and his men who had reached the door of the Gold Room in a body.

Unmasked crooks sought no quarter. They fought to kill. Those who had no guns were wielding chairs while their fellows pressed revolver triggers. It was an equal fray; one that would have broken the police attack, but for the enfilading fire that broke from beyond the curtains.

Clipping shots from The Shadow's automatics dropped aiming gun arms. Bullets intended for Cardona and his men were never fired. Aided by The Shadow's heavy fire, the men of the law came surging through. The door clanged beyond the curtains as members of Crime Incorporated went staggering backward through the room, sprawling across gilded chairs, staining tufted carpeting of orange with their crimson lifeblood.

Amid the hollow silence of a blue-draped room,

The Shadow's laugh sounded its parting knell. Crossing this empty chamber, The Shadow reached the further door. He entered another unoccupied apartment that had curtains of a different hue. From then on, his silent course faded.

IT was Clyde Burke who heard Joe Cardona's version of the fray at the Hotel Grammont. At headquarters, the next morning, the detective recounted the discovery that had followed the annihilation of Crime Incorporated.

"We've got the full details of the meeting," declared Cardona. "The guy that tipped us off—we don't know who it was—sure pulled a complete job. The place was wired with a dictograph.

"Up on the floor above, two stenographers were taking notes. Do you know who was with them— who hired them? I'll tell you. Howard Norwyn!

"He'd been hiding somewhere. He got word from an unknown friend to be on deck. From the reports, it appears that a guy named Richard Glade double-crossed the rest of the crew. It was when he told them 'I am the menace' that Norwin cut off the connection, acting on instructions from his friend."

"What became of Glade?" inquired Clyde.

"We don't know," responded Cardona. "He's the only one of the lot that got away. But we located his apartment. We landed those pictures that belong to the British Syndicate.

"Looks like Glade crossed himself, as well as the others. I can't figure it. But the important part is the way we're tracing the stolen stuff. We've landed Gaston Ferrar's jewels. We'll have everything else in a week, I'll bet. What's more, we've got Garry Hewes."

"Garry Hewes?"

"Yes. The real murderer of George Hobston. One of the crime crew was Culbert Joquill— lawyer with offices in the Zenith Building. We found a secret room in his place. Guess he didn't trust his own workers, for he had a statement there about Garry Hewes, with the guy's address. It was hidden with cash, and bonds of Hobston's.

"We trapped Hewes in his hotel room. He put up a fight; he got the worst of it. Confessed the murder while he was dying in the hospital. We knew Howard Norwyn was all right anyway, after he showed up with his dictograph reports, but the confession that Hewes made cleared Norwyn from all suspicion.

"And it all started from a tip-off," said Clyde, as he turned to leave the office. "Who gave it to you, Joe?"

"I don't know," asserted the detective, staring straight at the reporter.

Clyde Burke was smiling when he reached the street. He knew that Joe Cardona had wisely refrained from stating the source from which the word had come.

For Joe Cardona knew the power of The Shadow. He knew that The Shadow preferred to shroud his work in darkness. He knew that the master sleuth would aid him in the future, so long as his mighty hand could remain unknown.

Detective Joe Cardona, like the agents of The Shadow, knew the true being who had wiped out Crime Incorporated. Yet even they did not know the full details of the master fighter's war against that evil chain.

That record, hidden like The Shadow himself, belonged within the black walls of the secret sanctum. The facts concerning Crime Incorporated were preserved for the archives of The Shadow.

There, upon a single page of a massive tome was the heading, "Crime Incorporated." Beneath it, the dividend for which The Shadow had called, its full sum totaled in a single word:

"DEATH."

THE END

INTERLUDE by Will Murray

The Shadow vs. organized crime is the theme of this volume.

A year after The Shadow made his first appearance in print, a rival detective magazine ran the following editorial in its March 1932 issue:

> The sundown for the submachine gun terror has arrived—for fiction readers. The gangster story is on the wane. No longer does the swaggering mobster with his threat of "the spot" hold sway with American readers.
>
> Some time ago we predicted this and thumbed down on the gangster story.... The baffling, sinister mystery drama now rules the roost of detective fiction....
>
> A striking illustration of the gangster fadeout was evidenced in a motion picture I saw the other night. Three years ago that picture would have gripped the public. With a dozen bulletproof cars hurtling out to the kill, and the bristling machine guns poking out the windows under leering, slitted eyes—the public would have been spellbound. But not today. When that awesome spectacle was flashed on the screen—the audience laughed!
>
> And on the printed page, people have long tired of that worn-out prototype of he who now languishes in a federal prison.
>
> Well, friends, so much for fiction's sundown of the submachine gun.

The Shadow had led the way. A new type of pulp story was on the rise. It was variously called the "menace" story, "mystery–menace," "ultra-mystery" and other grim appellations. It was good old-fashioned melodrama updated for the Great Depression.

The unique innovation of The Shadow was that the sinister figure of menace which haunted most such melodramas had been transformed from a clichéd evildoer to an avenging nemesis of the wicked.

The Shadow's natural enemy was urban criminals. He was created with the simple objective to, in writer Walter B. Gibson's punchy phrase, "smash crime."

Prohibition had created the monster that grew into organized crime. Bootleg alcohol had fueled it so well that by the end of the 1920s, it was a greedy octopus strangling major U. S. cities.

In good times, the illegal bootlegger was seen as a kind of big-city Robin Hood who delivered a product once perfectly legal. But vicious gang wars in which innocent bystanders were callously slain, combined with the start of the Great Depression, drained the luster from public figures like Alphonse "Scarface" Capone, to name one who had enjoyed unchallenged celebrity status.

Alphonse "Scarface" Capone

At the pinnacle of his power, Capone ran a multi-million dollar operation employing over 400 people. It was an unincorporated corporation, and it was said that half of the Windy City's police force was on his payroll. Capone gave press conferences, opened up the first Chicago soup kitchen to feed the unemployed, and enjoyed unchallenged influence over the city. Despite his many crimes, local, state and FBI agents could not touch him. It took the IRS to bring down Capone.

The repeal of Prohibition in 1933 forced the mobster kingpins to seek other sources of income—principally vice, labor racketeering and extortion. One new avenue criminals opened up was the kidnapping for ransom racket. Kidnapping crimes became epidemic in New York City in the early

Charles "Lucky" Luciano

1930s. Once they began preying on the public instead of hosting them in their illegal speakeasies, the populace turned against them.

Newspaper scareheads proclaimed the rise of the organized super-criminal—masterminds who through political influence, public corruption and police impotence threatened to seize control of major cities such as New York and Chicago. Capone was the first of their kind and the model of all who followed. They were given a new official designation: Public Enemies.

A New York newspaper reported that, "Old forms of exploitation are rapidly returning, particularly in Brooklyn and Manhattan and conditions are now ripe for the super-criminal possessing business acumen and organizing and executive ability to construct a crime and vice organization which will put the underworld on top in this city as Capone had done in Chicago."

In the pages of *The Shadow Magazine*, the Dark Avenger confronted this ever-evolving threat with both guns blazing. Justice had a new face—and that unseen face lurked in the shadows.

Street & Smith's timing was perfect. Coincidentally, 1931 was also the year that a group of New York and New Jersey mobsters formed the National Crime Syndicate. This was the brainchild of gangsters Charles "Lucky" Luciano and Meyer Lansky. They actually instituted a board of directors known as The Commission to oversee operations. Luciano

Meyer Lansky

chaired this group, whose purpose was to settle disputes between competing crime families. Over the course of the 1930s, the Syndicate expanded to include Mafia families throughout the country.

The Syndicate's enforcement arm consisted of hired killers who were on salaried retainer and received bonuses for every hit. The press dubbed them Murder, Inc. Lansky and Benjamin "Bugsy" Siegel headed this sub-organization. Albert "The Mad Hatter" Anastasia, also known as the "Lord High Executioner," was their chief enforcer.

Against this backdrop, The Shadow took on a clone of Al Capone in 1932's apocryphal epic, *Gangdom's Doom*.

"It was to involve The Shadow in direct conflict with the Chicago mobs, which were then at the height of their power," Gibson recalled. "With The Shadow newly launched as a crime buster, the story would be a 'natural' even in another magazine."

Unfortunately, Street & Smith received a backlash of complaints from Italian-American readers,

Benjamin "Bugsy" Siegel

offended by what they saw as a convenient cultural stereotype. After that, Walter Gibson was instructed to portray organized crime in ethnically-neutral terms. This restriction led to some ingenious ideas.

Chain of Death was one of them. It was submitted on October 13, 1933 under the title of "Crime, Inc." It saw print in the July 15, 1934 issue of *The Shadow Magazine* with a particularly moody George Rozen cover.

Here, Maxwell Grant gave his own unique spin on the concept of an organized and incorporated criminal enterprise.

While Crime, Incorporated may or may not have been inspired by the National Crime Syndicate, its organization was more melodrama than Mafia. The concept of individual criminals organized so that each member only knows one other—hence the "chain of death"—is one Gibson will return to in future Shadow mysteries such as *The Hydra*.

This is also one of those cases where a cryptic code plays a major role. Codes and cryptograms were a big part of *The Shadow Magazine.* Its editor, John L. Nanovic, ran the Codes column that ran for years in its back pages. There he used the pseudonym of "Henry Lysing."

Devising the codes in his Shadow novels was Walter Gibson's responsibility, however. He confessed that it was sometimes a daunting task.

Writing a chapter on codes in his 1979 book, *The Shadow Scrapbook,* Walter singled out the code from *Chain of Death* as one of the most interesting, explaining, "It happens to be an ordinary type of cryptogram, but one allowing a special twist. In the story this code was merely the 'bait' that threw the experts off the trail of a baffling code...."

Students of mystery writing will recognize the influence of the famous Sherlock Holmes story, "The Adventure of the Dancing Men," on this particular puzzle.

By the end of the decade, George Rozen had moved on, and Graves Gladney had brought his own artistic vision to the series. His painting for our second selection, depicting the Master of Darkness creating his distinct silhouette in the form of a finger shadow covering a highly unusual insurance policy, is itself remarkable.

Death's Premium no doubt stems from Gibson's years working in an insurance company. In 1919, after graduating from Colgate College, he sold insurance for the Penn Mutual Insurance Company

in his native Philadelphia. Later, he worked with his brother Arthur typing policies at the Connecticut General Insurance Company. No doubt Walter absorbed a lot of inside information on the insurance game, because a great deal of technical material later found its way into the pages of *The Shadow.*

Death's Premium is a variation on Gibson's blockbuster 1937 novel, *Crime, Insured.* But what a variation! Only Maxwell Grant could conceive of and pull off such a complicated concept.

Here's how editor John L. Nanovic set up the story for Shadow readers in 1940:

> The life of Lamont Cranston is a dangerous one, for a great many of the crooks who meet The Shadow realize that the wealthy clubman, Lamont Cranston, is merely another guise for The Shadow. That is only one of the several disguised personages which The Shadow assumes, but it proves a very handy one because the real Lamont Cranston is usually on some big-game hunting expedition, and thus there is little danger of The Shadow meeting "himself," so to speak, when he is assuming that person's title. Once, some time ago, The Shadow found himself in an embarrassing position, however, for while he was being "Lamont Cranston" in New York, the real Lamont Cranston happened to be in an airplane accident in India, thus getting his name in the paper and putting The Shadow in a tough spot.
>
> Other assumed poses of The Shadow include Henry Arnaud, Fritz the janitor at police headquarters, his real identity as Kent Allard, famous aviator, and so on. All this is somewhat in the way of a slight preamble to the next novel, "Death's Premium," in which The Shadow makes very good use of these names. In order to smash a "death insurance" ring, The Shadow, in the pose of Henry Arnaud, insures the death of Lamont Cranston for a half-million dollars! The insurance company must prove the *death* of Cranston in one week or pay up!
>
> That's the basis of the "Death's Premium" novel, and you can tell by the setup that it's going to be a really fast-moving, thrill-packed yarn. It brings you a most unusual crime scheme, and one that makes The Shadow actually put his life up as a stake in order to break up the villainous work that is going on.

This ploy proved so shattering that after the gunsmoke cleared, The Shadow was forced to forever abandon Henry Arnaud—which had been his second most important running disguise after Lamont Cranston—as a reliable cover identity.

After seven years of continuous use, it had been compromised.

What more needs to be said? Except that *Death's Premium* was submitted on July 7, 1939, and published in the January 1, 1940 issue of *The Shadow.* Read it now! •

DEATH'S PREMIUM

THE SHADOW INSURES HIMSELF TO DIE— AND COLLECTS!

A Complete Book-length Novel from the Private Annals of The Shadow, as told to

MAXWELL GRANT

CHAPTER I
KEYS TO CRIME

EARLY dusk was deepening the grimy front of the old Hotel Thurmont when Ronald Parron sidled in from the front street. With quick, nervous eyes he darted a look about the lobby, then approached the desk and asked for the key to Room 312.

Parron was still glancing about after he received the key. The clerk took another look into the box, then told him:

"No messages, Mr. Hotchkiss."

At the mention of the name, Parron gave a jumpy start. He forced a smile to his twitchy lips, managed to mutter a thanks. Parron had just remembered that he was registered at this hotel under the name of "Hotchkiss."

Entering the elevator, Parron gave the operator a suspicious stare. Turned half about, Parron had his hand thrust to a hip pocket, where a revolver bulged. He regarded the elevator operator as a possible enemy, who might make trouble during the short ride.

The trip proved a safe one. On the third floor, Parron nervously unlocked the door of 312 and sprang into the room, his revolver drawn. He pawed for the light switch; failing to find it, he darted across the room.

Stumbling against a chair, he blundered into a bureau, where he halted, panting, at sight of a face that rose from the gloom.

It was a haggard face, pale in the dusk; a well-formed face that showed a trim mustache and sleek black hair. The face was Parron's own.

Sight of himself in the bureau mirror brought a laugh from Parron's lips. He fumbled for a lamp. His face looked less hunted when the lamp glow filled the room.

Drawing the window shades, the dark-haired man looked about him. Deciding that no intruders had been in the place, Parron tiptoed to a closet door and yanked it open.

With the same move, he covered the closet with his .32 revolver. Another laugh drifted from his lips when he saw that the closet was empty. Stretching, Parron reached eagerly to the shelf, brought down an oblong dispatch box of thin tinny metal.

The box was locked. Parron made no attempt to open it. He simply laid it on the bureau, then looked toward the telephone. He hesitated at making a call from the hotel room, but finally decided to do so. The number that he called had a Long Island exchange.

Parron recognized the voice that answered; but, in his turn, he used a tone that was different from his own. He spoke in quick, clipped fashion, and to complete the vocal disguise, he asked:

"Am I speaking to Mr. Renstrom? To Mr. Albert Renstrom?"

Receiving the affirmative reply that he actually expected, Parron pretended to doubt the other speaker's identity. Finally ending the bluff, he came down to business.

"All right, Mr. Renstrom," announced Parron rapidly. "I'm the man who sent you the letter that contained the key. I'm willing to send the box, too, if you're interested."

A low, earnest voice reached Parron's ear. Renstrom *was* interested; deeply so. He was ready to cooperate in any way possible. He had read the letter thoroughly, and would abide by its terms.

"It's a deal, Mr. Renstrom," decided Parron. "You'll have the box inside an hour. But remember—

you're to hold it until ten o'clock, as I specified in my letter—"

RENSTROM was interrupting with assurances. Smiling as he listened, Parron ended the phone call, tucked the dispatch box under his arm and stole from the hotel room.

He used the stairway instead of the elevator, and took a rear exit from the lobby. Spying a cab on the rear street, Parron hailed it and gave the driver Renstrom's address.

As the cab swung along, Parron studied an airplane schedule, choosing a plane that left Newark Airport at half past eight. If he missed that one, he could take another at nine fifteen. Where they went didn't matter to Parron. He was tapping a well-filled wallet in his inside pocket. His trip was going to be a long one.

It took the cab about half an hour to reach the Renstrom residence on Long Island. Telling the driver to wait, Parron alighted and went through a gate between high hedges. The porch light was on; as he neared its glow, Parron suddenly remembered a needed precaution. He paused, pulled the collar of his overcoat about his chin.

Peering upward, Parron squinted suspiciously at a window on the second floor. He thought he saw a face there; then, fancying that his imagination had tricked him, he hastened to the front door and rang the bell.

The door was opened by a white-haired servant who blinked at sight of the muffled visitor.

"For Mr. Renstrom," gruffed Parron, thrusting the metal box into the servant's hands. "Take it to him, right away."

With that, Parron was heading back along the walk. He took a quick glance over his shoulder as he reached the gate. The servant was staring stupidly at the box; there was no one at the upstairs window. Jumping into the cab, Parron told the driver to take him back to town.

During the ride the taxi driver became talkative. His head inclined toward the connecting window, he remarked:

"Tough about that polo player getting killed this afternoon. Read about it, did you?"

Parron winced; stared nervously.

"What polo player?"

"Young Reggie Chitterton," replied the driver. "Here's his picture"—the driver was thrusting a newspaper through the window— "but you won't be able to read it until we reach the bridge lights. Throwed off his horse, Chitterton was, and they found his skull fractured after they lugged him to the clubhouse. Dangerous game, that polo."

Stifling a groan, Parron managed to grasp the newspaper. He knew what had happened to

Chitterton, though the cab driver didn't. Parron could picture the whole case, and sum it up in one word:

Murder!

ELSEWHERE, keen eyes were studying the item that Parron did not have to read. Cut from the latest newspaper, the clipping lay beneath the glow of a bluish lamp. From darkness above the glare came a grim, whispered laugh, uttered by hidden lips.

The Shadow, master crime tracker, was in his sanctum, a black-walled room sequestered somewhere in Manhattan. To the clipping that told of recent death, he was adding others, of a similar variety.

All pertained to so-called accidents—the sort that would be checked by the law and classed as unavoidable. But behind such cases could lie the insidious hand of crime.

The Shadow knew!

He was visualizing what might have happened at the polo field, where Chitterton had suffered a fall during the second chukker. A felled player, carried to the clubhouse, would be in the hands of various attendants before a physician could arrive.

During that interval, much could happen, particularly if ghoulish killers were in wait, hoping for any break. Chitterton's death could have been murder—for a very definite reason. There had been too many others like it.

A hand moved from the light. There was a sparkle of a flame-colored gem: The Shadow's girasol. That rare stone, a magnificent fire opal, was The Shadow's only jewel. Returning to the light, the hand brought a square sheet of glossy paper.

The sheet bore a chart, with double lines. Graphically, those lines told their story. One traced the course of murder during the past year; it showed a slight decline when compared to previous periods of twelve months.

Crisscrossing murder's graph, the second line indicated cases of technical manslaughter. They had shown a surprising jump. From that, The Shadow had formed a definite conclusion; one which, so far, had not been noticed by the law.

Grouped together, the two styles of death did more than indicate a serious total. These statistics applied to New York City alone, and they were worse than any other, though the death wave was noticeable elsewhere. It was time that this particular chart reached the right man.

Forming his hands into an interlocking pattern, The Shadow held them between the light and the paper on the table. Supple fingers cast a silhouette upon the sheet. It was a hawkish profile, topped by a slouch hat, in miniature.

When The Shadow withdrew his hands the silhouette remained, shaded upon sensitized paper. Approaching the paper from the sides, The Shadow folded it and placed it into an envelope, which was already addressed to Ralph Weston, New York's police commissioner.

Sealing the envelope, the mysterious master reached for earphones that hung from the sanctum wall. Before his hand had touched the instruments, a tiny light gleamed from the darkness. A call was coming through, from the man with whom The Shadow intended to communicate.

Raising the earphones, The Shadow heard a steady, mechanical voice:

"Burbank speaking."

"Report!"

WITH that whisper, The Shadow pronounced his identity to Burbank, the contact man who kept in touch with active agents. For the past week, ever since The Shadow had learned of crime's increase, ardent workers had been aiding their chief in searching for men who might be murderers by trade.

Results had come at last. Burbank was relaying a report from Clyde Burke, one of the active agents. Clyde was on the staff of a tabloid newspaper, the New York *Classic*. It had been Clyde's job to visit nightclubs, gambling houses, and other places of a sporting reputation.

Other agents had prowled the underworld, without results. The fact that Clyde was coming through with information fitted with The Shadow's own conclusions; namely, that murder was being conducted on a deluxe basis, rather than through the hiring of ordinary mobsmen.

Killing meant thugs. Of that, The Shadow was certain; but he doubted that the lesser hands engaged in this game of supercrime would be found in the usual underworld dives. Through Burbank, he had instructed Clyde to be on the lookout for any man of better connections who held any converse with hoodlums.

Clyde had found such a man—one who did not visit thugs, but who had them come to him. At present, the man in question was at the Moonlight Club. He had just talked to a pair of tough-looking customers who had drifted to the bar. Apparently, the suspected man was awaiting the arrival of more followers.

The bluish light clicked off. Somber walls were stirred by a whispered laugh. Echoes faded, bringing silence to pitch blackness. The Shadow had departed by the sanctum's hidden exit. Real echoes, those, but they stood for imaginary ones.

Echoes like the *clank* of keys!

Ronald Parron held one key—to his hotel room.

Albert Renstrom had another key—to a mysterious metal box. The Shadow owned a third key, more potent than the other two.

It was the name of a man bent upon evil design. A key to coming murder!

CHAPTER II
MEN OF MURDER

ARRIVING again at the Hotel Thurmont, Ronald Parron entered by the front door. Riding up in the elevator, he did not bother to keep a hand on his revolver.

If crooks had learned his moves, so Parron reasoned, they would have attempted to block him long before this. As matters now stood, his work was accomplished. He was entering Room 312 for the last time, which was something that pleased him immensely.

Parron's enthusiasm waned when he pressed the light switch. Stiffening, he stared across the room toward a man who had been waiting in the darkness beside the bureau. Of their own accord, Parron's lips phrased the intruder's name:

"Rudy Waygart!"

The waiting man chuckled. His tone wasn't pleasant. It was an ugly tone, the sort that fitted Rudy Waygart. Sallow, lean-faced, with small gimlet eyes and sharp, bulging teeth, Rudy habitually wore a nasty expression that suited his disposition.

"Hello, Parron!" Rudy's voice was raspy. "I've been wondering where you've been keeping yourself. Up with those dukes of yours"—with a quick gesture, Rudy produced a revolver— "while I take care of that rod that's poking from your hip!"

Disarmed, Parron let Rudy shove him to a corner. Nervously, he was thinking how he could square himself with this unwanted visitor. His hands half raised, Parron nudged a thumb toward his inside pocket.

"I've got the cash right here, Rudy," he argued. "I was going to look you up, to pay off that poker debt. I was carrying a gun because I had so much money with me."

Rudy gave a satisfied grin, then glanced casually across the room, toward a suitcase. His tone became friendly as he asked:

"Going on a trip?"

Parron started to nod, then halted, horrified. Gimlet eyes, fangish teeth were combining in a leer. Chilled by a horrifying thought, Parron could find no words. It was Rudy who spoke.

"Thought that gambling was my racket, didn't you?" sneered Rudy. "Never figured I was in the same game you were. While you've been handling one end of it, I've been taking care of the other. You know what that means, don't you?"

Parron's lips moved as though trying to hold back the single word that summed the answer.

Murder!

It flashed through Parron's brain, an electrifying thought, and Rudy understood it. Pocketing Parron's gun, Rudy jammed his own revolver against the trembling man's ribs and rasped the prophecy:

"You're going on a trip, all right. A one-way ride, without a return ticket! You're the first double-crosser I've had to handle, but it's going to be a quick job!"

Prodded by Rudy's gun, Parron turned numbly toward the door. With a mock bow, Rudy reached left-handed for the knob, keeping Parron covered with his right, which held the revolver.

The door was ajar, something that Rudy didn't realize until he grasped the knob. Before he had time to guess the significance behind the fact, the door smashed inward. Struck by the barrier, Rudy was lifted from his feet, hurled half across the room. His gun went off in the air.

As he finished his backward sprawl, Rudy saw Parron tossed aside by an insurging shape of black moving with the speed and power of an avalanche.

The Shadow!

CRIME'S superfoe had trailed Rudy from the Moonlight Club. Outside the door he had overheard the killer's chat with Parron. Picking the timeliest moment, The Shadow had performed a move of twofold consequence: He had rescued Parron from doom's threat and had flattened Rudy, rendering the killer helpless.

The taunt of a shivery laugh came from lips that were concealed by the upturned collar of a black cloak. Below eyes that blazed from beneath a slouch hat brim was The Shadow's counter threat, the muzzle of a .45 automatic swinging toward Rudy Waygart.

At that instant came a clatter that sounded like an echo of The Shadow's incoming crash. Two window shades went whipping upward; as The Shadow wheeled, he saw forms lunging in from a fire escape. Coarse faces came into the light; tough fists were brandishing glittering revolvers.

Rudy's mobbies!

They hadn't been with the sallow killer when he left the Moonlight Club.

Rudy had sent the crew ahead, had posted them at the least expected spot. Rudy's plan, apparently, was to cut off any mad dash that Parron might make toward the windows. His cute idea had turned out bigger than he thought.

Murderous mobbies had the opportunity of a lifetime—a chance to bag The Shadow!

They overlooked one point.

Just as The Shadow's smashing entry and mocking laugh had revealed his presence, so did the crooks betray themselves by the noisy way in which they had disposed of the window shades. As they thrust gun muzzles into the room, The Shadow was wheeling toward the door. By the time they aimed, he was fading sideward, staying in the room instead of making toward the hall.

Tricked crooks changed aim. By then Rudy was coming to his feet, trying to block The Shadow's spinning course. Almost from the floor The Shadow

bobbed upward under Rudy's outthrust arm. He chucked the killer over his shoulders; flung forward in a sudden somersault, Rudy hit the floor again, half dazed.

Thugs held their trigger fingers, rather than riddle their leader. The brief delay was too long for their own benefit.

Two guns blasted. The first was the automatic that The Shadow had ready when he entered. The second shot came from the fringe of his cloak, where he had produced another gun. One clipped

**The Shadow bobbed upward under
the outstretched arm, chucked
the killer over his shoulders.**

thug sprawled inward from the window; the other sank back to the fire escape.

The Shadow had aimed while on the move. He didn't need to pick out his thuggish foemen; he simply fired at the window centers, and his method brought results.

Launching across the room, The Shadow reached the window that had disgorged a writhing crook. The Shadow suspected that there would be more than two, and he was right.

Gun to gun, he met another thug who was coming through the emptied window, and beat the fellow to the shot. Thrusting head and arm out through the window, The Shadow saw a fourth crook swinging from the far end of the platform.

The last mobbie was quick with his trigger; too quick. His revolver spurted a leaden slug that whined past The Shadow's slouch hat. The crook wasn't equal to the task of clipping a target three inches in width.

Gun muzzle close to the wall, one eye peering above it, The Shadow answered that blast. The impact of a .45 bullet jolted the last thug back across the rail.

Arms clawed, feet kicked high. The next token of that final fighter was the dull sound of a cracking skull that struck the cement alleyway, three floors below.

THE SHADOW heard the sound from midway in the room. He had spun about to look for Rudy Waygart. He saw the sallow murderer diving out into the hallway; from farther along came the fading clatter of running feet that belonged to Ronald Parron.

Fleeing, the rescued victim was showing maddened haste, thinking that Rudy was after him; but Rudy had forgotten Parron. The crook's sole reason for taking the same route was to escape The Shadow.

The chase led to the stairway, then down into the lobby. Rudy was twisting toward the rear route. The Shadow let the killer go, for a very important reason. Two loungers at the front of the lobby were springing up from chairs, to close in on Parron.

One glimpse of their faces told The Shadow what they were: triggermen that Rudy had ordered here as reserves. They didn't know that Rudy was dodging The Shadow; they thought that he was leaving the final work to them. Their guns were out, they were aiming, when The Shadow delivered withering shots.

The pair sprawled toward the front doorway. They were shooting as they fell; their shots were wide. Parron heard their shrieks. In response to some mental quirk, the hunted man paused at the sidewalk to look back.

A slumped thug fired, almost blindly, from the lobby floor. There was an echoing howl from the sidewalk as Parron staggered.

Speeding across the lobby, where all noncombatants had dived from sight, The Shadow reached the street, gathered Parron up and thrust him into the open door of a taxicab that had wheeled into sight as if summoned.

The cab was away with its wounded burden. Turned about, The Shadow looked back into the lobby. There was no more fight in the pair who had made that final thrust; both thugs were lying still. But Waygart was gone, to the rear street, and he had closed the trail behind him.

Two police officers were coming through from the back. Evidently Rudy had reached the street before they arrived. Seeing a cloaked figure on the lighted sidewalk of the front street, the two patrolmen raised a shout. It was answered from two directions along the front street.

The police were on the job. Too late to corner Rudy Waygart, they were in time to find The Shadow. They didn't stop to reason whether he was friend or foe. The cops had heard shots; they saw a fighter who held two guns. They opened fire.

Springing from the curb, The Shadow sought darkness across the street. Noting his course, the officers followed.

When they converged, they found themselves staring at a blank wall. Above was the sliding ladder of a fire escape against a dilapidated building; but it was beyond their reach. They decided that the man with the guns couldn't have gone by that route.

They were wrong. The Shadow had gauged the distance better than they had. He had reached the bottom rung with a high leap, and hauled himself to the floor above. The reason that flashlights didn't show him was because he was no longer there.

The Shadow had swung past the corner of the building. Away from sight of the police, he was crossing the low roof of a one-story garage, to reach the next street.

Two blocks from where Rudy Waygart had gotten in the clear, The Shadow knew that further pursuit of the crafty murderer would be useless, since a squad of police had come between. However, The Shadow had marked Rudy as a killer; and he had also started Ronald Parron on a route to safety.

Parron would talk, unless too seriously wounded. The fellow was anxious to get out of the murder racket represented by Rudy Waygart. What Parron knew might be sufficient to forestall all future crime.

There was a whispered laugh as The Shadow merged with darkness. Unfortunately, that mirth was premature. Crime's finish was not to be an early matter.

A long and arduous campaign lay ahead. More death was due before The Shadow could possibly trap Rudy Waygart and other men of murder!

CHAPTER III
THE LAW'S TURN

COMMISSIONER RALPH WESTON was at the Cobalt Club, his favorite place during evening hours. Swankiest of exclusive Manhattan clubs, the Cobalt boasted many wealthy members, who liked the special privacy it offered.

In fact, Weston had experienced some difficulty in joining the Cobalt Club. He had been accepted only through the efforts of Lamont Cranston, one of the most influential members. Behind that fact lay an important secret.

The man who posed as Lamont Cranston was actually The Shadow.

Knowing that constant contact with the police commissioner would prove valuable, The Shadow had pressed the point of Weston's membership. As Cranston, he had naturally gained Weston's full friendship and confidence. Whenever Weston was at the club, which was often, he welcomed Cranston's arrival.

Tonight was a case in point.

Commissioner Weston was busy in a telephone booth making a series of calls. He had received news of a gang raid at the Hotel Thurmont, and was alternately receiving reports and giving orders. When he emerged from the booth, Weston spied Cranston strolling in from the street.

Tall, easy-mannered, with a calm expression on his masklike face, Cranston approached Weston with outstretched hand.

"Good evening, Commissioner," he said in even tones. "You appear to be quite busy."

"I *was* busy," returned Weston briskly, "but my work is finished for a while. Suppose we go to the grillroom, Cranston."

"I shall meet you there, Commissioner. It happens"—Cranston's lips showed the faintest of smiles—"that I have a phone call to make, myself."

From the phone booth, Cranston watched the commissioner turn toward the stairs that led down to the grillroom. An attendant overtook the commissioner and handed him an envelope, which Weston pocketed somewhat mechanically.

By that time The Shadow was listening to a report from Burbank. The news was disappointing. Parron was dead.

Moe Shrevnitz, one of The Shadow's secret agents, was the driver of the cab that had carried Parron away from the Hotel Thurmont. Moe had headed directly to the office of Dr. Rupert Sayre—a friend of The Shadow. By then Parron was unconscious

from loss of blood. Sayre had attempted an immediate transfusion, but the victim was beyond hope.

No papers had been found on Parron, other than the banknotes that filled his bulging wallet. Crime's victim had failed to utter a single word before he died.

The Shadow told Burbank to arrange the further details. Sayre, of course, would report the case to the law. Moe's story would be that he had picked up Parron as a chance passenger; that upon noting the man's condition, he had stopped at the first physician's office he saw.

WITH the Parron angle temporarily closed, The Shadow went down to the grillroom. He found Weston alone there, for the place was being redecorated and there was only one table, in a corner.

"It looked like we'd run into a murder case," began Weston. "There was some shooting over at the Hotel Thurmont. But Inspector Cardona just phoned that it was merely a mob fight. We've cut down murder"—Weston was chuckling— "to the point where crooks are so badly off, they're killing one another—"

Interrupting himself, the commissioner stared at a sheet of paper that he had unfolded from an envelope. Clutching Cranston's arm, he found words:

"Look at this paper, Cranston!"

The Shadow leaned forward, gazed at the charted lines on the sheet. He remarked that they looked quite interesting, but not enough so to cause excitement or consternation. The commissioner stared at the paper again.

"It's gone!" he exclaimed. "But I saw it, Cranston! The outline of a hawkish silhouette, with a slouch hat above it!"

Cranston's eyes sparkled with interest. He took the paper, studied it in the light, then handed it back to Weston with a smile.

"It wasn't my imagination," argued Weston. "This is a message from The Shadow!"

Still smiling, Cranston lighted a thin cigar. His profile intervened between the match flare and the wall. Against the wall appeared the same silhouette that had faded when light struck the sensitized paper. It lasted for flickery moments, but Weston did not see the full-sized outline that marked Cranston's actual identity. The commissioner was studying the paper again.

For a two full minutes, Weston frowned, twitched at the tips of his pointed mustache. Then, flinging the paper to the table, the commissioner clenched his fists.

"Gad, Cranston!" he exclaimed. "The Shadow may be right. He usually is, you know."

Cranston shrugged. He was gazing idly at the sheet of paper, but did not seem to infer anything from it.

"Look how that secondary line has risen!" insisted Weston. "Like fools, we've been congratulating ourselves on the decline of the murder rate without checking the increase in cases that could come under the general head of homicide.

"If a tenth of those are actually murder, we're up against a huge problem. It would mean that the murder rate has almost doubled without our knowledge!"

Weston experienced a sudden change. He realized that The Shadow was doing more than merely helping the law. He was giving Weston a chance to actually carve the murder rate before the public realized that the police had been deceived.

Always impetuous, Commissioner Weston was seized with sudden desire for action, even though it might prove of a blind sort. Rising from the table, he strode out of the grillroom. Returning a few minutes later, he sat down with a triumphant smile.

"I just called headquarters," declared Weston. "Inspector Cardona isn't back there yet; but when he arrives, he's to call me right away. Do you know what's coming next, Cranston?

"I'll tell you. I'm going to have Cardona bring full reports on every case of chance manslaughter or accidental death that might, by the least shade of suspicion, be considered murder. We'll spend the rest of the night sifting those cases to the bottom.

"You're welcome to remain, Cranston, as long as you want, to see how the law operates. Too bad we can't have The Shadow here. He might enjoy it, also."

CASUALLY, The Shadow remarked that he would stay awhile, but that he was expecting a call from a friend that might take him elsewhere. Cranston frequently expected such calls. The commissioner had come to regard them as a common matter.

Actually, they were calls from Burbank, relaying reports of agents. Always, on a night when crime had struck, The Shadow had to be ready for quick countermoves. In this instance the chance seemed unlikely.

Tonight, Rudy Waygart and a band of henchmen had set out to finish a double-crosser. With Ronald Parron dead, it appeared that their full mission was accomplished. With Rudy's trail obliterated, The Shadow's best policy was to stay with Weston and note the commissioner delve into other murder cases that had been marked as closed.

Actually, that plan should have brought results. Instead, a freak occurrence was to thwart The Shadow's method.

At headquarters, a detective sergeant had left a note on Cardona's desk telling the ace inspector to call the commissioner at once. Entering the office, Cardona would have seen that message, had not the telephone been ringing when he arrived.

Answering the call, Joe Cardona lost the poker-faced expression that usually adorned his swarthy features. He knew the man who was on the telephone, recognized that whatever he said must be important.

Cardona's replies were a series of affirmatives; finishing with another "yes," the inspector planked the telephone on the desk, squarely over the note that lay there.

Looking for messages, Joe didn't notice the corner of the memo slip that poked from beneath the telephone. He strode from the office and out through the corridor, bound on a new mission.

At the door he ran into a wiry young man who was hastening in from the street.

"Hello, Burke!" snapped Joe. "Got your car outside? If you have, you're in luck."

Clyde Burke showed interest—the sort that befitted a reporter. He nodded that his car was outside.

"Drive me where I want to go," continued Cardona, "and I'll promise you a scoop, Burke."

They were riding in Clyde's coupé when Cardona explained why he hadn't used a police car. They were on the way to visit a man who didn't want Cardona's arrival to be conspicuous.

"His name is Albert Renstrom," explained Joe. "He lives out on Long Island. He's an actuary. You know—one of those fellows who does the figuring for big insurance companies."

Vaguely, Clyde remembered hearing of Renstrom. The man was the head of a national group of actuaries, which meant that Renstrom probably compiled statistics for many companies, rather than merely for one. But the next name that Cardona mentioned was more potent than Renstrom's.

"Thomas Merwood is out there, too," confided Cardona. "He got on the wire and said it was important that I come at once. When a big financier like Merwood says that anything is important, it must be."

Clyde agreed. Meanwhile, he was linking facts. He knew that Merwood handled gilt-edged investments, the sort that large insurance companies would buy. Naturally, in looking into the assets of such companies, Merwood would consult with someone like Renstrom.

As a result of such a conference, they had apparently uncovered something of consequence to the law. Something, perhaps, that pertained to the increased death rate that The Shadow previously had noticed. Knowing that The Shadow was seeking inside facts, Clyde was elated.

Clyde felt that luck was with him. Along with Cardona, he had stumbled upon a trail that he thought could lead to something highly important, even though it seemed remote from Rudy Waygart and the murderer's victim, Ronald Parron.

It never occurred to Clyde that he was crossing Parron's earlier trail; that at Renstrom's house it might be possible to obtain the very facts that a dying man had failed to tell!

CHAPTER IV
TEN O'CLOCK

ALBERT RENSTROM received the visitors in the downstairs living room of his spacious home. He made no comment when Cardona introduced Clyde. Evidently, Renstrom decided that Mr. Burke was another man from headquarters.

In fact, Renstrom seemed too concerned with matters of his own to worry about anyone else.

The actuary was a tall, stoop-shouldered man who looked quite frail and very nervous. His face was lean; his eyes had a fixed expression as they stared through large gold-rimmed glasses. While shaking hands he studied both visitors in an owlish fashion; then he licked his lips to speak.

Suddenly remembering that he was not alone, Renstrom turned and introduced Thomas Merwood, who was standing patiently by. The financier stepped forward, smiled as he spoke a deep-voiced greeting.

As tall as Renstrom, Merwood was much heavier of build. His broad face was square-jawed; his gray hair added dignity to his appearance. Merwood was calm, and his collected manner did much to soothe Renstrom. Nervousness ending, the actuary began his story.

"For some time," Renstrom told Cardona, "I have been observing a curious trend in the mortality rate among the policyholders of large life-insurance companies. The trend, I regret to say, has been upward.

"That fact is nothing to cause alarm, considering that the percentage is very slight. But the curious point is this: The increase in death has been restricted entirely to men in the higher-income brackets."

The final statement impressed Cardona. Promptly, Joe asked:

"Were all of them heavily insured?"

Renstrom shook his head.

"No," he replied. "None of them was overloaded. In fact, the opposite was the case. The payment of death claims was by no means in proportion to the increased mortality rate. On that account I did not give the situation the attention that it deserved."

Cardona was beginning to think that the matter deserved no attention at all when Renstrom produced a key from his vest pocket.

"This came yesterday," stated the actuary. "It was with a letter sent by an anonymous writer. The letter intimated facts that I would have regarded as preposterous, except that they tallied with figures at my disposal.

"The writer attributed many recent deaths to murder, craftily disguised. He said that if I would guarantee to press the issue, he would deliver a box containing documents that would prove the existence of an actual murder ring working throughout the country.

"I was to keep the letter secret until I heard further from him. He telephoned me this evening; I promised to abide by his terms. Half an hour later the box was delivered."

Cardona looked about the room as if he expected to see the box pop up from under a chair. It was Merwood who smilingly explained why the box was not on exhibit.

"Renstrom has it in the safe in his study," said Merwood. "The letter contained some provision about not opening the box until a certain time. What hour did it say, Renstrom? Eleven, wasn't it?"

"Ten o'clock," corrected Renstrom. "Until then I am honor bound to keep the box in my safe, as the letter specified. At that time I shall produce the letter and my own figures, along with the box."

"He won't listen to reason, Inspector," inserted Merwood. "I argued that he should place everything in your hands as soon as you arrived, but I haven't managed to change his decision."

The clock on the mantel showed twenty minutes past nine. Shrugging his shoulders, Cardona decided to wait until ten o'clock. But Clyde Burke was gripped by a sudden inspiration. Pulling out pad and pencil, he swung to Renstrom and Merwood with the question:

"How about it, gentlemen? Any statement for the press, while we wait? I represent the New York *Classic*—"

BURSTS of indignation came from Renstrom and Merwood. Answering them with impudent arguments, Clyde soon found himself unpopular with Cardona as well as the others. The upshot was an exertion of authority by Cardona.

Aided by an old servant, who came at Renstrom's summons, Joe marched Clyde to the front door and told him to be on his way.

Driving from the house, Clyde gave a rueful laugh. He had put himself in wrong with Cardona, and would have to square it later. But it had been the only way out.

Clyde wanted to find a telephone and get word to The Shadow. It was important that his chief be here by ten o'clock to learn facts firsthand.

Back in Renstrom's living room, Cardona was making profuse apologies. Renstrom was still indignant, angry because Cardona had brought a reporter here at all; but Merwood took the situation more calmly.

"No harm has been done," insisted the financier. "The few facts that Burke heard were not enough to make a newspaper story. The *Classic* will have to wait, like the other journals, until we issue a complete statement to the press."

As he finished speaking, Merwood turned toward the doorway to the hall. A girl was standing there; her face showed alarm. Noting that Cardona was a stranger, she gazed at him instead of the others.

Returning the stare, Joe was impressed by the depth and beauty of the brown eyes that met his, and the beauty of the girl herself. She was a brunette.

"Good evening, Miss Renstrom," said Merwood with a bow. "I am sorry if we alarmed you. This is Inspector Cardona. He was merely ejecting an unwelcome reporter."

"My niece," undertoned Renstrom to Cardona. Then, turning to the girl: "You may remain here, Janet. I am going to the study to gather some papers. I am not to be disturbed until ten o'clock."

Renstrom went upstairs. Janet chatted with the visitors, and her talk proved quite vivacious. Time went rapidly, and with it, Cardona began to have a hunch.

He remembered how nervous the girl had been until she learned exactly what had caused the commotion downstairs. At present, so Joe decided, Janet Renstrom was hiding something that she did not want her uncle or anyone else to know.

It was nearly ten o'clock when the brunette left the living room and went upstairs again. Strolling toward the hallway, Cardona glanced at his watch. Turning to Merwood, he grunted:

"About four minutes more. I guess we'd better wait the full time before we call Mr. Renstrom."

Actually, Cardona wanted those four minutes to listen for sounds from upstairs. He could hear Janet's voice in the upper hallway, and he caught enough snatches of her conversation to know that she was making a telephone call.

After the call was finished, Cardona thought that he heard another sound: the throb of a motor, outdoors. He decided that it must have been a car passing the house, for the noise faded.

Joe's guess was a bad one. There was a car outside, but it hadn't passed the house. It was stopped on the side street; a low-built sedan, its top no higher than the hedge that intervened between the sidewalk and Renstrom's premises.

Crouched in the parked car, four men were talking in low mutters. From behind the wheel came another tone, a smooth one. It was the voice of Rudy Waygart.

"SIT tight," Rudy was telling his new crew of thugs. "It isn't ten o'clock yet. You'll know when the time comes. I've given you the dope. Spread out, start shooting, then get back here. When we lam, we'll go in a hurry."

As he finished, Rudy gave a whisper for silence. He thought that he had heard a stir from the other side of the hedge. Staring out at pitch blackness, Rudy soon decided that no one was about. Nevertheless, he kept his gaze fixed toward the dim window of an upstairs room: Renstrom's study.

Below that window a blackened shape was moving upward. Gray stone walls were inky in the night. No eye could have discerned the ascent of the cloaked figure that was nearing the very window that Rudy watched.

A gloved hand clutched the windowsill. A slouch hat came up beside it. The Shadow was outside of Renstrom's window; still Rudy did not observe the black-clad arrival. The Shadow had chosen the side away from the light in Renstrom's study. The glow produced an optical illusion that Rudy could not observe from the car.

Thanks to the depth of the inner windowsill, there was a vertical streak of blackness along the opening. That narrow, shaded space looked like part of the wall. The Shadow was taking advantage of the projecting darkness to keep out of sight while he looked into the study.

He saw Renstrom at a desk stacked high with papers. The actuary had written something on a small pad and was staring at the penciled line. Then, with a nervous gesture, he crumpled the paper and looked for a wastebasket. None being at hand, Renstrom swung about in his swivel chair and began to turn the dial of a safe.

From somewhere in the house a clock began to chime the hour of ten. During the strokes Renstrom drew the safe door open, thrust one hand inward.

It was as if he had touched a hidden spring to produce a cataclysm. The whole room shuddered with a burst of tremendous light. The strokes of the clock were drowned by a deafening burst of sound that rose to a gigantic roar.

With that blast Renstrom was flung across the room like a discarded scarecrow. The door of the safe mouthed flame like the muzzle of a howitzer. Furniture was scattered into bits by the explosion.

The door of the room was shattered by the concussion. So were the window sashes above The Shadow's head. They were actually ripped to slivers by the blast.

The Shadow wasn't present to receive the spray of glass. Hurled outward by the explosion, he was a somersaulting figure in midair, his long arms sweeping wide as his gloved hands clutched uselessly to regain a vanished hold.

**Hurled outward by the explosion, The Shadow
was a somersaulting figure in midair.**

Shouts rose as the explosion's echoes faded. Crooks had seen the cloaked shape, revealed by the vivid glare. Returning darkness swallowed The Shadow below the gray stone walls; but watchers had marked the direction of his plunge.

Planned death, delivered to Albert Renstrom, had produced a greater prize. Tossed into the very midst of surrounding crooks, The Shadow had become crime's prey!

CHAPTER V
CLUES TO CRIME

FLASHLIGHTS glimmered as thugs thrust themselves through the hedge, seeking to close in upon The Shadow. Rudy Waygart, standing on the step of the sedan, was peering across the top of the hedge to direct the search.

With a triumphant snarl, Rudy pointed to something black that showed on the ground beyond the hedge. A crook scooped it up; the object was The Shadow's slouch hat. Eagerly, flashlights circled in an effort to find the hat's vanished owner.

One torch steadied. The man who held it saw something stir. He aimed his revolver; the others heard a gun bark. The shot wasn't from the crook's revolver. He was on the receiving end of that prompt blast. There was a cry, a staggery sound in the darkness. The flashlight struck the ground along with its owner.

Rudy saw the spot where the gun had spurted. He located the weird, challenging laugh that followed the report. Both came from the middle of the hedge, a dozen paces from the place where Rudy's car was parked. In a flash the murderer understood.

The Shadow's long hurtle hadn't ended in a disastrous crash. The cloaked fighter wasn't out of combat as crooks supposed. Instead of striking unyielding ground, to lie there senseless, The Shadow had landed in the high hedge. Wedged in the midst of springy branches, he had escaped with no injuries worse than scratches.

Diving away from the car, Rudy fired, hoping that his gun stabs would point out the direction to the others. He preferred to chance wild shots rather than run the risk of becoming The Shadow's target. It was lucky for Rudy that he dodged, for The Shadow promptly returned the fire.

Where Rudy's slugs merely clipped leaves from the hedge, The Shadow's whizzed close to the ducking murderer. Flattening beyond the car, Rudy decided to let his gunners handle the fray.

The Shadow chose that interval to wriggle from the hedge. Creeping along the ground, he was seeking the shelter of the house; from there he intended to bait his foemen. On the way he found the slouch hat that a crook had dropped. Clamping the hat on his head, The Shadow continued his crawl.

Things were changed suddenly when a flashlight bored from the window of Renstrom's study. Crooks were ducking when the roving glare reached them; floundering through the hedge, they rolled to safety below a low bank beyond.

Joe Cardona had reached the blasted room. Hearing gunfire outdoors, he had hurried to the window. Cardona was firing at the crooks as fast as his flashlight picked them out; but the range was long and Joe's aim too hasty.

The Shadow could have settled the fleeing tribe had he been in Cardona's position; but the ground level put him at a disadvantage. By the time The Shadow reached the hedge, Rudy was at the wheel of the car, driving away, while thugs clambered to the running board, dragging a wounded pal with them.

Only one man remained on the ground: the gunner that The Shadow had dropped early in the fray.

Reversing his course, The Shadow rounded the house to reach a lane at the rear. There was another car available: the one that had brought The Shadow here. He still had a chance of intercepting Rudy's crew somewhere in this neighborhood.

A big official car came along the front street, pausing as it neared Renstrom's driveway. It was bringing Commissioner Weston, for Cardona had remembered to call the Cobalt Club along about twenty minutes of ten.

As Weston's chauffeur veered toward the driveway, a sedan rocketed from the opposite direction. Foreseeing a crash, the chauffeur shoved the big car into reverse. Skidding, the sedan swerved alongside and stopped. Ugly-faced men poked gun muzzles from the windows, intending to avenge their recent defeat by murdering the police commissioner.

Rudy's crew never had a chance to fire. A limousine swung from the corner; a passenger in the back seat recognized the sedan and opened with a fire that sounded like a cannonade. Rudy knew who was bringing rescue, even though Weston didn't.

The Shadow!

WITH gunners slumping at the windows, Rudy yanked the sedan up into Renstrom's driveway.

With the car speeding forward, he saw a garage looming ahead. Jerking the wheel, Rudy swerved across the lawn in back of the house, tore a path through a hedge and bounced across the bank beyond.

Shoving the car into high gear, he took to speedy flight, carrying three sagging passengers with him.

On the front street, Commissioner Weston was shaking hands with his rescuer, who had alighted from the limousine. As they stepped into the glare of headlights, Weston was amazed to recognize Cranston, who had left the Cobalt Club sometime before him.

It turned out that Cranston had come to visit a friend in this vicinity and was quite as surprised as Weston at this unexpected meeting. He had heard a distant explosion, followed by gunfire, and had ordered his chauffeur to turn in that direction.

As for the rescue, Cranston calmly belittled it to a point where Weston decided that it had actually been anything but spectacular. Remarking that he had one of the commissioner's permits to carry a gun in the limousine, Cranston declared that the other car had fled the moment he opened fire.

Crooks had weakened; that was all. Weston agreed that such must have been the case. Had the commissioner been able to glimpse Rudy's passengers he would have realized that they had weakened to the point of complete collapse; that bullets, not lack of nerve, had accounted for their sudden disinterest in continuing the battle.

Together, Weston and The Shadow entered the Renstrom house. They found Cardona at the top of the stairs; the ace inspector wasn't surprised to see Cranston with the commissioner, for the two were often together.

Briefly, Joe explained what had happened; then led the way to the ruined study. A lamp was aglow on a half-shattered table that stood in the corner. Its light showed Renstrom lying close to the threshold.

The actuary's glasses were gone; his dead eyes had a bulgy stare. His fists were clenched, as though he had made a last mad effort to battle invisible enemies.

"The mob must have chucked a pineapple through the window," stated Cardona. "That's the only way they could have wrecked the place. I don't know why they started shooting afterward. They may have seen us through the downstairs windows and tried to clip us."

Merwood inclined to Cardona's theory of a bomb from outdoors. He had been with Cardona, in the living room, when the explosion occurred. Dashing up, they had met Janet on the stairway, in time to save her from a spill to the bottom.

The girl claimed that the whole house had been shaken by the blast. She kept repeating it and seemed too dazed to remember anything except that her uncle was dead. Merwood's sympathy seemed to soothe her, so the others left Janet with him while they entered the study.

None of Renstrom's papers remained. They had caught fire after the explosion; Cardona and Daniel, the old servant, had managed to extinguish the blaze, but had failed to salvage the documents that the law wanted.

The door of the safe was wide; its contents had been transformed to junk. Cardona suggested that the crooks had thrown the bomb in at an angle, knowing that Renstrom would be near the safe.

"They couldn't have souped the thing," argued Cardona. "Only Renstrom had the combination. Still they wanted the dispatch box that was in there and they must have gotten it. The box is gone."

Joe realized suddenly that he was disputing his own theory. He looked anxiously at Weston, fearing that the commissioner would call him for it.

Before Weston could speak, The Shadow offered Cardona a chance to display new headwork. Picking up a chunk of metal that lay on the floor, he handed it to the inspector. The thing was the lock of a cheap dispatch box.

Casually, The Shadow remarked: "You said that Renstrom had a key to—"

Cardona interrupted by hurrying to Renstrom's body; he brought back the key that he found in the dead man's vest pocket. It fitted the lock, which brought Cardona to the conclusion that the key was the right one.

By that time The Shadow was producing more fragments of the box.

"Odd, how the box seems to have blown outward," was Cranston's next remark. "Curious, too, the way the pieces scattered to all corners of the room."

"I've got it!" exclaimed Cardona. "The bomb was in the box! It was delivered here to get rid of Renstrom!"

JOE didn't notice the slight smile that appeared upon Cranston's lips. The Shadow had put across the point he wanted, giving Cardona credit for it. The box that Renstrom had received was a death device containing a time bomb set for ten o'clock.

Already The Shadow had linked this death with the affray at the Hotel Thurmont. Though he hadn't seen Rudy Waygart in the darkness, he had heard the murderer's voice.

Somehow, though, facts didn't quite fit. While Cardona was poking about for more clues, The Shadow picked up the lock and key to study them more closely.

In the hallway, Cardona found a knob from the shattered door. Bringing it into the room, he produced a small brush and a tiny bottle of powdered graphite. He was examining the knob for fingerprints, while Weston and Cranston were viewing Renstrom's body.

"Too bad," remarked the commissioner with a headshake, "that Renstrom was unable to leave us a single clue. He didn't even show that letter to Merwood—and now it's gone, along with all the papers that were on Renstrom's desk!"

"Not quite all, Commissioner."

With that comment, The Shadow stooped forward and gripped the fingers of Renstrom's clenched left hand. It took an effort to pry open the dead fist, but when it came, a crumpled paper fell to the floor.

Picking up the little wad, The Shadow handed it to Weston. The commissioner supposed that Cranston had noted a corner of the paper poking between Renstrom's fingers.

Weston unfolded the slip. It bore what appeared to be a word, and an odd one, penciled in capital letters:

ADICO

Deciding that the word was a name, Weston stepped out to the hallway to question Merwood and Janet. He asked if either had ever heard of a person known as Adico.

Both shook their heads. Daniel was there, also, but he was positive that Renstrom had never mentioned the name to him.

Cardona came from the wrecked study to look at the sheet of paper. Joe's fingers were covered with graphite that smeared the edges of the slip when he handled it. Passing the paper to the others, Cardona insisted that they study the name and try to jog their memories.

Merwood, Daniel, finally Janet, all insisted in turn that the name "Adico" still mystified them.

Cardona took the paper to a bright lamp on the hallway table, studied it, along with the knob from the study door. Laying both objects aside, he swung about, triumph registered on his face.

"There's one person who can tell us who Adico is," insisted Cardona. "We won't have to look far for the person in question. I mean someone who can tell us plenty besides; a person who had a lot to do with murder."

Shoving a hand forward, Cardona clamped his fingers on Janet's wrist and smothered the girl's startled outcry with the firm announcement:

"I mean *you*, Miss Renstrom!"

CHAPTER VI
THE MAN FROM THE DARK

AFTER a few frantic protests, Janet Renstrom became very earnest in declaring her innocence of crime. Taken at face value, Cardona's theory seemed wild. Of all persons, Janet seemed least likely to have played a part in her uncle's death.

Commissioner Weston evidently thought so. He insisted that Cardona produce proof before pressing the charge further. Obligingly, Joe showed the doorknob and the slip of paper, pointing out identical fingerprints on both.

"I found those prints on the knob," explained Cardona. "They looked like a woman's; that's why I smudged the note with graphite and let other people handle it. I was watching this girl very closely; those fingerprints are hers."

"Of course they are," agreed Janet. She paused to brush away tears that streaked her cheeks. "I stopped at the study door and was about to open it, just before I started downstairs. Then I thought I'd better make sure that it was ten o'clock before I disturbed my uncle. The clock began to strike when I reached the stairs."

The statement had the ring of truth; but Cardona did not accept it. He acted as though he expected Janet to produce an alibi.

"You made a phone call," Joe told the girl, "just after you came upstairs. Would you mind telling us where you called, and why?"

The color faded from Janet's face. Then, rallying, the girl replied:

"There was a message for me to call that number. Who it came from, I don't know."

"Do you remember what the number was?"

Janet pondered; at last she shook her head. She declared that the explosion and the shock of her uncle's death had driven such recollections from her head. Her nerve restored, she spoke in convincing style, but Cardona considered her statement to be an alibi.

So did The Shadow. He had learned what Cardona had noted earlier: that Janet was trying to cover up something.

Cardona decided to call the girl's bluff. Picking up the telephone, he gave a Manhattan number. The Shadow's keen eyes watched Janet's face, detected a tightening of the girl's lips, which neither Weston nor Merwood observed. Getting the number, Cardona asked for Room 312, and talked to someone there.

After a brief conversation, Joe thrust the telephone into Janet's hands and told the girl to speak. He added that she was to talk the way she had awhile ago, quietly, but in her normal voice.

With the slightest of winces, Janet complied. Cardona took the telephone from her and completed the conversation himself. Hanging up, he announced:

"That settles it. Do you know where this girl phoned, Commissioner? To the room at the Hotel Thurmont, where the shooting took place tonight. I left Markham there; he says she called just before ten and hung up on him. He recognized her voice again."

Swinging to Janet, Cardona demanded that she admit the truth. He expected defiance; instead, he encountered cool determination. Janet was quite prepared to tie Joe into many knots.

"Of course I called there," said the girl as though she at last remembered the number. "I was to ask for Room 312. The message said so."

Turning to Daniel, Cardona asked if the servant had given Janet any such message. Daniel shook his head. Promptly, Cardona snapped:

"Answer that one, Miss Renstrom."

"My uncle gave me the message," said the girl, her voice choking. "He had received the call and thought it was from one of my college chums. They often come to New York."

This time Janet was lying, and The Shadow knew it. Cardona suspected the same thing but couldn't prove it. However, he had made a good start. He asked if he could grill Janet further, and Weston finally agreed.

THEY went down to the living room, where Cardona began his quiz. He repeated previous questions, and Janet gave the same answers. Weston was standing at the doorway with Cranston. The commissioner heard his friend undertone:

"Sorry I can't stay until Cardona finishes. I wouldn't like to arrive home late for breakfast."

Commissioner Weston watched Cranston stroll out to the limousine. The big car drove away. Turning to Merwood, Weston saw that the financier was still smiling at Cranston's parting quip. By mutual agreement the two retired to the library, which was across the hall.

"I can't imagine what Janet could be hiding," declared Merwood seriously. "She cared a great deal for her uncle. I can't believe that she would have helped plot his death. Who was the occupant of that hotel room, Commissioner?"

"A man named Hotchkiss," replied Weston. "He disappeared, and we think that he may have been registered under an assumed name."

Merwood couldn't remember any friend of Renstrom's named Hotchkiss. He was saying so when Daniel appeared, admitting a pair of headquarters detectives. They had nothing new to report; Daniel had brought them to the library to avoid interrupting Cardona's questioning.

Grilling the girl was a tougher matter than Cardona had expected. Pacing the living room, Joe stopped at intervals to demand if Janet knew a man named Hotchkiss.

The girl shook her head each time; when Cardona suddenly shifted to the mysterious Adico, Janet wrinkled her forehead in perplexed fashion.

"Really, Inspector," she said earnestly, "if I could help you find my uncle's murderer, I would. I assure you—"

"I don't want assurances," interjected Joe angrily. "I want answers, and the right ones! I've wasted half an hour, getting nowhere. But I'm going to keep at it until I get results!"

A telephone bell was ringing. Daniel answered the downstairs extension, then came to the living room.

"For you, Inspector."

Cardona went to the telephone. From the hallway he could still see Janet, seated in a chair near a heavily curtained doorway. Despite the distance, Cardona observed a horrified expression come over the girl's face. He decided that she had thought of something that disturbed her conscience. Joe intended to make the most of it when he resumed the grilling.

What Cardona did not see was the gun muzzle that poked through the curtains within sight of Janet's eyes. Nor did he catch the raspy voice that reached the girl's ears:

"Stay as you are! Give me the nod when that cluck gets busy on the telephone."

Janet sat tight. She could hear Cardona shouting at the telephone, telling the caller to talk louder. The girl gave a nod; a folded paper skimmed through the curtains and landed in her lap.

"Open it," came the order. "Read it; then put it away. Remember what it says."

Trembling, Janet began to unfold the note. A sudden clatter stopped her. Cardona had flung down the telephone, was lunging into the room. He had spied the note and regarded it as new evidence.

With a shriek, Janet flung herself forward. The gun blasted from between the curtains; but the shot was late. Away from immediate harm, Janet forgot her own plight, fearing for Cardona. Desperately, she threw herself upon the inspector, hoping to hurry him out into the hall.

Cardona was already plucking the note from Janet's hand. With a quick clutch he grasped the girl's arm, swung her about and propelled her into the hall. Thrusting his hand into his pocket, he dropped the note and whipped out a gun.

All in the same move, Cardona was ducking for a table on the other side of the room, while the hidden gunner was spurting another shot from the curtains.

Men were coming from the library: Merwood, Weston, and the two detectives. Janet shrieked the words:

"It must be Adico—he's here!"

THEY saw Cardona lunging for the curtains. Like Janet, he had escaped the gunfire. Joe was ripping the curtain with bullets from a Police Positive, trying to down the man on the other side. But the invader was no longer there. He had cut through a rear room, seeking an outlet.

Detectives dashed along the hallway. Daniel was pointing to the pantry door. Yanking it open, the two detectives met the fugitive in darkness. They were slugging it out with him when Cardona arrived from another door.

Flashing a light, Joe hoped to find the mysterious Adico and settle scores with the killer. Again, the ace inspector missed his chance. The detectives were reeling back; Cardona's flashlight showed a swinging door. The foe was fleeing through the kitchen.

Daniel pressed switches that illuminated outside lights. Reaching the back door, Cardona could see for twenty yards, but he saw no sign of Adico, nor anyone else. The detectives appeared, coming from a side route, where Daniel had headed them, but they had seen no one on the way.

Rounding to the front of the house, Cardona and his reinforcements met Weston and Merwood, who had gone out through the front door. Joined by the puzzled Daniel, all wondered what had become of the enemy they sought.

The man from the dark had made good his escape. Remembering how Rudy had bashed through hedges, Weston decided that Adico had done the same. He set the detectives to work probing the sides of the lawn; then, with a rueful headshake, the commissioner decided that he had set that task too late.

Janet was seated limply in the living room when Weston and Cardona returned. Merwood came with them and gave the girl an approving nod. Janet smiled, realizing that her heroic effort in Cardona's behalf had squared her with the law.

Questioned, Janet told exactly what had happened, and gave a good description of Adico's raspy voice. When she mentioned the note, Cardona produced it and handed it to Weston, who read its contents carefully.

"This clears you, Miss Renstrom," decided the commissioner briskly. "You read it, didn't you?"

"I was starting to—"

"Read all of it," suggested Weston, handing her the paper. "But don't let it worry you. We shall guarantee you full protection against Adico, whoever he may be."

An hour before, the note might have given Janet a feeling of dread. Under present circumstances it did not trouble her. The explosion, her uncle's death, Cardona's questioning had stiffened her courage.

In fact, Janet smiled somewhat grimly as she read the note.

It seemed that men of crime had struck a snag at last. Janet Renstrom had escaped a murderous thrust; and with it—as Commissioner Weston testified—crooks themselves had cleared her of any complicity in their evil schemes!

CHAPTER VII
WITHIN THE CORDON

THE note was scrawled in red ink, as though the writer had disguised his hand. The blood-red color made Janet shudder, despite her restored confidence.

Somehow the vivid hue made the threat seem real, as Janet read:

> Do not inform the police that your uncle gave you the message to call the Hotel Thurmont. Failure to keep silence will bring death.
>
> ADICO

The message brought home two points: first, that Janet's previous testimony had been correct; second, that Adico was her enemy. Coming from a foe, the note helped the girl more than if a friend had sent it, for she had been under suspicion at the time when it arrived.

There was a puzzling factor in the message; one that caused Janet to feel somewhat stupefied. She kept staring at the crimson ink until Commissioner Weston approached and laid a reassuring hand upon her shoulder.

"You shall be amply protected," he assured. "I have instructed Inspector Cardona to place a police cordon here about the house. If Adico returns, we shall give him a warm reception."

It wasn't long before a squad of police arrived. Cardona posted them, then left in the official car with Weston, Merwood, and the two detectives.

Renstrom's body had gone out awhile before; as Janet stood on the front steps, saying good night to Merwood, she shuddered at the recollection of her uncle's last journey.

"You have all my sympathy, Janet," said Merwood in parting. "Remember that I counted your uncle among my best friends. Do not worry about danger."

"I'm worrying about you, Mr. Merwood."

"Because your uncle told me about the letter?" queried Merwood. "That is a minor matter, Janet. Evidently Adico has guessed that I did not actually see it, and that I have no idea who sent it. After all, the threat from Adico was delivered to you, not to me."

Commissioner Weston didn't quite agree that Merwood was entirely safe. He declared that the two detectives would accompany the financier to his apartment in Manhattan; that they would be detailed there, guarding Merwood until further notice.

With that they were off, and Janet walked back into the house. Daniel was serving coffee to two detectives in the living room. They were extras who would later relieve the men posted outside.

Going up to her own room, Janet undressed. Then, in nightie and kimono, she wrapped herself in a quilt and sat down in a chair beside the window.

A chill kept sweeping her in waves, and at last she realized its cause.

Fear of Adico!

Why?

As she labored with the mental question, Janet began to visualize the scene downstairs, at the time when the man had fled from behind the living-room curtains. She could picture the route that he had followed, through the dining room, then the pantry, finally the kitchen.

But how had Adico managed to disappear from the back porch?

Janet gained a sudden answer that explained her instinctive fears. The invader had disappeared because he had not gone to the back porch at all!

Janet remembered a door in the kitchen—one that led down into the cellar. She realized that Adico must have entered by the back door; that on the way through to the front he could have seen the route to the cellar and left it open for emergency.

Adico might still be in the house!

MADLY, Janet flung the quilt aside. She stumbled to a bureau, opened the drawer and drew out a tiny automatic that her uncle had once given her. Fumblingly, she loaded the gun.

What use was an outside cordon and police downstairs when Adico could easily come up by the back way from the kitchen and find Janet alone?

The note had promised death if Janet gave certain testimony, whether it was right or wrong. She had made the forbidden statement; namely, that her uncle had told her to call Room 312 at the Hotel Thurmont. At any moment, Adico's stroke might come!

Janet was tempted to shriek from the window; then realized that it would be folly. Better to talk to the detectives downstairs, tell them her suspicions and let them trap Adico.

Opening the door of the room, Janet turned toward the front stairs. Sensing something in the hallway behind her, she darted a look over her shoulder.

A figure from darkness made a sudden, amazing lunge. Two powerful hands gripped Janet. Whirled about, she actually felt that she was flying through the air.

Her rapid trip ended when she found herself half sprawled in the quilt-draped chair beside the window.

Janet's captor was a huge creature of blackness, ghostly rather than human.

A whispered laugh drifted through the room. Though weird in tone, it carried no menace. On the contrary it gave Janet a sudden lift of confidence; particularly as the gun in the visitor's hand was immediately withdrawn.

Janet made out the cloaked shape and hatted head of the singular visitor as he seated himself upon the windowsill.

Against the faint moonlight, the being in black was slightly visible from Janet's angle; but it would be impossible for patrolling detectives to observe his form against the darkness of the room.

Whoever he was, the stranger could not be Adico, the one enemy that Janet feared. The girl understood the reason for the swift action in the hall. Confronted by a gun, knowing that Janet would shriek for aid, the mysterious invader had but one choice: to overpower the girl.

At present his attitude was one of protection. At the window the cloaked personage was able to keep track of events outside and

Against the faint moonlight, the being in black was slightly visible from Janet's angle.

also watch the door of the room. Anxious to know his identity, Janet began:

"You... you are—"

"The Shadow!"

By his own pronouncement of the name, The Shadow seemed to speak of things mysterious. Thoughts flashed to Janet's mind; she remembered the talk of defeated crooks at the Hotel Thurmont; of battle outside this very house. She felt, somehow, that The Shadow must have remained in this vicinity after that. The thought caused her to blurt a question:

"Did you find Adico?"

The Shadow laughed. His low-toned mirth promised a remarkable answer, which promptly came.

"Not exactly," returned The Shadow. "I *was* Adico."

"You... you were—"

"I was acting in your behalf, to free you from the burden of unfair suspicion. You told an unwise falsehood when you said that your uncle had given you the message to call the Hotel Thurmont."

Amazed, Janet tried to figure how The Shadow knew. She realized that Adico was probably an imaginary person; that The Shadow had made the most of that supposed personality, merely to relieve her from the ordeal that Cardona had begun.

Further, Janet saw The Shadow's purpose. Knowing the truth, probably possessed of facts that the law had not learned, The Shadow had wanted to question her himself.

Janet didn't connect The Shadow with Cranston. Because of The Shadow's mysterious ways, she supposed that he had been listening in on Cardona's quiz, and thereby discovered the situation.

IT wasn't necessary for The Shadow to use Cardona's grilling tactics. He had already broken Janet's story; the girl was ready to talk. But before she could speak a word, The Shadow made a statement that amazed her.

"You knew that a man named Parron was at the Hotel Thurmont, in Room 312. That is why you phoned there."

Janet nodded.

"Ronald told me where he was," she admitted. "He asked me to keep it secret, saying that I would understand later. Tonight I saw him come to the house and deliver a box for my uncle. Daniel didn't know who it was, but I saw Ronald before he muffled his face."

"Parron delivered the box that caused your uncle's death. Yet you shielded him—"

"Because I knew that Ronald couldn't be responsible for what happened later. He never would have told me where he was if he had plotted my uncle's death."

There was logic in what Janet said. Moreover, it fitted with what The Shadow had himself discovered. Not only did he know that Parron had tried to shake loose from the murder ring that operated under the title of Adico; but The Shadow had evidence to substantiate the fact.

He produced the evidence: the little key and the lock of the shattered dispatch box. Janet had last seen those objects in Cardona's possession; she supposed that Joe had laid them somewhere and that The Shadow had picked them up.

Handing the articles to Janet, The Shadow remarked in quiet whisper:

"The key fits. Try to turn it."

The key fitted; rather loosely, it seemed. But it wouldn't turn the lock when Janet tried it. She couldn't quite grasp the answer, though she knew there must be one. The Shadow supplied it.

"Parron mailed the key," he stated, "and intended to deliver the box that it would open. Someone entered Parron's room and substituted a different box, loaded with a bomb, instead of documents pertaining to the murder ring.

"The fact that a killer named Rudy Waygart was waiting for Parron when he returned makes it obvious that crooks could have entered the hotel room while Parron was absent earlier."

Janet's expression tightened. Solemnly, she questioned:

"What happened to Ronald?"

"He is dead," replied The Shadow. "Our mission, therefore, becomes one of double vengeance. We must settle scores for the deaths of Ronald Parron and Albert Renstrom."

Bravely accepting the news of Parron's death, Janet gave prompt agreement to The Shadow's plan. His use of the term "we" inspired her with the hope that she could play a part in the coming campaign. The Shadow emphasized that very point.

"Parron was linked with a crooked gang," affirmed The Shadow. "When he learned that they dealt in murder, he tried to reveal it to your uncle, who was the proper man to explain the situation to the law.

"To protect himself, Parron did not reveal who he was. He probably had your interests in mind when he did so. Crooks managed to destroy the information that Parron sent your uncle. We must replace that information."

An excellent idea, thought Janet; but she wondered where they would begin. She was puzzled, too, about how she could help. When she put such questions, The Shadow answered them.

"Having known Parron well," The Shadow told her, "you can learn the names of persons who were friends of his. It is likely that some of his friends have died recently. I should like to know who they were, along with Parron's living acquaintances."

Rising from the windowsill, The Shadow drew a white envelope from his cloak and gave it to Janet. He said that it contained a simple code that she could easily memorize. She was to study it the moment that she opened the envelope.

"The writing will fade soon after you read it," cautioned The Shadow, "hence it will be unnecessary to destroy the paper. In giving me any names by telephone, spell them with the code letters. Always remember that someone may be watching you; therefore, trust no one."

Trust no one!

That thought dominated after Janet had watched The Shadow glide from the room to merge with the hallway's darkness. By no one, The Shadow had not included himself. That went without saying, and the fact was significant in itself.

Janet felt chilled no longer. She burned with eagerness to begin the task that The Shadow had assigned her. Nor had she forgotten the final words of caution.

She would trust no one but The Shadow!

CHAPTER VIII
THE FINGER POINTS

THREE days had passed; with them the excitement over the Renstrom murder had simmered down considerably. The police had obtained Parron's body from Dr. Sayre, and the clerk at the Hotel Thurmont had identified the dead man as the missing Hotchkiss.

Afterward, Parron's actual identity had been discovered, and it was generally conceded that he must have been a victim of crime. For there was no link between Parron and any known crooks.

In talking to reporters, Commissioner Weston declared that any rumor of a murder ring must be sheer exaggeration. It was probable, of course, that Parron had discovered the workings of some criminal racket that had death connected with it. However, assuming that Parron had informed Renstrom, it was probable that the latter had over-estimated the matter.

Renstrom was an actuary; his mind had been trained in terms of life and death, from the standpoint of statistics.

Along with that assertion the commissioner furnished an explanation for the murders. Having learned too much about things that did not concern them, Parron and Renstrom had been slain. But the manner of their death was, in itself, proof that a murder ring was not behind it.

The killers were bunglers. They had left dead mobsmen on the field. In short, when it came to murder, they lacked finesse. Claiming that the law had taken toll of almost all the mobbies involved, Weston declared that the case had resolved itself into a simple search for the leader who had headed the criminal band.

Privately, of course, Weston was troubled. In his office he frequently mulled over the chart that The Shadow had sent. Its conflicting lines bothered him, and he hadn't forgotten the fading silhouette that had been impressed upon the graphic message.

He believed, however, that by refraining from any mention of The Shadow, he would aid the cloaked investigator in the search for an actual master of murder.

Weston was still thinking in terms of Adico. As yet, neither the commissioner nor Inspector Cardona had gotten a lead to Rudy Waygart.

Meanwhile, The Shadow was considering a problem of his own. Janet had furnished him with the names he wanted. At first the list had been a disappointment. None of Parron's friends had died recently, nor did any of them appear to be important enough to be in danger.

Nevertheless, The Shadow had not discarded the list. Instead he had put certain of his secret agents to work upon it—such men as Harry Vincent, who had access to privileged social groups; and Rutledge Mann, an investment broker, whose clients were wealthy persons.

Likewise, in his guise of Lamont Cranston, The Shadow was actively checking on various deaths that looked suspicious, particularly among the select class covered by Renstrom's mortality figures. From such extended research, The Shadow had gained a very important fact.

Parron's friends were still alive; but some of their friends had met with sudden death!

FOR example, Reggie Chitterton. The polo player had a cousin, Alan Grake, who was due to claim Reggie's inheritance from their mutual grandfather. At present, Grake was abroad, had been for nearly a year. Attorneys were handling the inheritance for him.

There were other cases: a business rival of one of Parron's friends had died quite suddenly. A second instance: one of Parron's pals had owed money to a wealthy chum, presumably quite a large sum. But it had turned out to be very small after the chum in question was killed in an automobile crash.

Again both of Parron's friends were away. This proved a valuable link as The Shadow considered Janet's list. In his sanctum, The Shadow checked further facts and came to one that intrigued him.

From the list he chose a name, wrote it separately in ink of vivid blue:

CLAUDE JUBLE

The writing faded, while The Shadow gave a mirthless, whispered laugh. Then, on the same sheet of paper, The Shadow's hand inscribed the name of a man well-known to Juble, but not to Parron:

TYRUS VAYNE

Facts were definite. Claude Juble was the junior partner in an importing firm; his senior, Tyrus Vayne, was the real head of the business. Vayne & Co., it was called; but there was talk that it might, someday, be Vayne & Juble.

Then Vayne would retire and Juble would take over. Meanwhile, Vayne & Co. was gradually slipping. The business was moderate, but profitable. It might not be so in a few years if Vayne continued at the helm, for the senior partner was old-fashioned in his methods and persisted in continuing them.

For nearly a year, The Shadow learned, Juble had made no effort to push his own position, though he had done so before. Juble was simply keeping in the background, apparently quite content with Vayne's methods.

In fact, Juble was going on a vacation. He had intended to leave last week on a cruise, but reports of storms at sea had caused him to postpone the trip.

As Vayne's name faded from the sheet, The Shadow extinguished the sanctum light. Again a laugh sounded in the darkness. Though the curtained room was pitch black, it was still daylight outdoors. There was time for The Shadow to complete an important plan.

SOON afterward, a visitor was ushered into the private office of Tyrus Vayne. He introduced himself as Lamont Cranston, which produced a beaming smile and a warm handshake from the elderly importer. Vayne knew that Cranston was a millionaire globetrotter. The interview might mean business.

It did.

The business was much bigger than Vayne supposed. Idly smoking one of Vayne's best cigars, Cranston placidly proposed a deal that held Vayne breathless.

"On my coming trip to India," stated The Shadow, "I intend to buy a rajah's treasure house. It will cost me a considerable sum; perhaps"—he flicked the ash from the cigar— "it will run to half a million dollars. But that amount can be tripled inside two years, with your cooperation."

Vayne let his lips move silently before he managed to ask:

"Just how?"

"Your concern can import the gems," explained The Shadow, "and sell them at a tremendous profit, although the prices will be bargains here in America. The first purchase will lead to others; therefore it is advisable that we should organize as a new corporation."

Eagerly, Vayne agreed to the proposal. It was then that The Shadow brought up another angle. His tone was sympathetic as he declared:

"I intend to bring in other investors, Mr. Vayne. I am afraid that they will insist that a more active man head the new corporation. We shall need you in an advisory capacity, and you will share the profits, but young blood will be needed."

Vayne swallowed the bait in a single gulp. A generous man at heart, the old importer suggested the very thing that The Shadow expected.

"Wouldn't Juble do?" queried Vayne. "He's practically my full partner. He is young, capable, and knows the importing business. Ask anyone who knows; they will tell you that Claude Juble has a future in our trade."

"I agree with you," returned The Shadow. "Juble will be acceptable as president of the corporation. Provided, of course, that he will be satisfied with the salary that we are able to offer him."

"How much would that be?"

"Fifty thousand dollars." Naming the figure, The Shadow added, rather hastily: "Of course, we could guarantee an increase after the first year—"

No more was necessary. Vayne had almost collapsed behind his desk. Finally managing to grasp his telephone, he called Juble's apartment and poured forth the news. Finishing the call, he sat back and mopped his forehead.

"Juble intended to leave tonight on a cruise," said Vayne. "I told him to unpack instead. He wanted to come down here to the office right away when he heard your offer, but I suggested that he meet me at my penthouse.

"This is a wonderful chance for Juble, Mr. Cranston! You may think that your offer is an ordinary one, but I can assure you that it is far beyond what either Juble or I would have expected. Your associates must be very wealthy, like yourself."

The Shadow assured Vayne that they were. He named a few of the men that he thought would be interested, and decided to telephone them at once, to line them up as a board of directors. He purposely picked names that would impress Vayne.

Among them, The Shadow chose Thomas Merwood. The financier had lately been in the news, because of events at Renstrom's. Vayne promptly recognized Merwood's name, as The Shadow expected. There was another reason, however, why The Shadow called Merwood.

Weston and Merwood had discussed the possible existence of a murder ring. Like the police commissioner, the financier had expressed some doubt as to the extent of its activity. Both had agreed, however, that there might be something deep behind the mysterious Adico, whomever or whatever it represented.

According to The Shadow's calculations, Adico would be heard from again in connection with Tyrus Vayne. By bringing Merwood into the coming situation, The Shadow might make more progress toward his final goal.

CRANSTON'S limousine was outside. Vayne willingly accepted an invitation to ride home in the car, since it was on the way to the Cobalt Club. Dusk was deepening while they rode along, and all the while Vayne kept repeating his gratitude to Cranston.

The car paused in front of a secluded apartment house. Leaving it, Vayne entered the building. Before ordering the chauffeur to drive on, The Shadow looked upward to Vayne's penthouse, a dozen stories above the street.

In the penthouse, a lurking visitor was lying in wait for Vayne, this tragic evening. That visitor was death!

Only one person could prevent it. From beneath the rear seat of the limousine, Lamont Cranston was drawing garments of black that reposed in a hidden sliding drawer.

The Shadow was planning a daring course—one that meant risk for Vayne as well as for himself. A necessary course, however, for its purpose was to make crime show its hand.

If all went well, Tyrus Vayne would soon be expressing newer, greater gratitude to someone other than Lamont Cranston; at least, so Vayne would believe.

Vayne's thanks would be given to The Shadow!

CHAPTER IX
DEATH FINDS A WAY

DEEP in a comfortable chair, Tyrus Vayne smiled contentedly as he looked around the living room of his tiny penthouse. He was getting old, Vayne was, and he had realized lately that he looked it.

He felt, though, that today's conference with Cranston had relieved him of many years. Business worries were the thing that had aged Vayne. They were over, and he was actually sprightly.

A polite voice spoke. It was Harkin, Vayne's new servant. Rising from his chair, Vayne inquired:

"Dinner already, Harkin?"

"Not yet, sir," replied the servant. "It's Mr. Juble. He just phoned from downstairs. He's coming up."

Vayne met Juble at the elevator. Clapping his junior partner on the shoulder, he started him into the living room, talking all the way.

"It's the chance of a lifetime, Claude! The very sort of opportunity that I've dreamed about for years. I'm not too old to have a share of it, but you are the person who will really profit. You'd better forget about going on a cruise in order to be here when we form the corporation—"

Vayne stopped. To his amazement, Vayne saw a different Juble than he had expected. The young man did not show a single trace of enthusiasm.

Usually, Juble showed poise; tonight he was worried. Steady eyes had become restless; lips that customarily smiled were twitchy. Juble's whole expression was haggard.

"Why, tell me, what's the matter, Claude?"

Juble didn't immediately reply to Vayne's question. Half choking, he asked for a drink; Vayne had Harkin bring one. Gulping it in a single swallow, Juble clanked his glass on a table, then faltered the warning:

"You're in danger, Tyrus! Great danger... more than I can describe! You've got to go away... right off... in a hurry! Here"—he thrust an envelope into Vayne's hand—"take these tickets. Go on that cruise in my place."

"Nonsense!" returned Vayne. "Why, we're both needed here, to organize the new company. Cranston said so. They'll only offer you the presidency on my recommendation."

Juble's clutch tightened on Vayne's arm.

"That's just it!" said the young man hoarsely. "If anything happened to you, I'd—"

Vayne's eyes sharpened as Juble faltered. His own calm maintained, Vayne completed the sentence.

"You would lose out," he stated. "Am I right in inferring that your sudden concern for my safety is inspired wholly by your hope of personal profit?"

The words struck home. For the first time in their long association, Vayne was recognizing Juble's actual character. The fellow was a grasper; perhaps a plotter. In the past he had managed to hide such traits under a suave, agreeable manner.

Juble tried to offset his own betrayal.

"No, no!" he insisted. "*Your* welfare comes first, Tyrus. I'm nervous; but if you'll only give me time to explain—"

Vayne waited. He watched Juble's lips twitch, saw the young man's fists clench. At last Juble regained some of his suavity; he spoke steadily, though glibly.

"I made a serious mistake," he said. "I let someone sell me a proposition which seemed quite legitimate at the time. It wasn't until later that I realized what I had done. If I could only explain—"

JUBLE halted, interrupted by a dry comment which came from the doorway. The speaker was Harkin, the new servant. The man was pointing a gun at Juble and Vayne.

"No explanations will be necessary, Juble," inserted Harkin. "Instead, we would prefer co-operation. Tonight happens to be the deadline!"

Groaning, Juble sank to a chair. Harkin concentrated upon Vayne, who went slowly backward, hands partly raised as he stared, horrified, at the gun.

"It will be very quick, Mr. Vayne," announced Harkin with a leer. "Just a tap on the back of the head; after that you won't know that you are going over the rail on the outside roof.

"You are an old man. No one will be surprised to hear that you had an attack of vertigo and fell from the penthouse terrace. You have said yourself that the rail was too low, that it worried you.

"Two witnesses will support the accident story. One will be your friend and partner, Juble. The other will he an honest, trusted servant—myself."

Juble was on his feet.

"Don't go through with it!" he gasped. "I'll buy you off! I'll pay Adico more than is coming to me! Let Vayne live; by the end of a few years he'll be worth far more to me than if he dies!"

"More to you, perhaps," sneered Harkin, "but not to Adico. It's too late, Juble. You've told too much to Vayne."

Harkin had backed slowly toward the double door that led out to a little roof terrace. Alongside the servant were two other men, who had just come from the elevator. They were a murderous-looking pair, who were to serve as Vayne's executioners.

One had drawn a blackjack, preparatory to the "tap" that Vayne was to receive when he reached the rail. The other held a revolver; he covered Vayne, while Harkin stepped forward to open the doors. At that moment Vayne looked very pitiful, almost shrunken, as he stood hemmed in by the crew of killers.

Harkin extended his hand to open the double door. At that instant both sections of the double portal ripped wide. In from the darkness came the weird challenge of a shivering laugh that brought crooks full about.

Out of the blackness that formed the outdoor background they saw thrusting gun muzzles; above them, eyes that burned with righteous fury. Flat-footed, their guns unaimed, they stood petrified by that terror from the night as they voiced, in awe, his name:

"The Shadow!"

Scaling to the penthouse terrace, The Shadow had lain in wait to spring a perfect trap. This time he was outside; crooks were inside. Behind The Shadow was ample darkness into which he could fade if necessary.

As crooks let their guns hit the floor, The Shadow motioned Vayne aside. Nodding toward a telephone, he commanded in sibilant tone:

"Summon the police!"

Vayne obeyed. His words were terse across the wire. All the while, Juble was twitchy as he watched. He didn't belong to the crooked tribe who operated under the title of Adico, but his present rating was nearly as bad.

Conflicting thoughts were stirring Juble. At moments he was calculating upon flight, wondering if The Shadow would let him get away with it. At other intervals his expression tightened as he had flashes of hope that he might redeem himself.

At least he had tried to warn Vayne; even though his motives had been selfish, Juble had actually pleaded for the old man's life. Half risen from his chair, Juble glared at the helpless crooks as though he would like to slaughter them.

It was an act calculated to impress Vayne. Recognizing Juble's pose, The Shadow concentrated upon the crooks. They were the men who had to be watched; Juble could be disregarded as a factor. Such was The Shadow's verdict, until a freak of circumstances changed it.

One crook shifted. He was the fellow who had the blackjack; he hadn't dropped it like the others had their guns. At present the blackjack was as harmless as a baby's rattle, and The Shadow had let the thug keep his toy.

Gradually, the hand with the blackjack had slid behind Harkin. With the weapon out of sight, its owner was making his shift to start a bold leap toward The Shadow, who, in his turn, was awaiting the attack.

It would simply mean a bullet for the thug; and with the fellow sprawled upon the floor, Harkin and the remaining thug would be more cowed than ever. But Juble didn't see it that way. All that he recognized was a chance for actual heroics.

Springing from his chair, Juble struck the thug full force and reeled him forward. The crook tried to grapple with one hand while he swung the black-jack with the other. The Shadow let them tangle; in his turn he made a sidestep to keep Harkin and the other thug covered.

Just then the grapplers stumbled. Headlong, they pitched against The Shadow, almost pinning him beside the door. Bowling into them, The Shadow sent them sprawling; but, again, there was a freakish twist of direction. The staggering men formed a shield for Harkin and his pal.

Servant and thug grabbed for their guns.

Wheeling, The Shadow flung Vayne behind a huge chair in the corner, then pivoted to open battle.

Guns blasted loudly, their echoes magnified by the confines of the room. Harkin's pal slumped; but the servant reached the door and turned to fire again at The Shadow.

Juble had settled the fellow with the blackjack. Seeing Harkin, he made a spring for the murderous servant. The Shadow was twisting to a new vantage point, from which he could drop Harkin after the crook delivered another futile shot. Harkin was changing aim too slowly. Frantically he fired.

That shot should have missed The Shadow by three feet. Instead, it missed him by a dozen. It never reached the wall from which The Shadow whirled. An intervening target stopped it.

The target was Juble, finishing his lunge. He had come directly into Harkin's path of fire. Staggering momentarily, Juble pitched forward. The bullet had reached his heart.

Harkin was stabbing his gun forward for another shot. In finishing Juble he hadn't suffered the slightest delay in getting a new chance at The Shadow. But the black-cloaked fighter was working split seconds ahead of Harkin. The big muzzle of a .45 smoked a shot straight for the servant.

Sprawling, his gun unfired, Harkin rolled over dead. A weird laugh of triumph pealed through the room, to the accompaniment of snarls from two wounded thugs. With the echoes of that mirth came a metallic clang. It was the door of the elevator.

FROM his corner, The Shadow saw men in blue uniform dashing toward him. With a quick turn he swung through the open doorway to the terrace, and became part of the blackness beyond it. Only Tyrus Vayne was left to greet the police and tell them of crime's defeat.

For The Shadow had another mission; one that the death of Juble had produced. Like Parron, Juble was a man who could have told much about the murder racket if only he had lived. Chances were that Juble possessed evidence, in documentary form, relating to the mysterious Adico.

Mobsters hadn't intended to slay Claude Juble. Others in the ring—Rudy Waygart, for instance—would be late in learning that Juble had died. Even though the Adico organization was geared for speed, this time The Shadow held the edge.

Off into the night, The Shadow was traveling ahead of crime, hoping to get evidence that would mark an end to murder!

CHAPTER X
CRIME'S MOTIVE

A TINY flashlight twinkled in deep darkness. Its ray, a shining disk the size of a small gold piece, was moving low along the floor, roving from one object to another. Dwindling almost to a point, it settled on the lock of a steamer trunk—Juble's trunk, which he hadn't sent to the cruise ship.

The ray enlarged; into its area came a gloved hand holding a steel lock pick. The Shadow set to work upon the trunk lock.

A clicking sound—the trunk lid went upward. Within was a tray holding some scattered objects of apparel. Lifting the tray, The Shadow found the bottom of the trunk still packed. He probed among the articles that Juble had stowed there.

Time was short. That was why The Shadow had chosen the trunk as the first place to search. If Juble had any papers pertaining to crime's game, he would not have planned to go away without them.

Nothing was in the bottom of the trunk. The fact did not deter The Shadow's search. He knew that Juble might have foreseen a routine custom's inspection upon returning from the cruise. If so, the trunk would have some hiding place that would not ordinarily be suspected.

The trunk lacked trickery. The Shadow replaced the tray, began to examine it in minute fashion. The flashlight licked along a folded edge of cloth, the tray's lining, turned over one end and glued in place. Only The Shadow's eyes could have noted the frayed edge at one portion of the cloth.

Instantly, deft fingers were at work loosening the cloth. The edge came up to reveal a slit in the woodwork. The Shadow saw the folded edge of a white paper. Drawing it from the hiding place, he laid the paper in the tray, aimed the light full upon it.

It was the most remarkable document that The Shadow had ever viewed. It looked like an insurance policy; in fact it *was* one, except that its border was printed in black, instead of the customary green.

At the top was the amazing title:

AMERICAN DEATH INSURANCE COMPANY

The word "Adico" was explained. It was formed from the initials of the outlandish corporation, with the letter "C" of "Company" followed by the next letter, "O."

Below the title was the company's symbol, a skull and crossbones. At the bottom was the amount of the policy: one hundred thousand dollars. Spreading the folded sheet, The Shadow read its terms—in engraved printing, interspersed with engrossed hand lettering:

AMERICAN DEATH INSURANCE COMPANY herewith insures the death of Tyrus Vayne and agrees to pay the sum of $100,000 upon due proof that the insured is alive after ONE YEAR following the issue of this policy. This insurance is granted in consideration of a premium of $8,786.28, paid by CLAUDE JUBLE, who will become the beneficiary in the event that the insured should survive the stated term.

At the bottom, in smaller type, The Shadow read the statement: "Form SP2. Single premium, payable in advance." On a line in a lower corner appeared the date of the policy. It proved a highly significant find. The policy was just one year old. Its term would be up tomorrow.

DEATH insurance!

Outlandish that such a thing should exist, yet here was actual proof of it. Yet, as The Shadow analyzed the matter, he saw how logical the scheme could be.

Death insurance was simply the opposite of life insurance. Instead of a man insuring his own life, someone else insured his death. The case of Claude Juble and Richard Vayne was typical.

Juble wanted to take over the importing business before it dwindled and became valueless. Since Vayne was reluctant to retire, Juble had looked forward to his death. Juble had paid the sum of nearly nine thousand dollars to make sure that Vayne died within a year.

If Vayne didn't die, Adico would owe Juble one hundred thousand dollars. Therefore, Juble would be the winner in either case. In one instance he would acquire control of a profitable business; in the other, he would gross a hundred thousand dollars.

Naturally, the Adico outfit was out to make a profit of its own. Instead of running a legitimate insurance business, the sponsors had gone in for murder, craftily disguised. Premiums paid by men like Juble were accumulated by the strange insurance organization, while claims were seldom paid—if ever—simply because insured men, like Vayne, were always slated for death!

It was easy, now, to understand Parron's relation to the racket. Like any insurance business, Adico required selling agents, and Parron had been one. He had probably believed for a while that death insurance was as legitimate as any other form, though it appeared somewhat irregular.

The reign of murder; repeated deaths of men that Parron had insured—those tragedies had convinced Parron otherwise. That was why he wanted to get out of the game and expose it through Renstrom.

Reading the policy once again, The Shadow saw how cunningly it operated. The policy was Juble's receipt for a payment. If Vayne lived, Juble could present it and collect his hundred thousand. Adico would have to pay; otherwise Juble could make the policy public and expose the game.

Had Vayne died, Juble would have immediately destroyed the policy, since its existence would incriminate him in connection with the insured

man's death. Thus Adico was amply protected in all the policies it issued.

The Shadow had expected evidence of the sort he found, but the death insurance policy was far more remarkable than his actual anticipations. In fact, it improved The Shadow's own plans. He knew that he had put a decided crimp into the racket, confronting Adico with a most pressing problem.

Tyrus Vayne was still alive. Protected by the law, Vayne was beyond another murder thrust within the time allowed. But Claude Juble was dead, therefore unable to produce the policy or destroy it. As The Shadow had foreseen, crooks would certainly have to visit his apartment to reclaim the policy before police came here to have a look around.

The Shadow listened. From the street he could hear the throbs of traffic. Occasionally a car stopped near the apartment house. Any one of those cars might be bringing a squad of professional killers, headed, probably, by Rudy Waygart.

Tonight, mobsters would expect to find The Shadow. He had crossed their paths quite often lately. They would know that he had settled matters with Harkin and the others, up at Vayne's. They would probably suppose that The Shadow had also slain Juble, bringing about the present situation.

CALMLY, The Shadow turned the flashlight toward the edge of the trunk tray, to find if other papers were concealed in the niche. He found some; they were bills for various debts, made out to different persons.

Evidently, Juble had been running in the hole financially, another reason why he had been interested in the death insurance proposition when Parron proposed it.

On a sheet of paper The Shadow listed the names and totaled the amounts owed. They came to several thousand dollars; probably all honest debts. Fingering the slips, The Shadow was struck with a new inspiration—one that brought a soft laugh from his hidden lips.

Among loose papers in a desk drawer he found some printed billheads. He tore one away, then placed the pad beneath his cloak. Resting the flashlight so its glow showed the billhead, The Shadow filled it out as follows:

> To Mr. Claude Juble
> Owed to Henry Arnaud,
> for services rendered
> $3,250.00

Folding the faked bill, The Shadow tucked it in the niche with the rest. He replaced the death insurance policy where it belonged, then began a mending job of the frayed cloth that hid the secret hollow in the trunk tray.

Creaky footsteps were sounding in the hallway. Low voices mumbled; there was a *click* from the door lock. The Shadow recognized that arriving crooks were using a lock pick, not a key. It would take them a few minutes to get the door open. Carefully, The Shadow continued his job of mending the trunk lining.

He wasn't making it look perfect. On the contrary, he took pains to make the frayed edge just obvious enough to attract attention, yet not too crude.

The Shadow wanted crooks to find the death insurance policy and the papers that were with it!

Such a find would convince them that The Shadow had not arrived ahead of them; that their game was not discovered. Even The Shadow—so crooks would reason—would not be able to resist the temptation of acquiring evidence that was so damaging to Adico.

But The Shadow reasoned otherwise.

He was sure that he had learned enough to advance far with his hidden campaign. He had paved the way to further things, that might enable him to beat murderers at their own game, provided they did not guess that he had penetrated so deeply into their schemes.

The Shadow left the half-packed trunk unlocked. He wanted to help the mobsters accomplish what they had come to do. An unlocked trunk wouldn't rouse their suspicions. They would simply suppose that Juble had been in too much of a hurry to bother about locking it.

For Juble, hearing of Vayne's proposition to Cranston, had wanted his partner to live. The existing business had become unimportant compared to the new corporation that promised an initial salary of fifty thousand dollars. Vayne's death would have ended the deal, so Juble had done his utmost to prevent it.

All of which proved that The Shadow had sensed the secret behind the Adico racket, even before he had found the actual death insurance policy. The Shadow had suspected, at least, that men like Juble had paid cash for the murder of others, like Vayne. But, for the moment, he was dropping all such thoughts from mind.

The Shadow was confronted with a rather unique problem. Perfectly situated to battle incoming crooks, he was anxious, for once, to avoid them!

NEWLY formed plans required that The Shadow be gone before killers entered. He couldn't use the windows; they were latched, and they opened into a tiny courtyard that might prove an absolute trap. There was only one route: a circuit through the apartment itself.

Light suddenly streaked the room. The crooks had opened the door from the hallway. Against the glow, The Shadow saw the sallow, ugly face of their leader, Rudy Waygart. But Rudy didn't see The Shadow. All that the ace killer spied was fading blackness that seemed to retire reluctantly from the dim, incoming light.

Gun in one hand, flashlight in the other, Rudy sprang forward. Pressure of the flash switch threw a glare past Juble's trunk. Again blackness vanished.

Swinging the beam, Rudy spotted a closed door. He hurried across the room and tried it. The door was tightly shut. Deciding that all was well, Rudy began to inspect the room.

Noticing the trunk, Rudy examined it, gave a harsh chuckle as he ran his fingers along the turned-down cloth that edged the tray. He was congratulating himself upon a discovery that he thought was his alone.

Out in the hallway, a black-cloaked shape was moving away from a service entrance at the rear of Juble's apartment. A wraithlike form, it reached a stairway, unnoticed by a thuggish watcher that Rudy had posted as a lookout. Descending to a small lobby, The Shadow paused, listened for sounds from the rear of the hallway.

He heard them—shuffling noises that betrayed thugs spotted there. Rudy had brought his crew in through the back. It wouldn't do to try that exit.

Through the front entry, The Shadow reached the sidewalk; there, he came to a sudden halt as he sidestepped to a narrow stretch of outside brick.

The Shadow had flattened against the only portion of the wall that afforded complete darkness. Elsewhere, streetlights made the path too plain. Across the way The Shadow saw a parked car, much like the rakish sedan that Rudy had used in flight from Renstrom's. Such a car meant watching crooks.

Trapped between the outside watchers and the inside mob, The Shadow was faced by a new dilemma that threatened more than danger. His present position promised to ruin all the plans that he had formed against the murder ring!

CHAPTER XI
CROOKS OBLIGE

THIS was a time for clever strategy; a ruse of a sort that The Shadow had seldom tried. It meant slow-motion tactics, more difficult than rapid action, perhaps with risk of a most hazardous sort. Nevertheless, The Shadow resolved to try it.

Gunmen expected him. Still, they thought that they had reached the goal first. It was necessary to balance those facts; to preserve the illusion along with the real. Eyes toward the car across the way,

The Shadow watched for any motion within it. Seeing none, he began to edge out into the light.

He was watching across his shoulder, for he was moving backward. Inching away from the darkened doorway, The Shadow kept his cloaked form stooped forward. He had worked himself several feet rearward and was midway to another patch of darkness when he saw a motion in the car.

Instantly, The Shadow pressed forward a bit faster than he had retreated. He kept a free hand moving ahead, probing along the wall; but his other fist was under his cloak, gripping a gun. Seeing a gun muzzle glimmer, The Shadow made a quick dive forward.

Shots roared from the car. Those bullets peppered close to The Shadow. Chunks of brick bounded from his hat brim. He had beaten the opening barrage by inches only. Rounding the corner of the entry, he was momentarily safe as he heard the leather-lunged yell of someone in the car:

"The Shadow!"

Flattening on the entry steps, The Shadow caught the pounding of feet from the rear hallway. Knees doubled, he gave an upward spring, came into sight like a figure actuated by pistons. Guns blasting, he went back with the recoil, dropping away as revolvers spurted toward him.

A gunman plunged to the steps, clipped by one of The Shadow's shots. Others hurdled their sprawling pal, thinking that they had dropped The Shadow. They learned their mistake when they reached close range. Aiming up from a crouch, The Shadow gave the thugs both barrels.

There was a mêlée in the entry. Struggling crooks were grabbing for The Shadow's guns as he slashed them down with hard-slugged blows. He had crippled them to begin with; their fight was frantic, but useless. In fact, The Shadow was actually holding up two men who would otherwise have slumped.

He was making them keep up the semblance of a struggle; partly to mislead arriving reserves, also to keep human shields against any shots that might come.

Rudy Waygart was on the stairway. Glimpsing The Shadow, Rudy paused to pocket papers that he had taken from Juble's trunk, while he urged his followers to help the others get The Shadow. Two hoodlums had left the car across the street and were nearing the outer doorway to attack from that side.

With a twist, The Shadow actually flung crippled foemen into the path of Rudy's squad. With a fierce, challenging laugh, he swung for the pair from the street, sideswiping them with his gun-weighted fists. The two astonished crooks spilled in opposite directions.

The Shadow had gone easy with that pair. He wanted them to talk to Rudy later; to tell their leader that they had seen The Shadow coming into the apartment house, not out of it. His path cleared, The Shadow sprang across the sidewalk, out into the street.

Behind him came a piling group of would-be killers, who had disentangled themselves from the floundering men in the entry. At the rear was Rudy, again too wise to take undue chances with The Shadow.

Sure advantage lay across the street. There, The Shadow could find darkness; from it, employ sniping tactics, to thin out another of Rudy's ruthless but overzealous crews. Only a few yards to go—but the distance proved too long.

OTHER cars were swinging into the street from each end. One contained a reserve squad of crooks who began to shoot the moment that they saw The Shadow. The other, more distant, was a police car that promptly answered the fire.

Friend or foe, it didn't matter. The Shadow was caught between two fires. Still in the light, the smoking guns that projected from his fists were enough to mark him as the likely target for police as well as crooks. This wasn't the time to stop and offer explanations.

The opposite sidewalk could have been miles away, considering the chance that The Shadow had to reach it. Though he sped with longer strides, he came far short of his intended goal. In the midst of that first barrage, The Shadow made a twisting spring in air, landed on the paving shoulder first and rolled beneath the step of the empty sedan across the street.

Crooks passed him in their car, shooting as they went. Then they were tangled with the patrol car. Officers, recognizing crooks at last, began to shoot it out with them. Thugs who had come downstairs with Rudy saw their chance to reach The Shadow. Two of them took long bounds across the street.

They saw The Shadow rise, grip the door of the sedan and yank it open. Then, with a pitiful stumble, he rolled inside. A gloved hand gripped the door handle, gave a contorted twist that pulled it shut. But The Shadow didn't reappear at the window. Rudy saw his plight and yelled quick orders:

"Get him away! Make it quick! Finish him after you're clear!"

The two men sprang into the front seat, started the sedan and raced it around the corner. The patrol car had ditched the reserve crew and was after the sedan. Other police cars were whining into the street from the direction that the first had come.

Rudy and a few men with him supplied a barrage that made the first police car stop to return the favor.

Aiming up from a crouch,
The Shadow gave the
thugs both barrels.

With others coming up, Rudy knew that continued fight was useless. He and his companions fled through the apartment house and made their escape by the rear door.

Of two things Rudy was certain as he made his way to safety. He had obtained Juble's papers without the knowledge of The Shadow. Rudy could testify to that fact, personally. The other certainty was The Shadow's finish. Wounded, the cloaked fighter would have no chance against the two uninjured killers who had carried him away.

Rudy guessed wrong twice.

BLOCKS from the scene where strife had started, the man at the wheel of the sedan slackened speed and took a look from the window. The car was on a quiet street with a convenient alleyway nearby. A good place to dump a body and make a getaway.

Nudging a thumb over his shoulder, the driver grunted to his pal:

"All right. Give it!"

Eagerly, the man on the right leaned over the seat and probed with his gun in back. Finding an inert, huddled form, he poked it with his gun muzzle. Somehow, the muzzle caught; the gunman thought it had hooked in the folds of The Shadow's cloak.

Then the revolver began to twist about. With a snarl the thug fired; the blaze from the gun muzzle merely singed the cushions of the rear seat. A hand was gripping the crook's revolver; another fist came upward, took the hoodlum by the neck and yanked him into the rear.

Jamming the brakes, the driver swung from the wheel, shoving his own gun for a mass of rising blackness. Above came a swinging arm, its hand carrying a heavy .45, an empty gun that The Shadow was using as a cudgel.

Pressing his revolver trigger, the crook put in a shot that beat the gun's descent, but the gloved hand didn't falter. The last that the crooked driver heard was the sound of a hissed laugh in his very ear. Then came a skull-cracking jolt that produced light more vivid than a gun burst.

The Shadow opened the door of the halted sedan. He lifted his cloak from slumped shoulders on the rear floor. He had wrapped the first attacker in that garment when he hauled him over the seat. The man in front had blazed the death shot into the body of his half-gagged pal.

Garbing himself in the cloak, The Shadow pressed the slouch hat tighter on his head. Gliding away into darkness, he gave a parting laugh—a tone of sardonic mirth, that trailed from the enveloping gloom. Crooks failed to hear that mockery. One of the pair was dead, the other unconscious.

Like Rudy, they had fallen for The Shadow's final ruse, the best-staged of all. His spill, his crawl into the sedan, were calculated as a means of leaving a scene where odds were heavy against him, and chance of stray bullets too likely.

The Shadow had needed a car and someone to drive it while he kept low in back. Crooks had obligingly supplied him with both. He had let Rudy's pair of hand-picked mobbies carry him from the battle scene to a spot where he could settle them conveniently.

Perhaps, if Rudy Waygart had witnessed that later scene and heard the laugh that followed it, he would have felt less sure about the future. Crime would have trouble with The Shadow, skilled fighter who could turn defeat into triumph!

CHAPTER XII
CRIME'S NEW CLIENT

"CALL for Mr. Henry Arnaud—"

A man arose from a chair in the corner of the hotel lobby and stopped the bellboy who was passing him. Identifying himself as Mr. Arnaud, he let the bellhop conduct him to a phone booth, where a call awaited.

There, Arnaud spoke a dry: "Hello."

"Mr. Arnaud?" The voice was quick. "My name is Regar. Clarence Regar. I'd like to see you. My office is in the Ferwin Building. Could you come over, right away?"

"An urgent matter?"

"Yes." Regar's tone was emphatic. "It means money to you, Mr. Arnaud."

Agreeing to come at once, Arnaud stepped from the phone booth. As he walked from the lobby into daylight, Arnaud's full, shrewd-looking features underwent a momentary change. Strong sunlight gave his face a masklike appearance, seemed to mark full places that had once been hollows.

The effect was ended as soon as Arnaud stepped into a cab. Milder light, less revealing than the sun's full glare, made the face resume its fuller mold.

There was a secret to the face of Henry Arnaud.

It was a face built upon another, a disguise that no eye could discern except under conditions highly unfavorable to Mr. Arnaud. It bore but the slightest traces of a hawkish profile that ordinarily identified Lamont Cranston.

After the battle at Juble's two nights ago, The Shadow had registered at the pretentious hotel under the name of Henry Arnaud. He had foreseen a call like the one that came from Clarence Regar for very good reasons.

An organization named the American Death Insurance Co. was selling policies through agents. One of those agents, Ronald Parron, had died very suddenly. Like any insurance company, legal or otherwise, Adico would naturally turn Parron's business over to some other agent.

Parron had sold a policy to Claude Juble, covering the death of Tyrus Vayne. But Vayne was still alive, though Juble was dead. The term of the policy was over, and Adico owed money to the dead man, Juble. The death insurance company had to keep up its prestige. Therefore, one thing was certain.

The agent who was handling Parron's business would have to find some way to disburse the sum of one hundred thousand dollars among the heirs and creditors of the deceased Claude Juble.

Obviously, Clarence Regar was the man in charge of Parron's business. He had traced Henry Arnaud and called him, because among Juble's bills was one that bore Arnaud's name.

The Shadow found Regar in his office. The fellow appeared to be Parron's type, something of a society man. There the similarity ended.

Where Parron had been nervous, uncertain in manner and a trifle weak-faced, Regar was quite the opposite. He was cool and competent. His eyes were sharp, his lips suavely smiling, while his blocky chin gave him the challenging air of a fighter.

Regar eyed Arnaud steadily, yet failed to penetrate the face-filling disguise that the visitor wore. The Shadow had picked a chair near the window where the light struck him at an excellent angle. Regar was able to see changes that might flicker over Arnaud's countenance, without seeing through the face itself.

Producing the falsified bill that The Shadow had left in Juble's trunk, Regar passed it over with the question:

"Do you recognize this, Mr. Arnaud?"

"Of course!" The Shadow's tone was harsher, more brisk than the one he used as Cranston. "I made out this bill myself."

"May I ask what were the services that you rendered to Claude Juble?"

A hard smile registered itself on the faked lips of Arnaud. Regar saw shrewdness in the glitter of the eyes that peered through half-closed lids. The Shadow's tone was cold.

"In my own behalf," he said, "I should like to ask just why you are interested in any of Juble's transactions."

THE retort pleased Regar. In Arnaud he was recognizing a man of his own sort. He could foresee a heart-to-heart talk, crook to crook, which would make everything much easier.

"I happen to have a considerable sum of money," declared Regar, "which Juble entrusted to my care. It is my duty"—he shook his head sadly— "to pay off my dead friend's debts and turn over the remaining cash to members of his family."

Without a word The Shadow took a pen from Regar's desk, wrote something on the bill and extended it toward Regar. The sharp-eyed man stared at the writing; it was a receipt for payment.

With a bland smile, Regar reached into a desk drawer, brought out a stack of money and counted out thirty-two hundred and fifty dollars.

Pocketing the cash, The Shadow arose. He let his lips turn downward in an expression of disdain. Evidently, Henry Arnaud regarded the cash as a very trivial sum. Regar was quick to take advantage of the disappointment that Arnaud registered.

"You expected more, Mr. Arnaud?"

Turning toward the door, The Shadow paused. Meeting Regar eye to eye, he said in Arnaud's cold, harsh tone:

"This was chicken feed! If Juble had lived, I could have made this amount a hundred times over!"

Leaning back in his chair, Regar clasped his hands in front of him. Suavely, he suggested:

"Tell me more, Mr. Arnaud."

"Why not?" Arnaud's tone was a sneer. "Who can prove anything, now that Juble is dead? There's a lot of money in imports, Mr. Regar, provided that they come in duty free."

Regar gave a wise nod. He inferred that Arnaud was the big shot of a smuggling racket, with Juble the fence who disposed of the tainted goods. It fitted well with Juble's character, such crooked business, conducted under the protective name of Vayne & Co.

"Why do you suppose Juble wanted old Vayne to quit?" demanded Arnaud. "Not just because the business wasn't big enough for both. Juble wanted full control so he could work with me without anyone getting wise."

Regar was nodding sympathetically.

"Losing Juble was a setback," growled The Shadow. "He was a sap, to fail a legitimate proposition like he did. But I could still go places"— though half-closed, Arnaud's eyes flashed a glare— "if it wasn't for one man!"

Regar leaned forward.

"Sit down, Mr. Arnaud," he purred. "I have a proposition that I am sure will interest you. We call it death insurance."

FOR the next five minutes The Shadow was treated to a remarkable sales talk, explaining the Adico plan. It was very simple, and quite legitimate, as Regar put it, though the sales agent was constantly sneaking sidelong glances toward the much-interested Mr. Arnaud.

"One man troubles you?" purred Regar. "Very well, Mr. Arnaud, why not insure his death? By paying a premium of ten percent, with a percentage off for cash, you will collect the full amount, provided—"

"Provided that the man lives?"

"Exactly!" Regar smiled smugly. "If he lives beyond a period of one year, you collect. If he dies"—Regar spread his hands— "you lose the premium, but you get what you really want."

Flickering changes came over Arnaud's scheming face as he considered the merits of the proposition. Eyeing Regar shrewdly, he remarked:

"It seems that your premium rates are very low."

"They suit us," returned Regar. "Once in a while we pay off, as we are doing in Juble's case."

"You mean he insured his partner, Vayne?"

"Precisely! Usually our adjusters take care of such cases. In this instance they failed."

By "adjusters" Regar meant murderers. He was sure that the reference would please Arnaud, and apparently it did. Thickish lips formed a coarse smile as Arnaud's eyes glinted.

"I still think that I could buy out Vayne & Co.," remarked The Shadow, "and use it as a front for my own racket, with some stooge as a cover-up. But there's one man who could queer the deal, and I don't want to wait a year to get rid of him."

"Sometimes," returned Regar, "we issue special policies for shorter periods. Of course the premium is higher."

"What would it be for a policy covering one week?"

Regar squatted back in his chair. The request rather stumped him. The one-year period was a thin veil that made the death insurance business plausible, since there was always a chance that insured men, particularly elderly ones, would die within that time.

Arnaud was brazenly treating death insurance as what it was: a murder racket. He wanted to buy murder outright, without bothering with sham. He wanted prompt service and was willing to pay for it. To Regar it looked like the biggest sale that had ever come his way.

For the next few minutes Regar pondered over the risk. He was weighing everything that Arnaud had said. He knew that his prospective client had openly vowed himself to be a crook, but Regar was looking for a catch in the tale.

It struck Regar finally that Arnaud could not have known, could not even have guessed, that such a thing as death insurance existed, until Regar, himself, had mentioned it. Leaning forward again, Regar announced:

"We have a maximum rate of twenty-five percent that would apply to a policy on a one-week term. It would require a cash payment, with no discount. Of course, the man whose death you insure would have to be available, so that our adjusters—"

Regar paused. He saw Arnaud nod full understanding. Reaching for the pen, The Shadow wrote a name on a pad of paper, tore off the slip and gave it to Regar.

"This is the man."

"Very well," said Regar glibly. "You shall hear from me this evening, Mr. Arnaud. If the case is approved, the policy will be delivered. Of course, there is the matter of the amount."

Taking back the slip of paper The Shadow wrote a figure that actually startled Regar. Losing his suavity, the fellow gulped:

"You... you can pay the premium on this? All at once... when the policy is delivered?"

"That much and more," returned The Shadow, rising beside the desk. "I'm making it big, Regar, because I want results. I know how I'll stand"— he tapped the paper— "if that man dies. If he doesn't—well, your outfit can pay me off instead."

LEAVING Regar's office, The Shadow took a devious route, the sort that would shake any followers off his trail. He entered his sanctum at dusk, still wearing the guise of Arnaud under the cloak and hat that he had picked up on the way.

A while later, he left the sanctum. Riding in a limousine, The Shadow put his cloak and hat beneath the rear seat. When he alighted at the Cobalt Club he was wearing the calm, immobile features of the hawk-faced Mr. Cranston.

As Cranston, The Shadow dined with Commissioner Weston and two others—Vayne and Merwood—in the privacy of the half-decorated grillroom, where Weston had his special table. The commissioner was trying to get new angles on the murder attempt at Vayne's penthouse.

Vayne was sketchy on the details. The Shadow knew why. The old importer was trying to protect his dead junior partner, Juble, because of the heroic fight that the latter had put up. According to Vayne, Harkin and a pair of thugs had tried to kill him; that was all. Juble and a black-cloaked stranger had prevented it.

When questioned, Vayne remembered that crooks had called their foe "The Shadow," which Weston regarded as a very important point. But neither Cranston nor Merwood could supply any help in tracing further details.

Cranston stated quietly that he had intended to build up a large importing corporation, with Vayne & Co. as the nucleus. The proposition was still open, provided that Tyrus Vayne could find another man, as capable as the unfortunate Claude Juble, to become the president of the new concern.

Merwood stated that Cranston had called him, asking him to become a director. The financier was quite willing to serve in such capacity; in fact, if the corporation developed as well as Cranston expected, Merwood would be willing to buy stock in it.

As yet, however, Merwood wasn't sure that the market for imported gems could stand up under too great an influx.

Leaving the Cobalt Club after dinner, The Shadow entered his limousine and started home. But Lamont Cranston was no longer in the car when it arrived at the millionaire's New Jersey estate. Again cloaked in black, Cranston had become The Shadow; he had dropped off before the limousine reached the Holland Tunnel.

In his sanctum, The Shadow worked with make-up kit and mirror, adding the touches of a putty substance that filled his features and changed them from the thin visage of Cranston into that of Arnaud.

Later, he picked up Moe Shrevnitz's cab and timed his trip to arrive at Arnaud's hotel just before midnight. Wearing a tuxedo, Arnaud looked like a theatergoer returning from a show.

Regar was waiting in the lobby. The Shadow shook hands with the death insurance agent; then obtained a package that he had deposited in the hotel safe under the name of Arnaud.

With Regar, he went upstairs to a spacious suite. The appearance of the rooms indicated plainly that Arnaud was a man who could regard a few thousand dollars as the "chicken feed" that he had termed it.

About to open the package, The Shadow paused. He looked at Regar and inquired sharply:

"The policy?"

"Approved."

Opening the package, The Shadow displayed a bundle of currency. The notes were all of one-thousand-dollar denomination; he counted out a hundred and twenty-five of them.

Regar extended an envelope; while The Shadow was opening it, the crook wrapped the package of cash and bundled it under his arm. He left by the door, saying nothing further.

With Regar gone The Shadow stood alone, studying the document for which he had paid the sum of one hundred and twenty-five thousand dollars. It was a death insurance policy, promising payment of half a million dollars if the insured man lived beyond a week.

The sum, of course, would be payable to Henry Arnaud. The interesting thing was the name of the insured man, otherwise the victim, upon whose death Adico was staking a half million.

It glared from the whiteness of the policy, in black ink that symbolized doom, the name of the man who was to become the immediate target of killers like Rudy Waygart.

A whispered tone of mockery came from The Shadow's disguised lips, as he read the name: Lamont Cranston.

The Shadow had taken out death insurance upon himself!

CHAPTER XIII
THE HUNTED MAN

TWO days. No move from Adico.

Seated in the lounge of the Cobalt Club, Lamont Cranston was reading an evening newspaper. Outwardly, he was placid, but behind the outspread pages of the newspaper, keen eyes showed a sparkle as deep as the glowing girasol that adorned The Shadow's finger.

Deliberately, The Shadow was inviting murder. In tantalizing fashion, the killers who worked for Adico were ignoring the marked Mr. Cranston, although they certainly knew where they could find him.

Did they suspect that Cranston was The Shadow?

It did not matter. There was a better reason why the death organization was biding its time. Rudy Waygart, the ace killer, wasn't available for this important murder.

Shadow or not, Cranston was a man who might know a lot. A close friend of the police commissioner, he would probably recognize Rudy as a crook if the fellow walked into the Cobalt Club. It wouldn't do for Adico to start with a false move.

Things fitted with The Shadow's theory that the death insurance ring was nationwide. Other victims had been murdered in various cities, probably by killers who had learned fine points from Rudy. If Adico played its cards right, Cranston would probably meet with one of those specialists very soon.

Viewing the club foyer, noting that it was empty, The Shadow returned to his reading of the newspaper. Commissioner Weston had issued a statement claiming that the law had put the lid on murder and intended to keep it tightly clamped.

Superficially, Weston's statement sounded well. The commissioner argued that recent murders were the work of desperate mobsmen, who had been either killed off, or dispersed. Parron had been slain by massed invaders. A mob was on hand when Renstrom died from a planted explosion. Juble's death had come during a thwarted mob attack directed against Vayne.

The Shadow smiled. He knew the facts behind those cases, saw how they differed.

Rudy Waygart had used mob methods in finishing Parron and Renstrom, to hide the fact that many other victims—of a far different sort—were being handled much more neatly. No one had taken out death insurance on either Parron or Renstrom. They were simply persons who had learned too much about the murder ring.

Vayne was different. He had been insured. Murderers had tried to dispose of him in subtle fashion. It was The Shadow's own forcing of the issue that had made the case look like a mob attempt. Weston simply hadn't caught on to the situation.

In his statement, Weston bragged that the law had managed to successfully protect three threatened persons: Janet Renstrom, Thomas Merwood, and Tyrus Vayne, though all of them had definitely been marked for death.

Again, the commissioner was deluded.

Weston didn't know that The Shadow had faked the Adico threat against Janet. Nor did he realize that Merwood had never been in danger at all, since no one had insured the financier's death. As for Vayne, crooks no longer had a reason to kill him. His term had passed; his claim was paid off and scratched from the books.

Adico wasn't an organization geared for revenge. Its business was to make crime pay. It cost money to keep Rudy and such killers on the payroll. Their services were too valuable to be wasted.

There was no mention of Adico in Weston's statement to the newspapers. In fact, the commissioner had laid a definite taboo upon the name and did not like to hear it mentioned, even by Cardona.

Weston still thought that Adico was a person; until he gained some trace to the man in question, he preferred that the name should not be publicly disclosed.

EYES turned again to the foyer. The Shadow saw an approaching attendant. Meeting Cranston's gaze, the man nodded.

"A call for you, sir."

Impassive though his training had made him, The Shadow felt an actual thrill as he strolled to the telephone. He recognized that this call might be the forerunner of Adico's first thrust. From the moment that he heard the plaintive voice across the wire, he knew that his hope was realized.

"Cranston!" The tone was excited, though spoken in a guarded fashion. "It's Ladwin! I've got to see you!"

Despite its distress, the voice certainly belonged to Peter Ladwin. The man was an explorer, who had met Cranston in various foreign countries. Odd that Ladwin should be calling; he wasn't supposed to be in America at present.

"Ladwin?" The Shadow spoke in Cranston's tone. "I thought you had gone to Australia."

"I canceled my passage from 'Frisco," informed Ladwin, "and came here instead. I'm hunted, Cranston! My life is in danger! I can't risk coming to the club—"

"Give me your address."

Ladwin gave it. The Shadow left the club. By the time his limousine neared Times Square, he was no longer Cranston. As the car crept through the traffic of a gloomy side street its passenger issued silently from the rear door, thoroughly cloaked in black.

A tiny flashlight twinkled from between two parked cars. An odd color, that gleamed. It was green. A cab wheeled from its stand, slackened as the twinkle turned red. Sliding into the cab, The Shadow gave Moe Shrevnitz an address a few blocks from the one that Ladwin had mentioned.

Reaching the proper neighborhood, The Shadow continued his journey on foot. The district fitted Ladwin's story of danger. Usually, Ladwin stayed at an expensive hotel when he visited New York. On this trip the explorer had chosen dilapidated surroundings.

A safe setting in a way. Hunting for Ladwin in the forgotten sectors of Manhattan would be like looking for a dull-pointed needle in an oversized haystack.

But there was another side to that situation. Assuming that crooks had found a thread to their needle, Ladwin, they would have him boxed in a very unlovely position.

Alleyways, courtyards, empty doorways, untenanted houses, all made excellent lurking spots. In fact, this section had the look of a trap, which made The Shadow surmise that the hunted man, Ladwin, was actually bait, and Cranston the real prey.

Whatever the benefit that crooks might derive from the darkness of this neighborhood, The Shadow likewise shared it. The darker it came, the better he liked it.

Gliding unseen through narrow passages between brick-walled buildings, he hoped for an encounter with lurking thugs. If he found them, he intended to strew silently his path with them.

But there were no thugs. Entering the cellar of the old house where Ladwin was staying, The Shadow made his way to the second floor by a very gloomy backstairs. Stopping outside a room, he drew a glove half from his hand and knuckled a rap that seemed muffled in the hallway but which was sure to be heard inside.

A key turned. The door swung inward. A haggard, middle-aged man stepped backward with a gasp as living blackness entered. Gray eyes, frantic and fearful, met The Shadow's gaze. Then, rallying, Ladwin gasped:

"You... you're from Cranston?"

The Shadow's whispered laugh was an affirmative. Then, to inspire Ladwin's complete confidence, he tilted back his slouch hat and let the folds of his cloak collar drop downward.

SEEING Cranston's face, Ladwin gave a happy

gasp. He reached to the door, turned the key and removed it, and dropped it into his pocket. Licking his lips, Ladwin smiled.

"Stout fellow, Cranston!" he approved. "I hadn't dreamed that you could rig yourself up this way. Did you ever try the trick in the jungle? I'll wager that even a tiger would mistake you for a shadow!"

With Cranston's slight smile, The Shadow showed his approval of the banter. It was putting Ladwin at ease. His worriment lessened, the haggard explorer came to his story.

"I've received warnings, Cranston," he declared. "Someone kept calling my apartment in 'Frisco, saying 'Beware of death.' My mail brought clippings telling of accidents. One day I received a letter with big words scrawled in red pencil.

"It said: 'Look out for Adico'—and the voice mentioned the same name when it called again. I didn't tell the police because I was intending to sail for Australia. Then came a crudely typed letter, in red, telling me that death lurked aboard the liner. That's why I didn't sail."

Calmly, The Shadow inquired why Ladwin had come to New York. The hunted man explained very simply that he had received a final call, stating that a friend in New York could aid him.

"I have few friends in New York," asserted Ladwin. "In fact, you were the only one I was sure of, Cranston. That's why I came East by plane, hid myself here, and called you at the club."

Added up, Ladwin's story produced an obvious face value. Ladwin could be classed as a death insurance victim, scheduled to die soon. Someone— perhaps a person like Parron—could have tried to warn him against an Adico murder.

Meanwhile, the Adico crowd itself might have seen a special value in Ladwin. Placing him as a friend of Cranston, he would be the right man to use as unwitting bait. Even if Ladwin outlived his term, it would be worthwhile to pay off on his claim, in order to dispose of a half-million-dollar victim like Cranston.

There was another angle. By bringing Cranston and Ladwin together, the Adico workers could murder both at once.

Looking about the place, The Shadow saw it was a little apartment. There were two doors, beside the one that he had entered. Opening one, The Shadow found an empty closet. Ladwin opened the other to display a small lighted bedroom.

As with the living room, windows were bolted shut, and Ladwin had drawn the shades.

"If you can get me out of here, Cranston," Ladwin pleaded, "I'll be safe. I've hired a plane; it's waiting at Newark Airport. But I'm worried for fear that enemies may be on watch. Did you see anyone outside?"

"No one."

Ladwin sighed relief. He opened a small suitcase, took out an envelope and carried it to the living room.

"This contains the papers I mentioned." Ladwin crossed the room, laid the envelope on a table, and turned on a lamp. "You can look them over, Cranston, while I'm getting packed."

He pushed a chair to the table. The Shadow sat down and opened the envelope. Ladwin hurried back into the bedroom, closing the door behind him. Spreading the papers, The Shadow paused. His keen ears had caught the faintest of *clicks*.

Listening for any repetition of the sound, The Shadow heard something else. Again, it was a noise that ordinary hearing would not have caught. In fact, The Shadow might not have noted it, except for the fact that he had strained to a listening attitude.

Tilting his head in different directions, The Shadow gained a position wherein the sound became more audible. It was a low, steady hiss, and The Shadow located its source. The sound came from the table lamp. Leaning forward, he drew a brief breath.

No odor was perceptible; but the hiss was certainly caused by an escaping gas. The Shadow felt the effects of the vapor; it gave him a temporary dizziness. Steadying, he tilted back his head, drew in a relieving breath of fresher air.

The first sound was explained. The click had come when Ladwin locked the bedroom door, from the other side, just as he had previously locked the door to the hall. Reaching to a window shade, The Shadow pressed its edge aside, noted the greenish tinge of the pane beyond.

Unbreakable glass, in metal frames, painted to look like wood. Arranged for Ladwin's own protection? Not quite! It was Ladwin who had pointed The Shadow to the corner table and had then turned on the special lamp, so that the flow of gas had begun.

Peter Ladwin wasn't a hunted man at all. He was a murderer deluxe, in the employ of the Adico ring. Chancing to be one of Cranston's friends, he had been summoned to New York to engineer the most important murder that Adico had undertaken!

A whispered laugh came from The Shadow's lips. Though low, subdued, its sibilance drowned the faint hiss of the death gas. The Shadow's mirth was a veto against doom!

CHAPTER XIV
CRIME OVERPLAYED

WITH the end of ten silent minutes, a key turned sharply in its lock. Confident that caution was no longer needed, Peter Ladwin opened the door from the bedroom and peered through. His face was worried no longer; it was gleeful.

The smile on Ladwin's puckered lips told that he had taken a deep breath of the clear air in the bedroom. Suitcase in one hand, he was holding a key in the other, ready to move to the outer door and make his own safe departure.

First, however, Ladwin had time to look at the victim who lay slumped upon the corner table. There was something else that Ladwin wanted, too: the batch of papers that contained clippings and other evidence.

Approaching, Ladwin reached across a slumped cloaked shoulder and clutched the envelope. It was empty. The smile left his compressed lips. He put the envelope in his pocket, along with the key that his hand already carried.

Setting down the suitcase, he dived his hands toward The Shadow's cloak, to make a rapid search for the missing clippings.

The slouched form shifted as Ladwin jogged it. The slouch hat fell to the floor. Two stacks of magazines tumbled from a sofa pillow on which they rested; the black cloak slipped floorward with them.

A dummy figure!

Using articles at hand, The Shadow had improvised a sham for Ladwin's benefit. It hadn't required much imagination on Ladwin's part for him to be deceived.

But with his discovery, Ladwin's imagination was highly stirred. Clutching up the cloak and hat, the startled crook turned toward the outer door, ready for a mad escape.

A laugh greeted him from another direction. Wheeling, he saw the closet door swing wide. He was facing Cranston, who held a leveled automatic. But the mockery that Cranston's lips exhaled was the whispered mirth of The Shadow!

Burning eyes told their story. By using the closet as a waiting place, Cranston had made himself immune from the gas.

Listening, he had waited until Ladwin came from the bedroom. Drawing his own breath later, The Shadow was in condition to outlast the foiled murderer as they faced each other in the gas-laden room!

Quivering, Ladwin extended the hat and cloak. It was the only way that he could make a plea for mercy. Any attempt to speak would have meant inhaling the death gas. Plucking the garments from Ladwin's hand, The Shadow gestured his gun toward the outer door.

Eagerly, Ladwin produced the key. He sprang to the door, managed to steady his fumbling hand long enough to unlock it. Almost out of breath, he clutched the knob feebly, pulled the door halfway inward and pitched headlong across the threshold.

The gas hadn't gotten Ladwin. He was simply out of breath. One deep swallow of the free air revived him instantly. Rolled to an elbow, he looked back, saw The Shadow stepping around the door.

With snakelike speed, Ladwin displayed a return of his murderous skill. Driving one foot through the doorway, he kicked the door fully inward.

The flinging barrier sideswiped The Shadow, sent him sprawling half across the room. Coming to his feet, Ladwin lunged inward, drawing a gun. He intended to use the weapon as a cudgel, before The Shadow could grab up the automatic that had clattered from his grasp.

One stunning blow would be enough; the gas would do the rest. Finding Cranston, the police would suppose that a fall had caused the blow that Ladwin intended to strike.

WHAT Ladwin didn't notice was The Shadow's free hand. It happened to be beneath the cloak and hat.

Swinging, bringing the garments with it, the hand caught Ladwin's descending wrist, gave a twist that carried the murderer off balance, thanks to the force that Ladwin was putting behind the slugging blow.

Then The Shadow was on his feet heading through the doorway, while Ladwin, rolling toward the table, was fumbling for the gun that his hand had failed to hold. As he came to hands and knees, he saw the door swinging shut.

It was The Shadow's turn to need air. He had to have it before he could settle Ladwin.

Seeing his own gun handy, Ladwin grabbed it up and aimed for the slammed door. He intended to riddle the thick wood with every bullet that his revolver contained, spraying the shots so that one, at least, would be sure to clip The Shadow.

Ladwin fired his first shot.

The roar that came was louder than a cannon's. Its result would have done credit to a six-inch shell. The tiny apartment exploded in one titanic blast.

Ladwin had forgotten that the odorless death gas was inflammable. Either that or he hadn't realized how fully it had charged the atmosphere.

Like a mammoth bomb the whole room ripped outward. Steel window frames were twisted like weak wire; their unbreakable glass was flung to the next roof. The door to the hallway, splintered from its hinges, was broken into chunks that scaled along the hall.

Interior walls were shattered; the whole house quivered and sagged on its foundations. Great tongues of flame licked from the windows to the roof and roared along the inner hall. As the licking fire vanished, bricks began to rattle down upon the front sidewalk, while the rear courtyard received a veritable hail of masonry.

Flattened by the explosion, The Shadow felt the scorching flame ride over him like a mass of billowy surf. He had escaped Ladwin's bullet; the passage of the fiery gas was too brief to do him harm. Nevertheless, he was staggering as he went down the tilted front stairway. The force of the concussion had jarred The Shadow badly.

People were shrieking from other windows in the wrecked house. They were safe, though they didn't know it, for the flames had dissipated too rapidly to start a serious conflagration. No one in the house saw the staggering figure that went out through the front door carrying a cloak, a hat, and a gun.

That sight was reserved for two men in a roadster, who had swung their car in from the corner. Turning on their headlights, they saw someone falter into the glare, then make a stumbling retreat toward the house.

"It's Ladwin!" voiced one. "He oughta have lammed sooner. Let's get him away quick, and flash the word to the crew."

"Yeah," agreed the other as they were clambering from the car. "We'll be dodging smoke eaters, along with coppers, if we don't make it swift."

They reached the man on the sidewalk, steered him toward the roadster. Headlights showed his face imperfectly; it was grimy. Accepting him as Ladwin, the thugs were more interested in the articles he carried. They paused, plucking at the cloak and hat.

"Cripes!" ejaculated one. "That guy Cranston musta been The Shadow!"

"Looks like it," rejoined his pal. "We'd better make sure he's croaked. Hey, Ladwin—what about it?"

The thug shook the groggy man who had come from the house. A face turned squarely toward the headlights. The crooks saw the countenance more plainly.

"This ain't Ladwin—"

"It's Cranston!"

"The Shadow!"

MENTION of the dread name stirred its owner to action. The Shadow voiced a laugh that carried challenge, though its mockery was off key. Swinging blindly into battle, he slashed one crook aside with a hard gun-hand swing, met the other in a grapple.

They rolled in front of the roadster's headlights. The Shadow could hear the approaching clatter of the thug that he had swept aside. Gun poked past the shoulder of the man who grappled him, The Shadow fired repeated shots. A yell told that one of his stabs had reached the incoming crook.

A revolver was swinging toward The Shadow's head. Too late to ward off its stroke, he made a quick sideward move. The descending revolver clanged a metal bar—the car's front bumper. Losing the gun, the crook made a backward grab to regain it; then swung in again.

Knees doubled, The Shadow drove both feet upward. They met their human target, hurled the thug into a backward somersault. Grabbing the roadster's bumper, The Shadow hauled himself to his feet, scooped up his hat and cloak, then stumbled into the car.

Putting the throbbing motor into reverse, he zigzagged it backward toward the corner. The two gunmen were shooting, but their aim was bad. One was wounded, the other winded; they couldn't follow the car's erratic course. Then they were meeting troubles of their own.

A patrol car was roaring down the street from the opposite direction. The thugs turned to greet it. As they opened fire, they were met with shots. One succumbed from bullets; the other, the thug that The Shadow had wounded, lost his balance as he twisted toward the curb, and went shrieking beneath the front wheels of the patrol car.

Undisturbed by the jounce that their car took, the officers went after the roadster, not knowing who its occupant was. They were overtaking it when a sedan slashed across their path. Brakes shrieked as guns talked. The police sprang from their car to take shelter against overheavy odds.

The thing that saved them was the steady shooting that came from the corner where the roadster had turned. His daze ended, The Shadow had come from the captured car to snipe the gunners who were trapping the police. The sedan took suddenly to flight, carrying away its crippled crew.

Covering more blocks in the roadster, The Shadow abandoned the car in a side street and started for his sanctum. Arriving there, he brought papers into the bluish light. They were the clippings and other items that Ladwin had asked him to examine.

This was The Shadow's first opportunity to get a good look at them. Among them he found an interesting link. One showed a picture of a California convict named Lucky Engriff, who had escaped from San Quentin Prison.

In two group photographs—one showing a street riot in San Francisco; the other a crowd at Coney Island—The Shadow picked out the same face. He noted that the New York clipping was of later date than the one from 'Frisco.

BY a process of deduction, The Shadow came to a remarkable conclusion. These clippings, presumably sent to Ladwin by a mysterious person who wanted to help him, indicated that Lucky Engriff was connected with the murder ring; that the escaped convict had gone to San Francisco and later to New York.

That part was simple. The remarkable point was that the evidence was bona fide. The Shadow was sure that Engriff was in New York; that he was actually employed as a killer in the death insurance racket.

The reason was this:

Ladwin, playing a false part, needed genuine evidence to support his singular story. Evidence so strong that The Shadow would recognize it as real. It had been necessary to keep The Shadow fully occupied with the papers during the ten minutes that it took the gas to fill the death room.

Anything flimsy would have been too risky for Ladwin. As for Engriff, he would willingly have allowed such damaging evidence to reach The Shadow's hands, because Ladwin expected to get those papers back. The Shadow remembered that Ladwin had made a grab for the envelope as soon as he approached the table where the death lamp stood.

All members of the Adico ring would soon know that Ladwin had died instead of Cranston. They would wonder whether or not The Shadow had kept the evidence incriminating Engriff. The man who would wonder most would be Lucky Engriff himself; moreover, the escaped convict would be particularly eager to do something about it.

By all calculations, Engriff would be the next man to seek Cranston's life. He would demand the appointment, and the Adico organization would have to approve it, in return for Engriff's cooperation with Ladwin.

Leaving the sanctum, The Shadow went into a laboratory that adjoined it. When he returned, he placed a sheet of glossy paper beneath the bluish light. On the paper were imprinted photostatic copies of the three newspaper clippings that pertained to Engriff.

Twisting his hands into the right position, The Shadow interposed them between the light and the paper. As on a previous occasion, a hawkish silhouette impressed itself upon the sensitized sheet.

Folding the paper, The Shadow sealed it in an envelope. He turned off the blue light.

A laugh trailed out in the solid darkness—

CHAPTER XV
CRIME TRIES AGAIN

THEY were dining at the Cobalt Club, Commissioner Weston and his friend Lamont Cranston, in the otherwise deserted grillroom. Despite new worries that perplexed him, Weston gave a satisfied smile as he leaned back in his chair.

"I hope that the house committee keeps on haggling," he declared. "The more time they waste choosing new decorations, the longer we can have the grillroom to ourselves. If they want my opinion, I would say to leave the place as it is.

"Ladders, paint buckets, paper all over the floor—it suits me, Cranston. It gives me privacy when there are no other diners about; and, candidly, Cranston, all this mess is no worse than the old decorations. Remember when the place looked like a tropical garden, with palm trees and parrots? Bah!"

The Shadow remembered. The parrots had particularly annoyed Weston because everytime the commissioner raised his voice, he had been imitated by croaks from a dozen cages. Weston's tone was the exact pitch that parrots liked to mimic.

"Yes, I like it as it is," repeated Weston. "After the waiter is gone, I can hold conferences here. Tonight, for instance, I am expecting Inspector Cardona—"

There were footsteps from the stairway that led down into the grillroom. Cardona's stocky figure came into sight. Approaching the table, Joe handed the commissioner an envelope.

"It was at your office, Commissioner," said Cardona. "It came after you had left."

Unfolding the contents of the envelope, Weston gave a rapid exclamation:

"Look quickly! Both of you!"

Rising from his chair, Cranston unfortunately jostled Cardona. They were too late.

"It's gone again," Weston told them. "The profile of The Shadow! It was there on the paper, plainly visible!"

Cardona was looking at the glossy sheet. What he saw was interesting enough.

"This looks like The Shadow's work, all right," asserted Joe. "Those photographs aren't fading out. I wonder how he got this dope, Commissioner."

There were arrows with the photographs, pointing out Engriff's picture in the groups. Weston saw the combination, and asked:

"What do you know about this fellow Engriff?"

"He's dangerous," replied Cardona. "I had a full report on him from San Q. They don't know he's headed East, though. Engriff used to be one of those daredevil guys that jump off cliffs and take rides on skyrockets.

"Working as a stunt artist, he was, until that got too tame for him. He went in for gang stuff—just for the excitement, he said. They got him on a second-degree charge, and he went up for twenty years. Only, he got out."

"The time of the big break, wasn't it?"

"Yeah. Somebody smuggled in some dynamite, and the cons blew a hole in the wall. I always figured that Lucky was the bird who planted the charge."

WESTON was showing renewed interest in the photostats. Suddenly he slapped his broad hand on the table. Jarred dishes added echoes to the thump.

"This fits with last night's mystery!" exclaimed the commissioner. "Ever since we identified Peter Ladwin by scattered articles from his suitcase, we have been wondering why a man of his repute was in hiding.

"Ladwin came from San Francisco. So did Engriff. Perhaps Ladwin feared the fellow and was living in a squalid neighborhood to avoid him. We must work on that theory, Inspector. Engriff may be responsible for other deaths."

Turning to Cranston for approval, Weston received a nod. Quietly, The Shadow stated:

"Perhaps Engriff murdered Parron—"

"And Renstrom!" exclaimed Weston. "The explosion at Renstrom's is a case in point. Perhaps Engriff was behind Juble's death. Maybe Vayne could give us some clue—"

Mulling over matters, Weston became more and more convinced that he was right. The law had not yet linked Rudy Waygart with the mobbies who had shown up—some of them to stay—on the scene of every crime.

Dying crooks had refused to talk when questioned. They claimed they didn't know who they worked for, or what the racket was. They had lied to protect Rudy, but on the second count they told the truth. None of Rudy's gorillas had ever heard of Adico.

The Shadow voiced no objection to Weston's theory regarding Lucky Engriff. He preferred to have the law go after Lucky, rather than Rudy. By The Shadow's calculations, Lucky was to be heard from very soon.

"Yes," repeated Weston, "we must talk to Vayne."

"We can do that quite easily," declared The Shadow. "Merwood and I are calling on Vayne tonight to talk over the importing office. I don't suppose that Merwood would object if you came along, Commissioner. Why not ask him?"

"I shall do so."

Weston shook a bell that brought a waiter, who went to get a special telephone that plugged into a floor socket recently installed in the grillroom. Calling Merwood, Weston told the financier about the new evidence that the law had received.

"Merwood is willing to postpone all other business," declared Weston as he laid the telephone aside, "and he is anxious to be present when we talk to Vayne. He hopes that we are on the trail of the man who murdered Renstrom. We shall start at once and stop for Merwood on the way to Vayne's."

OUTSIDE the Cobalt Club, they chose Weston's official car instead of Cranston's limousine. When they stepped into the big car, Cardona did not come along. He explained that Sergeant Markham was parked around the corner in a headquarters car.

"We'll follow you, Commissioner," said Cardona. "I may need Markham later."

Most persons would have felt secure while riding in the police commissioner's official car. Not so The Shadow. He knew that he was marked for death so long as he persisted in appearing publicly as Cranston.

The Shadow would have preferred his own limousine, or Moe's taxi, even though the trip was short. Nevertheless, he made no objection to Weston's insistence that they ride in the official car.

After all, The Shadow was quite prepared for any trouble. In special pockets under his tuxedo jacket, he carried a brace of automatics. His coat had been fitted for them.

Weston was commenting on the Engriff theory. He did not notice that Cranston was observing every corner that they passed; even scanning each darkened doorway as they rode along the avenue. Folded arms gave Cranston the semblance of calmness, but his hands, tucked beneath opposite elbows, were gripping the handles of the automatics.

The official car swung into a narrow one-way street that led toward the apartment house where Merwood lived. With a side glance through the window, The Shadow saw Markham's car follow. There would be no trouble from the rear; but up ahead—

It came. A terrific shriek of fire apparatus, accompanied by the clang of bells. A hook-and-ladder truck, loaded with a dozen firemen, had swung into the block. It was bucking traffic, as it had a right to do, shrilling its warning for other vehicles to clear the path.

People were scurrying along the sidewalks. Among them The Shadow saw a stoopish man who had been close to the curb in a position to note the commissioner's car when it passed.

There was ample room to avoid the fire truck, and plenty of time to be out of its way. Weston's chauffeur swung the big car toward the curb where he could park it. The rapid swerve, the application of the brakes produced a jolt.

Oddly, Cranston was flung forward. Weston didn't realize that his friend had made a deliberate lunge. The commissioner couldn't see what happened next, for Cranston's body blocked the sight. One hand speeding forward, The Shadow grabbed the wheel, yanked it from the chauffeur's grasp.

Veered to the right, the car climbed the curb, shot across the sidewalk and made an angled plunge into the hollowed entrance to a basement that was protected by a flight of stone steps.

Both Weston and the chauffeur were hurled to

the lower side of the car as it crashed, but Cranston did not share their experience. Swinging about, he caught the handle of the high door on the left, yanked it downward.

Throwing his weight against the reluctant barrier, he went headlong as the door swung outward, to land in the trough of the uptilted step.

Strange though the course of the car had been, the fire truck matched it. As the car veered to the right, the truck lurched to the left. Its wheels grazing the curb, it was bound for the very spot that Weston's car had left!

The Shadow had averted a terrific wreck by supplying a minor mishap instead. He had placed the official car where the roaring, cumbersome truck could not reach it, saving Weston's life, the chauffeur's, and his own.

THAT was not all The Shadow did.

He had one gun drawn as he flattened on the step. Looming almost upon him, The Shadow saw the fire truck and the driver at its wheel. He stabbed a shot straight for the driver. The man flipped backward from the wheel, losing his helmet as his hands flung wide.

Still The Shadow's gun was stabbing shots, aimed for the truck crew, as the vehicle careened past, completely out of control. They were firing in return, those firemen, but their shots were high, wide, and scattered.

No marksman, however capable, could have found any target while the truck was riding wild. Front wheels climbed one curb, jolted away and headed across the street.

Yelling men were forgetting their guns to hang on. Others, a few who had intercepted The Shadow's bullets, were losing their hold and falling to the street.

Markham's car dodged the massive hook-and-ladder truck by taking to one curb as the uncontrolled juggernaut climbed the other. The truck struck the front of an empty store, bashed in the show window and half a ton of bricks surrounding it. Ladders were ripped to splinters as the truck crashed through.

With the shattered equipment went falling figures. A few of them came to their feet, still clutching guns. They heard a sound that followed the echoes of the crash.

It came from near the commissioner's car:

The laugh of The Shadow!

Strange, taunting, it branded enemies for what they were: not firemen, but thugs. Crooks engaged in one of the most daring murder attempts ever made in Manhattan.

Who would have suspected that a hook-and-ladder truck, bound apparently toward a fire, was a fake vehicle that had come from a deserted garage on a murder trip?

Only The Shadow!

The truck had passed a dozen traffic cops, but none had challenged it. The Shadow had personally put a finish to its mad career, by settling the thug who drove it. He had thinned its crooked crew with bullets; the crash had settled several more. At present, The Shadow was dealing with the stragglers, who were still enough to make trouble.

Tuned to The Shadow's shots came those from another gun. Cardona was out of Markham's car; he had heard The Shadow's laugh. Pelting mobsters from the rear, Cardona gave The Shadow satisfactory aid. Wildly shooting mobbies sprawled under the double fire. No more shots came from the vicinity of the shattered truck.

When Commissioner Weston climbed from his canted limousine, he found his friend Cranston seated, dazed, upon the higher step. Cranston didn't remember just what had happened. He had heard shots, a crash, a strange, weird laugh.

Cardona was beckoning from along the street. Together, Weston and Cranston joined him, Stepping over the stilled forms of recent foemen, Cardona shouldered through the smashed wall, toward the front of the hook-and-ladder truck.

Beside the fake truck lay the battered driver. Cardona turned a flashlight on the dead man's face, which was still in recognizable condition.

Though it wasn't necessary, Joe pronounced the name:

"Lucky Engriff."

CHAPTER XVI
THE SIXTH DAY

COMMISSIONER WESTON was considerably worried, and he wondered why. Dining at his table in the grillroom, he began to count the names of persons under his special protection.

The list included Janet Renstrom, Thomas Merwood, Tyrus Vayne; all were amply safe. Detectives were still on duty at the Renstrom home. Merwood had servants who were capable and loyal. In his turn, Vayne had hired a reputable private detective to help investigate Juble's death, and the man was serving as Vayne's bodyguard.

Finally analyzing his worriment, Weston decided that it was Cranston's safety that disturbed him.

Cranston had admitted an acquaintance with Ladwin, the explorer who had died a few nights ago. Classing Ladwin's death as murder, with Lucky Engriff the killer, Weston concluded that the crook-manned fire truck had been directed at Cranston.

Through such erroneous reasoning, Weston had

actually struck the truth; but he was far from guessing crime's motive. Cranston was wealthy, but there seemed no logical way whereby crooks could profit through his death.

Had true facts been told to Weston, he would have considered them too fanciful to believe.

An organization called Adico, flinging murderers at Cranston, to save itself the payment of half a million dollars to a man named Arnaud!

Murder for profit, yes; for Adico, if it succeeded, would retain the one hundred and twenty-five thousand dollars that Arnaud had paid as premium. Still, the case was amazing.

Quite as amazing as something that the Adico group did not know; namely, that Cranston and Arnaud were the same man, and that both were The Shadow!

Tonight was the sixth night. Adico had played two aces—Ladwin and Engriff—only to lose both. Despite Weston's qualms, Cranston had shown skill at taking care of himself. But Weston, in his ignorance, was quite relieved when he saw his friend enter from the grillroom stairway.

Cranston was seated at the table when Merwood arrived, accompanied by a chauffeur who politely left after having safely conducted his employer to the police commissioner's presence. Soon afterward, Inspector Joe Cardona appeared.

"I am sorry, gentlemen," said Weston with a smile, "that I must ask you to conduct a business conference under police supervision. But murder is in the air; it might strike anywhere, even here, if we did not take proper precautions."

Merwood gave a worried nod, turned his broad face toward Cranston and queried anxiously: "Where is Vayne?"

"We expect him shortly," interposed Weston. "Ah! I believe this is Vayne now."

ENTERING from the stairway, Vayne was followed by a private detective who answered to the name of Hapthorpe. Advancing eagerly to the table, Vayne turned first to Cranston, then to Merwood, and exclaimed:

"Excellent news! I have just heard from a man who can give our importing corporation the international status that it requires. You have heard of Mailleaux Frères, the jewelry wholesalers in Paris?"

There were nods from Cranston and Merwood.

"This man represents them," continued Vayne, rubbing his hands. "His name is Georges Daux, and he is staying at the Hotel Marleigh. He says that Mailleaux Frères have read reports of our prospective enterprise and would like to buy a share in it."

"Why didn't you invite him here?" inquired Merwood.

"I felt that he should talk to Cranston first," replied Vayne. "Daux wants to know about the jewel purchases. He spoke as though he would like to ask some confidential questions that only Cranston could answer."

The Shadow arose, turned in leisurely fashion toward the stairway. He spoke in Cranston's style.

"I shall go over to see Daux," he said. "Meanwhile, Vayne, you can talk with Merwood regarding the details of our company's incorporation."

Weston came to his feet in alarm.

"I can't let you go alone, Cranston!" Weston's tone showed horror. "Anything might happen! I tell you, murder is everywhere!"

"Cranston can take Hapthorpe," suggested Vayne. "I have found him to be a very good bodyguard."

Weston studied Hapthorpe. The private dick looked brawny, but sluggish. Weston shook his head.

"Hapthorpe can stay here," he decided. "Inspector Cardona can go with Cranston. By the way, Cranston, where is that gun you had the other night, at Renstrom's?"

"Out in the car, I suppose" was Cranston's smiling reply, "unless somebody stole it while my chauffeur was asleep."

"Better stop and look for it. Take it along. You may need it."

SMALL, but exclusive, the Hotel Marleigh was more of an apartment house than a hotel. It had an ample lobby, which Cardona eyed thoroughly when he and Cranston entered from the limousine, and the place looked quite innocent.

There was a dapper clerk behind the desk. He phoned up to the suite where Daux was staying, then announced to Cranston that the guest was ready to receive him.

The Shadow and Cardona entered an automatic elevator which had a modern type of hinged door. The metal door was swinging shut when Cardona pressed the button for the fourth floor. Smoothly, the elevator began its upward journey as soon as the door had closed.

Reaching the fourth floor, they were greeted by Georges Daux, a middle-aged man with thin, dark hair, sparkling eyes, and a polished French manner.

"Ah, Monsieur Cranston!" exclaimed Daux. "This is indeed one great pleasure! Monsieur Vayne had told me that I should expect you. Votre ami—that is, your friend"—he looked questioningly at Cardona— "he is one who is also interested in jewels, oui?"

"In a way, yes," replied The Shadow. "Show Monsieur Daux your bracelets, Inspector."

Cardona produced a pair of handcuffs, flashed them along with his badge. Daux tilted back his head and laughed.

"Ah, bracelets! You have a sense of humor, Monsieur Cranston. But why"—he shrugged, spread his hands— "why should you need a police inspector with you when you visit me?"

The Shadow blamed it on Weston, explaining matters as he and Daux strolled into the suite, with Cardona close behind them. Daux's rooms were quite pretentious, befitting the foreign representative of so important a firm as Mailleaux Frères.

Two stocky servants were in the living room. Indicating them, Daux remarked:

"I, too, require protection, *messieurs*. That is why I always have these men with me. Look!"

From a table drawer he brought a fistful of jewels, strewing them on the table. Rings, pendants, gem-studded brooches, made a valuable array that The Shadow estimated as worth upwards of fifty thousand dollars. Yet Daux treated brilliant diamonds and richly colored emeralds as if they were mere samples of his wares.

"One thing is wrong," he said gloomily. "The price. It is too high. We must give more for less, to satisfy the American trade. If you can buy jewels cheaply in India, Monsieur Cranston, we could do very much."

The Shadow nodded. He glanced toward Cardona, who had taken a corner chair and was buried in a magazine that he had picked up from the table.

"I believe that I can talk freely," The Shadow told Daux. "Let me tell you something about the gems that I intend to buy."

Daux listened, fascinated by the tale that followed. It began with a boar hunt, wherein Cranston had saved the life of a rajah. Next came the details of political intrigue which Cranston had spiked, thus keeping the rajah on his throne.

In return the rajah had conducted his benefactor to a secret underground chamber where a jewel-studded Buddha squatted mid heaps of fabulous gems.

"Ancestors of the rajah placed that wealth in the Buddha's care," declared The Shadow, "that it might someday be awarded to a man who, according to a yogi's prophecy, would come from a far land to save the throne."

"Ah!" Daux nodded, wisely. "You were the man of the prophecy, *n'est pas?*"

"I was. But having no armored truck available, I left the jewels in the rajah's care. On my next trip to India, I intend to claim them."

"And they will cost you nothing?"

"Only transportation and custom duty. Beyond that, all will be profit. Does it interest you, Monsieur Daux?"

It interested Daux exceedingly. He chattered about the jewel market in Europe as well as America. He assured Cranston that Mailleaux Frères would pay a large sum in advance for the privilege of selling the gems in France and other portions of the continent.

THE interview ended, Cardona came promptly to life, indicating that he had been alert while reading the magazine.

Taking the magazine from Cardona, The Shadow studied the illustration on the opened page, then scanned half a dozen paragraphs printed in French.

"Very, very funny!" The Shadow chuckled in Cranston's style. "Don't you think so, Inspector?"

Cardona shook his head; remarking that he didn't read French. The Shadow handed the magazine to Daux, suggesting:

"Translate the anecdote for Inspector Cardona."

Glancing at the page, Daux opened his lips in a gleaming smile, that turned to an almost convulsive laugh.

"Ah, it is rare, this story!" he exclaimed, amid his laughter. "You must take the magazine, with my compliments. Inspector Cardona can hear it when you translate it for your friend the commissioner."

Daux was conducting his visitors out to the elevator, thrusting the magazine in Cranston's hands as they went. Still chortling, he shook hands, then opened the elevator door. Bowed into the car, The Shadow and Cardona could see Daux's laugh-wrinkled face through a little glass window as the door was closing.

Cardona was thinking that the magazine anecdote must have been a very funny one. The Shadow wasn't thinking of the magazine at all, even though he had it tucked beneath his arm.

The Shadow knew that Daux's mirth was a sham; but behind it lay cause for future jest, of a Satanic sort. Daux's farewell to his visitors was a prelude to death. Mere moments would prove it—moments dependent upon mere inches that the elevator door would have to travel before it was fully shut.

Death to The Shadow unless, by display of rapid skill, he could halt the closing trap and turn doom back upon another of the Adico murder makers, Georges Daux!

CHAPTER XVII
DEATH REVERSED

CARDONA was pressing a button as he heard the door bump to a close. On the opposite side of the little window, Daux was doing the same. His fingers were at the wall button which ordinarily brought the elevator to the fourth floor.

The button stayed in when Daux pushed it. Eyes toward the little window, Daux expected to witness a sudden disappearance of the faces on the other side. His laugh was changing to a leer that revealed his evil design. Then the leer had wiped itself away, to be replaced by a frantic scowl.

Daux was springing back from the elevator door as if it had scorched him. He was yanking a revolver as he went; his eyes, beady, glary, saw the reason for his mistake. The door hadn't fully shut. It had stopped with less than an inch to go.

A rounded chunk of metal blocked it—the muzzle of a gun that The Shadow had thrust into the crack at the final instant.

Daux aimed for that muzzle, pressed the trigger of his own gun. Finding a half-inch opening between a metal door and a cement wall was too much for a marksman on the move, as was Daux.

The wedging gun answered before Daux could fire again. Flames from the .45 automatic bored a bullet straight through the killer's forearm, into the ribs beyond it. Daux's twisty dive became a tumble. He hit the floor with a yell.

Servants were bounding from the apartment. They saw The Shadow shouldering from the elevator, carrying his smoking gun. Their own hands whipped into sight with weapons, but The Shadow's moves were quicker. His .45 was mouthing staccato bursts as he sprang forward. Well-aimed shots floored Daux's servants.

Amazed by Cranston's unusually swift action, Cardona wondered where he came into it. Joe was out of the elevator, too, but there weren't any targets left. However, Cardona's disappointment wasn't to be long-lasting.

Doors ripped open along the hall. Men with guns took aim at Cranston as he hurtled past. Hearing the clatter, he came full about, dropping to his knees and one extended hand. With his other fist he jabbed quick shots up into the very mouths of blazing revolvers.

Cardona didn't have to duck. Not only was he far behind, but Daux had shoved out a foot to trip him. Flat on the floor, Cardona witnessed the display of bursting guns. He could hear the smack of ricocheting bullets as they jolted from the walls.

Gunners were sagging back into their doorways, but Cranston was still delivering shots. That whirl, that drop of his, had carried him below the level of the hasty fire. Nevertheless, he hadn't clinched the victory. His gun was empty.

Surviving thugs sprang from their doorways. Cardona saw Cranston lunge up to meet them, heard the clash of metal as the attackers reached their prey.

Joe couldn't shoot because of Cranston, but he saw his chance to enter the slugging conflict with these killers who had bolstered Daux's murderous servants. Heaving himself into the mêlée, Cardona clouted hard at every head he saw.

ODD, how Joe missed those swings. He didn't realize that other blows were landing ahead of his. The Shadow was already hammering away when Joe arrived.

Bowled back by a rush of half-staggered crooks, Cardona suddenly found himself beside Cranston. Together, they drove their stubborn foemen along the hall.

Shots were roaring, almost in Cardona's ear. Joe could feel the whiz of bullets that skimmed past his face. He saw Cranston give a momentary jolt, knew that his companion had been hit. It couldn't be serious, though, for Cranston was keeping on, as they slashed at rising men who came into their path.

Fortunately, the mobsmen were shooting wildly, from complete desperation. Cranston had softened them considerably, first with bullets, then with hard-slashed blows. Fighters were dropped all along the hallway. Only three remained, and they were trying to escape.

An intercepting figure came up to aid them. It was Daux, clutching his gun in his left fist. He was mouthing oaths, and they weren't in French, as he tottered toward Cranston. Shoving the revolver ahead of him, Daux pulled the trigger just as a long arm finished a hooked swing.

The Shadow's gun hit Daux's as it blasted. The shot found the hallway wall. So did the revolver, carried from Daux's fist by the weight of the empty gun that thwacked it. Spun half about, Daux came squarely into the path of another spurting gun: Cardona's.

Without waiting for Daux to fall, Cardona pivoted toward the elevator. Joe didn't see what happened behind him. He thought that Cranston only had one gun; instead, the commissioner's friend was carrying two.

The Shadow was finding his opportunity to draw that second automatic; and crooks, fearing the straight-aiming Cranston, didn't wait for more battle.

One had yanked the elevator door wide open. He dived into the car with the others. The door was closing when bullets smashed against it. Through the window, with its wired, shatter-proof glass, crooks were giving a farewell leer. Then, with the thump of the door, faces were wiped from sight.

The wall button was still pressed. The mere action of starting the car had produced what Daux had intended earlier. The elevator, with its groggy crew of criminals, had taken a plunge to the bottom of the shaft!

Stopped by the door, Cardona was gripped by a long-held suspense. His head was pounding from the action of the fray; perhaps that was why he fancied that he heard a vague sound, much like a whispered laugh. A tone that meant The Shadow— for Cardona had heard such mirth in the past.

Then the whispery taunt was drowned by a muffled clangor far below. The elevator had struck cement deep in the basement; with the rising reverberations of the crash came trailing, dying shrieks. Like Daux and his crooked servants, the last of crime's reserve crew had gone to doom.

It was death, in reverse, thrown back upon those who served the brain who planned it.

LOOKING about, Cardona saw Cranston leaning against the wall, one hand clamped just above his knee. Waving Joe away, The Shadow gave a slight smile and pointed toward the floor.

"Pick up the magazine, Inspector," he said dryly. "I want the commissioner to see it. Don't worry about this leg of mine. It's not more than a flesh wound. Find a stairway, and I'll manage to hobble down."

Joe found the stairs, kept close to Cranston so that his companion wouldn't stumble. On the way, Cardona remarked:

"Say! That story must be a mighty funny one."

"It's not humorous at all," returned The Shadow. "It happens to be a serious description of the bookshops along the River Seine, in Paris."

"But you laughed at it—"

"And so did Monsieur Daux."

They were at the bottom of the stairs before Cardona suddenly caught the inference.

"Then Daux wasn't a Frenchman! You guessed it, and tested him out! But what about those trick words he was using?"

"They were the sort that a fake Frenchman would use," returned The Shadow. "Daux probably culled them from a dictionary that I saw in the corner. He should have improved his pronunciation before he tried them. When I found that he couldn't read French—"

Cardona's nod told that he knew the rest. Joe understood, at last, why Cranston had been so prompt with the gun that Weston had advised him to carry along.

They were half across the lobby, The Shadow leaning heavily on Cardona, when suddenly a jerk sent Joe stumbling to the right. Cranston had made a sudden shift; with all his weight he was lunging his companion toward a cluster of chairs beside a pillar.

They were rolling when a revolver barked from twenty feet away. Its bullet flattened against the pillar just above their heads.

Not bothering to draw his automatic, The Shadow pulled its trigger. The gun was beneath his coat, but it was pointed at a backward angle, its muzzle underneath his arm. The shot scorched through the cloth, met a marksman who was bounding forward from a chair to take new aim.

The killer had been stationed in the lobby, ready in case Daux failed. Clipped by The Shadow's bullet, the man staggered about and started for an exit at the back of the lobby, where a pair of thuggish companions leaped out to aid him.

Shooting together, The Shadow and Cardona met the incoming thrust. As they fired, more guns opened up from the front door of the lobby. Patrolmen had heard the earlier gunfire from the fourth floor and had reached the scene. Dropping their wounded burden, the thugs fled out through the back.

The man who had tried to kill The Shadow was riddled with police bullets when Cardona reached him. He wasn't an ordinary crook, this fellow. His features were shrewd, intelligent; they marked him as a man of craft, like Daux.

Hobbling up, The Shadow viewed the dead face on the floor. Although he recognized it, he couldn't say so. Not while he was Cranston, though, as Arnaud, The Shadow might have spoken the dead man's name: Clarence Regar.

Seated alone in the hotel office, while waiting for a physician to arrive and attend his wound, The Shadow gave a low, meditative laugh that no one else could hear. Ladwin, Engriff, Daux—they were the types that The Shadow had expected as messengers of death.

Regar was different. He belonged to the selling end, not to the murder corps. The fact that Regar had been pressed into such service could mean one thing only: that Adico had run out of expert killers, with the exception of the missing ace, Rudy Waygart.

One night more. It would be murder's last chance. Adico would bank everything on that final thrust, and Rudy would necessarily be in it. He had to be, since there were no more of his caliber left.

The Shadow knew!

CHAPTER XVIII
CRIME'S DOUBLE TRAIL

THERE was much news the next day. Headlines shrieked of murder, twice foiled. The law had victory to show for itself, so Commissioner Weston was releasing facts galore. He openly admitted that a murder ring had been at work, but claimed that it was entirely suppressed.

The statement carried logic. Weston had withheld it, the night when Lucky Engriff had met with grief; for Lucky, an escaped convict, was not important enough to rate as the head of a craftily managed murder ring. But Georges Daux and Clarence Regar were of sufficient caliber to hold such status.

Daux, it turned out, was a clever confidence man, who had operated under several aliases; while Regar, well known socially, actually had a mysterious office in Manhattan which he had probably used for illicit transactions.

Classed as a team, they formed a competent pair; but why they dealt in murder was a puzzle. Weston sidetracked questions on that score, declaring that the law was investigating and that he would issue a statement later.

The commissioner refrained from mentioning Adico. Privately, he told Cardona that it was probably a name that applied to Daux and Regar combined. No papers of any consequence were found, either in Daux's hotel suite or Regar's office.

In the morning newspapers, Joe Cardona was the hero. It was noon when Clyde Burke slouched into Joe's office, parked himself on a corner of the desk and queried:

"Anything for me, Inspector?"

"Outside, newshound," gruffed Cardona. "You gummed one scoop I tried to shove your way!"

"The Renstrom story? I was trying to help you, Joe. I figured I was postponing the conference by sticking around. That's why I had myself kicked out."

Clyde spoke earnestly, and Cardona actually believed him. Apologetically, the inspector muttered:

"I guess I was too dumb to see it, Burke. If there's anything I can do for you—"

"Now, we're getting somewhere! Give me the lowdown on last night, Joe. Didn't Cranston do just about as much as you did?"

Cardona hesitated, then nodded.

"He did more," admitted the inspector, generously. "I wanted to give the story out, but the commissioner said to lay off. Listen, why don't you follow your own hunch and keep after Cranston until he gives you the whole thing?"

"You'll corroborate it?"

"I'll have to," returned Cardona with a grin, "if Cranston starts the ball rolling."

By mid-afternoon the *Classic* was on the street with its scoop. Cranston's picture dominated the front page; he was rated equally with Cardona in the smashing of the murder ring. Immediately, Cranston's New Jersey home became the goal of dozens of reporters, all anxious to go Burke's story one better.

Cranston's physician, Dr. Sayre, dispersed the mob of newshawks, telling them that his patient would have no more to say until after he had conferred with the police commissioner, at ten o'clock that evening.

LATER that afternoon, Janet Renstrom was sitting in the living room of her home, staring moodily at the darkening sky. She felt that she should be happy, but, somehow, she wasn't.

Murderers had met deserved death, but Janet wasn't convinced that either Daux or Regar had planted the bomb that killed her uncle. Maybe Lucky Engriff had done the deed; but if so, there was certainly someone else who had given the order.

Evening was approaching, and in this house all evenings were gloomy. Janet had stayed at home constantly, because The Shadow had ordered it. He knew that her life would be in jeopardy, if the Adico group guessed how much she knew. Since The Shadow had not informed her otherwise, Janet decided that the head of the murder ring must still be at large.

A ring from the telephone bell brought Janet to her feet. Hurrying out into the hallway, she scrawled letters quickly on a pad. It was a simple rearrangement of the alphabet, based upon a few key words, with the rest of the letters in rotation: the code that she had memorized before it faded, that night when she talked with The Shadow.

But it wasn't The Shadow, or the methodical-toned speaker, Burbank, who sometimes called in his stead. Someone had simply gotten the wrong number. Janet was hanging up when she heard the doorbell ring.

Daniel came from the pantry. Crumpling the code slip in her hand, Janet let the servant pass and watched him open the front door.

The visitor was Thomas Merwood; Janet tossed the slip into a wastebasket beneath the telephone table and hurried forward with a glad greeting.

Merwood's visits were about the only relief in the monotony of Janet's existence.

They went into the living room: after a short chat, Merwood brought up the matter of the murder ring. He was enthused at first; then he shook his head.

"We still haven't found out who Adico is," he said. "Maybe the name is a mere myth, but it should certainly have some bearing on the case."

"Aren't the police investigating further?"

"I don't know, Janet," replied Merwood. "Commissioner Weston talks as though the case were closed. Of course, there's Vayne; he has hired a private detective named Hapthorpe, who is supposedly looking into Juble's death, but they don't seem to be getting very far."

There was silence; then a voice came from the radio, which Janet had turned on earlier. A news commentator was on the air.

"*Flash!*" came the voice. "*Lamont Cranston, new hero in the smashing of the mysterious murder ring, has just staged another exploit. Leaving his home as darkness settled, he successfully dodged a cordon of reporters who have been camping on the grounds of his New Jersey estate.*

"*Cranston's physician announced that his patient has gone for an excursion to be free from all annoyance. He says that Cranston will call on Commissioner Weston at ten o'clock this evening, and will issue no statements until after the conference.*"

Merwood gave a broad smile.

"A clever fellow, Cranston," he said approvingly. "He was the real factor that settled those murderers, last night. Cardona admits it, but Weston won't."

"Tell me, how badly was Cranston wounded?" Janet asked.

"Not seriously," replied Merwood. "He must certainly be in good shape to dodge those reporters. Wait—"

He paused, his hand lifted. It was the radio again, the commentator was reading a very testy statement from Commissioner Weston.

It referred to the coming conference with Cranston, which would be held at the Cobalt Club. All reporters were to stay away, the commissioner warned. After the conference, Weston would issue a general statement to the press.

"He wants to muffle Cranston," decided Merwood as he rose. "I hope he doesn't succeed. I think I'll call Weston and give him my opinion on the subject."

Janet was listening to the radio when Merwood returned to the living room, shaking his head.

"To put it candidly," said the financier, "Weston is a conceited lout. He says that he cannot allow his personal regard for Cranston to interfere with facts that concern the law."

"You mean he won't believe what Cranston really did?"

"Weston shapes truth to suit his own designs," returned Merwood. "However, he can't prevent me from dropping in on that conference. Both Vayne and I have the privilege of calling at the Cobalt Club whenever we choose, because it is the only place where we can talk business with Cranston."

HALF an hour after Merwood had gone, Janet received the call that she expected. It wasn't The Shadow's whisper; the voice was slow, calm-toned, very much like Cranston's.

It gave her the coded message, letter by letter, with pauses between the words. Remembering the paper that she had tossed into the wastebasket, Janet used it to decode the message. It read:

SWIM TO BOAT OFF DOCK AT NINE

Such instructions promised real adventure. Janet could understand why The Shadow ordered it. Obviously, The Shadow knew of Weston's present mood; how the commissioner was ready to challenge anyone, even his friend Cranston.

It wouldn't do for her to leave the house openly, for detectives who patrolled the ground would insist that she wait until they called Weston. He would probably taboo any trip.

Shortly before nine, Janet went up to her room. Disrobing, she clad herself in a modern bathing suit that consisted of trunks and halter. Wearing bathing slippers, she stole down the backstairs, out the kitchen door and across the lawn, to the opening in the rear hedge, where the path began.

Something stirred amid the brush. Crouching beneath the hedge, Janet felt very helpless; her costume was so scanty that she feared her figure would be revealed by its whiteness. Fortunately, one of the detectives came past the slice in the hedge. The noise from the brush faded away.

Taking the path, Janet hurried toward the dock that extended into the Sound, positive that she had escaped some lurking enemy.

The Shadow must have known that crooks would be about tonight. The boat would be her one refuge, for Janet knew that The Shadow had agents in his service, and such men would certainly be on board the craft.

In the dim phosphorescence of the water, Janet saw the outline of an anchored cabin cruiser. Kicking off her slippers, she took a prompt dive from the end of the short pier, made swift strokes for the waiting craft. Her approach was heard on board.

Friendly hands came over the side, helped Janet to the deck. The motor was thrumming; as Janet looked back she thought she saw a figure stooping near the end of the pier. She had evidently outraced some follower along the path.

She couldn't see the faces about her, but she heard the courteous voices which directed her to the cruiser's tiny cabin. It was lighted; closing the door, she stood alone and looked about. Everything was prepared for her, from towels to a complete supply of apparel.

Dressing, Janet found that the clothes were all her proper size. The dark dress with its long sleeves was excellent for this secret excursion, yet attractive in itself. So were the black kid shoes that went with it.

Stepping to the deck, Janet saw the glow of Manhattan lights looming up ahead. The cruiser sped beneath big bridges and swung in toward a deserted pier, where Janet observed the lights of a waiting taxicab.

She smiled at the clever way in which The Shadow was transporting her to Manhattan for a special meeting, leaving detectives guarding an empty house.

ELSEWHERE, The Shadow was receiving his own report of Janet's trip. It came across the wire to the sanctum. Burbank gave the details in his methodical tone:

"Report from Vincent. Janet Renstrom left house at three minutes of nine. Swam to cabin cruiser moored offshore."

There was a pause; then:

"Report from Hawkeye," announced Burbank. "He has located hideout occupied by Rudy Waygart. Hideout empty."

"Reports received."

With that statement, The Shadow studied a curious clock upon his table. It was formed of moving dials, registering hours, minutes, and seconds. Gauged to exactitude, that clock was The Shadow's guide on all expeditions wherein the time element might prove a vital factor.

The clock was registering very close to ten. Whatever the significance of Burbank's reports, there was very little time to deal with them, considering the appointment where, as Cranston, The Shadow was to meet Commissioner Weston.

Instructions, though, could go to agents. The Shadow voiced brief orders for Burbank to relay. Knowing that Janet was inbound to Manhattan, having learned that Rudy was at large, The Shadow was making certain changes in his plans. He was allowing for a double trail, knowing that both would have a bearing on coming events.

This was the night for crime's last thrust. Until ten, all servers of Adico would have to bide their time, so far as Cranston was concerned. They had their victim tagged for doom; but his whereabouts were unknown. In slipping the reporters at dusk, The Shadow had also dodged any watchful crooks.

In so doing, The Shadow had postponed all combat until a scheduled hour. He had given crooks time to weave their strategy, introducing whatever cunning factors they could design. It did not matter who became concerned in it, or why. All trails, whether of Adico's making, or The Shadow's, would meet at one destination.

There, all would depend upon The Shadow's prowess. Should other lives be threatened, The Shadow could protect them by saving his own. He knew that his battle of last night had told crooks the true identity of Lamont Cranston, even though the law had not found out.

Crooks, bonded in a common cause of evil, would be operating with one slogan: "Death to The Shadow!"

The Shadow had his own slogan:

"Death to Adico!"

CHAPTER XIX
CRIME FROM WITHIN

COMMISSIONER WESTON was dining later than usual. Many things had detained him at the office—freak phone calls, crank interviewers, bothersome reporters. There had been trouble, too, when he reached the club. Some argument among the waiters.

The usual man who served meals in the grillroom was absent tonight. A stupid substitute admitted being new to the club's ways when Weston questioned him.

Later, the waiter proved his inefficiency by serving Weston's steak without the mushrooms.

"They were delivered late, sir," the waiter tried to explain. "The chef hasn't finished cooking them. But I'll have them very shortly."

The mushrooms arrived. Weston stared, as if to push them aside, then observed their appetizing look. He spread them on the remainder of his steak, tasted them and liked them. The chef had certainly made amends for his delay.

While Weston ate, the new waiter watched with a pleased smile. Stepping through a doorway, he stopped near a stairway that led up to the kitchen. There, he whisked off his apron, coat, and false shirtfront, handed them to a sallow man who stepped in from a basement entrance.

"All right, Koko," whispered the arrival. "Get going and fix your alibi. I'll do the rest."

Weston stared when the sallow man entered the grillroom wearing the waiter's outfit. The fellow was carrying a half-filled brandy bottle and a glass. He poured a drink; the commissioner began to swallow it. Then, muttering thickly, Weston objected:

"I didn't order brandy!"

"You said brandy, sir," returned the waiter, in a smooth tone. "But there may have been a mistake."

"A mistake?" Weston made a wide clutch at the waiter's arm; gripping it, he pulled himself to his feet and stared at the fellow's face. "*You're* the mistake! You aren't the waiter"—the commissioner was swaying as he spoke— "who was here before."

Steadying, Weston grabbed the fake waiter by both shoulders, glared at a pair of tiny, gimlet eyes. With a big-toothed smile the sallow man shoved his hand hard against Weston's chest, sent him reeling back into his chair.

Weston reached for the brandy bottle, as if to swing it like a club. He couldn't find it with his hand. Rolling his head sideward to the table, the commissioner gave a half-crazed laugh that gave out while his lips were still in motion.

Just then the service door swung open. A girl stepped into the grillroom, stared in surprise as she saw Weston rise, reel about in his chair, and flop with another maddened laugh. She looked toward the waiter in alarm.

The girl was Janet Renstrom. She was taken aback by the false waiter's ugliness. He wasn't just homely; he looked vicious. Weston must have thought the same, for he came up in his chair, staring with eyes that showed dilated pupils.

"What... what are you?" shrilled Weston. "A man or a monster? Get out of here, you devil"— making a mad grab, he knocked over the brandy bottle— "before I... before I—"

"Before what, Commissioner?"

The ugly man snarled the question as he leaned toward the table, where Weston's coat sleeve was soaking up brandy that had poured from the bottle. Shakily, the commissioner managed to uptilt his head, as it wobbled from side to side.

"Before I—" The commissioner paused, managed momentarily to control his curious spell as he demanded: "Who are you?"

"Rudy Waygart."

WESTON squinted as he tried to study Rudy. He muttered that he didn't know him.

Janet began to shrink toward the door; she had thought first that Rudy might be a detective, but now she was sure he wasn't. Spying her retreat, Rudy whipped out a revolver.

"Stay where you are, Miss Renstrom."

"Why'm I drunk?" moaned Weston. "Brandy? Bah! Don't want it. Didn't drink it." He knocked the bottle to the floor, pawed at the tablecloth and pulled it toward him. There was a clatter as his face flattened amid the dishes.

Janet was staring at Rudy's gimlet eyes beyond the gun muzzle. Something in their ugliness told her a horrible truth.

"You're the man—"

"Who planted the pineapple in the box that Parron took to your uncle?" Rudy's tone was sneering. "You guessed it. Neat job, wasn't it?"

Janet gave no answer. Rudy's snake eyes held her helpless. Their glitter was more terrible than the glint of the gun.

"A neat job," repeated Rudy. Then, with a gesture toward the table: "So was this. The commish looks like he's drunk, don't he? Only he isn't.

"You look like a doll with education. Ever hear of a mushroom called the *Panaeolus*? No? Well, I've got the name straight, anyway. It's one of the poison kind, only it isn't deadly. That's what the commish had for dinner."

Weston heard the mention of the mushrooms. Slapping at the dish, he knocked it from the table. The dish crashed the floor; Weston began to mouth a cackly, hysterical laugh, as horrible as any that Janet had ever heard.

"It makes a guy act drunk," informed Rudy. "That's the best thing about the *Panaeolus*. It's why we fed it to his nibs. His friend Cranston is due here soon. He's going to get croaked"—his free hand sweeping sideward, Rudy whisked a revolver from beneath Weston's coat— "with this gun!"

Janet understood as she saw Rudy pocket his own revolver, that Rudy intended to murder Cranston, then pin it on the commissioner. Talk of a disagreement between the two friends would make it bad for Weston. Found in an intoxicated condition, gun in hand, the commissioner would have no alibi.

"It's getting him good," jeered Rudy as Weston gave a hysterical gargle. "He's due for a crying jag pretty soon. He won't even remember what happened. Nobody, not even that wise guy Cardona, will figure that Weston was anything but drunk, the way this joint stinks of brandy!"

Something that Rudy said made Janet forget Weston's plight. Being framed for murder was one thing; to become a victim could be worse. Cranston was slated for that fate; so was Janet!

The Shadow's agents hadn't brought her here. Those men on the cabin cruiser were crooks. They had managed to trick her with a faked message; their courtesy had been a sham, to dupe her into coming here.

Remembering the man that she had dodged along the path, Janet realized that he must have been a watcher posted by The Shadow.

"Guessing things, aren't you?" jeered Rudy, poking the gun closer. "Yeah, we're going to croak you, too, with the commissioner's gun. You know too much, cutey. You've talked to The Shadow!"

The Shadow!

He, too, must be slated for death; therefore, he could only be Cranston. The thought struck home to Janet; she wondered if it had occurred to Rudy. Her nerve suddenly steeled, the girl decided to test him.

"One death should be enough," she said bravely. "Let Cranston live. It will be easier. If you kill me, the commissioner will be blamed. That seems to be your main motive."

Rudy pursed his lips in solemn manner, gave a very approving nod.

"A game kid, aren't you?"

Encouraged, Janet returned the nod. She was moving forward boldly to the very muzzle of the gun, almost daring Rudy to fire. Through her brain was running the thought that if Rudy used that gun he would have to leave in a hurry, before the club attendants arrived.

That would mean life—for The Shadow!

SUDDENLY, Rudy's impressed look vanished.

With the ugliest of snarly laughs, he sped his loose hand forward, slapped it upon Janet's arm. With a vicious wrench that made Janet gasp in pain, he swung her around between himself and the stairway that led up to the foyer.

The finish of Rudy's twist dropped Janet to her knees. She didn't try to rise as he stepped back beside Weston's table. Instead, she looked up, pleading, hoping that further entreaty might still have avail.

"Go ahead—beg," sneered Rudy. "You won't be the first dame that made me try to change my mind. Maybe it works out in the sticks, but not in this town, where a new crop of dolls comes in every week. Anyway, you look too educated to make a hit with me. I like dames dumb."

Stepping forward with two long strides, Rudy planted the gun muzzle squarely against Janet's temple.

"Try to get smart," he told her. "If you do, I'll tap you so hard you'll need a new permanent wave! I can knock you cold, you know, and give you a couple of bullets later, so you won't be helping Cranston any if you start anything before he gets here."

Motionless, Janet waited. The gun muzzle seemed to freeze her entire forehead, numbing her brain by its penetrating coldness.

"That's it," gibed Rudy. "Sit tight. Maybe you figure Cranston can fake a sneak in here; but I'm telling you he can't. He's got a game leg, for one thing, and—"

As Rudy reached that point, a puff of light flashed from the bottom of the stairway to the foyer. It didn't alarm the murderer. Keeping the gun point squarely against Janet's head, Rudy turned toward the disappearing glow and grated a welcoming laugh.

Against the new white plaster of the grillroom wall, Rudy saw The Shadow. Sight of the cloaked figure merely provoked the killer to further mirth.

"Hello, Cranston!" Rudy greeted. "Trying to kid me with that get-up? We figured you'd pull the Shadow stuff tonight. That's why I had a guy named Koko plant a flashbulb, with a thread to set it off, right there at the bottom of the steps."

The Shadow's figure was clearer. Rudy could see the burn of steady eyes. There was a gun beneath them, its muzzle pointed straight for Rudy; but the killer's former fear of The Shadow was gone. Watching Janet as he spoke, Rudy gave new invitation.

"Keep coming, Shadow," said the crook. "The closer you get, the better you'll see. Only, don't get too close, because when you do, I'm liable to touch this hair trigger. You wouldn't want to see this doll get croaked, would you, Shadow?"

The Shadow was approaching with a slow, impressive glide. A whispered taunt issued from his hidden lips; the mockery filled the room, bringing echoes from every wall.

Its shudder seemed to grip Rudy and bring a tremble to the bold crook's shoulders. But Rudy's gun hand stayed right where it was, its weapon still clamped to Janet's head.

Summoning his full bravado, Rudy repeated his snarl in all its ugliness. He spoke as though he held full command, totally disdainful of the gun that covered him.

"Close enough, Shadow!" reminded Rudy. "I mean it when I say I'll shoot!"

The Shadow halted. Rudy's lips widened their grin of triumph. He had accomplished something that no crook had ever hoped to do, Rudy had, in making The Shadow obey him. Crime's master foe was baffled. Rudy had The Shadow wondering.

Yes, The Shadow was wondering.

He was wondering why Rudy, formerly quick to dodge from danger, was so confident on this occasion. But that problem didn't keep The Shadow wondering long. Quickly he grasped the answer.

For once The Shadow's silence was more to be dreaded than his laugh, though Rudy did not guess it. Through silence The Shadow was building to the stroke that might produce crime's doom.

Silent strategy could bring a later laugh.

The Shadow's laugh of triumph!

CHAPTER XX
THE MASTER HAND

IT was a strange, unprecedented scene.

Commissioner Weston, slumped drunkenly across the table, a dupe prepared to receive murder's blame. Janet Renstrom, kneeling on the floor, awaiting death from a gun muzzle pressed against her forehead. The Shadow, standing rigid, silent, unwilling to press the trigger of his gun.

The center of that scene was Rudy Waygart, the missing murderer who had so suddenly reappeared, to take control over both The Shadow and the law.

It was too much glory for any lone crook; particularly one like Rudy Waygart.

Plainly, Rudy was counting upon more than his own prowess to put up such a front. Rudy stood for Adico and all the strength of the insidious murder ring. Rudy was the last of the aces; The Shadow had disposed of the other three: Ladwin, Engriff, Daux, with Regar as an ace in the hole, to boot.

There would have to be a trump card in Adico's pack, all ready to be played; otherwise, Rudy wouldn't be going through with his present action. The Shadow knew of such a trump, had hoped that it would be used tonight. This was his chance to find the brain of Adico!

Calmly waiting, The Shadow concentrated upon Rudy. There was a flaw in the killer's situation. Suppose Rudy should fire the gun that he held pressed to Janet's head. The shot would be the last he ever gave. The Shadow would drop him before the gun could end its recoil.

Rudy was counting upon important aid.

It couldn't come from the service door beyond where the killer stood. Mobbies might be lurking there; in fact, they probably were, for Rudy always carried a gun crew along.

But they would not help—The Shadow could riddle them the moment they appeared. And Rudy not only knew it; he had seen such things done in the past.

Aid could arrive from one spot alone—from the stairway behind The Shadow, the steps that led down from the foyer to the grillroom!

The Shadow had strolled through the foyer as Cranston, carrying cloak and hat across his arm, like ordinary garments. He hadn't put on the black garb until he reached the darkened stairs, for the simple reason that there were too many persons in the foyer. People like club members and attendants.

The Shadow had recognized them when he passed. They weren't crooks; they couldn't be. Still, someone was coming to those same stairs, to cut off The Shadow's retreat; otherwise, Rudy wouldn't have a chance.

Another murderer, appointed to kill The Shadow? No!

It couldn't be. The Shadow saw the entire setup. If Commissioner Weston was to be framed for the double murder of Janet and Cranston, *both* shots would have to come from the same gun— the revolver that Rudy had borrowed from the commissioner's pocket!

Two shots from that gun.

The first would be fired at The Shadow, not Janet. Rudy couldn't risk it otherwise. The ruse was clear, though only The Shadow could have so quickly divined its cunning phases.

Rudy still was the actual menace.

Whoever else came into the picture would do it only to distract The Shadow, so that Rudy would be clear for action. By shooting The Shadow first, Rudy could easily settle Janet afterward. *Provided that Rudy's bullet found The Shadow!*

A LAUGH almost escaped The Shadow's lips. He had the links he wanted. Rudy wouldn't move until the aid arrived. Crafty aid, geared to trick even The Shadow; for it would be through pretended stealth, which he would actually be supposed to detect.

Such was crime's setup. Did it have a loophole?

Yes. One that crooks had overlooked: Janet's temporary safety! The girl wasn't scheduled for instant death, as Rudy was trying to make it appear. Janet was The Shadow's trump card; a small one, but strong enough to take an ace!

The Shadow's eyes steadied on the girl's, for Janet's gaze was turned in his direction. The girl caught understanding from those glowing orbs. She saw The Shadow's free hand move toward his other wrist, clamp tightly there.

Despite the pressure of Rudy's revolver, the girl managed to give a perceptible nod. By clutching his own gun hand, The Shadow signified that she was to grab at Rudy's, the moment that action began. Rudy didn't catch the signal. His eyes no longer met The Shadow's.

The flash to Janet was timely. Already, The Shadow could hear the token he expected: a creeping sound from the stairway; cautious, guarded at first, then with a slight stumble—the planned giveaway that The Shadow could not ignore.

With a fierce laugh The Shadow wheeled in a wide, eccentric circle. There was an instant scramble as the man on the stairs sprang upward, away from the path of aim. He had been sneaking down the steps sidewise, ready for that quick bound toward the top.

As The Shadow spun about, Rudy whipped his gun from Janet's forehead and aimed for the black-cloaked fighter. With the crook's shift, another hand was on its way: Janet's.

Grabbing Rudy's wrist, Janet yanked it just as the murderer tugged the trigger. Rudy's misdirected shot went two feet wide of its cloaked target.

One bullet wasted. Rudy's harsh snarl meant that it didn't matter. Cuffing Janet's chin with his free hand, Rudy flattened the girl on the floor. The thwack that Janet's head took made her see a flash of light as vivid as Rudy's gun burst.

There was such a blast; but it didn't come from Rudy's revolver, though the crook was jabbing the weapon toward The Shadow. With all his confidence, the murderer had lost his chance.

The Shadow hadn't halted his whirl to go after the marauder on the stairway. Completing his rapid spin, the cloaked avenger was aiming at Rudy again, firing as he came! The whirl had taken less than a full second; and The Shadow, concentrating solely upon Rudy, had picked his target with precision.

Tongued flame was like a vivid arrow pointed close to Rudy's heart. The slug from a .45 jarred the ace murderer, sent him reeling against the table where Weston had lifted a distorted face to stare with grotesquely livid eyes.

As Rudy bounced from table to floor, The Shadow's laugh pealed anew. That laugh, telling that The Shadow had succeeded, meant that Rudy had failed.

MASS attack was due. Driving for the service door at the rear of the grillroom, The Shadow thrust Janet toward a safe corner, then shifted in the other direction to shove Weston from his chair.

As the commissioner flattened beneath the table, the rear door lashed open. Thugs jammed through, headed by Koko, the crook who had served the mushrooms.

The Shadow served them bullets hot from a pair of gun muzzles. The charging tribe disintegrated into wild, excited grapplers who grabbed at The Shadow's guns, tried to sledge him with their own.

From her corner, Janet saw The Shadow reel backward. Frantically, the girl made a scramble for Rudy's lost revolver, hoping to aid her rescuer.

She didn't guess The Shadow's latest ruse.

He was letting disorganized thugs carry him to the front of the grillroom; in fact, he was dragging some of the wounded along to make a show. He wanted to bait the man who had acted as decoy on the stairway.

Near the steps, The Shadow shook thugs aside, purposely stumbling over one falling figure, he staggered to the steps, acting as though he couldn't quite point his gun upward.

The Shadow's limp helped. He had strained his injured leg during the rapid fray; he had merely to put his weight on it to make his stumble real. He was on one knee, but still dangerous, there at the bottom of the gloomy steps, when a figure came lunging down upon him.

Stiffening, The Shadow met a bulky, desperate antagonist who came with a powerful surge. A slashing gun skimmed the brim of the slouch hat; failing in the stroke, the final killer went berserk and tried to plant the muzzle against The Shadow's head.

Warding off that move, The Shadow jabbed his own gun toward the other man's heart; a flinging hand dashed it aside.

Then they were locked, circling about the grillroom until they came up against Weston's table. The Shadow's hat was tilted back, the face of Cranston showed beneath the lifted brim. His opponent recognized it and throated a savage challenge.

The Shadow recognized the broad face that was eye to eye with his. He answered the challenge with a mocking laugh, an invitation to battle, wherein death to one would mark the victory of the other.

This was the meeting that The Shadow had long sought, an open encounter with the master hand who managed the affairs of Adico. He wasn't surprised at the face he saw, for The Shadow had long ago guessed who the real brain was.

It was Janet who voiced an amazed outcry as she recognized that glaring face so close to Cranston's.

The master hand of Adico was Thomas Merwood!

CHAPTER XXI
CRIME'S FULL PROOF

LIMPING, wearied from his furious fray, The Shadow was at a physical disadvantage against a burly opponent like Merwood. The head of Adico had strength, along with a superhuman fury, inspired by his last chance to save the death insurance racket.

He was fighting for half a million dollars, Merwood was, the sum represented by Cranston's scalp. Proof that The Shadow was not only human, but the very man that Adico wanted to kill, was all Merwood needed to show himself a fighter far more extraordinary than any of the dead murderers who had served him.

Always a cool calculator, Merwood was keeping his wits as he tried to wear The Shadow down. Like Cranston, Merwood had come into the Cobalt Club openly, as was his right.

He had intended to be a chance witness to a double murder, which he could blame on Commissioner Weston. Even now, Merwood might turn the outcome to his own design.

If he could kill The Shadow, then Janet, it would be easy to plant the death gun on Rudy and claim that all killing had been the result of a mob fight.

Making Weston the goat had been a good idea, but it wasn't essential. As long as the commissioner wasn't in condition to give accurate testimony of what had happened, Merwood's story would stand.

He had to work swiftly, did Merwood, for people would soon be pouring into the grillroom. Sounds of battle had carried up to the foyer, and would certainly bring police. Probably The Shadow was banking on it. With that thought, Merwood doubled his already forceful strength.

Head tilted backward, The Shadow could feel the steady pressure of Merwood's gun hand. The Shadow, too, was getting his gun muzzle slowly into position toward Merwood's body; but the slow-motion duel was uncertain. Either hand might win, if this kept on, and The Shadow didn't intend it to be Merwood's.

Craftily, the Adico master was keeping The Shadow turned toward Janet, so the girl couldn't put in a shot from Rudy's revolver. But the girl still had a value in this fray; one that The Shadow had understood from the start. It was the thing upon which the cloaked fighter banked in this moment of emergency.

Janet heard the words that hissed from Cranston's lips:

"To the foyer! Up the stairs! Quick—get started! Get clear!"

The girl hesitated. She didn't want to abandon her rescuer. Then she caught the commanding glint of the eyes that peered from Cranston's strained face as he actually wrenched his head so he could see her across a cloaked shoulder.

Though she didn't guess the purpose, Janet followed orders. Turning, she dashed full speed for the stairs. She heard Merwood raise a bellow, realized its meaning as she ran.

Merwood couldn't let Janet get away!

Slated for sure death, the girl had been introduced to the entire situation. Even if Merwood triumphed against The Shadow, Janet's testimony would mark the financier as the real head of the murder ring.

She knew about the *Panaeolus* mushrooms; a chemical analysis of the innocent-looking dish would prove Janet's story and discredit Merwood's.

As Janet neared the stairs, Merwood did what The Shadow had been working for all along. The master crook let fury overplay his wisdom. Twisting his gun away from The Shadow, Merwood aimed for Janet and fired.

Merwood was reeling as he pulled the trigger, for The Shadow, too, had reserve strength and was using it. The bullet pinged the wall, a yard wide of Janet; the girl reached the stairs.

Savagely, Merwood tried to get his gun back at The Shadow. Another muzzle was already pressing home. The Shadow's .45 spoke; it drove a bullet into Merwood's side, just as the big man's gun spouted a futile blast across a cloaked shoulder.

This time, Merwood reeled alone.

Gun fist lowered, his other hand clamped to the wound above his hip, Merwood was trying to find The Shadow. He heard a mirthless laugh, but couldn't see its author. The tone might have come from anywhere, the way it reverberated from the grillroom's enclosing walls.

BY the time that Merwood turned toward the rear of the room, The Shadow was through the service door. His gun muzzle, poked through a crack, was covering Merwood's staggery course.

The crook didn't see the gun's mouth. But he heard the clatter of footsteps from the stairs. They were too loud to mark Janet's return; besides, the girl would not be coming back.

Nevertheless, Merwood turned. Into the scene of carnage came Inspector Joe Cardona, a pair of bluecoats close behind him.

Merwood saw only Joe, greeted him with a spasmodic snarl. Sight of Merwood, one hand gripping a gun, the other clutching a blood-gushing wound, had made Cardona pause.

Too late did Cardona recognize that Merwood was a killer, not a victim of crime. Too late, that was, for Cardona to beat the coming shot. It was another gun, already trained, that came to Cardona's aid. Flame spat from the crack of the service door as The Shadow fired.

Merwood jolted forward, upward, clipped in the spine. Convulsively, his fingers tightened on his gun; the trigger snapped. A bullet carved the plaster above Cardona's head, sent a shower of debris downward.

From that splatter of plaster came a three-gun volley as Cardona and the officers fairly riddled the killer whose stagger had all the semblance of a murderous lunge.

A laugh whispered through the grillroom, as Joe and his companions stooped above the dead form of Thomas Merwood.

Solemn, mirthless, that departing knell marked more than the death of a master murderer. It told the end of Adico.

Leaving by the basement exit, The Shadow blinked his flashlight. Signals answered his varicolored flashes; he was met by agents who had arrived to cut off the flight of Adico's reserves, a sortie that had never come.

But Harry, Hawkeye and the others had met Janet as she scurried dazedly along the street. They had put her in Moe's cab; it was waiting nearby.

Soon, The Shadow was riding to a new destination, with Janet as his companion. The girl said that she had simply kept going after she dashed out from the Cobalt Club. She had remembered The Shadow's instructions to get clear.

Calm again, Janet heard The Shadow's whispered account of Merwood's death, spoke her willingness to aid in the followup that was required. They reached a big apartment house; there, The Shadow left the taxi.

Soon, signal flashes gleamed from high above. Red, then green; finally, there was a yellow glimmer as the light disappeared. Janet entered the apartment house, went up in the elevator and rang boldly at a door.

It opened. On the threshold was a dapper servant whose face switched to a sudden scowl when he recognized Janet. His sharp cry carried a tone that the girl in her turn recognized. This man, like the rest of Merwood's servants, had been one of the smug crew on the cabin cruiser!

Janet realized now that Merwood was able to send her the fake message in The Shadow's code, telling her to board the cabin cruiser, because he had probably found the code symbols in the wastebasket when he had gone to make a phone call. Janet had dropped the code there when Merwood had last come to her home.

BEFORE the dapper servant could yank a gun, men sprang into the corridor from doorways where they had waited. They were The Shadow's agents; they had come here, too.

Sight of drawn guns sent Merwood's servant scurrying into the apartment shouting the alarm. Crooked flunkies rallied, only to be greeted from a weird laugh that came from an opened window.

They turned to see the silhouetted form of The Shadow. Guns opened on them as they frantically tried to aim. As they fled, The Shadow followed them, drove them into a reception committee of his agents, who gun-slugged them senseless.

Merwood's chauffeur was among the slumped group; from the hallway, Janet recognized him as the taxi driver who had brought her from the dock to the Cobalt Club, where he had guided her in through the basement entrance.

The Shadow's agents whisked Janet out to Moe's cab. They were away before police arrived. But up in Merwood's apartment, where groans of groggy crooks alone disturbed the silence, The Shadow remained busy making a search.

He found the evidence he wanted: papers gathered by Parron, among them death insurance policies marked paid. Merwood's own records were there in full, and when The Shadow blasted open a strong-box with a gunshot, he discovered a huge stack of cash funds.

The Shadow did not count the cash in full. Thumbing a stack of bills of thousand-dollar denomination, he took five hundred of them and left the rest. It was Adico's final payment, the half million owed to Henry Arnaud; a collection on the expired death insurance placed on Lamont Cranston.

Tearing the last page from a big ledger, The Shadow wrapped the money in it. The page carried the only records of the transaction which The Shadow had conducted under two names.

Moving to the window, The Shadow swung across the sill. He was gone, into outer darkness, when the police entered Merwood's apartment.

At the hospital where Commissioner Weston had undergone a session with a stomach pump, physicians decided that the patient could receive visitors.

Propped in bed, Weston smiled a weak greeting to Lamont Cranston, who was accompanied by Tyrus Vayne. He asked them to listen while Inspector Cardona read a full report on the Adico racket.

It developed that Merwood's books were complete except for a single page, which probably accounted for a shortage in the recorded funds. In all, however, the police had gathered more than two million dollars; some in cash, the rest in gilt-edged bonds.

"Fancy it, Cranston!" exclaimed Weston. "The books show more than two hundred and fifty names, all insured for at least a hundred thousand dollars each. At premiums averaging ten percent and more, Merwood's racket had brought in more than three million dollars.

"Only one name was written off as a loss." Turning to Vayne, the commissioner added: "That was yours. Of course, there were heavy expenses. Killers like Waygart, Engriff, and Daux received sizeable salaries, and were authorized to hire thugs.

"Ladwin was a murderer, too; something we hadn't guessed. It cost them money to rig up his hideout as some sort of trap, and they spent a lot on the fake fire truck that Engriff drove. Daux's jewels were a loss, too, for we appropriated them.

"Agents like Parron and Regar operated on commissions, and surprisingly small ones. Once in the racket, they couldn't object. When Parron tried to get out, Merwood made an example of him."

The books showed that the vast majority of the death insurance policies were unexpired, which amounted to the saving of nearly two hundred lives throughout the nation. With murderers obliterated, the law could concentrate upon a roundup of hiding salesmen and scared clients who had insured friends for death.

"We owe a lot to The Shadow," conceded Weston. "He cracked the racket wide open and ruined it. We have cause to be elated."

CRANSTON didn't look elated. The commissioner asked him why.

"I'm thinking about Merwood," said The Shadow in Cranston's customary tone. "We should have seen through him almost from the start. You took his word for it, that he hadn't seen the letter that came to Renstrom.

"He must have seen it and it probably told a lot. Because only Merwood could have guessed that Parron sent that letter. Learning about the box, Merwood had Rudy substitute the one that contained the bomb."

Nodding, Weston suggested that Merwood might have sent the Adico note to Janet. He saw Cranston smile, but didn't guess that the note had been important in another way.

"You called Merwood," reminded The Shadow, "the night we learned about Engriff. Only Merwood could have sent Lucky after us with the fire truck. It was Merwood, too, who told Daux to call Vayne—"

"To lay another trap!" exclaimed Weston. "Hoping to get me, Cranston, along with you and Cardona!"

Again The Shadow smiled. He preferred that the commissioner should keep his theory that Merwood liked revenge as well as profit. It fitted with recent events at the Cobalt Club, where Merwood had again shown such traits.

The fact that Cranston had been the only target, with Janet as bait to trap him, did not occur to Weston. He didn't know that Cranston had been to the club at all, during the evening. The commissioner did not guess, nor did Cardona, that the missing page of Merwood's ledger listed Cranston's name, insured for death.

At the doorway, Cranston shook hands with Vayne.

"Sorry, Vayne," he said, "but I can't go through with that importing proposition. I have a friend, though"—his tone made Vayne brighten— "who might supply cash to help your present company. You'll hear from him; his name is Henry Arnaud, and he tells me that he has a few hundred thousand to invest."

All visitors had left when Commissioner Weston found a folded sheet of paper on the table beside his bed. Chafingly, he thought that Cardona had mislaid some of the Adico records; but Weston learned otherwise when he unfolded the sheet.

Its sensitized surface was blank, except for a dark-shaded silhouette that showed a hawkish silhouette. Vaguely, from blurred recollections of his hazy evening at the club, Weston recalled that same profile in life.

The Shadow!

THE END

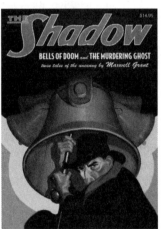

Walter B. Gibson (1897-1985) was born in Germantown, Pennsylvania. His first published feature, a puzzle titled "Enigma," appeared in *St. Nicholas Magazine* when he was only eight years old. In 1912, Gibson's second published piece won a literary prize, presented by former U.S. President Howard Taft, who expressed the hope that this would be the beginning of a great literary career. Building upon his fascination with magic and sleight of hand, he became a frequent contributor to magic magazines and worked briefly as a carnival magician.

He joined the reporting staff of the Philadelphia *North American* after graduating from Colgate University in 1920, moved over to the *Evening Public Ledger* the following year and was soon producing a huge volume of features for NEA and the Ledger Syndicate, while also ghosting books for magicians Houdini, Thurston, Blackstone and Dunninger.

A 1930 visit to Street & Smith's offices led to his being hired to write novels featuring The Shadow, the mysterious host of CBS' *Detective Story Program*. Originally planned as a quarterly, *The Shadow Magazine* was promoted to monthly publication when the first two issues sold out and a year later began the twice-a-month frequency it would enjoy for the next decade. Walter eventually wrote 283 Shadow novels totaling some 15 million words.

Gibson scripted the lead features for *Shadow Comics* and *Super-Magician Comics,* and organized a Philadelphia-based comic art shop with former *Evening Ledger* artists. In a 1942 *Bill Barnes* comic book story, he foresaw America defeating Japan through the use of a U-235 atomic bomb.

He also found time for radio, plotting and co-scripting *Nick Carter, Chick Carter, The Avenger, Frank Merriwell* and *Blackstone the Magic Detective*. Walter also hosted ABC's *Strange* and authored scores of books on magic and psychic phenomena, many cowritten with his wife, Litzka Raymond Gibson. He also wrote five *Biff Brewster* adventure novels for Grosset and Dunlap (as "Andy Adams") and such publishing staples as *Hoyle's Simplified Guide to the Popular Card Games* and *Fell's Official Guide to Knots and How to Tie Them*.

No one was happier than Walter Gibson when The Shadow staged a revival in the sixties and seventies. Walter wrote *Return of The Shadow* in 1963, and three years later selected three vintage stories to appear in a hardcover anthology entitled *The Weird Adventures of The Shadow*. Several series of paperback and hardcover reprints followed, and Gibson wrote two new Shadow short stories. He was a frequent guest at nostalgia, mystery, comic, pulp and old-time-radio conventions, always delighted to perform magic tricks and sign autographs as both Gibson and Grant, using his distinctive double-X signature. His last completed fiction, "The Batman Encounters—Gray Face," appeared as a text feature in the 500th issue of *Detective Comics*.

Walter Gibson died on December 6, 1985, with a *Shadow* novel sitting unfinished in his typewriter. "I always enjoyed writing the *Shadow* stories," he insisted a few years earlier. "There was never a time when I wasn't enjoying the story I was writing or looking forward to beginning the next one." Walter paused and then added, a touch of sadness in his voice, "I wish I was still writing the *Shadow* stories."

Richard E. Wormser (1908-1977) served as an assistant editor of *The Shadow Magazine* in 1931 and worked briefly for Gibson as researcher/proofreader on early Shadow novels. The Princeton graduate went on to write 17 Nick Carter pulp novels and hundreds of short stories and novelettes under a variety of pen names including "Edward Friend" and "Conrad Gerson."

His first hardcover novel, *The Man with the Wax Face*, was published in 1934 and followed in 1935 by a sequel, *The Communist's Corpse*.

After Hollywood adapted several of his pulp stories beginning with "It's All in the Racket" (filmed in 1936 as *Sworn Enemy*), Columbia Pictures enlisted Wormser as a staff screenwriter. Twice hired and fired by legendary studio boss Harry Cohn, Wormser also pounded out B-movie screenplays for Republic, Universal, Warner Brothers and RKO, and later teleplays for *Lassie, Colt .45, Zane Grey Theatre, Cheyenne* and *77 Sunset Strip*.

The prolific wordsmith also wrote more than a dozen movie and TV paperback novelizations including *The Wild Wild West, McLintock, Thief of Baghdad, Major Dundee, Torn Curtain* and the 1967 Green Hornet novel *The Infernal Light*.

Wormser won Western Spur awards for *Ride a Northbound Horse* in 1964 and *The Black Mustanger* in 1971, and was honored with an Edgar Award for *The Intruder* in 1973.

"I have published endless words, on tons of paper; square miles of the great northern pulp forests have been denuded on my account," he recalled near the end of his life. "In reparation, I served three years in the U.S. Forest Service, but I'm afraid I'm still indebted to our wooded acres." •

THE AVENGER by Kenneth Robeson

A-1: Justice, Inc. & The Golden Hoard
A-2: The Sky Walker & The Devil's Horns
A-3: The Frosted Death & The Glass Mountain
A-4: The Blood Ring & Stockholders of Death

DOC SAVAGE by Kenneth Robeson

D-1: Fortress of Solitude & Devil Genghis*
D-2: Resurrection Day & Repel*
D-3: Death in Silver & The Golden Peril
D-4: Land of Always-Night & Mad Mesa
D-5: The Spook Legion & Submarine Mystery
D-6: The Polar Treasure & Pirate of the Pacific
D-7: The Lost Oasis & The Sargasso Ogre
D-8: The Sea Magician & Living-Fire Menace
D-9: The Majii & The Golden Man
D-10: Dust of Death & The Stone Man
D-11: Cold Death & The South Pole Terror
D-12: The Squeaking Goblin & The Evil Gnome
D-13: Brand of the Werewolf & Fear Cay
D-14: The Man of Bronze & The Land of Terror*
D-15: The Red Spider & Cold War Stories
D-16: Secret in the Sky & The Giggling Ghosts
D-17: The Czar of Fear & World's Fair Goblin*
D-18: The Monsters & The Whisker of Hercules
D-19: The King Maker & The Freckled Shark
D-20: The Thousand-Headed Man & Gold Ogre
D-21: Hex & The Running Skeletons
D-22: Mystery Under the Sea & The Red Terrors*
D-23: The Fantastic Island & Danger Lies East
D-24: The Black, Black Witch & WWII stories
D-25: The Red Skull & The Awful Egg
D-26: The Annihilist & Cargo Unknown*
D-27: Murder Mirage & The Other World
D-28: The Metal Master & The Vanisher
D-29: The Mental Wizard & The Secret of the Su
D-30: Quest of the Spider & Mountain Monster
D-31: Devil on the Moon & I Died Yesterday*
D-32: The Feathered Octopus & The Goblins
D-33: Quest of Qui & The Devil's Playground*
D-34: Man Who Shook the Earth & Three Devils
D-35: Meteor Menace & The Ten Ton Snakes
D-36: The Phantom City & No Light to Die By*
D-37: Mystery on the Snow & Peril in the North
D-38: Murder Melody & Birds of Death
D-39: Poison Death & They Died Twice

*Also available in James Bama variant cover editions

THE SHADOW by Maxwell Grant

S-1: Crime, Insured & The Golden Vulture
S-2: The Chinese Disks & Malmordo
S-3: The Red Blot & The Voodoo Master
S-4: The Murder Master & The Hydra
S-5: The Black Falcon & The Salamanders
S-6: The Shadow's Justice & Broken Napoleons
S-7: The Cobra & The Third Shadow
S-8: The London Crimes & Castle of Doom
S-9: Lingo, Partners of Peril & The Grim Joker
S-10: The City of Doom & The Fifth Face
S-11: Road of Crime & Crooks Go Straight
S-12: Serpents of Siva & The Magigals Mystery
S-13: Six Men of Evil & The Devil Monsters
S-14: The Grove of Doom & The Masked Lady
S-15: The Shadow Unmasks & The Yellow Band
S-16: City of Crime & Shadow Over Alcatraz
S-17: The Fate Joss & The Golden Pagoda
S-18: The Unseen Killer & The Golden Masks
S-19: Voodoo Trail & Death's Harlequin
S-20: The Blue Sphinx & Jibaro Death
S-21: The Plot Master & Death Jewels
S-22: Tower of Death & The Hooded Circle
S-23: Smugglers of Death & The Blackmail King
S-24: Washington Crime & Quetzal
S-25: The Gray Ghost & The White Skulls
S-26: Vengeance Is Mine! & Battle of Greed
S-27: The Python & The Hawk and The Skull
S-28: Master of Death & The Rackets King
S-29: The Shadow's Rival & The Devil Master
S-30: The Sealed Box & Racket Town
S-31: The Dark Death & House of Shadows
S-32: The Silver Scourge & The Book of Death
S-33: The Strange Disappearance of Joe Cardona & The Hand
S-34 The Blackmail Ring & Murder for Sale
S-35: The Condor & Chicago Crime
S-36: Crime Rides the Sea & River of Death
S-37: The Third Skull & Realm of Doom
S-38: Dead Men Live & Dictator of Crime
S-39: Face of Doom & The Crime Ray
S-40: The Crime Clinic & Cards of Death

THE WHISPERER by Clifford Goodrich

W-1: The Dead Who Talked & The Red Hatchets
W-2: Six Pyramids of Death & Mansion of Missing
W-3: Murder Queens & Kill Them First!

www.shadowsanctum.com/pulps.html